ACTION!

ROBERT CORT

ACTION!

A Novel

Random House / New York

Copyright © 2003 by Robert Cort

All rights reserved under International and Pan-American Copyright Conventions.
Published in the United States by Random House, an imprint of The Random House
Ballantine Publishing Group, a division of Random House, Inc., New York, and
simultaneously in Canada by Random House of Canada Limited, Toronto.

RANDOM HOUSE and colophon are registered trademarks of Random House, Inc.

Grateful acknowledgment is made to Henry Holt and Company, LLC,
for permission to reprint an excerpt from "The Road Not Taken," from *The Poetry
of Robert Frost,* edited by Edward Connery Lathem. Copyright © 1916, 1969
by Henry Holt and Company, copyright © 1944 by Robert Frost.
Reprinted by permission of Henry Holt and Company, LLC.

Library of Congress Cataloging-in-Publication Data
Cort, Robert W.
Action! / Robert Cort.
p.   cm.
ISBN 0-679-45232-X (alk. paper)
1. Hollywood (Los Angeles, Calif.)—Fiction.
2. Motion picture industry—Fiction.   I. Title.
PS3603.O6895   A27   2003   813'.54—dc21   2002026578

Printed in the United States of America on acid-free paper
Random House website address: www.atrandom.com
24689753
First Edition

Book design by J. K. Lambert

For my wife, Rosalie

and

Althea Horner, mentor and friend

CONTENTS

1948

CROSS
SEAS

Harry Jastrow popped the hinge on his gold and porcelain pocket watch. Twenty-two minutes remained until his call to action—too much time to kill and too little to run for cover. Behind its towering bronze doors the Supreme Court stood impregnable. Settle down, Harry. You're pleading a case, not storming a beach. Regardless of who wins in there, no one dies—just like the movies.

"Your Honors, the Department of Justice has accused the chief executives of Paramount Pictures, RKO, Metro-Goldwyn-Mayer, Twentieth Century–Fox, and Warner Bros. of multiple violations of the Sherman Anti-Trust Act. But my clients are not corrupt monopolists. They are, in fact, pioneers who have carved out a new industry. . . ."

"Dad, you're mumbling."

Harry smiled reassuringly at AJ, his twelve-year-old son. "I'm rehearsing."

"Could you do it inside? I need to use the bathroom."

They marched into the building expecting to confront history; instead, they bumped into Bette Davis mugging for photographers in front of a bust of John Marshall. Was that Clark Gable talking to reporters by the Scales of Justice? The Great Hall looked like the lobby of Grauman's Chinese Theatre at a world premiere. In lieu of a bullet, Harry bit his bottom lip. He had warned the moguls who ran Hollywood that they couldn't manipulate the American judicial system like an audience in Peoria. But they'd told him nine old guys in long black robes couldn't keep their hands out of their pants when Lana Turner winked at them from the front row.

Mel Cantwell, Harry's Washington-based co-counsel, elbowed through the crowd. "Who's responsible for this circus?" Harry indicated a longshoreman costumed in a three-piece suit—Spyros Skouras, president of Twentieth Century–Fox. Cantwell mopped his brow with an already damp handkerchief. "The justices hate grandstand plays."

"Don't worry, Mel. I'll be so riveting they won't notice."

"Dad, Mr. Cagney says hello." AJ returned from the men's room, struggling to comb his unruly hair. "I look like Einstein."

"You look handsome." Harry felt guilty because he'd used the last of their Brylcreem to tame his own black mop.

"Sir?" The head of publicity at Warners interrupted. "We need you for a moment."

Harry checked his watch again, for more than the time. His father had stolen it off the corpse of a Russian nobleman who'd frozen in an ice storm outside St. Petersburg. Too bad Poppa wasn't alive to see where it had ended up. Ten minutes remained. "Let's go."

The publicist escorted him into the courtroom to shake hands with Paul Muni and Lana Turner . . . in a low-cut blouse that might just do the trick. Harry listened dutifully to Muni. "You have to be bold, Jastrow, bold in your speech, bold in your being. That's how I played *The Life of Emile Zola*. I'd have won the Oscar if Metro hadn't bought it for Spencer Tracy."

"A grave miscarriage of justice." Harry's irony sailed past the actor. "Why don't you folks get seated. Show's starting any second."

He nudged his son toward the appellant's table, but a man with a bald pate and wire-rimmed glasses intercepted them. Adolph Zukor, founder and chairman of Paramount, had spent his life creating an industry that didn't exist the day he kissed the ground at Ellis Island in 1888. "Bubbala, look how big you've grown!" He squeezed the cheeks of his favorite grandnephew. "Did you help your father prepare for today?"

"He didn't need help," AJ declared proudly.

Zukor nodded. "Your dad is going to do great! He's so honest those judges couldn't not believe a thing he says when he says it."

The courtroom grew still. Static electricity welded Harry's suit to his skin. His son and Zukor scurried to the gallery as the marshal's "Oyez" thundered.

Chief Justice Frederick Vinson pounded his gavel. He reminded Harry of a "hit 'em hard" football coach. "We will hear arguments this morning in the case of *United States of America versus Paramount Pictures, et al.*"

Robert Wright, the deputy attorney general of the Anti-Trust Division, rose to address the Court. His puritanical upbringing as the son of the demanding architect Frank Lloyd Wright had stripped him of compassion. Like many of his WASP colleagues in the Justice Department, he resented the eastern European Jewish immigrants who wielded untrammeled cultural influence over his country. This was his chance to cut the Horatio Algerbergs down to size. "I have prosecuted scores of businessmen for violations of the Sherman Anti-Trust Act, but none has been so deliberate and deceitful a defendant as the so-called Big Five motion picture studios."

"*Basd meg!*" Zukor cursed in his native Hungarian, while Skouras muttered an unflattering epithet in Greek.

Wright glared in their direction. "The Big Five not only produce and distribute virtually all the movies made in America, they also own a significant number of the nation's theaters. They have used their monopoly power to harm independent exhibitors. And who are these exhibitors? They are small businessmen—families, for the most part—working to keep their one theater in operation. The FBI conducted a secret, fifteen-month investigation of five hundred towns which conclusively proved the industry's guilt. The trial jury convicted the Big Five on all counts. Now the defendants are demanding a reversal. We ask that you order the studios to sell *all* of their theaters and exit the exhibition business *permanently*. Divorcement is the only remedy that will curtail their abuses."

"Off with their heads!" "Hang 'em high!" "Fry the bastards!" That was how "divorcement" translated to panicky movie executives. Economic catastrophe loomed because the studios earned most of their profits from their theaters. In typically understated fashion, *Variety,* Hollywood's newspaper of record, had labeled today's hearing Armageddon.

Harry knew that the Big Five had played far over the edge of legality for decades, so three months ago he'd negotiated a settlement with the Justice Department that would have allowed them to maintain ownership of a limited number of theaters. But the moguls were too greedy to lose *any* profits. They'd rejected the compromise and assigned Harry the mission of keeping the Court from approving Wright's draconian request.

He'd reminded everyone that, as a studio executive, he hadn't tried a case in years. But his bosses and colleagues had argued that no one knew more about the issues than him—including their attorneys, who'd lost in the lower courts—and no one presented a more true-blue image of the industry. Insiders whispered that if Harry succeeded, he was destined to head a studio. But that prospect meant nothing today. It was the specter of failure that gripped him. The bigwigs had a habit of pumping up their expectations only to wind up bitterly disappointed. He feared joining those actors marked for stardom who'd disappeared after the movies that were supposed to make them stars died at the box office.

For fifteen minutes Justices Black, Jackson, and Burton lobbed softball questions at his opponent. Harry exchanged disbelieving looks with Cantwell. Did the justices intend to invite Wright over for tea? In the face of the Court's obvious sympathy, Harry waived his opening statement to devote full time to questions from the skeptical judges.

William O. Douglas fired first. "Dimitri Glendakis built a state-of-the-art theater in Fresno, California, but no major studio sold him a single feature. Is that how your clients reward excellence and innovation?"

"Our attorneys advised Mr. Glendakis, before he broke ground, that we could not provide films for his proposed theater because we had preexisting obligations to other theaters in that zone."

"Weren't those 'preexisting obligations' to your own theaters?"

"And to the theaters of other companies," Harry responded. "But we did offer him three other areas in which to build."

Vinson cut to the government's most damaging assertion. "Mr. Jastrow, how do you defend the practice of block booking? It sounds to the Court suspiciously like a dictatorship."

"We admit to selling in blocks of ten to fifteen films. We specify exactly which films are to be shown on what dates and for how many weeks. Otherwise, the independent theater owners would cherry-pick our highest-profile product. Then the studios couldn't make movies that look less commercial up front—we call them 'sleepers'—because there wouldn't be guaranteed play time."

"If those movies are so marginal, perhaps you shouldn't make them at all."

"Each year sixty percent of our movies lose us money. Unfortunately, before we make them, we don't know *which* sixty percent."

The courtroom burst into laughter. Harry maintained a straight face, but the echo of his son's giggle buoyed him.

"The motion picture business is one of the riskiest in America. Each of the major studios produces approximately thirty films annually at an average cost of two million dollars and spends millions more in marketing. The exhibitors bear *none* of this risk. If the public doesn't come, they return our prints at no cost."

The more probing the questions from the bench, the more unflappable Harry became. Skepticism switched to curiosity. Zukor, Skouras, and the stars edged forward, anticipating a Capra moment. Go for it, Harry told himself, like Jimmy Stewart in *Mr. Smith Goes to Washington.*

"Early in this century—when movie producers didn't own theaters—there was chaos in our industry: product shortages, bankruptcies, broken contracts, illegal combines. For the past thirty years the studios' ownership of theaters has created prosperity, and the peace has allowed our filmmakers to create the first truly American art form. That progress will wither if the Court grants the Justice Department's request and obliterates the core structure of the business. We admit that abuses have occurred. But we urge you to abandon the overkill of theater divorcement and concentrate instead on more limited solutions."

The moguls mobbed him. "You're the greatest counterpuncher since Tunney," Skouras proclaimed. "We're going to beat those fuckers."

"Watch your language." Zukor pointed to AJ.

"Sorry. Your dad's a genius, kid."

Trying to mimic the adults, AJ shook his father's hand.

That made Harry feel like a hero.

They burst onto the steps of the Supreme Court building, bracing against the chill winter winds, just in time to see officials from the Justice Department slapping Bob Wright's back for a job well done. Reality trumped elation. Court was a crapshoot—and it would be May before the Big Five learned if their dice had rolled lucky seven or snake eyes.

=

AJ studied the room-service menu at the Hay-Adams Hotel with the intensity he applied to a multiple-choice quiz in Miss Alder's math class. Rule 1: Eliminate obvious no's. That killed oatmeal, because he hated the lumps, and eggs, because he'd eaten them scrambled, boiled, and shirred on the train coming east. Rule 2: Go with a choice that makes sense. It was Rice Krispies with a banana . . . until he ignored Rule 3: Avoid unknowns. AJ didn't recognize the name, but he enjoyed an adventure, so he ordered toast, bacon, and coffee for his father and smoked kippers and a glass of milk for himself.

In fourth grade he had abandoned his given name because he intended to win the Academy Award and thought that "Produced by Albert Julius Jastrow" would look old-fashioned on the screen. Alternatively, if he joined the PGA tour, "AJ Jastrow" would fit better on the trophies. Only his father knew his golf ambition, because Mom would have brained both of them. AJ Jastrow, Esq.—after Dad's triumph yesterday, he had to consider the law. He'd heard Miss Turner tell Mr. Cagney how his father's square chin and Roman nose reminded her of a Jewish Clark Kent. AJ checked his jawline in the mirror. He looked more like Jimmy Olsen.

"Son, are you ready?"

"I've got to finish packing."

"Well, hurry up. I've got a couple of surprises for our last day."

When room service arrived, a black waiter with gray hair and a gold front tooth laid out gleaming silverware on a linen tablecloth. He set two plates in front of the Jastrows and removed the domes with a flourish. AJ had assumed kippers were a sausage, not a relative of the herring. They looked and smelled like the soles of his old sneakers. But he'd ordered them, so he tasted a bite, which was so salty that he had to gulp down the milk. The combination reminded him of castor oil.

"Something wrong?"

"No, the kippers are really good . . . for kippers."

"Let's skip breakfast and get doughnuts at our first stop."

His father's bad knee—the one shot up in the war—froze in the cold, but together they hiked up the marble stairs to the Lincoln Memorial. Dad whispered, as if he were in temple, describing how the thirty-six marble columns represented each state on the day the president died. The statue of the man seated in his chair made AJ feel small. "Why does Lincoln look so sad? He *won* the Civil War."

"He wanted to take his family back to Illinois, but there was still a big job left to do. Maybe he knew he would never see home again."

Usually Dad gave more details. The heroes of American history were his heroes, unlike AJ's; he preferred the Yankees. The words carved into the wall intrigued him. "With malice toward none and charity for all." It was from the Second Inaugural Address. He didn't know what it meant but decided to learn more about Lincoln so that he could understand why his father so honored him.

The second surprise topped the first. Instead of taking the train, Dad had booked them two seats on a flight to Chicago. When they arrived at the airport, AJ was sure the cabdriver had made a mistake.

"It's going to be the only way to travel, so I thought you might want to try it."

"Dad, are you . . . I mean, are we . . . really? You're not kidding?"

"Scout's honor."

As they bumped down the runway, his father looked more nervous than before the hearing. I bet he wishes we'd taken the train, AJ thought. Then they were airborne and the whole city appeared below, the white marble of the monuments brilliantly reflecting in the sun. This was the best day of his life.

CHAPTER 2

Harry proudly considered himself a Los Angeleno from New York, unlike most transplants, who viewed themselves as New Yorkers temporarily living in Los Angeles. The expatriates still rooted for their Yankees and Dodgers, longed for subways and sidewalks, and savored the memory of a water bagel, while Harry embraced L.A.'s unique gifts, like bright lavender trees. So on the first Monday in May he detoured through Hancock Park to admire the blooming jacarandas. A block from the Paramount lot he heard distant chanting.

"Bingo! Bingo! Bingo!"

A Cadillac Sixty Special sat like an ambushed stagecoach amid a boisterous, sign-toting crowd. As the studio's senior vice president for business affairs, Harry had signed the check for the car, which was a gift to Bing Crosby, Paramount's number one box-office star. The actor was backed against the front fender signing autographs for members of his fan club who were there to wish him luck on the start of production of *A Connecticut Yankee in King Arthur's Court.* He appeared amiable, but with every kiss and quip, his eyes darkened a shade until sky blue had time-lapsed to midnight. As Crosby edged back to the driver's seat, Harry swerved his Oldsmobile to the curb and dashed across Melrose.

A Paramount patrol guard named Mike Inman greeted the Caddy. In his slate gray uniform with the mountain logo stitched in blue across his heart, Mike considered himself the studio's first line of defense. "Great to see you back, Mr. Crosby."

"Right. What stage am I on?" There were two dozen humpbacked structures as cavernous as airplane hangars.

"Number ten. Those folks sure do love you."

"That's why they start fan clubs," Crosby replied curtly. "Don't you know by now that I hate crowds? How could you stand there with your thumb up your ass while they badgered me?"

"People arrived really early, so I thought—"

"If you jerkoffs can't give me some simple protection, I'll work at Warners."

From twenty yards away Harry saw the guard ball his fists. He was enough of a loose cannon to pound dents into the actor's syrupy-smooth features. "Hey, Bing! Can't you make it to work on time?"

Mike cooled it, and Crosby stuck his head out the car window. "Jastrow, get your butt over here."

Harry did, and got a juicy smooch on the forehead. He had negotiated all Bing's deals with Paramount—and helped get him off scot-free after Crosby had pushed a piano out the window of a New York hotel suite during one of his benders. "How's your game?"

"I shot a seventy-seven at Bel Air yesterday and took Astaire for a C-note."

"Thank God we're putting you back to work. You'll get too good to play with me."

"I'm already too good. But your swing cracks me up." Crosby glanced at his watch. "Damn, I *am* late!" He stepped on the gas and disappeared onto the lot.

Inman sucked up the exhaust, then stared plaintively at Harry. "I guess you want an explanation?"

"What's to explain? It's the first day of shooting, so Bing feels miserable that he's neglecting his kids, and you've been a sourpuss for the last six months."

"You noticed?" Mike's missing sense of humor was a casualty of his battle to kick binge drinking.

"Hey, there are *no* secrets around here." At least not from me, Harry thought. In addition to his other jobs, he was in charge of all operations on the lot and proud that everyone from secretaries to electricians sought him out with complaints, comments, and confessions. "Do us both a favor. In the future when you see Der Bingle, dig a hole and hide!" Inman was so grateful for not being fired he shook Harry's hand till it hurt.

Circling the lot checking the movies in production, Harry paused at Old New York Street, which was dressed as a turn-of-the-century slum. One of the studio's top art directors, Fritz Kreter, was supervising the placement of rotting piles of garbage and screaming for more squashed fruit. Harry watched an apprentice hang tattered sheets to dry on lines between the buildings. "Hey, Fritz, the laundry's wrong."

Kreter paled. "What's the problem, Mr. J.?"

"It needs to look sadder."

In their make-believe world, there was always a solution. "Greta, add slack to the line." The now-drooping laundry looked pitiful—and authentic. "How'd you know?"

"I was there."

=

The Lower East Side of Manhattan, where Harry had grown up in the decade before World War I, was a squalid, crowded, and cacophonous breeding ground for broken spirits. He'd escaped the slum through books, reading everything from dime novels to an old edition of Plato's *Republic.* But his idylls were short-lived, because some young tough just off the boat was always prepared to take what little he had. Defending the street corner where he sold the *New York Herald* cost him more bloody noses than he could count. That penchant for dreaming— matched by a willingness to duke it out—proved ideal career training for the movie business.

Only when he became a parent did Harry realize how little he knew about his folks. A month after he'd arrived from the Ukraine, Isaac Jastrow got a job laying bricks. He did it twelve hours a day, six days a week for the rest of his life, while his wife, Esther, hemmed dresses for the uptown German Jews who came to her neighborhood for bargains. On Sundays the Jastrows made babies, five in total, all of whom died young, except their firstborn son. Because his parents lacked the time and energy to understand their new world, Harry interpreted it for them. He shaped every significant family decision and grew addicted to dispensing advice. When he learned that businessmen rarely made strategic moves without consulting an attorney, his career plans crystallized.

After graduating first in his class from NYU law school, Harry chose real estate law, accepting the mantra of Jewish immigrants that said owning property was the key to prosperity. In the midst of the Great Depression, however, his only prosperous client was the Broadway Theatre Company, which owned fifty screens in the five boroughs. Its president invited him to a premiere of *Come On, Marines,* a comedy about soldiers who rescue shipwrecked glamour girls. The poster looked dumb, but why hurt the man's feelings?

Halfway through the movie, Harry escaped for popcorn, but he halted before reaching the concession counter, his breath taken away by the sight of a woman waiting there—arms akimbo, shoulders back, hair flowing in the breeze of a table fan. Fleetingly they locked eyes. Somehow she looked familiar, but that wasn't possible. He could never have forgotten so miraculous a beauty. She paid for her Tootsie Roll, took a healthy chomp, and had sashayed away when it hit him—she was in the movie. He had an instant to catch her. "You're Mary, the nutty redhead with the big boobs."

The young woman turned and stared. "Excuse me?"

"You are, aren't you?" His mouth swept him down the drain. "If you're not, I'm truly sorry. I probably shouldn't have said anything. But it wasn't an insult. Mary—the character, I mean—is a knockout." He squinted. "It *is* you. Can I have your autograph?"

She burst out laughing. "Are you always so suave?"

"No one's ever used my name and *suave* in the same sentence."

She signed a napkin *Maggie Nolin* and handed it to him. "Is this what you want?"

"For starters." He couldn't believe how bold he was in her presence—and how sexy it felt. Where was the insecure guy from Hester Street?

Maggie tossed her candy aside. "Let's blow this place."

She'd probably played a gangster's moll in an earlier film, Harry figured. "Don't you have to stay for the press or the producers?" he inquired. "If you do, I'm happy to wait."

"No, I pretty much go where I want, when I want. Otherwise, I get into a rotten mood."

Tonight she wanted ice cream. He suggested Rumplemeyer's, near the Plaza, which allowed a long walk uptown to impress her. As she finished *his* sundae, Maggie confessed that her real name was Margaret Rose Kimmel. Although she'd grown up in Chicago, she qualified as a fringe member of Hollywood royalty because her mother was Adolph Zukor's youngest sister. But her real hero was her father, who'd died when she was twelve. He'd been the city's district attorney and had taken her to court for big trials. Harry tasted the hot fudge on her lips when they kissed good night.

"Tell me something, Mr. Jastrow." The bombshell actress vanished. "Are you going to turn out to be another of the cads I always find so appealing?"

"No one's ever used my name and *cad* in the same sentence."

They kissed again . . . this time, whipped cream.

Four months later Harry and Maggie married at Temple Emanu-el on Fifth Avenue. She chose New York over Chicago to accommodate her uncle Adolph's busy schedule. At the reception Zukor offered Harry a position in the studio's legal department. It paid twenty-two dollars more a week, and his bride thought he might enjoy it. Within a year he'd restructured the leases on all Paramount's theaters—saving the company hundreds of thousands of dollars—and had negotiated the purchase of two independent theater chains. He quickly gained expertise in the legal thicket of relations with exhibitors and became known as "Zukor's boy." Meanwhile, Maggie's acting career bottomed out, and after giving birth to AJ, she settled into the long-running role of wife and mother. The same day they purchased a house in Brooklyn, the chairman handed Harry a ticket on a train west to interview for a position under Barney Balaban, the studio chief and Zukor's heir apparent.

In 1939 the Paramount lot could barely contain a thriving thirty-acre city in which five thousand people scrambled to film fifty-five movies. Harry's first impression was of the bikes. Everyone pedaled somewhere, delivering something that someone else needed ten minutes ago. Sweating in his heavy tweed suit, he asked his guide if he had time to change. Instead, the young man directed him to the wardrobe department, where a savvy dresser fit Harry in the same tropical glen plaid that Bob Hope had worn in *The Cat and the Canary.*

At fifty Barney Balaban resembled everyone's rich uncle. Dressed in subtly blended shades of gray, the chief greeted him formally. Balaban was cautious about Zukor and preferred hiring executives with unquestioned loyalty to him. "Adolph tells me you're a legal eagle . . . and a mensch."

"He's being kind."

"Adolph? I don't think so." Balaban assessed him from head to toe. "I like your suit."

Welcome to Hollywood.

Film executives invariably broke the ice discussing movies they'd seen recently, a topic that revealed both taste and access to screenings. "What did you think of *Gone with the Wind*?" Balaban asked.

"My wife couldn't make the screening. She threatened divorce if I went without her."

"It sets a new standard. Selznick did a magnificent job."

"In New York we screened *The Wizard of Oz,*" Harry offered. "It's magical."

"It's not going to do any business." To players like Balaban, a film's box-office performance defined its quality.

"Whether it does or not, it's still a wonder."

Harry's boldness scored. At the end of the interview Barney gestured to the scripts neatly piled in his office. "We're creating art here. The novel is finished. People don't have the time to read. They want their stories in two-hour chunks. And radio's peaked. This is our time." He paused ceremonially. "I'd like you to join me in making the next five years the best ever for Paramount."

This was Harry's *beshert,* the uniquely satisfying "meant-to-be" that all men seek but few find. Two hours later he called Maggie and told her to hire a moving van.

=

Two *years* later his dream almost came to an abrupt end.

Hours after the Japanese bombed Pearl Harbor, Harry enlisted in the Marines. In early 1942 he was officially commissioned a second lieutenant—unofficially, cannon fodder. Guadalcanal, New Guinea, New Britain—he landed on some of the sorriest real estate on earth. But that didn't stop the Japanese from killing and dying to protect it. Once ashore, combat was chaos, ordered only by the dual goals of keeping his platoon alive and curing his crotch rot and dysentery.

Then came Tarawa. It was supposed to be a cakewalk, but just to reach the beach he wound up humping seventy pounds of pack and weaponry through a quarter mile of knee-deep water under a hailstorm of enemy mortar fire. By the second day he could smell death in his canteen water. Body parts bobbed obscenely in the ocean. On the final day of the battle, his point man disappeared. Dodging machine-gun fire, Harry found the soldier sinking in quicksand. Saving him was like pulling taffy. Just when he'd succeeded, a Japanese sniper in a breadfruit tree shattered his knee with a single rifle shot. The field surgeon fused it too tightly, but since the guy had operated on twenty men that day and saved only six, Harry never complained.

He earned a Purple Heart, which his son displayed to all his friends, an honorable discharge—and a bonanza for his career. With so many young men off fighting, the corporate pyramid at Paramount was underpopulated. He rose rapidly to a seat among the handful of men who determined what made America laugh, cry, and cheer.

=

A nineteenth-century Spanish don would have felt at home in Harry's office. The scrolled sofas and chairs were deeply upholstered, and intricate mosaic tiles decorated the floor. Entering through the back door, he set his briefcase down on an antique desk once owned by General Santa Anna and studied the flash reports from key Paramount houses. Thursday was Dish Night in theaters around the nation, so admissions on the Randolph Scott western *Albuquerque* should have ticked up, but the offer of free Melmac had failed to spur much activity. The headline in *Variety* proclaimed, PAR'S $31,668,709 NET PROFIT IN '47 SECOND ONLY TO '46.

But it was old news. All over town, 1948 was shaping up as a lousy year. Box office for the industry was down 19 percent in the first quarter. That projected to a loss of a billion admissions by year's end. Harry hadn't expected a continuation of the bonanza of the war years, when Americans had packed theaters to escape from death and destruction, but the accelerating slump was alarming. With their survivors' mentalities, Zukor and Balaban hunkered down, assigning him the job of cutting the studio's overhead. Every day he fielded calls from agents irate at his canceling the contracts of writers, directors, and producers who'd loyally served Paramount for years. He assuaged and explained—but felt guilty as hell.

While the studio kissed off the little guys, the big shots told it to get lost. Balaban wanted to make a five-year deal with Cary Grant, so yesterday Harry had called his agent. "Why would I do that when I can gouge you on each new picture?" he'd laughed. And stars like Grant weren't satisfied with huge salaries. With Uncle Sam taking nearly 90 percent in taxes, they demanded "ownership" to get more favorable capital-gains treatment. The contract system was kaput. Five years from now all the talent would be freelance, driving up the prices for the guys in demand.

By nine A.M. Harry was already buzzed and bothered, so when his secretary, Anita Benitez, entered the office, he put on a positive face. "*Como estas,* Anita?"

"*Muy bueno,* boss. How was your table last night?" The Jastrows had celebrated Maggie's thirty-fifth birthday at La Rue on the Strip; to get a table, Anita had harassed owner Billy Wilkerson until he'd guaranteed them his personal booth.

"Perfect! About nine o'clock, Bogie walked in with Lauren Bacall and saw us sitting in 'his' spot. It was as if the king of England had found a couple of commoners eating bag lunches on the throne."

The phone rang. "Mr. Cantwell calling from D.C."

Harry grabbed the receiver as Anita discreetly slipped out.

"Hold on to your hat. The decision's coming down today."

Harry took deep breaths. "Are you sure?"

"Yes . . . well, almost."

"I thought they'd forgotten about us." Or hoped they had. "Any hint of which way it went?"

"That it took them so long is a good sign. It meant they listened to you. I'm headed over to the Old Ebbit to sweat it out. I'll phone as soon as I hear."

There was no time to collect his thoughts because Harry was due at his weekly staff meeting with Balaban and the other senior movie executives. He decided not to alert anyone until he had decisive news, in case Mel's information proved wrong. Gathering his files, he glanced at a photo on his desk of his family on a vacation in the Baja, their arms around the three-hundred-pound marlin they'd landed after a two-hour fight. Harry did a quick calculation. If he floored it, he could reach the Mexican border in three hours. In Ensenada it was easy to get new identity papers, then disappear into the hills. . . . The picture frame crashed to the floor. He cut himself on the broken glass.

CHAPTER 3

"*S*heket!"

AJ blinked under the stony stare of Rabbi Leon Ginsberg. "I made a mistake, huh?"

"Do you not understand the meaning of the word *silence*?"

AJ shuddered. Everything about the new rabbi was creepy—his German accent, the cloud of cigarette smoke suspended over his steel-wool hair, even the thick soles of his shoes, which looked like they could stomp someone to death. After escaping the Nazis, Ginsberg had been unemployed for a long time because there were too many émigré rabbis for the Jews in America. Maybe that's why he was always in a bad mood. After finally getting a job at Beth Israel Temple, he had cracked down on the Hebrew school's lax standards. It was just AJ's luck to be among his first guinea pigs.

"You are butchering our language."

He suspected that the rabbi was right, but it was hardly a crime. "Sorry, sir."

"Call me *Rabbi.* I am not a general. How old are you?" He knew the answer because he was testing AJ for his bar mitzvah in three weeks.

"I'll be thirteen on May twenty-second, Rabbi."

"Thirteen?" Ginsberg feigned disbelief, but the guy was no Edward G. Robinson. "I have *yeladeen* who read Hebrew better. Your instructor warned me that your preparations were shoddy. But what I am hearing simply will not do. Open your prayer book and try again."

"Baw-ruck a taw—"

"Bah-ruch."

AJ hated failing. He had always reached milestones ahead of schedule, crawling at six months and walking at ten. By the time his family had moved to Los Angeles, he already knew how to read, so the principal had proposed skipping him directly into second grade. His parents had hesitated, but AJ had seen a chance to reach middle school a year early and had convinced them. He'd studied hard, competed aggressively, and held his own with his older classmates. But Hebrew seemed like a waste of time—after all, no one spoke it—so he shirked assignments.

"Ku-ma a-do-noy, vei-fut-zu."

"Ve-YA-fut-su."

"Right. I knew that. *Ve-YA-fut-su, oy-be—*"

" '*Oy-be*'? I don't see any '*oy-be.*' I see an *oy-ve-khah.*"

Ominous silence. "Should I continue?" The man puffed and puffed on his cigarette, silently choosing his next form of torture. Maybe Ginsberg had learned his third degree from the SS. AJ decided to focus on something other than his interrogator, which was how Richard Conte had handled his inquisition in *A Walk in the Sun.*

Golf was his favorite pastime, so AJ stared out the window to Los Angeles Country Club, across the street, and imagined the approach shot on the hole that bordered Wilshire Boulevard. He'd never played the course, because no Jews or film people were members, but after passing it on the way to school every day, he guessed he needed to hit an eight-iron from the bottom of the hill. The rabbi looked to see what had him so entranced. A foursome in knickers walked down the fairway. Boy, it must drive Ginsberg nuts after all the Nazi persecution to wind up a wedge shot away from another group of anti-Semites.

"Look at me, Albert!"

The man was meaner than Himmler. "Yes, sir—I mean, Rabbi."

"We Jews are the chosen people. Do you understand that?"

Dad said people were special because of what they did, not how they were born. "I'm not sure I agree with—"

"It would violate my covenant with God to bar mitzvah anyone who did not care enough to learn the language of his blessed forefathers."

AJ slumped in his chair. "You're not going to . . . you mean—"

"It isn't *that* bad. You'll attend my Torah tutorials this summer and we'll postpone your bar mitzvah until the fall."

He'd never envisioned so harsh a sentence. Ginsberg left the room to inform AJ's mom, who was waiting downstairs. His folks would have to explain to everyone that the party was off because their son was lazy and irresponsible. They'd have to cancel their vacation to the Canadian Rockies to stay home while he went to summer school, instead of summer camp. How could they trust someone who failed because he didn't try? Although AJ prided himself on being too old to cry, he did so. Now he was weak as well as worthless. He choked on his shame until breathing was like sucking air through a soggy straw.

"Did I hear you say my son is dumb?" In all his misery, AJ took heart hearing his mother's voice through the door and quickly wiped his eyes on his jacket sleeve.

"You misunderstood me, Mrs. Jastrow." The rabbi reentered his office.

"Oh. Then maybe you're saying *I'm* dumb."

With her rich red hair and canary yellow dress, his mom looked like the flame at the tip of an explosive fuse. Ginsberg retreated as if she might blow at any moment. "I didn't say that either of you is dumb. Your son simply isn't ready."

"He's almost thirteen. He was ready for his bris, he'll be ready for his bar mitzvah. It's a matter of showing up."

"No, no! It doesn't work that way. Albert cannot chant his haftorah. He can't even read it." He emphasized the words as if talking to a foreigner.

Maggie wheeled around. "AJ, why can't you chant this . . . this thing?"

"I have a block. "

"A block? Well, buster, you better *un*block because two hundred guests are coming to hear you knock their socks off. And like any performer worth his salt, you're going to give a hell of a show. I don't want to hear excuses about not being ready."

"Mrs. Jastrow, three weeks is insufficient time for a student of Albert's modest abilities."

" 'Modest abilities'?" She advanced until she was inches from his face. "AJ has always been an A student. So if he can't do his havatorah—"

"Haftorah."

"Exactly . . . then maybe it's not his fault; maybe the problem is the sorry educational approach employed by this temple."

"I agree, that's why I'm insisting—"

"Herr Ginsberg, I read your C.V. when we hired you. I understand you studied in the most distinguished seminaries in prewar Europe. We must look like country bumpkins to you, but frankly, you'll fare better if you remember that most of us in Hollywood prefer a more jovial Judaism." He started to interrupt again, but she shushed him with a wave of her finger. "My husband and I have made a nonrefundable deposit for the ballroom at the Hotel Bel-Air three weeks from tomorrow. We're celebrating AJ's birthday that night and you're cordially invited. If you can also bar mitzvah him that morning . . . perfect. If you can't, we'll survive." AJ thought his mother was finished. "Unfortunately, if you insist on canceling the bar mitzvah, my Uncle Adolph—as in Zukor—will be deeply disappointed. AJ, come on, you've got a *real* school to get to."

Her topper had checkmated the rabbi. The temple's elders wouldn't offend the chairman of Paramount just because his nephew didn't know an aleph from a gimel. AJ could see the man fume, but the anger had a shade he couldn't identify. On the way to their car AJ's relief was replaced by embarrassment that he needed an adult's help. "Mom, how am I going to learn this thing?"

"We'll write it out phonetically and you'll memorize it. That's how I did it when I played a Spanish prostitute on Broadway. But whatever you do, don't tell your father."

"Definitely not." AJ could already picture his downcast eyes. "Thanks."

"Oh, fiddle-faddle."

She loved to imitate Vivien Leigh in *Gone with the Wind*. People said they looked alike. As his mother drove west on Wilshire, AJ glanced back at the temple. Was Ginsberg staring at them from his window? Then it hit him—the rabbi's expression in the office was the same one Rhett Butler wore just before he carried Scarlett O'Hara up the stairs to the bedroom. His skin crawled at the idea that a strange man found his mom sexy. But it didn't faze her. "That rabbi's a bully," she warned. "I don't ever want to hear of you bullying anyone. It's a miserable trait."

CHAPTER 4

"Gentlemen, we have a crisis." Barney Balaban grimly waved a letter in front of the three top vice presidents in Paramount's movie division. "An hour ago I received this special delivery from Ted Gamble."

"What the hell does he want?" Harry spoke too quickly, his pitch too high. Gamble was president of the Theatre Owners of America, the organization of independent exhibitors whose antitrust complaints had fueled the Supreme Court case. Did he have a scoop on the verdict?

Balaban put on thick reading glasses. " 'Dear Barney, I'm writing to you and the other studio chiefs about an issue of grave concern to my constituents. Television aerials are sprouting on roofs across the nation. Although there are only a million sets in home use, the medium eats away at our audience like a cancer. But we can halt its spread if we act together immediately.' "

Harry smiled ironically. Next to divorcement, nothing incited anxiety among movie executives faster than a discussion about TV.

" 'People are already complaining about the sorry programs available on television. How many hours of professional wrestling and bad variety acts can anyone watch! The station owners have only one recourse. They have begun offering hefty sums to independent producers for the rights to show their old films. Fortunately, the overwhelming supply of such movies remains with bastions like Paramount. *We ask you to announce publicly that your studio will never sell or license its old films to any station.* This stance will starve TV to death. Best regards, Theodore Gamble.' "

"The guy's overreacting," Frank Freeman growled. At six foot five, with a shock of white hair, Paramount's head of production resembled a snappish polar bear. "Movies are the finest entertainment known to man. Television can't touch us."

"Isn't that what vaudeville impresarios said about radio?" Balaban asked sourly.

"And what silent movie stars said about the talkies," Harry added. "No one can halt a technology as powerful as television."

His certainty was born of personal experience. Six months ago the Jastrows had splurged, spending four hundred dollars to buy a ten-inch Dumont. Maggie couldn't keep enough coffee and Danish for visitors who came by for a peek and stayed for hours, and AJ's popularity at school soared with his daily reports on last night's shows. With TV in the family, Harry and Maggie stayed home more often, cuddling in front of the set in the dark. Harry still had carpet burns on his knees from "christening" the family room while the national anthem signaled the end of the day's programming. God help the movies when the men who returned from the war discovered that television was an aphrodisiac.

"Am I hearing you right, Jastrow?" Paul Herzog lived to fight. At thirty-seven, he was in charge of Paramount's theaters and selling film to exhibitors. His muscled arms, washboard stomach, and broken nose were holdovers from his years as an amateur middleweight. "Are you saying that we should ignore the growth of TV?"

"No, I'm saying we need to accept it and find a way to make it work *for* us," Harry replied. "Gamble's got his head in the sand."

"Have you ever sold any film?"

"You know I haven't. But people in our industry feel I know something about exhibition."

"What you know is what's printed on contracts. I sold film—person to person, house to house. While you were attending some Fancy Dan college, I traveled the Midwest, sleeping in fleabag hotels, eating overcooked pork chops, getting to know local exhibitors."

"For the record, Paul, I went to City College. What's your point?"

"These men are scared. You would be too, Jastrow, if you had every dime invested in a building that could be crawling with cobwebs next year. They're our partners and when you're under attack, you don't desert your allies. That's how we won the war. Eisenhower understood that."

"And Eisenhower just sold his rights to television," Harry countered. Ike's sale of *Crusade in Europe* to ABC for a twenty-six-part teleseries distressed the studios. "How can you talk about loyal partners? The exhibitors sued us."

"Gentlemen!" Barney hated confrontation. He grabbed a bear claw from a pile of pastries and began wolfing it down. "The question is what do we do about this demand."

"We could certainly use the licensing revenues to prop up our profits, especially if box office continues dropping," Harry noted. "And the movies in question are so old they're practically worthless."

"That's shortsighted," Herzog countered. "And I'll tell you why."

"I'll bet you will," Harry muttered to himself.

"Television may be here to stay, but licensing will cannibalize business from our own theaters." He smiled at Harry. "Assuming we still own theaters after the Supreme Court decision."

"Don't even raise that specter." Balaban turned white. With his jaundiced eyes, he looked like the glass of buttermilk from which he sipped. "I won't tolerate negative thinking on that subject."

"Tell Gamble to get lost," Harry advised. "This is an internal Paramount matter."

"Jastrow, you're missing the big picture—literally. TV's future isn't in the home. The stations will never make enough money from advertising to provide decent entertainment. And nothing looks good on that tiny box anyway." Paul circled the conference table, selling his idea as if it were next year's blockbuster. "TV's future is in the theaters. Hear me out. If we install large-screen television—I'm talking forty feet wide—in our showcase houses, we can broadcast special events like the Joe Lewis–Jersey Joe Walcott fight. People will pay a huge premium to see that kind of event, especially with a television picture that's bigger than life. I've convinced the independent exhibitors to go with us on this. Let's not anger them over the licensing issue and take the chance they'll oppose us on theater TV. My advice, Barney, is to make the declaration they want loud and clear."

The round had ended, but Harry kept punching. "The whole value of TV is its convenience in the home."

"Suppose you're right about the future, Harry," Freeman interrupted. "We should buy ABC before Fox does."

"The FCC will never let a studio own a network. But we can accomplish the same thing by providing the programming. No one can do it better than us. Licensing our old films is a perfect stopgap until we can gear up for original TV production."

Herzog recoiled as if struck by a low blow. "That's abject surrender— like selling A-bombs to the Russkies."

"What did you say?"

"Maybe lawyers like you don't love movies, Jastrow, but us guys in the trenches damn well do."

"What the hell do *you* know about trenches?" A 4-F deferment had kept Herzog out of the war, despite his fighting shape.

Paul hovered. "Don't you dare question my courage!"

Harry rose to defend himself. "Then don't insult my loyalty."

"Sit down, both of you!" Balaban shouted. "I will not tolerate this kind of behavior." When the intercom buzzed, Barney caught his breath. "Harry, your secretary says there's an urgent call."

===

The connection was so bad that at first Harry couldn't understand what Mel Cantwell was saying. He heard "seven to one," but was that for or against? The static cleared. "We were scorched. They upheld the lower-court ruling and sent it back to the judge to establish procedures for divorcement."

Harry's weak knee caved. "Bob Wright won't quit until he makes us sell every one of our theaters."

"That's the word."

Harry wanted to curse the Court, but his sense of equity didn't allow him the satisfaction. "If you were on the bench, Mel, how would you have voted? Hollywood had a hopeless case."

"I know that, you know that." Cantwell's voice cracked. "Let's hope your bosses reach the same conclusion."

CHAPTER 5

AJ rolled the dice. Double threes teetered precariously on the edge of the board—and hung there. It clearly wasn't his family's day. He walked his top hat six spaces, till it landed on Boardwalk. "I'm busted, Ray."

Ray Stark savored a victory in Monopoly as much as the thrill of signing a hot new client. "You played with a lot of smarts, kid, but you should have built hotels on Marvin Gardens when you had the chance."

"I didn't have enough cash."

"You had the cash, but not the guts to use it."

That hurt. Ray's postmortem reflected his philosophy that you conquered the world before it conquered you. Although he and Dad looked at those things differently, they were best friends. The Rabbit—Ray had gotten his nickname because of his outsized teeth and cheeks and Munchkin size—was like a mischievous older brother. A few weeks ago he'd tried to sign an actress named Sarah Campbell, but Sarah's niece, Bunny, was visiting for the day, so Ray had asked AJ to come along to keep the girl busy. He held Bunny's hand on the Ferris wheel and plied her with cotton candy while the Rabbit retired to a nearby motel for his meeting. All hell broke loose, however, when his mom found out, screaming that Ray was going to hell for using a minor as a beard. That didn't make sense because AJ was still too young to need a shave.

"Another game, kid?"

"I hope those guys on the Supreme Court die. Dad did great, but they had their minds made up. I bet the attorney general paid them off."

Ray laughed. "You're watching too many gangster movies. How about hearts?"

It was that or homework. "Deal."

=

Shortly after seven P.M. Harry pulled into a driveway two streets above the Beverly Hills Hotel, killed the engine, and stared at his New Orleans colonial. Sandwiched between a new French Regency and a half-finished Georgian, the house somehow fit perfectly. Maybe the lush foliage knitted the styles together. Because of the boom in postwar construction, it had taken two years to build and had consumed much of the Jastrows' savings. Ninety-nine nights out of a hundred it was his haven. But tonight it was a two-story headache with a thirty-year mortgage. For the right offer, he'd sell on the spot, take off to a deserted island, and live under palm trees and stars.

Harry's fantasies of escape had begun in the war. Before each battle he planned his exact route, even took the first steps, then remembered the guys who counted on him—and the fate of the soldier in *The Red Badge of Courage.* His commanding officers bragged that no one hung tougher than Lieutenant Jastrow. But the urge to run and hide had accompanied him back to civilian life, growing more frequent the higher Harry rose at Paramount. Last week he'd skipped out of work early, driven to Long Beach, and watched ships steam from the port to faraway places. That was just crazy. He needed to talk—but to whom?

Balaban had reacted to the verdict by disappearing into the bathroom for fifteen minutes. When he'd emerged, he'd instructed—no, ordered—Harry to call Robert Wright and cut a deal in which Paramount sold a partial interest in their wholly owned theaters to the independents. It was the compromise Harry had previously proposed but

Balaban couldn't hear it. They had to move, Barney claimed, before Warners or Fox got the same bright idea—as if those guys weren't already scheming to save their butts.

When Harry trudged into the kitchen, Maggie was loading their dishwasher. The damn thing was a waste of money because you had to scrape every plate clean before putting it in. "You must be wrecked," she said softly.

He welcomed her hug, sudsy hands and all. "The news is all bad."

"AJ's playing cards with Ray. I'll get him so you guys can work. Come up as soon as you're finished." She started to leave. "Here's the good news . . . I love you."

Harry's immediate concern was that the verdict would provoke a steep sell-off in the stock of Paramount and the other majors, so he had called Stark earlier, seeking advice on the best angle to place on the Court decision. Although he was now a successful agent, Ray had started as a publicist at Warner Bros. and possessed shrewd instincts for dealing with the press. Harry scanned his draft release, which expressed "profound disappointment" with the ruling but emphasized the studios' "respect for the law"—as if they had a choice. An "acceptable compromise" would hopefully enable them to maintain control of most of their theaters. Harry added a line stressing the solidarity of the companies.

"That should calm down Wall Street," Stark noted.

"What are you doing with your portfolio?"

"Selling every movie stock I own."

Harry smiled for the first time all day.

"I covered Vince Golden at *Variety,* as well as Peter Dames at the *Journal,*" Ray explained. "*The New York Times, Box Office,* everyone's putting a good face on it." He paused uncomfortably.

"What's bothering you?"

"I got this strange call from Mark Sillman at *Film Weekly.* I didn't pay much attention because the guy's a maverick and the paper's a rag, but he got a tip that the studios were furious that their legal team blew the case. He mentioned Cantwell in D.C.—and you."

"Me?"

"Especially you—something about your not being aggressive in going after Bob Wright at the hearing. I killed the story, saying I spoke to Nick Schenk at MGM and Jack Warner and they blamed Truman because he hates Hollywood. Sillman bought my explanation." Stark paced the room. "But we need to find out who fed him the information before they feed you to the fish."

"Check out Spyros Skouras," Harry advised. "When I proposed my settlement idea, he complained I was a 'fellow traveler' with exhibitors."

After bidding Stark good night, Harry dialed Zukor in New York.

"Shalom. This is Abba Eban speaking." Eban was the representative to the United Nations from the provisional state of Israel, which was days away from declaring its independence. Arab troops from five countries had massed on Israel's borders. In their desire to assimilate, most moguls shunned any connection to Zionism. The polo-playing Louis B. Mayer even denied having Jewish blood. But Zukor staunchly supported Israel. Harry apologized for calling late.

"No problem, Mr. Jastrow. We operate on Holy Land time here. I'll get Adolph, but I'm sorry to hear of your defeat today. I understand it was a monumental injustice."

Bombs could fall on Tel Aviv, but Hollywood's grief grabbed the spotlight. "I appreciate that," Harry replied.

"We helped rally this country through the war," Zukor whined. "Where's the thanks?"

"Politicians have notoriously short memories."

Zukor was silent for several seconds. "The real loss, Harry, it's not the money . . ."

"No, sir?"

"All of us—Marcus Loew, Bill Fox, Carl Laemmle, the Warners—we started with theaters. They were how we connected to the audience. You sit on your ass night after night, next to other people sitting on their asses, you get to know what people want."

"We can still go to theaters, Adolph."

"It won't be the same. But maybe it won't be such a big problem. Barney says you think you can make a deal to save us."

Now the deal was Harry's idea! It was useless to drag any mogul into reality. "I'll do my best."

"Give my love to my gorgeous niece and say hello to the bar mitzvah boy."

=

Upstairs in their bedroom Maggie spread cardboard cutouts of table assignments across their bed while chain-smoking Viceroys. Harry hated her habit but didn't understand the pressure the bar mitzvah created.

The biggest headache was seating—not the number of guests but their egos. Hollywood was a company town, so any event, even the birthday party of a thirteen-year-old, functioned in part as a business conclave. Since Paramount was paying for half the affair, she tried to arrange a few tables that might inspire a movie. She seated her friend Olivia de Havilland next to William Wyler, whose next film was *The Heiress*. The director wanted de Havilland as his leading lady and would have five courses to make his pitch.

The other problem Maggie faced was the strict caste system in the business. If it was violated, some people would sulk in the powder room all night. Unfortunately, perceptions of what caste you belonged to differed. And then there were the "untouchables." Harry was friendly with senior agents such as George Wood of William Morris, superagent Myron Selznick, and Ray. But Maggie struggled with where to seat them. The stars they represented considered their agents beneath them. So did most studio executives, who regarded the "ten percenters" as parasites. If she stuck them with civilians, like AJ's orthodontist, they'd have nothing to talk about. On the other hand, if the agents shared a table, they might eat each other rather than the roast beef. She installed them at table 20 and prayed for the best.

"This is an even bigger mess than I thought." Harry entered the bedroom, yanking at his tie. At first Maggie thought he hated her seating choices but then realized that he remained preoccupied with the Supreme Court ruling.

"How so?"

"I don't know. But my instincts tell me I'm in trouble." Now he couldn't get the knot out of his shoelace.

She studied him. "You're feeling guilty, aren't you, that you couldn't save their arrogant asses? You think *you* screwed up."

"I told them to compromise . . ." He rubbed his eyes. "Somebody else should have pleaded the case."

Harry's exquisite sense of responsibility left him vulnerable to a world willing to take advantage. The best remedy was a kick in his butt. "That's bullshit! No one could have done a better job. If Balaban and Uncle Adolph point a finger in your direction, tell them to look in the mirror!"

Harry kicked his shoe across the room, walked over to the bed, and picked up a cutout of the Paramount "exec table." "Seat Barney next to my mother. He won't mess with me again."

Maggie removed the girdle she didn't need, slipped on one of his threadbare oxford shirts, then turned on the radio. Patti Page was singing "Every So Often." Leaning over to kiss him, she made sure her breasts rubbed his chest. It was clear what he needed next.

"Honey, I'm really tired."

"You only think you are." She patted the bed.

Harry swept the bar mitzvah onto the floor and urged her back on the pillows.

≡

From the fourth tee at Riviera Country Club, Harry saw the swells on the Pacific Ocean. Gaping sand traps guarded the green 230 yards to the west, giving the hole a reputation as the toughest par three in America. Harry swung as hard as his reconstructed knee allowed. The ball banana-arced to the right, directly into the prevailing wind, and failed to carry the lip of the last bunker. "Another day at the beach."

"How do you do it?"

"Do what?"

"You know." AJ shrugged. "Stay calm."

"If I didn't, I couldn't lecture you." Last year AJ had broken a nine-iron heaving it into a drainage ditch after a sculled shot. Harry had made him pick it up and walk back to the clubhouse. He wasn't allowed to play again for a month. That was punishment for both of them, because nine holes together in the fading Sunday sunlight was their favorite time of the week. When AJ was six, Harry had given him a cut-down set of clubs as a Chanukah present, and they were in the middle of a lesson when the news of Pearl Harbor reached the coast. His son had outgrown the clubs, but they remained on display in the garage, like bronzed baby shoes.

AJ stepped to the forward tees and threw grass in the air. It blew back in his face. "Lot of wind up there."

"It won't stop you, son." AJ was the youngest golfer in the club's history to break eighty, and Harry was so proud that he sometimes asked him to fill out a foursome with his business friends.

The boy's drive bored through the wind, bounced once on the green, and began rolling. Thirty feet from the hole it appeared to come up short, but the topspin kept it going and the slope of the green directed it on target. Harry grabbed AJ, hugging and slapping his back. "It's going in! It's going in!"

"Dad! Did it drop? Did it?"

From the distance it was impossible to tell, so they ran as fast as they could lugging their bags, then dumped them and sprinted the final fifty yards, until they saw . . . the ball hanging on the lip, a half inch from elation.

AJ sagged. "One more lousy revolution. How could that happen?"

To be thirteen and not know the answer—his son would learn about life soon enough. "I know what you're feeling." Harry thrust his arms around him. "But by the time you're my age, you'll have ten holes in one—make that twenty."

AJ seemed unconvinced. "Let's find yours, Dad."

Harry's ball had come to rest in the jagged footprint of a previous visitor to the trap. "Why people can't take thirty seconds to rake after they've finished hitting."

"Give yourself a drop," AJ offered graciously.

"What?"

"Okay, okay, I know. Play it as it lays."

"Lies."

" 'Lies' doesn't sound right."

"You 'lay' your club down, but the ball 'lies.' " Harry insisted upon proper grammar because the phrase described the fundamental rule of golf. Wherever and however your ball landed, you did the best you could with it. Harry hacked at his Titleist, and it exploded, flying into the cup without touching the green. He celebrated by meticulously raking his divot. They collapsed on the hillside to savor birdies reached through unlikely routes. "Capricious game," he mused.

"Capricious game," AJ agreed. "What's 'capricious'?"

"Sometimes things happen for no apparent reason, as if the golf gods were teasing to see how we handle the good and bad." He watched the boy memorizing *capricious* for one of those vocabulary tests in *Reader's Digest*. "So, who do you like in the Open?" Riviera was set to host the national championship next month.

"It's got to be Hogan," AJ said. "He owns this course." The incomparable Ben Hogan was his son's hero. "Dad, do you still think I should go into the business?"

"Sure. We're going to be partners, right?"

"Absolutely. That's what I want. I even came up with a name for our company last week in math class: J-Squared Productions, but written J to the second power."

"I love it! When you have a son, we can change the name to J-Cubed. So what's bothering you?"

"I guess my question is . . . will there be a business to go into?"

It's amazing, Harry mused, how much a kid could pull from the ether, or from *Variety* . . . or from eavesdropping on Ray Stark. He stared out to the ocean. "Remember our fishing trip to Baja?"

"Uh-huh."

"We headed south out of Cabo and came to that juncture where the waves pounded against each other."

"The captain said they were fifteen feet high."

"The phenomenon's called 'cross seas.' It happens when the waves from one sea smash into the waves from another. There was no line, but you could imagine where the Sea of Cortés ended and the Pacific Ocean began. The water must have been six or seven degrees warmer in the sea."

AJ nodded. "And a lot bluer."

"That's because the Sea of Cortés is sheltered by land on three sides. The movie business has been sailing in that kind of sea. Now it's hit the Pacific. All the protections we've counted on—owning our theaters, owning the stars, owning the audience—they'll soon be gone. But that doesn't mean the business can't sail on without them."

"I guess so."

"If you're still up for it when you finish college, we'll start J-Squared. We can build our offices right near here so we can go play a few holes at lunch."

AJ stared dubiously at the empty fields and endless eucalyptus trees of the Pacific Palisades. "I'm not sure people will want to visit us in the boonies."

"It won't always be like this." Unfortunately.

"Would you mind if we quit? I've got stuff I need to work on."

"Sure." Harry masked his disappointment. He would have played all night.

CHAPTER 6

Paul Herzog never deigned to visit his colleagues, so when Anita announced that he was pacing in the outer office, Harry's skin prickled. During the war the instant itch had proved a reliable early-warning sign of lurking danger. And in the two days since the Justice Department had rejected his fool's-errand compromise, the halls of Paramount reminded him of those miserable atolls in the Pacific, booby-trapped by nature and the Japanese.

"Barney and I decided you should see this before it appears in the trades." Herzog forked over a press release. Its headline read, NO PAR PIX ON VIDEO PER BALABAN.

Harry skimmed it, his feet dancing nervously in the well of his desk. "Paramount has no intention of offering its old films to television on either a licensing or sales basis, because the interests of our exhibitors are the first consideration of the company." It was a defeat for him and the company. Take the high road, Harry. "Congratulations, Paul. For all our sakes, I hope your advice was right."

Herzog smiled tightly. "As a kid I had rheumatic fever. The doctors told me I couldn't play sports."

"Really?" Harry couldn't think of any information less relevant.

"So on Saturdays I went to matinees to watch movie stars overcome obstacles bigger than mine. They're the ones who inspired me to believe I could do anything." He leaned across the desk until Harry felt the air stream between the gap in the man's front teeth. "When the going gets tough, Jastrow, the tough get going. Regardless of our past disagreements, we have to stand shoulder to shoulder."

Harry imagined Herzog as a young boy, standing in front of a mirror memorizing a new cliché each day. "Those would be admirable sentiments, Paul, if we were fourth and long with thirty seconds to play. But this isn't a football huddle where one guy calls the plays. I intend to say what's on my mind."

Herzog abandoned his pep talk. "Balaban asked me to head up the team to dispose of our theaters, and I need you to run revenue projections." He removed a thick file from his briefcase. "Get started on these. Also, Barney approved my idea to broadcast a Crosby concert next year on theater TV. You need to introduce me so I can propose it to Bing."

"He prefers 'Mr. Crosby' if you're not his friend." Harry's two-by-four failed to graze Herzog.

"Stop by my office when you've got all the information—the sooner the better."

Harry deposited Paul's assignment in the wastepaper basket, then thought better of it. The meeting had unnerved him. The guy was too damn cocksure. And why had Barney sent an emissary rather than delivering his news in person? There was no cause for panic, he told himself, even as he sensed the enemy outflanking him.

=

"I'm finished."

"Was something wrong with the chicken?" Maggie asked.

"It was delicious." Harry pushed aside his half-eaten dinner. He had no appetite, even for her freshly baked seven-layer cake. "Paul Herzog's out to get me."

"That sleazy sales guy? Are you sure?"

"Ray took the reporter at *Film Weekly* to dinner at the Brown Derby and got him so drunk he copped to who spread the rumor about my 'screwing up' at the Court. It was Herzog."

"You should knock his block off."

That was always her solution—to everyone and everything that stood in her way. Harry avoided conversations about corporate politics whenever he could, but this time Maggie had a right to know. "I've got to be careful. Herzog's sly. He told Balaban that the exhibitors had targeted Paramount for a boycott because of my role in the Supreme Court case. It was a lie, but the boss believed it and caved on the TV issue."

"Have you talked to Barney?"

Harry shook his head. "He's home with gallstones."

"Call him there."

"No, I'm going to low-key it for a while."

"Passive resistance?" She regarded him skeptically. "Like your friend Gandhi."

"He's not my friend, but he did defeat the British empire."

"And look how he wound up." She sealed the chicken in a bell-shaped container and stored it in the fridge.

Harry escaped the kitchen—and their skirmish. He closed the door to his tiny home office, which was off-limits to Maggie and AJ, and cracked open a notebook filled with his large, scrawling handwriting. After returning from the war he'd resolutely refused to discuss what he had endured. So many men had died or suffered worse fates. It was time to get on with life. And maybe he could have put the horror behind him if it wasn't for Hollywood's war movies. They ripped the scab off his experience and deluded the public with their ridiculously romantic visions. He wasn't sure if the screenplay he was writing was an exposé or therapy, but it portrayed combat as madness in a way no one else had done. Lest anyone discourage his efforts, he wrote in secret.

Tonight he reached the turning point of his story, inspired by the real-life events of March 6, 1943. His alter ego, Lieutenant Farber, was scouting enemy positions when a camouflaged Japanese soldier emerged from behind a fabulous rhododendron—looking like a clown with flowers sprouting from his helmet—and fired point-blank. *Click, click, click.* Thank God, nothing worked in the stinking jungle. *Banzai!* The Jap charged and Farber stuck out his bayonet.

Perspiration dripped down Harry's forehead, causing the ink from his fountain pen to bleed down the page. No loss—his attempts at writing the character's dying words were nothing but cross-outs. In that final moment he'd wondered what the real soldier had said. Was it good-bye to a beloved wife? Or "Get the fucking blade out of my gut"? Harry had killed from afar, but that was the one time he'd cleaned a man's intestines off his rifle.

It was macabre, but now he was hungry—no, ravenous—so he headed to the kitchen. When he opened the plastic container, it whooshed. The drumstick was perfect. But even if it kept stuff fresh, who was going to buy a product called Tupperware?

=

Three days later he arrived at the studio early, just as *Chicago Deadline* completed its night shooting. Harry waved to a weary Alan Ladd, headed home at his day's end. "Are you okay, Mr. J.?" Mike Inman asked from his guard post.

"I'm fine."

"Damn right you are." He raised the barrier and waved him onto the lot.

Unlocking his office, Harry reached for the trade papers tucked under the door. In the left-hand column of *Variety*, above the fold of the paper, the headline read, EXEC SUITE FLUX AT PAR. He blanched but forced his way through the article. "A shakeup in top management may be imminent at the Gower Street studio, informed sources are speculating. Gordon Stern, until recently head of business affairs at RKO, appears headed to the Admin Building. Stern's arrival would be part of a reorganization long favored by prexy Barney Balaban for two senior vice presidents to head all functions under him. Production would remain the fiefdom of Y. Franklin Freeman, while all marketing, business, and legal execs, including Stern, would report to Paul Herzog. The Big Loser in the shakeup appears to be Par vet Harry Jastrow, currently a VP at the Herzog and Freeman level. His future looks cloudy at best."

No wonder the guard had been so solicitous—Harry was seconds from tumbling off Paramount Mountain.

=

Harry camped in Balaban's anteroom until the president arrived. "I'm glad you're here," Barney lied. "I was going to call you."

"I don't think so."

He beelined for his desk—an eight-foot-wide mahogany bunker. "I don't know where they get this garbage."

Harry wasn't letting him off the hook. "Not from you?"

"Absolutely not."

"Sid Victor wouldn't print that story without confirmation." Victor, *Variety*'s editor, took pains not to embarrass the majors, since their advertising kept the paper profitable.

"I didn't take his call," Barney reported precisely.

"And I didn't even *get* a call. That only leaves Herzog."

"It wasn't him. I know you dislike Paul, which is too bad because he feels you two could be friends if—"

"Please! So if it's not him?"

"Maybe this Gordon Stern?"

"It wouldn't have made the trades without a Paramount source giving it credence."

"You underestimate the chutzpah of reporters these days. But I'll phone Sid and let him know we're furious."

"And make him print an immediate retraction?"

"That would just dignify the whole thing." Like any studio chief worth his perks, Barney danced out of a dilemma with spins, dips, and jitterbugs.

"Is the story true?"

"You know better than that."

"Yes or no?"

Balaban took off his glasses and wiped them meticulously. "If you're going to cross-examine me, maybe I should hire a lawyer."

"How about Gordon Stern? I hear he's available." Harry's frustration made him dizzy. "Barney, within an hour everyone in this town is going to think my middle name is 'Loser.' So spare the strokes and jokes. I'm upset."

"You're upset? Well, so am I!" In an unexpected counter, Balaban tangoed from behind his desk. "I've got stockholders on my ass asking why their dividend is shrinking. The bankers are bellowing to cut costs. The government's stolen our theaters, no thanks to you. The agents rob us blind. And yesterday Zukor accused me of ruining his colossus. If that weren't enough, the men I depend on are trying to cut each other's balls off! It's killing me!"

Harry let the tantrum subside. "I'm sorry if I'm a pain in the ass. But I've got a mortgage and a boy who outgrows his clothes on an hourly basis. So I need to know if I should be looking for another job."

Barney's shoulders slumped. "I had dinner with Stern. Paul knows him from some boxing gym downtown and thought Gordon could be an asset to Paramount." He paused. "I felt Stern was impressive. But nothing—I repeat, nothing—is decided."

Harry strode down the hall. He might as well keep walking—because he was out on his ass. Balaban was probably waiting until after AJ's bar mitzvah before announcing the reorganization. He'd reacted too slowly. Maybe his wife's "take no prisoners" philosophy was right. But then one line from Barney's tirade echoed in his brain—the line about Zukor. Maybe that was his wedge. Hell, he had nothing to lose.

=====

The ripples of her husband's troubles reached Maggie at the Hotel Bel-Air, where she was conferring with Monsieur DeLoach, the catering manager. Ten in the morning was early to sample baked Alaska, but Maggie insisted on tasting every item on next Saturday's menu. "Perhaps a trifle less sugar in the meringue." He bristled. "Otherwise everything's fine." She gathered her belongings.

"*Pardonnez-moi,* Madame Jastrow, but I was wondering . . . if you wouldn't mind writing the hotel a check for the balance of two thousand dollars." His eyes shifted to a copy of *Variety* on the desk.

Maggie read about her husband's fate with horror. Then the implication of DeLoach's request struck her. "You're worried we'll stiff you?"

The manager looked smug. "No, no, not worried . . . perhaps a *trifle* concerned."

"Monsieur DeLoach, if I could find another hall for this bar mitzvah on short notice, I would." Her tone rechilled the melting ice cream. "But since I can't, let me make it clear you'll be paid in full so long as every item is perfect. You are a smarmy little man to whom I will never speak again."

His apology was still ringing as Maggie made a right on Stone Canyon. She only managed the corner of Chalon before yanking the car to the curb to let her rage subside. Harry must be so miserable. She fought an urge to drive to the studio because it would only embarrass him. Calling Uncle Adolph was inappropriate, so she was stuck doing nothing. Then she remembered there was one person she could help.

===

Half of AJ's classmates were industry kids who knew whose father was who, whose mother was having an affair, even which actors were losing their hair and needed toupees. There was a pecking order by parental status—and the resentment to go with it—so when AJ found a copy of the *Variety* article taped to his desk, there were too many suspects to interrogate. He forced himself to remain calm through English and social studies, but then his mom arrived to take him to lunch. Although she assured him that the story was malicious gossip, she wasn't as good an actress as she claimed.

When he came to bat that afternoon against Roosevelt Middle School, the opposing catcher, Joey Battaglia, regarded him with a nasty grin. "Hey, it's Son of the Loser."

Sensing trouble, the umpire shouted, "Play ball!"

AJ had seen old newsreel footage of Ty Cobb, so he knew exactly how to answer the insult. But he needed a pitch he could hit. Sure enough, with the count three and one a lame curve floated toward the plate. AJ drove it deep to left. He never considered stopping, despite the third-base coach frantically waving him off. The relay throw beat him to the plate by ten feet, so AJ began his slide up the base path. He raised his spikes high in the direction of Joey's thighs. As they collided, AJ dug in. The catcher's scream meant he'd struck soft flesh. When the dust settled, the ball was rolling on the ground and Battaglia was crying like a stuck pig. "Get a tetanus shot, Joey, because I keep my spikes rusty on purpose."

"You're out of here, Jastrow," the ump shouted.

"Fine, but the run scores." In the dugout his teammates stared at the blood on his uniform. "What? What?" The fury in his eyes backed them off. He picked up his glove and stormed away.

C H A P T E R   7

Dear Adolph,

Barney has apparently decided that my continued presence at the studio is detrimental. Although he's my direct supervisor, you hired me and I treasure our long relationship. Paramount is your creation—and it is in dire straits. I have a specific vision of how to rescue it that I want to articulate only to *you*. If you find my ideas compelling, I stand ready to help implement them. Otherwise, I'll tender my resignation next weekend at the bar mitzvah and relieve the studio of any further contractual commitment to me.

> Sincerely,
> HEJ

G rand gestures were popular in studio boardrooms, where executives welcomed the same kind of unexpected plot turns that made their movies so popular. Knowing that there was tension between Adolph and Barney, Harry sensed his note would grab the chairman's attention. Whether it would save his job was another matter, since people whispered that Zukor was too old and out of the loop to take on Balaban.

Two weeks of body blows had unleashed an aggression that fueled Harry's manifesto on how he would run the company. It was unvarnished and lacked the collegial tone of his life.

1. Paramount is in the *storytelling* business—not the *movie* business. All the talent on our lot, from writers and directors to grips and makeup artists, combine to weave tales on film. But whether we project those tales on screen or broadcast them over the airwaves is irrelevant. The studio must embrace the

medium of television by aggressively selling our old movies to the networks.

2. I propose a new unit be created under Frank Freeman dedicated to creating programming for TV. The shows would borrow the radio format of continuing characters in a weekly series and could utilize marginal actors still under contract to the studio.

3. During the past three decades "going to the movies" has become a habit for Americans. The very phrase indicates that the audience pursues the *activity* rather than focusing on specific films. In the past we could depend on people filling our theaters, week in and week out, regardless of what Hollywood offered. Those days are gone forever. In the next decade every film will have to stand on its own. Production on all B movies should cease at once—those are the first films TV will emulate. We should produce half the number but lavish more value on each.

4. Star casting will continue to be vital, but we need to sort the wheat from the chaff—a category that includes overpriced legends such as Clark Gable, Jimmy Cagney, and Joan Crawford.

Harry supported his vision of the future with forty pages of arguments, graphs, organization charts, and financials. He previewed it only for Maggie. She applauded his ideas—her only objection was to his offer to resign. Since his contract had thirteen months to run, she argued, why risk a year's salary over a matter of principle? But he insisted and dispatched the memo so it would reach Zukor before he boarded the train to Los Angeles for meetings at the studio in advance of the bar mitzvah.

Waiting drove Harry into a funk. He was in his office when he spotted a manila envelope on his desk marked PERSONAL AND CONFIDENTIAL. The absence of a postmark indicated that it had originated on the lot. He sliced it open and flipped through a set of eight-by-ten glossies. His face betrayed nothing, but it took him three tries to hit the button on the intercom.

"Yes, boss."

"Find Ray Stark—pronto."

=

The Rabbit surgically cut the chocolate swirls out of a marble cake in the Jastrow kitchen while Maggie studied photographs of Paul Herzog, captured candidly screwing another man in the butt. Her face was a mask of clinical detachment. "To get into that position, you'd have to be pretty limber. I wonder if his partner's a dancer."

Harry marveled at his wife's shrewdness. "His name is Billy Sanchez. He appeared in three Busby Berkeley musicals till he ripped his Achilles tendon. According to a carbon of a lease agreement, included in the package, he lives in a pied-à-terre paid for by Herzog. I had no inkling Paul was a homosexual, but clearly the word was out in some circles."

"Whoever the Weegee was did a hell of a job," Stark said admiringly. "It's a nice artistic touch the way he framed the can of Crisco in the lower left corner of the butt-fucking shot."

"And I thought it was only for frying chicken." Maggie guffawed, and Ray joined in.

Harry didn't—he found the pictures deeply distressing.

"They were sent by this security guy on the lot, this Mike Inman?" Stark asked.

"I had a hunch, so I checked the handwriting on the envelope with the handwriting on his job application. You don't need an expert to tell they match."

"Why'd he play Good Samaritan?" Ray firmly believed there were only trace amounts of nobility in the average Angeleno.

"Mike's a sot. A year ago a cleaning lady discovered him dead drunk in the stateroom set of *Road to Rio* with his face buried in the crotch of Gale Sondergaard's stand-in. I saved his job by getting him enrolled in one of those new Alcoholics Anonymous chapters. He's been on good behavior ever since."

"And extremely appreciative," Stark noted dryly. "There's one tricky problem. How do we get the pictures into the right hands without being traced? You don't need Balaban thinking sweet Harry Jastrow is a vindictive son of a bitch."

"I disagree." Maggie downed a shot of Scotch. "Meanness is the only quality he responds to. Dump them in his lap."

"Hold on," Harry cautioned. "Nobody's dumping anything. If Zukor and Balaban see these photos, they're going to explode. Your uncle Adolph hates fags, and Barney's paranoid that the code people are in the wings."

"So?"

"So Herzog will be fired on the spot."

"Exactly." Maggie checked with Stark, who seemed equally mystified. "The only bad news is he'll probably land a job at MGM."

Harry shook his head. "The talent can screw each other sideways if the public doesn't find out. But this is terminal for an executive. Herzog will be blackballed in this town."

His wife threw up her hands. "By your own admission, the son of a bitch is trying to ruin you. You've got a family to support."

"You don't have to remind me of my responsibilities."

"Apparently I do. You've devoted the best years of your life to Paramount. What kind of job do you think is waiting out there?"

"I still intend to win this fight. When Zukor gets my memo—"

"Your memo—your 'vision of the future'? Give me a break. Uncle Adolph probably never read it. Oh yeah, and how responsible was it to kiss off forty thousand dollars with that asinine offer to resign." She grabbed the marble cake to keep Ray Stark from picking. "Now I know where my son gets his disgusting habits."

The phone rang. "Mom, it's Grandma Rita," AJ shouted from the top of the stairs. Maggie left to take the call.

Stark took a swipe at the icing. "This memo of yours, I hope it's a real page-turner."

They sat in silence until Maggie returned. "Uncle Adolph's not coming. My mom spoke to Aunt Lottie, who says he got off the train in Chicago with the flu and is going to stay there for the weekend."

Harry called it as they all saw it. "Barney made the decision to axe me and Zukor doesn't have the stomach to attend the execution."

Ray cracked his knuckles with the vigor of a fighter with his gloves off. "But the good news is they're going to change their minds when they find out that Herzog's a pillow-biter. I'll have copies of the photos made first thing in the morning."

His offer was a call to arms. Harry locked and loaded his rifle, switched off the safety, and sighted the enemy in the crosshairs. All it would take was the slightest pressure of a single finger . . . and more hate than he possessed. His voice filled with resolve. "I detest Paul. But I will not ruin his reputation because he's a fairy."

His friend protested. "If the positions were reversed . . ."

"Save your breath, Ray." Maggie was acid. "I married a fucking moron."

Harry saw the anger coming—but those words carried utter contempt. "Because I'm not willing to stoop to his gutter level—that makes me a moron?"

"Okay, how about a coward?" Maggie stalked past him.

=

AJ remained hidden behind the sofa while his father and Ray said good night. The only kid he knew whose parents were divorced was Johnny Offerman, who was shy and weird, probably because he was ashamed. That's how AJ felt after sneaking downstairs and overhearing the fight from the living room. It made him tremble. His parents argued, but never like this.

He couldn't believe the things his mom had said. You didn't talk like that to someone you loved. And Dad wasn't a moron. Maybe she was drunk . . . or temporarily insane? If so, they wouldn't get divorced, because his father forgave. AJ struggled to comprehend the issues. Without seeing the pictures, he knew that a fairy was a disgusting person. But his father felt that wasn't reason enough to hurt this Mr. Herzog. It was Dad's job at stake, so he got to make the decision. But suppose Mom was right and Dad couldn't support them. . . . Of course he could. AJ was doubly shamed at doubting him. If he made less money, the family would spend less. He could give up golf lessons. The idea of helping made him feel better.

But then he heard a chilling sound. Peeking between the cushions, AJ saw what he hoped not to see. His father was seated at the kitchen table. Tears streamed down his face. His body shook. The only time AJ had seen him sob like that was at *The Best Years of Our Lives*. Dad had won the Purple Heart, so Mom's other accusation couldn't be true. But why didn't he stop? AJ's cheeks were wet.

He sneaked upstairs and buried his head in a pillow, which didn't help. Nor did counting the knots in the knotty pine paneling. He went to his closet and opened up the box with his baseball cards. Near the bottom, underneath Joe DiMaggio, he found what he was looking for. AJ had harbored a crush on Elizabeth Taylor since seeing her twice in *National Velvet*. He'd gotten her autograph once at a party, and though she was three years older and famous, she wasn't the least bit stuck-up. So staring at pictures of Liz in a scanty bathing suit made him feel guilty. He'd paid a kid in the ninth grade two weeks' allowance for the shots. The one he preferred showed her looking over her shoulder with a playful smile.

At first AJ wondered if there was something wrong with him because he loved looking at her bottom. Now he was sure he was sick because all he could think about was squeezing it. Maybe he was as sick as Paul Herzog. God—suppose someone took pictures of him now? But then it happened—like it always did. AJ carefully flushed the tissues into the toilet. Minutes later, he was asleep.

CHAPTER 8

Harry slogged through the days preceding his son's bar mitzvah. Passivity masqueraded as civility in the movie business, but the way his Paramount colleagues ducked contact because of his fall from favor proved more hostile than a punch in the nose. The costs of the party flowed in at double his estimates. Five hundred dollars for the band was mad, but so was another knock-down-drag-out brawl with his wife. Harry asked old law school friends to scout job openings back East. They responded positively, but did he really want to be general counsel for a grocery chain or a savings bank?

AJ came into his parents' bedroom sticking out his neck. "Dad, can I get a little help with my tie?"

"Is *please* in your vocabulary?"

"Please."

"Only in California can a boy become a man and still not be able to knot his own tie."

"Hey, hey . . . it's not a noose," AJ complained as Harry yanked on his collar.

The boy was an hour from his big performance—give him a break, Harry. "You're right. Let's try it together." Hand in hand they pulled over, under, then through. The simple contact soothed both of them.

"Do I have time to practice my speech again?"

Harry removed his treasured timepiece. "No. We need to get going, but you'll be fine." AJ nodded solemnly. "Today is the last day I'll be wearing this, son. Tomorrow, it's yours."

"Dad, no . . . you love that watch."

"I love you a lot more." He hugged him, kissing AJ's hair carefully so as not to muss it. "My father gave it to me for my bar mitzvah—and it was *all* he had to give. Promise that you'll give it to your son."

"Right, it'll be a family tradition." AJ looked over his shoulder and wolf-whistled.

Edith Head, the doyenne of Hollywood's costume designers, had personally designed Maggie's outfit. Her royal blue silk suit ended midcalf, with slits up her legs rakish enough to make the congregation at Beth Israel take note. But the designer's pièce de résistance was Maggie's matching hat, a faux yarmulke that contrasted dramatically with her red hair. For all its uncertainties and overruns, today was her production.

"Thank you for the compliment." She kissed AJ on the forehead, then sent him off to wipe away the telltale lipstick.

Neither Harry nor Maggie said a word . . . until he offered, "You look stunning."

"I'm tired of being angry," she said flatly.

"Me too."

"But I still am."

"Me too." He sighed. "We've always dealt with the world differently, Maggie. But until Monday I thought we valued it the same way."

She started to speak but didn't. His wife was a car without reverse.

They heard AJ's footsteps in the hall. "We'll figure it out—one way or the other," he said quietly. "Let's enjoy today." They held on to each other long enough for AJ to see. His smile was worth their brief truce.

=

As AJ was helping Rabbi Ginsberg remove the Torah from the Holy Ark, a rumbling in the rear of the synagogue distracted worshipers. Harry had turned to tell people to keep quiet when he realized that the commotion was marching down the aisle—Adolph and Lottie Zukor. They took seats in the row behind the Jastrows. Harry was incredulous. "I thought you weren't coming."

"Miss my grandnephew's bar mitzvah?" Zukor boomed.

"Shoosh! We took a flight from Chicago so we could make it," Lottie explained sotto voce. "But he still has a head cold. Now his ears are stuffed—he's deaf as a doornail."

As Harry looked back to the *bima,* he noticed that his wife was pale. "What's wrong?"

"With all that was going on, I didn't want to say anything," she whispered. "AJ's really terrible."

"How terrible?"

"Say the prayer for 'break a leg.' "

Harry groaned. When he dared to peek, the rabbi had pointed to the place in the Torah where AJ began his *aliyah*. But his son didn't look frightened. He had that unmatched focus he displayed over a four-foot putt. And from the first note he clearly required no assistance, divine or otherwise. His chanting gripped the congregation. "What are you talking about?" Harry asked.

At the kiddush reception directly after the ceremony, the proud parents smothered their son in hugs. Maggie couldn't resist. "How'd you do it?"

"After my tryout, I tried memorizing the passage like you said, but it felt wrong. So I borrowed against my bar mitzvah loot and hired a student at UCLA to tutor me."

"Every freedom fighter in Israel is proud of you," Zukor interrupted. He handed his grandnephew an envelope stuffed with cash. "Don't spend it all in one place."

After AJ and Maggie disappeared to count, Adolph pulled Harry aside. "I read your manifesto. A regular Karl Marx you are . . . and long-winded. You believe we need to make big changes?"

"Adolph, what we do in the next year will determine the course of the business for the next twenty years. Unless we control television and make it work *for* us, other people will step into the void—agents, the advertising agencies, and the networks. None of them is our friend."

"Barney thinks you're disruptive."

"I am. The status quo won't hold."

"A few of the ideas make me think that you're not so smart."

"Which? Tell me—"

"Relax. All this commotion is not good. Anyway, I think you are on to something." Zukor closed his eyes for such a long beat that Harry thought he'd dozed off standing up. "We had disasters like this in the early days. Did I ever tell you about the fire?"

"The one that burned down the Twenty-sixth Street Studio?" The 1915 blaze in New York had wiped out every piece of film equipment Zukor owned.

"I didn't have a pot to piss in. Or a window to throw it out of. But did that stop me? No! I turned that riding academy on Fifty-sixth Street into an even bigger studio." He stood taller. "I'll work out your problem somehow. Paramount without you isn't Paramount to me."

"Thank you."

"But try not to be such a pain in the ass. We got to compromise . . . be a team."

"I'll try."

Harry watched as Zukor strutted back to the buffet, then stuck his hand into the chopped liver and licked his fingers clean. Those fingers that had been picking and blowing his nose all day.

That simple act—so ruthlessly crude, so effortlessly arrogant— convinced Harry that it was time to leave. Not Hollywood—Hollywood was his home. But Paramount wasn't. It couldn't be home with the people who lived there. What kind of job could he find? Maybe better, maybe more of the same. Harry intended to find out. He could always start a company and wait for AJ to grow up. His letter of resignation sat in the right-hand drawer of his desk. On Monday he would hand it to Adolph. But not until Balaban and Herzog learned they'd lost.

=

The swans in the pond at the entrance to the Hotel Bel-Air ignored the black-tie crowd arriving for AJ's reception. Their indifference impressed the guests. Hollywood coveted class—especially WASP class— and as Ray Stark noted, those birds didn't have a Jewish feather on them. As a former florist at Forest Lawn Mortuaries, he'd personally designed the floral centerpieces and arrived early to supervise their placement.

Harry had a secret crush on Jean Howard, Maggie's best friend and the event's official photographer. To him, the former Ziegfeld girl was more alluring than the screen personalities she regularly captured at work and play. Right now Jean was focused on lining up a shot of the family in front of a fountain salvaged from a seventeenth-century Spanish mission. She called for her assistant to move the fill light to the left, and from behind the trunk of a banana palm stepped Naomi Riordan.

At fourteen she had joined the Beat Generation before America knew it existed. Wearing black slacks and a black turtleneck, Naomi secured her dark brown hair with an ivory barrette, exposing a face so untouched by the sun that AJ imagined her walking with a parasol. Her complexion was the gift of Coos Bay, Oregon, the rainiest town in the West. Naomi was Jean's niece. At the age of six she'd taken a photograph of the funeral service of her pet turtle. It won first prize at the county fair and launched a passion. Now she adjusted the light, edged Harry back, angled Maggie to emphasize her gold choker, then arrived at AJ. She raised his chin, straightened his tie, then flicked an eyelash from his cheek. "You must be the bar mitzvah boy."

"Man . . . officially I'm a man, as of noon today."

"My mistake."

His eyes trailed as she swayed out of frame.

"Hey, AJ, want to look in the general direction of the camera?" Jean requested. Harry and Maggie stifled giggles.

=

AJ loved the hora because it was communal—and didn't have a lot of steps to remember. The diameter of the circle expanded with each chorus of "Hava Nagila," a song with the fierce energy to make people lose their inhibitions. AJ clasped his mom's left hand, while she linked with her mother-in-law, then Fran Stark. As they kicked into high gear, he glanced to the bandstand, where a new singer was taking the microphone. It was so cool that Bing Crosby was performing at his bar mitzvah.

Amid the mounting madness, Uncle Adolph produced a dining room chair. Tradition demanded that the celebrants hoist the man of the moment above the crowd. His dad raised one leg, while Zukor, Ray, and Frank Freeman raised the others. From his high vantage point AJ spied Naomi across the room poised to capture the scene with Jean's Rolleiflex. He waved his arms over his head like the new bantamweight champion of the world, but by the time the chair revolved, she had retired to the gardens.

"Hava nagila, hava nagila . . ." The song and dance became a whirling dervish. His golf coach replaced Uncle Adolph just before he keeled over, but he was as tall as Mr. Freeman, which forced his father and Ray to lift him higher. The chair wobbled and his father flinched and gripped his left arm. "Dad, are you okay?"

"I pulled a muscle. I'm fine." He signaled for Bert Silberdick, their accountant, to sub for him.

The song exhausted the guests, but not AJ. He dashed like a star halfback through the parade of waiters entering the ballroom with platters of roast beef and Yorkshire pudding. Naomi was sitting pensively on the steps of the hotel's honeymoon cottage, blowing perfect smoke rings from her cigarette, when he arrived. "I looked silly up there," he began sheepishly. "But you can't avoid it. I bet they carried Moses around like that at his bar mitzvah."

"At thirteen everyone thought Moses was an Egyptian prince—

including Moses. And you didn't look silly. You looked happy. I was envious."

"Aren't you happy?"

Naomi shrugged. "Come on, I want to take your picture."

"Again?"

"For the first time." She directed him to a doorway where a dim bulb cast a half shadow over his face. "You have your father's cheekbones and forehead, your mom's nose and eyes. It's amazing what an equal blend you are. It all comes down to your chin. If it develops a jut, you'll look like your mom; if not, your dad. Either way, you're going to be handsome."

"Thanks. I feel better already."

"Make fun. I'm shooting a number of boys—sorry, men—your age. Then I'm going to sketch how they'll turn out. In thirty years I'll track all of you down and check my predictions."

"Can I take a picture of you?" He wanted a memory of this moment.

"I'm the doctor, not the patient."

"Then how will I be able to remember you?"

Naomi put down her camera. She edged toward AJ, never losing eye contact, then took his face in her hands and kissed him. He'd heard rumors about French kissing but had never tried it. Naomi had, and AJ was used to following a strong woman, so when she opened her mouth, he was barely a beat behind. Soon their tongues touched. She tasted warm and salty. AJ thanked God he'd skipped the Caesar salad. "Are you staying in L.A.?" he asked, coming up for air.

"Nope. I'm flying to Portland in the morning. And I'm too old for you." AJ guessed that his moment had passed. She read his mind. "If you're wondering, it wasn't the best kiss I've had, but it was the best 'first kiss.' "

=

Harry stumbled like a drunk around the deserted swimming pool at the far end of the property. He abandoned his theory that he'd dislocated his shoulder because the pain had spread to his chest and his breathing had gone shallow. A wave of nausea engulfed him and he puked into his own distorted reflection in the water. "Calm down!" The shock of his voice echoing through Stone Canyon broke his panic, and he limped back to the reception. But the pressure intensified and he tripped down the flagstone steps, bruising his elbows and ripping a hole in the knee of his tuxedo.

When he recovered his balance, Harry was back in combat. Someone lurked. *"Banzai! Banzai!"* A mortar shell rocketed from a palm tree, blowing a hole through him. Harry tumbled and rolled, finally settling on his back. He saw stars—hundreds, thousands. Now that he was off his feet, he felt better, thank God, because he wasn't ready to leave this earth. There were too many joys to revisit and discover for the first time: playing the Riv on a summer afternoon; laughing till he hurt at the next Hope-Crosby comedy; meeting AJ's bride; balancing his grandchildren on his knees . . . and making love to the love of his life. He had to find Maggie, to see her coppery hair one more time, to say he could never stop loving her.

=

AJ read Naomi's sigh as a sign that she enjoyed his caress. But just as he ground his body into her, the honking swans broke the mood, so he took her hand to explore why the damn birds wouldn't shut up. A cluster of hotel guests had gathered near the pond. Two uniformed bellhops sloshed through the water, making their way to a log. Then AJ realized the log was someone doing the dead man's float. But this guy—and now he could see it was a guy—wasn't swimming.

Naomi wanted to take a picture and he didn't want to be a chicken, so they pushed forward. The bellhops got the man on his feet, but their bodies shielded his identity. People buzzed and ran for help. From inside the ballroom AJ heard the band playing "Did You Ever See a Dream Walking?" Rescuers reached the bank, but the man slipped from their grasp and plunked back into the water. When they pulled him up, he was covered in mud and water lilies. AJ searched for Naomi, but like one of those crime photographers, she was already at the scene.

Now AJ saw that the victim wore a tuxedo, which meant he was a bar mitzvah guest. He had to find out who so that he could tell his folks. Then he heard a tortured wail from Naomi.

"What? Who is it?"

Her scream went silent. When the bellhops flipped the man into the light, AJ understood. Varicose veins crisscrossed his father's neck, his face was red as if he'd held his breath too long—or not long enough—and there was mucus dripping over his lip, like a kid who'd blown his nose without a tissue. But the horrible thing was that his dad, who was always full of energy, was so still.

This can't be. That just looks like him.

AJ barreled forward, but somebody grabbed him. The rescuer attempting artificial respiration yelled that he needed space. Women screamed. Was one of them his mom? Despite AJ's thrashing and kicking, the guy held him with a gorilla's grip. He got so dizzy he couldn't fight. He fell over, but it took forever to hit the ground. A long fall would kill him, which was okay, because then he could say good-bye to Dad—or be with him forever.

CHAPTER 9

The chimes at the front door woke AJ early Sunday morning. He had a sluggish headache and his throat was sore from crying. At least discomfort proved he was alive. The dingdongs threatened to drive him wacko, so he raced down the stairs. No one seemed to be around. He opened the door, expecting a policeman or another doctor.

"Are you the Jastrow kid?"

AJ gaped. Was he dreaming? No, the guy in the cap had the right menacing stare and stance. He was definitely . . . "Ben Hogan?"

"The same. I hear you might give me a good game. Are you ready to play?"

How could this be?

"Your father's going to join us, if that's okay?"

Of course—playing with Mr. Hogan was the special present Dad had teased about.

"Cat got your tongue?"

"He's dead . . . my dad's dead." It was the first time AJ had said it out loud.

"Sweet Jesus." Hogan instinctively removed his golf cap. His face was more gentle and vulnerable than opponents claimed.

"He had a heart attack last night and drowned."

"I'm sorry. I had no idea." There was no escape shot from this deep rough. "You get a rain check. We'll play whenever you're ready."

"I don't think it would be fun anymore—I mean, golf without him."

Hogan bent down till they were eye to eye. "I don't play with just anyone, even if they pay a lot of money. Your pop had to convince me. You know what he said?"

AJ didn't want to hear. Dad was gone, that was that.

"He said you practiced hard like me, digging balls out of the dirt until your hands were blistered. Let me look." AJ shyly put up his callused palms. "He didn't lie. But the thing that did the trick was when he said you had heart—more heart than anyone he knew. You're not going to disappoint him, are you?"

"No, sir."

"That's better. See you next month."

Heart. Honor. And guts. His dad had respected those qualities above all. AJ remembered Ray saying last night that someone had to pick out clothes to bury Harry in. He went upstairs and poked his head into his parents' bedroom. Mom was snoring away—an earthquake wouldn't wake her—so he slipped quietly into the closet and rummaged around. There must have been twenty suits, none of which felt comfortable, so he decided to lay his father to rest in his favorite beige cardigan and brown corduroys.

=

An hour before the Jastrow funeral, officials at Forest Lawn scurried to provide folding chairs for the overflow crowd. "You could steal the studio blind this morning," Frank Freeman reported upon entering the private family room at the back of the chapel. He squeezed his massive arms around AJ. "I wish you could hear the wonderful stories people are telling about your father."

They could keep their stories. He chatted politely, then broke away to check the clouds. Why hadn't he brought an umbrella for himself and his mother? Catching his reflection in the window, AJ reflexively fixed the crooked knot in his tie. He should have learned his father's technique when he had the chance. People tried to be helpful, but most whispered the obvious: "She'll be so lonely." "A boy needs a father." "It couldn't have happened at a worse time."

The dumbest conversation was between his dad's secretary and Grandma Esther. Miss Benitez wailed that his father was so young—his death wasn't possible. But his grandmother said it was inevitable. She explained how her husband, Isaac, had died at forty-nine and that neither one of his two brothers had celebrated a fiftieth birthday. Harry's grandfather had died at forty-six, and a truck had run over Harry's brother Martin when he was sixteen. The litany sounded like a stupid Gypsy curse, the whole idea that Jastrow men didn't live long because they were too good for the world.

Rabbi Ginsberg sat down beside him. "How are you doing?"

AJ shrugged. "Okay. The hotel never found my father's pocket watch."

"Excuse me?"

"They dragged the pond, but it wasn't there. I think it was stolen. But how could anyone do that? Dad should have it with him."

The rabbi looked helpless—like everyone else. "We'll need to go soon. You don't have to give a speech. No one expects you or your mother to talk at a time like this."

"I know. I want to."

"I'll call on you at the beginning, it will be easier."

"Last—I'll go last."

=

Maggie flushed the bottle of Miltown down the toilet in the ladies' room. Better to burst out crying than be lobotomized like last night. Christ, she'd barely recognized her son after the doctor tranquilized her with a hypodermic that could have numbed a horse. Despite the drugs, the truth was clear. She was a middle-aged widow; she had a son on the threshold of adolescence; and she had no career. The combination made her persona non grata in Hollywood.

And what was she supposed to do about the new electrician who claimed that the guy who'd wired their house was an imbecile? Or the gardener who warned that the oak tree in the front yard was ready to snap and crush the guest bedroom? She had to cancel their reservations at Lake Louise but didn't know where they were booked. She and Harry had worked out such a perfect division of labor that her husband's sudden absence made her useless.

Bless Harry! And damn him! He was beyond irreplaceable—he was inconceivable. Her husband had lacked an instinct for survival—he'd been too decent for an indecent business. That was why she'd tried so hard to toughen him up. But her efforts had been for naught. Was she being too kind to herself? Had her badgering contributed to his death? That had been her first thought upon gazing into his lifeless eyes. But people didn't die of broken hearts; they keeled over from blocked arteries.

She had to believe that. She had to move on. Maggie had too many responsibilities to allow herself the luxury of grief.

=

His father's funeral was AJ's first. People were sad but also . . . scared. The mood made him feel like the last, lonely victim in a horror movie. The courage he'd summoned vanished, and he waved to the rabbi that he had changed his mind. But it was too late—the prayers began. As the congregation rose, AJ rose with it. He sat when they sat. After a few moments he heard Frank Freeman speaking about Dad.

"Almost a year ago Barney Balaban and I decided to do a movie on Mahatma Gandhi's life. We gave Harry the unenviable job of optioning his rights. There was endless correspondence through go-betweens. Just before the negotiations concluded, the phone rang in Harry's office and an operator said a party was calling from Delhi. Anita buzzed Harry, who was in the middle of a fight with Charlie Feldman. For you civilians, Charlie's the toughest agent in this town. Harry couldn't get rid of Charlie, who was screaming bloody murder on behalf of Marlene Dietrich, but he had Mahatma Gandhi holding on line two. Finally, Harry hung up and without missing a beat said smoothly, 'Sorry to keep you waiting, Mr. Gandhi.' The two of them talked for half an hour. The highlight of my life was my friend explaining profit participation to the holiest man in the world."

The mourners released their tension in gales of laughter.

Somehow, Dad was back. AJ turned to his mom, relieved to see that even she grinned.

"They were just about to hang up," Freeman continued. "Then Gandhi said, 'I do not know you, Harry Jastrow, but all my life I have relied upon my ability to judge men from the smallest of details. Your voice is a good voice. Your words are true.' He was correct. You could always trust Harry."

Rabbi Ginsberg called on Adolph Zukor to give Harry's eulogy. Harry's death, the chairman noted, was a terrible blow to Paramount, which needed men of vision in these blind times. AJ glanced at the studio contingent. Next to Mr. Balaban and Mr. Freeman sat a stocky man whose face AJ recognized as the man in the pictures he'd sneaked a look at. The guy seemed impatient, as if this was the last place on earth he wanted to be. AJ decided to take care of that.

Paul Herzog's body rose like a marionette. He levitated above the congregation. "Go ahead—scream, you sleazy bastard. No one can hear you," AJ shouted, his cheeks flushed. He whipped Herzog from the chapel and deposited him in the basement where they stored the empty coffins. "Would you like the solid mahogany or maybe the teak? I know the prices because I selected one." Herzog pleaded for mercy but AJ nailed the coffin shut, the blows of the hammer synchronizing with the beats of his heart. "So you don't like tight places? Neither did my dad." Utilizing X-ray vision he watched Herzog suffocate. "Here comes my favorite part." As AJ thrilled to the feasting worms . . . Ginsberg summoned him to the altar. He wiped the sick grin from his face before the mourners could see.

Dad, please be with me.

"My father was great. In fact, he was so great at everything I worried I would never match up. That's why my favorite time was when we played golf. You see, he was . . . kind of bad." AJ waited for the nervous laughs to subside. "I don't mean to brag, but I'm sort of good, so it gave me hope. The big thing for Dad on the course was honesty and acceptance. 'Play it as it lies,' he used to say. That means that even if your ball winds up in some impossible place, you have to play it exactly how you find it. You're not allowed to move it or improve it or hit a mulligan— even if it got where it got through some really lousy break. I feel my family got the worst break ever. Although I still don't like that rule, I'm going to live by it."

His mouth dry, he walked the twenty-six steps back to his seat.

=

After the gravediggers laid Harry's coffin in the ground and family, friends, and associates returned to their limousines, Maggie and AJ remained at the grave site. Just to the left was a small marble tombstone with a Star of David. It bore the inscription "Emily June Jastrow, July 1, 1940–July 3, 1940." Maggie visited Emily every month, to keep her company. Now she would have her father by her side. "I wish you could have met your sister, AJ. She was sick from the minute she was born, but still, she was so, so beautiful."

"Dad explained."

How had he explained a baby choking on her umbilical cord? Or a life of forty-eight hours spent all in a coma? There was no explaining that or the misery when the doctors said Maggie could never have another child. She wanted a little girl more than anything in the world. Let her husband and son cavort together on the golf course. With a daughter she would share those secret parts of her life that men could never understand. But that dream was not to be.

"Can we go back to the car?"

She gripped his hand firmly. "It's just you and me, kid." But that would be more than enough.

＝

On June 1, AJ accompanied his mother to Paramount to clear out his father's office. Miss Benitez had laid everything out, from diplomas to a photograph of Dad dressed as an Indian. Pulling AJ aside, she handed him a sealed manila envelope. "I typed this for your father, and I know he would have wanted you to have it."

"What . . . ?"

"Not now." She glanced warily at his mother, who was busy selecting keepsakes.

"Thank you." AJ joined her. In a broken picture frame he saw a picture of Stretch, the marlin from Mexico. He remembered his father talking about "cross seas" and the movie business. Did that idea apply to his life as well?

Construction workers entered the office to make measurements in order to expand the office for its next occupant. When his mom asked who that would be, Miss Benitez changed the subject but finally admitted it was Paul Herzog. He and Frank Freeman were the new executive vice presidents, with long-term contracts for lots of money.

"I hope Paramount goes bankrupt," Mom declared.

That night AJ rested on top of the covers, agonizing over what he had heard in the office. Paul Herzog's triumph was like the Nazis occupying Europe or the Japanese bombing Pearl Harbor. AJ might be powerless to strike back now, but it wouldn't always be that way. He opened the envelope from the office. Inside were eighty pages of an unfinished screenplay. It was almost four A.M. when AJ reached the last scene. The hero crouched behind sandbags, waiting for an artillery barrage to subside before leading his squad on a mission behind enemy lines. The script was the best thing AJ had ever read. He picked up an imaginary M-1 and launched blistering gunfire at the unseen enemy.

＝

Maggie sat in the passenger cabin of a DC-6 revving at the end of a runway. For Christ's sake, take off already. She had to get out of Los Angeles before the town crushed her—and, more important, her son. For weeks he had been morose and uncommunicative, unable to climb out of the tragedy of his father's death. He needed a new start.

Harry had left fifty thousand dollars in savings and a hundred thousand dollars of life insurance. Ironically, Balaban had offered to pay the remaining year on his contract. She'd wanted to tell him to stuff it up his ass, but it might come in handy for AJ's college. After selling the house, Maggie calculated they had enough money to live comfortably, but it would be easier in the conservative Midwest, so she chose Chicago, where she'd grown up. Her son greeted the news without argument.

Finally, the wheels rolled.

Once airborne, the plane flew west over the Pacific, as if the pilot had lost his sense of direction, before banking right. AJ opened *The House on the Cliff,* one of those Hardy Boys mysteries he devoured, never bothering to look out the window. As the desert came into view, Maggie sat back, relieved that their life in California was over forever.

A SCRATCH
ON THE
NEGATIVE

awn was still a promise as AJ approached the eighteenth tee at Pebble Beach, visualizing the shot he intended to hit hours later. To his left, surf pounded the saw-toothed coastline like shelling from a Navy destroyer, the foamy explosions pockmarking his rain gear. "It all comes down to this final hole." His hushed voice mocked the melodrama of a TV announcer. "With a one-stroke lead Jastrow has to make sure that if he errs, he does so toward the rough on the right." AJ swung his imaginary driver. "But that ball has split the center!" He tipped his cap to a gallery of barking sea lions.

Striding down the fairway, AJ sensed something apocalyptic, as if the Pacific had gouged the edge out of America in this very spot. Pebble had seemed safer on his first visit, in 1947, when he'd caddied for his father in Bing Crosby's Clambake—a golf tournament over the legendary courses on the Monterey peninsula in which the best pros in the world were paired with Bing's golf-addicted buddies from Hollywood. AJ had hit a few shots, which had caused Crosby to joke that he'd be a better partner than his dad. After leading Northwestern to the NCAA finals last spring, AJ had received a congratulatory telegram from Bing, along with an invitation to play in the 1957 event. He had dreamed about his return to the West Coast ever since.

Golf was less a game for AJ than a test, requiring a premium on his preparation and practice. Despite thousands of past successes, he always worried about the next shot. Even a two-foot putt held the specter of disaster. But he fed on the stress, and this morning his appetite was voracious. Standing on the final green, AJ rolled balls from every angle toward a maintenance worker, who stuck the flag in a newly cut hole. Satisfied he had a feel for the break and speed, he headed to breakfast in the clubhouse.

=

"You don't swing like a dentist," AJ said admiringly as he shook hands on the first tee with his professional partner, Dr. Cary Middlecoff. The tall Tennessean had won the U.S. Open after abandoning his dental career.

"That's fortunate, 'cause I wasn't too handy with a drill. You know Ken Venturi?"

AJ greeted a man his age. "You were amazing at last year's Masters."

"Until Sunday." Venturi's collapse in the final round had kept him from becoming the youngest player to win the famed tournament by a single stroke. "Have any of you seen Todd?" The absentee in their group was Ken's celebrity partner, Mike Todd, whose production of *Around the World in 80 Days* had opened to rave reviews in New York and was favored to win Best Picture at this spring's Academy Awards.

Middlecoff spit. "He's probably back at the lodge banging his fiancée."

"I'd take a hole in one with Liz Taylor before eighteen with us," Venturi replied.

They stared when AJ didn't laugh with them. "Not my type," he alibied.

Seconds later a golf cart bore down, bucking to a stop by smashing into a black tee marker. Mike Todd popped out like an uncapped fire hydrant.

"Which of you guys is Venturi?" Ken raised his hand. "I hope you're a winner, because I'm not here for my health." Todd handed out cigars, as an afterthought tossing one to AJ.

"What's your handicap, kid?"

"Scratch, sir."

"Impressive." He turned to the pros. "My father gave me a kick in the ass, not golf lessons."

What's this guy's problem? AJ wondered. He returned the cigar. "Thanks, but I don't smoke."

"Good for you." Todd genially lit up. "It's a filthy habit. Let's make this interesting. How about a side bet, say a fifty-dollar Nassau between the teams?"

Middlecoff and Venturi agreed.

"And what say we amateurs play a fifty-dollar Nassau with automatic presses against each other? I'm a duffer, so you need to give me a stroke a hole."

The plane ticket to California had used up most of AJ's savings. A bad round could bankrupt him. "I'm in," he squeaked.

Todd took the honors. "I'll use my chipper." The club, a cross between a one-iron and a putter, was so short he had to bend directly over the ball. AJ smirked—the poor guy looked like a hunchbacked gnome—but he gulped when Mike smashed his drive two hundred yards down the center. It wasn't the shot of a high handicapper. "The motherfucker sandbagged us," Middlecoff whispered.

AJ launched his drive into a copse of cypress trees. That could happen to anyone, he reassured himself. His attempt at a heroic recovery pinballed off trunks and branches, remaining stymied.

Now Todd wore the twisted grin. "I'm in for par. How about you, AJ?" he asked.

"Seven."

"Listen, I know you're shitting your pants, but it's only money. I made two fortunes by the time I was your age—and lost them both. You know what it taught me? Absolutely nothing!" Mike found his own joke fabulously amusing.

After three holes AJ felt like the victim in a train wreck. Middlecoff took pity. "Shorten your backswing. And show the bastard you still got some fight left."

AJ finally put a drive in play on the fourth and caught up with Todd. "Is it true what Dr. Middlecoff said—you're a film producer?"

Todd seemed incredulous at AJ's ignorance. "Producers are a dime a dozen. I'm a showman."

"There's a difference?"

"A producer makes movies *he* likes. A showman makes movies the *public* likes."

"What's it take, sir, to be a showman?"

"Flair and balls. It's all about flair and balls."

AJ nodded as if absorbing the wisdom of the ages.

As the foursome arrived at their second shots on the sixth hole, a gale built off the Pacific. AJ deftly combated it with a low knockdown practiced on the windswept plains of the Midwest, but Todd's chipper failed him. After he sliced two shots in the direction of Japan, Mike rummaged through his golf bag.

"No balls," AJ observed.

Todd glared. "Did you say 'no balls'?"

"Yes."

"You're saying *I don't have balls*?"

"Sorry, Mr. Todd, you misunderstood. You're a showman, so of course you've got *those* kind of balls." AJ glanced at his crotch. "I was wondering if you had this kind." He held up his Titleist. "Because I've got extras."

Todd never made another smooth swing. On the sixteenth green he faced a sloping five-foot putt to keep the match alive. If he missed, AJ won four hundred dollars. Todd spit out his cigar. But just as he took the putter back, a gust blew the half-chewed Havana directly in front of the cup. The ball hit it squarely, knocking the cigar into the hole; the ball remained on the lip.

"Fuck me and my molars," Middlecoff exhaled.

Mike removed a fat money clip to pay off both his *and* Venturi's losses. "Kid, that was a hell of a performance," he said admiringly, counting out AJ's share.

"Thanks. I'm lucky the course fits my game."

"It wasn't your swing that beat me. It was your *cabeza*. Not many people can figure out how to mind-fuck Mike Todd. I was pissed that Crosby stuck me in a foursome with a nobody just because he was jealous my first movie did more business than any of his. Now I'm glad."

When they reached the par-three seventeenth, Mickey Rooney was preparing to drive to the hourglass green jutting into Carmel Bay. The other celebrity in his group, Johnny Weissmuller, of *Tarzan* fame, and both pro partners had already hit. Rooney's three-wood started straight, but the wind jacked the shot wildly left. "Goddamnit!" He smashed the turf. "I deserved a better fate."

"A thousand dollars says you can't hit the green with four more," Todd challenged.

Mick motioned for his caddie to hand him another ball. His next three drives landed in tall grass. His ruddy complexion darkened to purple when he dribbled his last chance off the tee. "You miserable cocksucker!" He hurled his club thirty yards, where it broke in two against a lone pine. "You suckered me, Todd. Only a pro hits that green in these conditions."

"Another five hundred says I can." The voice belonged to AJ, but he had no idea how it had escaped his lips.

Mike's eyes sparkled. *"That's* flair and balls, baby."

But was he showman or show-off?

"Who the Christ are you?" Rooney demanded.

"AJ Jastrow," Todd interjected. "He's an amateur, but another five hundred says he stiffs it inside thirty feet of the pin in one shot."

Rain slashed them at a sixty-degree angle, while the wind wailed like a Scottish bagpiper gone berserk. Mick motioned to AJ. "Go ahead, sucker."

"It'll be like landing a plane on a carrier in the middle of a typhoon," Venturi observed to the guy standing next to him.

"A night landing at that," replied Charlie Feldman, casting his eyes to the dark, violent sky. AJ remembered his dad saying Feldman had once taken Darryl Zanuck for fifty thousand dollars in an evening of poker. So he wasn't surprised when Charlie, smelling a sure thing, kicked off a speculative wave of side betting by offering even bigger odds.

When AJ swung, he was sure that he had aimed too far right. He bent to retrieve his tee, not bothering to follow the flight. Then he heard the most unmistakable—and incongruous—yell in the world. "Ay-Jaaaaaaay!" "Tarzan" Weissmuller beat on his chest as the ball hit the green and slid to a stop ten feet from the hole. Todd lifted AJ into the air and crushed him with a bear hug. "That's my boy! That's *my* fucking boy!"

=

"Where are we headed, Bing?"

"Gibson's Gulch," Crosby replied as he navigated Monterey peninsula's Seventeen Mile Drive from the middle of the road. He puffed contentedly on his meerschaum, filling the Eldorado convertible with smoke that smelled like tangy barbecue sauce. "Actually, Lawson Little's house. The pros nicknamed it because Lawson mixes the best Gibsons west of St. Louis."

Phil Harris, the bandleader-reborn-as-comedian, rode shotgun. He looked to AJ, luxuriating in the backseat. "For three weeks before the tournament he fills his basement with gallon jugs, then goes down once a day to give a half turn so the vodka won't settle."

Little's house boasted glass windows overlooking the Pacific and more sofas than a furniture store. Perched on their arms like provocative mannequins were dozens of ravishingly beautiful women. AJ looked over his shoulder as a sultry blonde with a wealth of cleavage and skimpy Capri pants beckoned him over.

"The girls think you're the best-looking guy here."

"You're making fun of me."

"The word is you're one of those professional golfers," she flirted. "But I'm sure I saw you at a casting session. Weren't you in *East of Eden?*"

"Actually, I'm a first-year law student at the University of Chicago." The blonde screwed up her scooped-out nose. "Wrong answer, huh?"

She smiled thinly. "Probably works better at homecoming. We're after big game."

But the stars and golf pros couldn't have been friendlier. At dinner AJ swallowed inside stories about Hollywood and the PGA tour as greedily as the steamed clams, spicy chili, and garlic bread. The highlight of the evening occurred when Crosby and Hope performed a customized version of their song-and-dance routines. They roasted everyone in attendance. When it was AJ's turn, they mocked his "Joe College" crew cut and the fact that he had picked the pockets of the two shortest guys in the tournament—Todd and Rooney. AJ beamed as if he had just tapped into their exclusive gentlemen's club.

His stomach cramped up around midnight, so he hitched a ride with Gordon MacRae, who'd recently starred as Curly in *Oklahoma!* Shit-faced, they belted out Rodgers and Hammerstein songs all the way back to the Del Monte Lodge. AJ sprinted to his room. He didn't even bother to switch on the overhead light because he was too busy tugging down his trousers on the way to the john. But when he was seconds from salvation the bathroom door opened from inside, illuminating a stark-naked girl who appeared unfazed by his presence.

"Hi, I'm Janey. I'm a present from Mr. Todd." AJ uncramped. She pursed her lips, noting his state of undress. "Jeez, I thought I was supposed to be a surprise, but I guess there was a change in plans. No problem." With that she pushed him backward till he flopped on the double bed.

AJ was in the worst of binds. All his life he'd needed privacy when he went to the bathroom, virtually never using public toilets. On top of that, he was sexually inexperienced, having slept with only three women. Fearful that a hooker would report his lack of expertise to Todd, he vowed to meet the challenge. Unfortunately, midway through AJ's inaugural blow job, his stomach spasms returned with a vengeance. His body trembled, which the intrepid Janey interpreted as positive feedback. But when she stroked his balls—something no girl had ever done—he lost control and let loose with a thunderous chili-infused fart.

She staggered on her haunches. "You . . . you . . . you nauseating pig!

He told me you were a sweet college kid. If that's what they're teaching, I'm glad I didn't take the SATs." She retreated to the bathroom, slamming the door.

"Janey, I'm sorry. Please come out."

"So you can shit on my head?" The young woman emerged fully dressed and bolted for the hall. "Movie people are all the same."

AJ started to chase her but decided to seek relief in the bathroom instead. Sitting blessedly on the commode, he reveled in his trifecta—doubling his net worth, golfing into Clambake history, and grossing out the sexiest woman he'd ever met.

=

The next morning AJ was suffering a hangover so heinous he could barely tolerate the sound of his club whacking the ball. Back at the clubhouse, he encountered his benefactor. AJ ordered a Coke and cautiously thanked Mike for his surprise.

"You deserved her. Janey's great, isn't she?"

"The best I've had," AJ replied truthfully.

"She played an Indian princess in *Around the World.* I'm giving her a bigger role in my next one."

"She's not . . . she's not a prostitute?"

"Hell, no. She's actually the granddaughter of a friend of mine."

"Did she . . . did she—"

"Say you were great? No." AJ feared the worst. "She said you had a huge cock and were a bit of a freak. In Hollywood, that's the best reputation you can have." Mike winked. "Talk about reputations, I understand your dad was quite a guy."

"You knew my father?"

"No, but Crosby said he was the best executive around and that if God hadn't taken the day off, Harry Jastrow, not Barney Balaban, would be running Paramount today."

"You bet he would."

"What are you doing with your life?"

"I'm in my first year of law school. This summer I've got an internship at Skadden Arps in Washington."

"That sounds . . . secure. We all need lawyers—because everyone else has one. What kind of law?"

"I don't know yet. I've only taken contracts, civil procedure, and real estate, which were kind of dry."

"Don't bullshit a bullshitter."

AJ laughed. "Okay . . . parched. I'm hoping criminal law is more fun."

"Good luck. No interest in the business?" To movie people, there was only one.

"I dreamed about it as a kid, but I've decided I should do something more serious. My mother's got me running for Senator Dirksen's seat when he retires."

"But you still go to the movies?"

"Since they built the Old Orchard, it's my second home."

"What's the best thing you've seen recently?"

"I loved *The Bad Seed*. Patty McCormack was fantastically evil. And *The Seven Samurai* . . . whoa!"

"I'm meeting Kurosawa next month to see if he'll do an American movie."

"That would be fantastic. He's got an eye like John Ford. And when that actor . . . something Mifune . . . gave his speech about how the samurai had robbed and pillaged for too long, I was on my feet shouting, 'Yeah!' "

Todd rested his fist on his chin. "Have you ever heard of *Don Quixote*?"

"Cervantes! I read *Quixote* for my Spanish lit class."

"It's my next film. How would you like to work on it?"

"Huh?" From enemy to employer in twenty-four hours? "That's awfully nice of you, but as I said—"

"You said, 'I should do something more serious.' 'Should' is somebody else talking. I heard the pizzazz in your voice talking about movies. And there's nothing more important you can do with your life than entertain people."

"My mother visited Hollywood last year and said times are bad."

"Not 'bad.' Terrible! That's the opportunity. The studios are a joke. They make and sell movies the way they did thirty years ago. They'll go belly-up one of these days, but the big bosses—the Warners and Cohns and Zanucks—won't care. They're old men who created a one-generation business. They lived selfishly and they'll die selfishly. Forget the studios. The future of the movie industry lies with independent producers like Stan Kramer, Sam Spiegel, and me. We finance our own projects and make them the way we want. It's a brand-new ball game. And I can tell—you *have* to be a part of it."

AJ walked back to the lodge with his head far above the next gale brewing to the west. A job offer in Hollywood was the last prize he'd imagined collecting at the tournament.

≡

May 2, 1957, was Maggie's forty-fourth birthday. To celebrate, her son invited her to the Palmer House, the most expensive restaurant in Chicago. After spending hours at Marshall Field's, she selected a Norman Norell silk taffeta dress with a wide black belt. They had to add another notch because her waist was so tiny. Friends wondered why so stunning a woman had never remarried. After Harry's death she'd dated the available men—mostly older widowers—but found the prospect of them touching her repellent. Only in the last few years did she touch herself. Maggie loved sex, but couldn't recapture her appetite. She joked that by the time she saw her husband in heaven, she would need to get laid *really badly*. Until then, her best man was her date for the evening.

As she applied makeup, Maggie listened to the closing stock market report from Wall Street. Her investments, especially in technology companies like IBM and Haloid, had performed spectacularly in the bull market, and she considered taking some profits and buying AJ a new Thunderbird. Not the red one he coveted, because red was his only bad color, but the white, which was classier and would stand out against his olive skin. He was a terrific kid—and on his way to becoming a famous adult. The move to Chicago had been a brilliant stroke. She'd raised him away from the corrupt values of Hollywood and oriented his future to the power centers of the East. People could cluck about her grandiosity, but in her heart, she was the mother of the first Jewish president of the United States.

≡

Go ahead, tell her. She'll understand. Even if she doesn't, AJ braced himself, she's your mother—what's the worst she can do? "How's your duck, Mom?"

"Fantastic. You haven't touched your lamb. If it's too rare, I'll call the waiter—"

"The lamb's fine."

"You're nervous about D.C., aren't you?"

"That's what I want to talk about. You see, I'm—"

"They're going to love you. That reminds me, I'll call Triple-A tomorrow and get a route map."

"Ask for one going west."

"Excuse me?"

"I'm not going to Washington." He caught her attention with that punch. Now he had to finish the combination. "Mike Todd offered me a job in Los Angeles. He's going to pay me a hundred and twenty-five dollars a *week*!"

"What are you talking about?"

"I'm talking—no, I'm not *talking*. I'm actually doing it—dropping out of law school. I'm going to make movies . . . well, someday. Hooking up with a real showman is a once-in-a-lifetime opportunity."

"AJ, this is insane."

"No, insane is staying in a place that makes my skin crawl. After I returned from Pebble Beach I realized I didn't belong in law school. The casework bores me. The students are like pod people from *Invasion of the Body Snatchers.* I hate how the professors pit us against one another. Every day I get sicker at the prospect of spending my professional life talking out of both sides of my mouth. When Mike visited Chicago last week for the local premiere of *Around the World,* he said he was serious about his job offer."

"And you're prepared to give up a future you've dreamed about for years?"

"You did the dreaming, Mom."

He'd struck a low blow, but it was too late. "Are you accusing me of pushing you to become a lawyer?"

"I didn't say 'push.' But a lot of decisions I've made in the past . . . well, they haven't always been what I wanted. Like attending Northwestern. If it had been up to me, I'd have gone to Stanford. Or staying in Chicago for law school rather than going to Harvard."

"Living home saved us money. Was that such a terrible sacrifice?"

"No. And I never complained. But for my future I need to follow *my* dream."

"And *your* dream is to go into a business that's dying, if it isn't already dead."

"People like Mike are turning Hollywood around."

"My girlfriend dated Todd when he produced on Broadway. He was a two-bit hustler then, and dollars to doughnuts, he still is!"

"He's flamboyant. If you knew him like I do, you'd feel differently."

"Now he's your close friend?" She took a gulp of wine. "You'll wind up with nothing when this ridiculous adventure fails."

"It's not going to fail!"

"I could kill Bing Crosby for twisting your head. I'm calling him right now."

AJ pinned her wrist to the table. He could never cross the California line if she called anyone. "I'm sorry this is such a surprise. It was to me too. But think about it—the signs have always been there. English was my favorite subject. I've been writing short stories for years. And God knows I love movies. It's in my blood. You remember how Dad and I planned to build a studio together. I think he'd tell me to follow my instincts."

"Into a business filled with the scum of the earth? Into the business that killed him?" She shook her head. "I don't intend to buy another black dress."

"Mom, you're being melodramatic."

"You're too young to recognize your mistake. Call Mike Todd tomorrow and tell him no."

"I called him today and told him yes."

Maggie collected her purse. "The discussion is over. If you go to Hollywood, you go it alone—without any help from me. And by the way, you're a coward for telling me this in a public place rather than at home."

Now he knew how his father had felt. Be thankful for small favors: at least she'd skipped the "fucking moron."

CHAPTER 11

Pink's recipe was classic—plump, chewy, hickory-smoked hot dogs served on soft, buttery buns and topped with condiments that cleared your sinuses. AJ had remembered them fondly while exiled in Chicago and had made the take-out shack on La Brea his first stop upon returning to Los Angeles. He had introduced Mike Todd, who'd become addicted and assigned him to buy the franks for the staff luncheons. It wasn't glamorous, but any paying job in Hollywood these days put you ahead of the game.

The year he'd left town there were five billion movie admissions. Last year the number was two and a half billion. In less than a decade profits had fallen by 60 percent. To generate extra cash, a few desperate studios drilled wells to pump oil that lay thousands of feet below their soundstages. No other American industry had ever suffered such a devastating decline so precipitously. It was perversely pleasing to AJ that his father had been prescient in forecasting the turbulence in Hollywood. Television had stolen a huge chunk of the movie audience, while the studios stood idly by and watched agents, advertisers, and independents control the new medium. Ironically, even the exhibitors who'd won in the Supreme Court had lost in the end. Their downtown movie palaces died because the middle classes deserted the cities, but the exhibitors lacked the cash and credit to build theaters in the suburbs.

AJ glanced at his note: eight dogs with mustard and relish, three with ketchup, two with sauerkraut, and one plain for Liz. Shit! As he tried to figure the missing order—he knew he needed fifteen—AJ hooked a left into the parking lot. He zipped up his Cubs jacket and got out of his secondhand Chevy. The June gloom had descended with its annual vengeance. Like a three-martini lunch, the thick low clouds hung around until late afternoon, flattening the landscape and souring the populace.

The guy in line ahead of him was a perfect example. "I don't belong here," he groused to a woman whose head was buried in her purse. "I'll go nuts if I don't get back to the city."

"So order a 'New York dog' and make believe you're at Nathan's." The girl's search hypnotized AJ. Not the search itself, but the way she arched her back and shook her long auburn hair out of the way and balanced on a foot so delicate it seemed unlikely to support her. He strained to see her face, but it remained hidden. As she bent over, her cuffed, faded Levi's rode up her athletic calves and tightened around her slim bottom. "I think you're lonely for Neile. Why don't you go to Vegas? You'll be there in three hours, the way you ride."

The guy glanced at a pristine Harley in the space next to AJ's Chevy. "And fuck up my carburetor with sand? If I'm bored here, imagine me on the Strip. Steph, what the hell are you looking for?"

She removed a pack of Clorets and popped a couple in her mouth. "I'm having the spicy dog with extra onions, so I thought I'd get a head start. Want some?"

Her friend looked dubious.

"I'll take one, if you have extra," AJ blurted out. The couple looked as if he'd materialized from outer space. "Your idea makes a lot of sense—I wouldn't have thought of it."

She studied him for a seeming eternity before shaking two into his palm. "A man who recognizes genius. . . . I'm Stephanie Salinger."

"AJ Jastrow."

Stephanie shook his hand with a firm grip. "And the guy staring through you like a fluoroscope is my friend Steve McQueen, the biggest undiscovered star in Hollywood."

"I'll tell my boss."

The actor evinced his first sign of interest. "You're a casting agent?"

"No, but he told me I should always check out new talent."

"Who's 'he'?"

"Mike Todd." Among the town's upwardly mobile, a boss at Todd's level raised AJ's status, even if his function was retrieving hot dogs. Predictably, the girl's eyes widened. They were one shade lighter than blueberries. In the time it took to reach the counter, Stephanie invited him to a party Saturday night. In return, AJ offered two tickets for *Around the World in 80 Days.*

The gruff McQueen requested a third for his wife, who was due back from Las Vegas next week. AJ had hoped Neile was Steve's girlfriend, but wife was better. Stephanie Salinger was available. At least it seemed so, because the way she hopped on the back of McQueen's bike and slipped her arms around his waist made AJ wonder. He hung back so that they wouldn't see his boring wheels. Then he remembered that the order he had forgotten was his own, so he returned to the back of the line. He wasn't leaving without his extra-spicy chili dog.

≡

AJ's phone rang at five-thirty A.M. When the same thing had happened two weeks ago, he'd thought his mother had taken sick. Now he didn't flinch and his stomach remained settled. "Hey, Mike."

"Did you find him?" A month ago Todd offered the part of Sancho Panza, Quixote's faithful servant, to the Mexican actor Cantinflas, but he'd passed because the role was too similar to the one he played in *Around the World.* Mike had then ordered AJ to locate the actor so he could make a personal appeal.

"His agent and publicist stonewalled me, so I hired this private eye in Mexico City."

"You're shitting me."

"Señor Julio Ago. The guy sounded creepy, but he called at midnight to say he had tracked Cantinflas to Tijuana. He's attending a bullfight tomorrow." AJ yawned. "I mean today."

"Pick me up at seven. And brush up on your Spanish."

AJ showered, half-expecting Todd to blast into the bathroom and hand him a towel. It made sense that his first movie had been *Around the World,* because Mike identified with Phileas Fogg, the lead character played by David Niven, who accepted a dare that he could circumnavigate the globe in record time. Don Quixote reflected another aspect of the producer's personality: his outsized dreams and desire for nobility. Initially, AJ's job had involved researching the details of seventeenth-century Spain to inform the script and production design of the movie. Once a week he and Mike lunched, talking for hours about the themes of the book and the tragedy of its hero. Increasingly, Todd had AJ shadow him throughout the day. It made his learning curve steep, even if the hours were awful.

They were thirty minutes from the Mexican border when Mike awoke from a nap. "Is your mother still on the rag about your leaving?"

AJ ignored his crassness. "She's an iceberg when I call."

"So don't call."

"I'm all she's got."

"She *wants* you to believe that. And you want to because it makes you feel special. Your mother will squeeze guilt out of you until you show more spine than a sponge. I'm not a big fan of mothers. Junior's gave him a hard time."

"I think your son's great," AJ replied. Mike Jr., who was as self-effacing and quiet as his father was self-promoting and garrulous, was the company's chief of staff.

"He likes you too. Everybody does, except Guy." Fifty-year-old Guy Biondi was Todd's gofer extraordinaire. "He's paranoid I'll get rid of him. But I won't, at least not until I see how you work out. You've got the cash, right?"

"A thousand in tens and twenties."

"You ever fight a bull?" AJ shook his head. "Good experience for making a movie."

Two hours later they walked where AJ had never expected to set foot—the center of the Toreo de Tijuana at Agua Caliente, the city's foremost bullring. Mike had managed to bribe the local promoter for the opportunity to present Cantinflas an award, which was actually a trophy they'd picked up at a pawnshop in the Mercado Hidalgo. AJ felt like Sancho Panza—solidly in tow but distressed by his boss's bizarre behavior. It didn't help that he spotted blood in the sand where the last bull had died. Since Mike didn't speak Spanish, AJ interpreted. The feedback through the ancient microphone jolted the crowd. Mike looked to a nearby box, where Cantinflas sat in shock.

"Today is the happiest day of my life." AJ couldn't believe that Todd had stolen Lou Gehrig's farewell at Yankee Stadium. "Because I have the chance to present the United Nations Fellowship Award to a great performer, a great man, and a great Mexican—your very own Cantinflas." AJ tripped on the translation, but Mike was on too much of a roll to notice. "His work in *Around the World in 80 Days* created goodwill throughout the globe. In his honor I'm establishing a foundation to educate deserving Mexican children who come to America." People stomped, forcing Cantinflas to acknowledge the tribute. "I only hope we can work together in the future to bring more joy to the world."

The ride home took six hours because AJ had drunk too much tequila and refused to drive faster than forty miles an hour. Cantinflas hadn't accepted the part but had agreed to give it serious consideration when the script was ready. "We've got him," Todd said confidently.

"Isn't he eventually going to realize that there's no such award?"

"Nobody checks on good news. Shit, the U.N. should give him one. He's done more for international relations than they have."

"And the foundation?"

"It's a great idea. I'll put up ten grand. You did such a good job, keep whatever money we didn't use on bribes."

The two hundred dollars would come in handy, but the offer left AJ feeling more like a bagman than a producer in training.

=

"We're going to throw the biggest birthday party New York's ever seen."

Todd's staff blinked en masse.

"Boss, your birthday was last month."

"Thank you, Guy. I didn't know that. Who can tell me what happened on October fifteenth one year ago?"

"The premiere of *Around the World in 80 Days*."

Todd rewarded his son with a stogie. The movie's reserved-seat road-show release in big cities had proved a fabulous success, Mike explained, but with *Around the World* opening nationwide in late October, the publicity from a party could blow the box office through the roof. They would have to drop their other activities to make it happen.

There were a thousand problems—but not a word of warning. Like most cult personalities in Hollywood, Todd surrounded himself with people who believed his genius was their salvation. A few were sycophants, but others were born executors who admired his ability to formulate the big idea that eluded them. Mike fed on their zeal.

"The question is where do we hold the party."

Guy Biondi might be Dopey or Sleepy but never Bashful. "They got this giant new amusement park in the New Jersey Palisades."

"The press aren't schlepping to Jersey. Don't be a schmuck all your life."

"How about the Fifty-ninth Street Armory?" The suggestion came from Bill Doll, whose job as Todd's publicist rendered him redundant.

"Too militaristic."

"In Chicago we'd hold this kind of bash in the Madhouse on Madison." Everyone looked at AJ blankly. "Chicago Stadium . . . where the Blackhawks play?"

"That's brilliant. We'll give people skates," Biondi joked, "and watch them fall on their asses."

Todd beamed. "The Madhouse on Madison. That's it! We'll hold our shindig at Madison Square Garden. Eighteen thousand of my intimate friends in the prime indoor venue in the world."

=

Over the next two weeks AJ developed a crick in his neck spending morning, noon, and night on the telephone arranging entertainment for Todd's "Garden Party." Mike's notion was to use different nationalities to highlight the theme of *Around the World*. AJ managed to book twenty-one folk-dancing troupes representing as many cultures to perform before dinner, but he faced a touchy problem. "The Armenian belly dancers from Hoboken won't appear if the Turkish sword dancers from Queens are on the floor."

"So promise exclusivity." Todd moved on.

AJ didn't. "They'll see each other. I can't just lie to them."

"Of course you can! Both of them want to be there, right? It's only their bullshit history talking."

"There's a holocaust in that history."

Todd turned tomato red. "I didn't hire you to give me a lecture from some fucking college history course!"

Those in shouting range swiveled to see AJ sweat and sway like a schoolboy caned on the hands. He swallowed his self-respect and grinned, as if to say "No big deal." But it was.

AJ was still unnerved when he ran into Art Cohn in the parking lot after work. Mike had hired Art to write his biography because he believed his own life story was so valuable a property it would be the basis for a great movie—and a legacy for his son. Maybe Todd was right, but AJ couldn't believe any man had that much chutzpah. "Has Mike always been so . . . unstable?"

"I interviewed guys who knew him back in Minneapolis when he was Avrom Goldbogen, guys who backed his plays on Broadway, men who took his marker in high-stakes gin rummy. They all made the same observation: Mike only feels alive when he's hanging on the edge, forty stories in the air."

"It doesn't scare him?"

"Nah. Because he never really believes he'll fall—no matter how many times he's chewed concrete."

Based on *his* one fall, AJ hated the taste. He couldn't simply write today's incident off as "nothing personal." Heading home, he decided to be so professional that Mike would never have reason to attack him again. And if that meant keeping his mouth shut more than he liked, so be it.

For a hundred dollars a month he rented a studio apartment in a gracefully shabby Art Deco building in Hollywood called the Ravenswood, where Mae West, the sex symbol of the '30s, had once lived. AJ had sexual ambitions of his own—number one being Stephanie Salinger. Their dates had been great, even the ones when her unemployed actor friend tagged along. But tomorrow night McQueen's wife was due to fly into L.A. from Vegas, where she was starring in *The Pajama Game* at the Desert Inn, so AJ counted on having Steph to himself.

He fretted that she would hate his decorating choices—cinder-block bookshelves and painted plywood tables. To liven it up, maybe he could buy some flowers or, better still, a bushy plant, although he couldn't keep anything green alive for more than a week. Flopping down on his mattress on the floor, AJ decided that his first priority was to get that brass bed he'd spotted in a secondhand store on Highland, and maybe the afghan that went with it. . . . Without warning he yawned loudly. Work was a hell of a lot more exhausting than school. In the past month he'd scalded his hand cooking spaghetti and bleached the color out of his best madras shirt. He wasn't a gifted homemaker, but bachelors weren't supposed to be. What mattered was that he was coming and going as he saw fit and on his way to big things in the movie business.

CHAPTER 12

AJ sat on the horn, weaving through traffic, jumping lights. His big day had started with both a dead battery and a flat tire and now he was late for a barbecue at Ray Stark's. Turning west on Santa Monica, he glanced at the Fox lot and recalled his day at the Supreme Court when Spyros Skouras had boasted that the studio system was impregnable. Last week the banks had forced Skouras to sell most of Fox's back lot to real estate investors, who intended to construct apartments and stores in a development, anachronistically named Radio City of California.

Skidding to a stop in front of a mini-mansion in Holmby Hills, AJ handed his keys to a valet. Apparently, the good times weren't completely history, because providing someone to park your guests' cars—even with dozens of spots available—remained de rigueur. In the acre of garden that constituted Stark's backyard, AJ whistled at a bronze sculpture by Henry Moore next to a Rodin. "Your place is like the Louvre."

"It's the Hollywood dream—win big early, then play with the house's money." Ray patted his shoulder. "I expect you to do the same." A few months earlier Stark had surprised the town—and caused Ava Gardner to weep—by resigning as a senior agent at the Famous Artists Agency. He had been traveling ever since, generating projects for Seven Arts, his new production company. Ray looked AJ up and down, an affectionate, amazed grin spreading across his face. "After all this time . . . it's great to have you back here. How's the job working out with Todd?"

"Mike's one of a kind."

"Did I hear someone use the devil's name in vain?"

Stark did the honors. "AJ, meet S. J.—Perelman." The bespectacled writer had won the Academy Award for his screenplay of *Around the World in 80 Days,* but the only time AJ had heard Mike mention the writer's name, he'd spit in disgust.

"The next time you see that sinister dwarf, send him my best wishes."

Now he understood why. "The boss can be hard to get along with."

"You are working for a man who has no peer in his profession. And that profession is to humiliate and cheapen his fellow man, fracture their self-esteem, convert everyone around him into lackeys, hypo-crites, and toadies, and thoroughly debase every relationship, no matter how casual. I suggest you shed his company soon because his enormity grows on you like a fungus."

It was a blistering indictment, even in a town where venom was the vernacular. As a writer, Perelman was smarter and angrier than most people, but AJ knew enough to give the attack credence. "Don't worry, kid," Stark reassured him as they walked away. "Some people would say the same thing about me." He then edged AJ over to a man with sun-nier advice on the vagaries of life in Hollywood.

Ronald Reagan was taller in person than he appeared hosting CBS's *General Electric Theater* on Sunday evenings. "I'm the local poster boy for surviving job insecurity. Back in 1952, I was president of the Screen Ac-tors Guild, but I couldn't get an acting gig. After twenty pictures, the studios figured they'd given me enough screen tests." Reagan indicated a petite brunette in a nearby cluster of women. "Nancy and I were new-lyweds and struggling to pay the mortgage on this beautiful parcel of ranchland I've got near Santa Barbara. I went riding in the hills to fig-ure out what else I might do, but I couldn't imagine anything I enjoyed as much as acting. So we let fate—and MCA—take its hand."

The fourth member of their group laughed like a man paid 10 per-cent to do so. Taft Schreiber was the right-hand man of MCA's topper, Lew Wasserman. AJ recalled his dad describing the talent agency as an octopus, and in the years since his death, it had grown more tentacles. Schreiber explained how MCA, which produced *G.E. Theater,* had con-vinced the appliance maker to give Reagan a try. "Since you became their spokesman, Ronnie, sales are up in all divisions."

"Thanks, Taft." Reagan turned back to AJ. "My advice, son, is make sure you love this business. If you do, believe in yourself, play for the long haul . . . and get yourself a good agent."

"I didn't think that agencies were allowed to produce shows and movies," AJ commented as he and Ray wended their way to another clump of guests. "Doesn't the Screen Actors Guild prohibit it because it can be a conflict of interest?"

Stark nodded. "They do prohibit it, but you can apply and get a waiver. I got tired of applying and being rejected. That's why I quit to produce full-time."

AJ was perplexed. "But MCA got a waiver for *General Electric The-ater*?"

"And for their other twenty hours of television. MCA's the only agency with a *blanket* waiver from SAG."

"Which they got back in 1952 . . . ?" AJ hastily sewed two and two together. "So MCA convinced Reagan to push the blanket waiver through when he was president of SAG. That's why they had to land him the G.E. job."

"Go to the head of the class. A lot of competitors are furious; so are the studios. Rumor is, the Justice Department is trying to prove that Wasserman got a sweetheart deal."

"I bet everyone's just envious they didn't think of it first."

Ray smiled amiably. "I certainly am." They approached a man who was whispering in the ear of a handsome blonde. "Rabbi, look who I've tracked down for you."

Hollywood encouraged reinvention—an actor's stock-in-trade—but the metamorphosis in Leon Ginsberg stunned AJ. The man's German accent was almost undetectable. He sported a dazzling tan, highlighted by a white Lacoste shirt. AJ recognized the blonde as Eve Arden, who'd recently starred in the CBS comedy *Our Miss Brooks.* "Albert Jastrow, how are you?" Ginsberg pumped his hand and bragged to Arden, "This young man gave a speech once that moved me to tears. I said to myself that he would do great things one day. And he has."

"Sorry, Rabbi, but I haven't done anything yet, great or otherwise." AJ remained cool until he could figure out why Ginsberg was interested in him.

"Phi Beta Kappa, University of Chicago law school, now an important job with Mr. Mike Todd? I hear all about you from this man." The rabbi gave Stark a Hollywood hug, the appearance of which suggested intimacy, though it signified nothing more than "good to see you." "Ray and Fran are valued members of my new congregation in Brentwood. Lots of people in your business belong, above and below the line." It startled AJ to hear a rabbi use an insider's terms to describe the division between actors, producers, writers, and directors and the technical crew on films. "By the way, how's your mother?"

"She's fine. Back in Chicago." They made small talk until AJ apologized for having to leave early for another engagement. Curiously, the rabbi walked him to his car.

"AJ, I wonder if I can do both of us a favor." Magically, a script appeared. Ginsberg announced that he had written the story of his adventures in Europe—his harassment by the Nazis and the good deeds he'd done for people before escaping to America. The title was *Exile*. Todd was the perfect producer, Ginsberg reckoned, because he'd demonstrated a bent for internationally based projects. After working for Mike, AJ was used to people slipping him scripts, whether they were members of the Writers Guild or pumped gas at the Esso station. "We'll consider it right away, sir."

=

"Is that the worst idea for a movie you've ever heard?"

Stephanie sucked the cherry in her mai tai. "Second worst. Steve wants to do a film version of *An Enemy of the People*. When I told him Ibsen doesn't sell tickets in Omaha, he said, 'With me in it, it will.' Someday we'll probably find out."

His father had once advised AJ to find a girl with a good appetite. Steph fit the bill. She took the last sparerib, swiped it through the duck sauce, and systematically cleaned the bone. The Formosa was her favorite Chinese restaurant. She relished the crowd, the character, and the Cantonese cooking. AJ, on the other hand, found the food greasy and the place itself a dark and dingy hangout for actors whose careers were on hold. "Everyone here looks like they blew today's audition."

"They probably did." She cheerfully surveyed tonight's diners. "But they'll all be back at it tomorrow."

Born and raised in Cincinnati, Steph had headed west two years ago after attending Ohio State and was already a sought-after script supervisor. Her job was to make sure that everything the actors did in a scene matched the action in previous takes and to report inconsistencies to the director. Unlike most girls, who cared only about marriage and family, Steph was determined to succeed professionally. AJ found that sexy.

"I still haven't gotten my invitation to Todd's party," she kidded.

AJ recounted Perelman's blast and the incident over the dance troupes.

"What's the real problem—his ordering you to lie or humiliating you?"

"The latter, I'm afraid. I'm used to awards, not abuse."

Steph smiled. "The award you deserve is for the thinnest skin in town."

"You don't understand how vicious Mike can be."

"Don't I? In the last film I worked on, an American named Danny

Blaylock played a British spy. In his key scene he completely forgot his English accent. We were behind schedule, so the director yelled, 'Cut, print, let's move on.' When I reminded him about Blaylock's accent, he screamed, 'You stupid bitch, you tell me one more time how to do my job and I'll make sure your skinny ass never sits next to a director again.' "

"I hope you told him to go to hell."

"I wanted to. I also wanted to cry, but instead I walked away. After lunch he tried smoothing it over, but his apology was so awkward I stopped him and said, 'Thanks for the compliment.' He looked confused. 'About my butt being skinny,' I said. 'I always think it's too big.' Last week he called to ask if I'd be script supervisor on his next film."

"You should *direct* his next film."

"Right. There are precisely two female members in the DGA. Anyway, AJ, that's not my point. A lot of the guys we work for would be committed to loony bins if they did anything else. My dad's a pharmacist. Can you imagine if he called his assistant a 'stupid bitch' because she reminded him that the prescription was supposed to say two pills once a day rather than one pill every other day?" AJ burst out laughing. "The insanity comes with the talent—or vice versa. But if you take their outbursts personally, you won't last here. And that would make me very unhappy."

AJ pushed aside their plates to kiss her—and kept at it until the flatulent Harley in the parking lot announced Steve McQueen's arrival. The actor entered, alone and pissed, and explained that Neile couldn't make it to Los Angeles because of her understudy's broken ankle. McQueen sucked down a beer. "Be smart, Jastrow, stay single. I love my wife, but if she were my girlfriend right now, I'd tell her to get lost."

AJ headed to the men's room but, glancing back, noticed that McQueen's head was buried in the crook of Steph's neck. She giggled at something he said—or was he nibbling on her ear? AJ stormed around drying his hands. He wasn't sure if he was jealous because he cared so much about Steph or because he felt inadequate next to Steve, who figured to be phenomenal in bed.

When he returned, two guys were hovering over the table looking pissed. One was a linebacker for the Rams who accused Steve of having seduced his girlfriend in an acting class; his lankier buddy egged him on. McQueen's only response was a cocky smile. The guys left hurling threats. "I've got to get out of those classes," Steve sighed. "They're like bordellos. Man, do I need a job."

After being discharged by the Marines, McQueen had done some undistinguished stage work in New York. Hoping to build a career in movies, he'd come to Hollywood with his new bride, Neile Adams, a successful dancer. He had managed a few TV credits, but his only movie role was a bit in *Somebody Up There Likes Me*.

The crash of breaking glass from outside froze them. Steve guessed it was the headlight on the Harley. He vaulted to his feet and was out the door, even as Steph pleaded with him not to do anything crazy. AJ promised to mediate. Outside, the linebacker circled McQueen, viciously swinging a tire iron at his head, but the actor was a born street fighter and a scarred veteran of juvenile detention centers. He edged in, reducing the man's advantage.

AJ was scared. "Guys, cut this out. Let's talk about it."

"Fuck you!"

McQueen charged, took a glancing blow, and flattened the man against a tan DeSoto parked next to the Harley. He was beating the crap out of the linebacker when his friend showed up with a Louisville Slugger. He took dead aim as if Steve's head were a hanging curveball.

AJ slammed the guy from behind, sending the bat twirling like a majorette's baton. The man attacked him with a flurry of punches, one opening a cut that bled into his eye. AJ had no experience in street brawls, so he improvised, blocking most of the blows with his elbows. Then one connected with his right ear and all he could hear was Niagara Falls. The idea that he was deaf triggered a rush of adrenaline. AJ threw haymakers without caring if he got hit—so long as he hit back harder. He ripped flesh off his knuckles when he smashed the guy's front teeth, more when he broke the man's nose. He heard screaming, which meant his deafness wasn't permanent. Someone powerful grabbed his arms as the two attackers stumbled backward, disappearing into the night.

Eventually he realized that the person restraining him was on his side. Steve talked him down, assuring him they had won. The pain in his body asserted itself. "Jesus! Ow! That fucking hurts!" AJ waved his hands to get rid of the sting.

Steve looked over to Steph. "You want to help me with the champ?" She rushed over to examine AJ, whose obscenities continued unabated. "If I hadn't seen it with my own eyes . . ." McQueen laughed out loud. "College boy here? Un-fucking-believable!"

=

"He's your friend for life now," Stephanie shouted from the bathroom of AJ's apartment as she soaked his shirt before the bloodstains set.

"Then I better take a crash course in jujitsu." AJ applied an ice pack to the side of his head. His jaw ached when he talked, but his hearing was back and the emergency room doctor had stitched his cut. Still, he shook. He couldn't tell if the fight had altered his personality or revealed it. "It's a good thing the Irish don't run Hollywood," he observed ruefully. "There'd be fistfights in the commissary every day. Or, worse yet, the Italians. We'd see blood and bodies on Rodeo Drive."

Steph plopped down on the bed. "The Jews run it, so there's constant whining."

AJ bristled.

"Hey, no offense, I'm Jewish myself," she added.

"No offense taken. You think all Jews are whiners?"

"Only the males."

"That's not—"

"Come on, I've been listening to Jewish men complain about their mothers and wives and girlfriends since the crib."

"You prefer the strong, silent type?"

She thought for a beat. "I don't think in those terms. Why do you ask?"

"It's just that . . . well, you seem to like Steve an awful lot."

Steph placed her arms protectively across her chest. "I do like him. So what?" When he said nothing, her eyes narrowed. "You're wondering if maybe he and I . . . ? One of those punches must have damaged your brain."

"You're right. It's none of my business."

"Oh my God. You're not wondering—you actually believe I slept with a married man whose wife is one of my best friends."

"Steph, don't get so angry. It's just that . . . well . . . I'm *interested* in you."

"What are you *interested* in? Finding out if I'm an easy lay? Or finding out if I'm a virgin?" Given the size of his apartment, she reached the door before he could react. "The most important thing to me is being able to trust the person I love. I hate the idea of cheating. So go to hell. And make sure you change your bandage tomorrow."

He leaped from his bed to stop her. "I was being an insecure asshole. I apologize."

"Apology accepted. Good-bye."

If this woman walked out . . . if he never saw her again . . . that was unacceptable.

"I'm *interested* in you because I absolutely, positively, and unconditionally adore you."

"That's better." She kissed him hard on the lips.

It hurt, but he wasn't about to complain.

CHAPTER 13

The captain's voice crackled from the cockpit over the public-address system of TWA's Flight 49. "Ladies and gentlemen, passengers on the right side of the aircraft now have a bird's-eye view of *Sputnik.*"

Over the wingtip of the DC-7 the pulsing lights of the Russian-made shooting star blinked an impenetrable code. Was it televising pictures of America back to Moscow? Could the satellite be rigged to drop a bomb? After World War II AJ and his generation had assumed that America ruled the world because it possessed the coolest technology. That belief now seemed a child's fantasy, despite President Eisenhower's assurance that *Sputnik* yielded the Communists no military advantage. If the United States orbits one, AJ wondered, maybe it could transmit movies from Hollywood all over the planet. Todd would love the idea because he always counseled to "think big."

AJ was en route to New York for the *Around the World in 80 Days* bash. Mike bragged that it would join the pantheon of the city's celebrations, from V-J Day to the Dodgers' first World Series triumph. At a meeting with CBS last month he'd introduced AJ as a researcher from Northwestern who'd conducted a consumer poll showing record levels of viewer interest in the party. Based on the detailed data, the network had agreed to broadcast the event live on national television. Todd was elated—indifferent to the fact he'd made up every number.

The plane banked sharply to the left to avoid a band of thunderstorms over central Illinois. As lights from the suburbs of Chicago appeared to the north, AJ's concerns shifted to the stop he'd make there on the way back from New York. It was past time to patch up his quarrel with his mom. He had so much to tell her about his adventures in Hollywood, but their sporadic phone calls never exceeded the three-minute minimum. How would she take the news that he was in love? Hopefully, it wouldn't be a replay of the Dara Berkowitz incident. Dara had been Tri-Delt's homecoming queen. AJ had really liked her, but all his mother could say when they met on prom night was that the girl laughed like a hyena. After that, AJ couldn't listen to Dara giggle.

No, this time was going to be different. Even Mom had to love a girl who could work a twelve-hour day, go surfing at sunset, and cook dinner. Steph could even argue politics, which she did fiercely, having worked for Stevenson in the 1956 election, while AJ was president of the campus Young Republicans. Although they hadn't made love, he knew sex with Stephanie would be terrific. Five hours and he already missed her. With another three to go, he decided to get some sleep. He was sure to need it in the days ahead.

The marquee outside Madison Square Garden read CLOSED TONIGHT FOR A LITTLE PRIVATE PARTY. Mike's black-tie affair was so hot a ticket in New York that AJ had to travel to Queens to rent a tuxedo. When he reported for work at five A.M. on "T-Day," he hung it on a rack in their makeshift offices above the Howard Johnson's at Fiftieth Street, but since then he'd consumed so many bagels out of nervous energy he wondered if his cummerbund would still fit.

Mike Jr. rushed over. "You have to rush to La Guardia to pick up Hubert Humphrey." The Minnesota senator was tonight's keynote speaker. "All the limos are booked."

"Sorry, Junior," AJ demurred. "I've got a problem with the Mummers." With their wild costumes and antics, the Philadelphia band was at the top of the bill, but two hours earlier their captain had threatened to withdraw unless AJ met his demands to fix their bus.

"I'll handle it," Guy Biondi offered.

Biondi couldn't find his ass with both hands, but Junior brooked no debate. "Hell, Humphrey may be president someday, and he's an old friend of Dad's from their Milwaukee days."

On the drive from the airport the senator never stopped talking, heaping equal praise on the National Guard for protecting black schoolchildren in Little Rock and Mike Todd for exemplifying the American dream. If this guy got elected president, the nation was in for a four-year headache. Escorting Humphrey inside the Garden, AJ found Todd atop a ladder on the main stage, instructing a mob of performers, waiters, cops, and television crew on what would happen that night.

"Here's the order. First come the bands, followed by the folk dancers, elephants, Boy Scouts, and Senator Humphrey. We finish with Elizabeth cutting the cake. I can't be any clearer than that, can I?" People raised their hands with dozens of follow-up questions, but he left Junior to tidy his mess.

Todd hugged Humphrey and introduced him to Elizabeth Taylor. Her violet eyes finally shut the senator up.

"Mike! Mike! Hold on." AJ recognized Walter Cronkite and Byron Palmer, the director of the CBS special, dashing across the floor.

"Hey, Walter, doesn't this beat sitting behind the anchor desk?" Todd asked jovially.

Palmer pounced. "What the hell kind of a bill of goods did you sell us? The broadcast is three hours away and not one of my guys knows what's going on or when. You promised us a trainload of celebrities, but I don't have a clue who's showing up."

"That's absolutely unacceptable, Byron. You should have had the schedule this morning. Jastrow, I told you the list of guest stars was to be on Mr. Palmer's desk by ten A.M."

"I . . . I . . . I'm not—"

"No excuses!" Todd swung back to Palmer. "I'm plagued by incompetents. If you'll excuse me for a moment, I'll get this under control." Mike grabbed AJ and shielded him with his body. "Go to the office, type up a list, and get it to this schmuck as quickly as you can."

"I have no idea who to put—"

"It doesn't matter. We're winging it. 'Byron Bureaucrat' needs a list, so get him one. Meet me at the Ripley to let me know what we promised."

A few hours later AJ was stewing in his third bourbon and branch water at the bar of a low-rent hotel near the Garden. He hated the taste but thought it gave him an air of sophistication. And it got him drunk quickly. Mike arrived arm in arm with David Niven, dancing a jaunty rendition of "New York, New York." Niven shook AJ's hand and assured him how lucky he was to be working for an unparalleled impresario. "I didn't want to do this movie in the worst way, but your boss wouldn't take no for an answer. Now I'm rich. Stick with him and it could happen to you."

"Hey, sorry about earlier, but my plan worked perfectly," Mike joked. "Palmer's a pig in shit. I just got off the phone with Sinatra—he's actually coming, so you're not totally full of it."

It was scant solace. AJ was sick of lying every minute of every day. He was sick of Todd's rationalizing, sick of being dragged into his boss's cycle of bullshit—and sick of ducking a confrontation. As soon as this crisis passed, AJ intended to tell Mike what his limits were.

=

The evening's unsung hero was designer Vincent Korda, who'd beguilingly transformed Madison Square Garden. His theme was "Around the Garden, *Around the World.*" A replica of the Sphinx replaced the home bench of the Knicks. As guests circled the arena sipping Dom Pérignon, they visited the Leaning Tower of Pisa, the Taj Mahal, and the Matterhorn. But the champagne was the first omen that all was not right around this world. It was supposed to be free, but the waiters—furious because Todd had screwed them on their rate—scalped the bottles at five dollars apiece.

"The Star-Spangled Banner" announced the onslaught of the bands. With butterflies in his stomach, AJ sent out his first group, thirty Alsatian accordionists in lederhosen. Although he planned to launch two bands per minute, he'd failed to calculate their members gawking and playing to the TV cameras.

Mike was strutting in blissful ignorance when AJ and Palmer forced their way on stage to explain the problem. "So it takes longer, what's the big cockamamie deal?" Gritting his teeth, Palmer reminded him that the CBS broadcast would finish before the stars of the movie and the other celebrities appeared. "Okay. Cut out the rest of the bands and dancers."

AJ knew people had rehearsed for months, but this was no time to argue their case. He resorted to the Big Lie one last time. Assembling the leaders of the remaining bands, he announced a change in plans: they would march *after* the speeches and food.

"You expect me to believe that bullshit?" AJ recognized the towering man dressed in a cape of huge peacock feathers as Tommy Lombino, captain of the Mummers. "Jastrow, you promised to get back to me, but I didn't hear a fucking word . . . so fuck you."

AJ spied Guy Biondi shrinking into the crowd. "Guy, didn't you—"
"We're marching *now!*"

AJ tried blocking the exit and knocked over a Mummer on stilts before two guys with vulture masks flattened him. The band moved in slow motion, playing Dixieland tunes on their banjos and trombones. Todd ran to intercept them or kill AJ—whichever he managed first.

The collision occurred at the Eighth Avenue end of the Garden. Todd screamed for the cops to evict Lombino, who responded by threatening to have his band strip off their outfits. "And believe me, Shorty, they ain't got jockstraps on underneath." When Mike threatened to sue, Lombino sneered and signaled the band to keep marching. Palmer threw down his headset, shouting that the rest of the broadcast was canceled.

Todd charged AJ like a midget bull elephant. "I told you to cut the fucking bands."

"I tried."

"Bullshit. In all my years, I've never seen a bigger loser."

Poor choice of words. "What did you say?"

"One more idiotic failure and you're out. I'm only patient to a point, then—"

"I quit."

"You what?" Todd lost his rhythm mid-rant.

"I'm through." AJ stormed away, loosening his black tie.

Todd whipped him around by the shoulders. "You think you can quit on me? *You're fired!* No one will hire you when I've finished ruining your reputation!"

AJ took a step forward, causing Mike to take one back. Then another and to the left. They looked like a dance pair working out a routine. "Keep him away," Mike beseeched. No one sympathized. He stumbled, but AJ grabbed him by his lapels, as if they were performing a dip, then lifted him off the ground.

The crowd roared.

"Please! Don't hurt him!" It was Mike Jr.

AJ eyed the frightened Todd. There were a thousand things he wanted to say, but none of them would make the slightest impact, so he marched his former boss across the floor and dumped him on his butt in front of Art Cohn. "Another chapter for the bio."

=

By the time AJ had hiked to the Pierre, there were already urgent messages from reporters at two New York papers—and his mother. He dialed her first. "Are you okay?"

"I'm better than you."

"What's going on, Mom? What's 'urgent'?"

"Well, it's not every day that a mother sees her son in a vaudeville act on live television. I couldn't hear what was being said, but Walter Cronkite gave a pretty fair blow-by-blow." AJ broke into a sweat. Byron Palmer must have exacted revenge by televising the altercation. "Todd looks even nastier than I thought. But don't worry, we'll figure out a plan when you get here."

"Mom, I'm going straight back to L.A. I want to find another job as soon as possible."

Disappointment seeped through the line. "You already know how I feel. Let me know when I can catch you in prime time again."

Her sarcasm stung, but there was no point being prideful when he might have to eat crow. AJ stared out his tenth-floor window but saw only the blackness of Central Park. In school he'd regularly been voted most likely to succeed, but in the real world . . . how about class clown?

The phone rang. He hoped it was Steph, who was working on a night shoot. But the guy on the line said his name was Harold Klurfeld from Walter Winchell's office at the New York *Daily News*. "Mr. Jastrow, I'd like your version of the 'heavyweight bout at the Garden.' "

"Huh?"

"I've already got a quote from Mr. Todd saying that you're 'a troubled youth who was drinking heavily earlier in the evening.' The bartender at the Ripley confirmed his allegation."

Apparently the worst moments of AJ's life—his dad's death and now his sacking—were fated to be public. "I'd really appreciate it if you wouldn't run that. I wasn't drunk, but it's a private matter between Todd and myself. Your story would add to my embarrassment."

Klurfeld guffawed. "Get used to it, kid. Humiliation is mother's milk in your line of work." Claiming he had a deadline, the man abruptly hung up. AJ had a deadline as well. He had to use the rest of his round-trip ticket before Mike canceled it. Without replacing the receiver, he called TWA and made reservations on the morning flight to the coast.

CHAPTER 14

The *Garden Party* earned a lousy Nielsen rating on the West Coast, so other than two matrons at a Hughes checkout counter who wanted to know what Mike Todd was really like, no one recognized AJ as the disgraced screwup. Maybe notoriety would have helped—without it he was just another job hunter in a town with double-digit unemployment. AJ aggressively pursued every rumor of an opening, but suffered more slammed doors than Willy Loman.

The studios had instituted a hiring freeze, with the ironic exception of Paramount, which advertised for a script analyst. A hundred hopefuls applied. In the initial interview Joe Fuchs, the hoary story editor with a complexion the color of phlegm, quizzed AJ about old films. He had seen all of them with his folks and passed the first hurdle by correctly identifying Victor Fleming as the director of *Treasure Island, Test Pilot,* and *Tortilla Flat.* His next test was to prepare notes on the studio's upcoming project, *I Married a Monster from Outer Space.*

AJ dissected the holes in the story and even suggested alternative lines for the corny dialogue. Dropping off his assignment, however, he froze at the sight of Paul Herzog, deep in discussion with a steely Jack Palance, who starred in Paramount's *The Lonely Man.* They looked like a pair of criminals plotting a heist. Barney Balaban's refusal to retire as president had made Herzog the longest-running understudy in town. AJ fled the lot, wondering if working for the enemy would make him a disloyal son. He decided not to worry, because getting the job was still a long shot.

His work was so impressive, however, that Fuchs showed it to his boss, who ordered the scriptwriter to implement the suggestions. Joe promised to call AJ with a formal offer within forty-eight hours. Then . . . nothing, not a word for a week. AJ phoned repeatedly, but Fuchs was invariably "down the hall" or "in conference." AJ guessed what had happened, but to make sure he sneaked onto the lot and surprised his prey in the men's room. After checking that no one was eavesdropping in the stalls, Fuchs admitted that when AJ's name came up, the big boss told him to hire *anyone* else. Although the Harry Jastrow incident was long in the past, Herzog was taking no chances.

With Christmas approaching AJ widened his search, seeking employment as a production assistant. Unfortunately, the studios were financing fewer films and many of those were shot out of town, and frequently out of the country. "Runaway production" left Hollywood with a surfeit of experienced workers, and AJ's college degree proved a hindrance, since no one valued education when the job was bringing coffee to the director.

So he was thrilled to land a gig as Danny Kaye's stand-in on *Merry Andrew,* a circus musical starring Kaye and European import Pier Angeli. He arrived on the MGM lot full of enthusiasm—the only person in a good mood. Everyone else wore black armbands to commemorate the recent death of Louis B. Mayer, Metro's founder and boss for thirty years. On the set AJ paid close attention as director Michael Kidd rehearsed a scene in which Kaye courted Angeli under the big top. When Danny departed for hair and makeup, AJ took his place, inches from the Mediterranean beauty. She purred hello with her marvelous accent, but before he could trot out his limited Italian, Pier departed with a flirtatious *"Ciao."* Her stand-in's breath reeked of cheap whiskey as she babbled about her upcoming auditions. The cameraman circled them, thrusting a meter next to AJ's nostrils, then barking orders at his gaffer, who adjusted the lights to cast precisely the shadow that flattered the left profile. Kaye reappeared, and AJ drifted into oblivion.

Shot after shot, hour after hour the routine never varied. No one said a word to him other than "Keep your head up" or "Don't move." When he suggested that a scene might play better if Kaye's character moved to his left so the Fat Lady could also be in the frame, the director stared as if he were Mr. Bumble and Oliver had asked for "More." By wrap, AJ felt less essential than the greensman who fed the elephant.

His frustration was high and his spirits low as he exited the Egyptian Theatre with Steph after seeing *The Incredible Shrinking Man.* "That was idiotic," he groused.

"Come on. The scene where he lances the giant spider with the straight pin—I heard you shout. The special effects were wonderful."

"Not to me. But that's because I already know what it's like to feel two inches tall." He recounted his dismal day as they drove to the San Gabriel Valley to try the new In-N-Out Burger. They joined a line that drifted around the restaurant.

"I'm sorry." She shook her head. "The job was a mismatch. A stand-in needs to be invisible, and you have too much . . . presence. There'll be something else."

He took a deep breath. "Between takes today I wrote a letter to the dean of my old law school to see if he'll let me return next year."

"You're quitting Hollywood?"

"Hollywood's quit on me."

"You hated law school."

"At least I was decent at it." They finally got their order, and he immediately began chain-eating French fries.

"AJ, why can't you understand that it's only a matter of time till others discover how talented you are?"

"You're the one who doesn't understand. You've got a job that puts you in the center of the action. The whole *Gunsmoke* crew depends on you. Hell, James Arness sent you flowers. You've made it."

"And you will too." Steph wiped relish off his upper lip. "If it's necessary, I'll chain you to your bed until you come to your senses."

The look in her eyes said she loved him. He knew it did. And that knowledge turned his day—and his life—upside down. Even bad was good because it proved they belonged together. "This isn't the most romantic setting." He tapped the Formica table and pointed to their Cokes. "But I have to say this now. Steph, I love you."

"You do?"

"I have from the first day we met."

She grabbed her jacket and purse. "Why don't you finish your burger so we can get out of here."

Later, after they'd made love for the first time and Steph slept soundly in his arms, AJ made a mental note to apply for a California driver's license. She wouldn't need the chains—he was never leaving this state again.

=

With his girlfriend working overtime, AJ phoned Steve McQueen and the two went to check out *Sweet Smell of Success*. They'd become unlikely buddies after the fight at the Formosa. With AJ, Steve felt safe venting his endless frustrations. For his part, AJ decided that if he'd known McQueen in high school, he'd have gotten into more trouble and had a lot more fun.

A thousand cars packed the Sepulveda Drive-In for the seven-thirty show. As the only male twosome in their section, AJ suspected that he and Steve looked like a couple of homos. Then he felt a wet tongue on his neck and remembered why they were there. From the backseat

Thor, McQueen's German shepherd, slobbered on him. Steve refused to leave the dog at home, so they'd hid him in the trunk until they parked.

"He loves you," McQueen marveled. "I wish he liked Neile." Thor was a bone of contention in Steve's marriage. Neile argued that their life was too unsettled to own a dog; she already saw her husband infrequently and didn't want to share his affections. But for Steve, who'd grown up without a family, the animal was a surrogate child. Sensing that Neile disliked him, Thor did his business next to her pillow while she slept. It was the final insult, since Steve had bought him with Neile's paycheck. "God didn't intend a wife to make more money than her husband," he griped.

The comment struck AJ close to home. "No work on the horizon?"

"A TV pilot about a bounty hunter. But I'm not doing the idiot box. It's death for an actor."

"I think you're selling television short, Steve. Sure, they do mindless stuff, but some of the shows are better than a lot of movies. Can I read the script?"

"Be my guest. You'll see that it's just another oater."

=

Fedoras outnumbered trilbies two to one as the hat of choice among William Morris agents. AJ calculated the ratio while sitting in the lobby of the agency's headquarters in Beverly Hills. For an important meeting with his representatives, McQueen had asked AJ to accompany him for moral support. Both wore black, AJ in a suit and Steve in jeans and a T-shirt. They looked like a public defender and his client.

Along with its rival MCA, William Morris was Hollywood's preeminent talent agency. Originally founded by its namesake as a booking service for vaudeville acts, by midcentury the Morris office represented talent in every area of entertainment. The agency's motto read, "No Act Too Big . . . No Act Too Small (Our Small Act of Today Is Our Big Act of Tomorrow)." Presently, McQueen was the smallest of their "acts," and if his wife hadn't been a valued client, they would have dropped him from the roster.

A secretary escorted them to a large conference room, where they sipped coffee from bone china cups. McQueen was palming the silver spoons when Sy Marsh and Stan Kamen entered, apologizing for being late. "My time's cheap," Steve said scornfully.

Marsh promised to change that. A lanky man in his early thirties, he talked and moved with the audience-pleasing exuberance of the song-and-dance man he'd once been. Kamen, in contrast, was more reserved, polished, even gentle—he reminded AJ of Henry Fonda. The two men were cordial to him, while trying to figure out if he was their client's drinking buddy, bookie, hanger-on, alter ego, or God knows what else.

Their agenda was to convince Steve to do an episode of *Trackdown,* a western that starred Robert Culp. The episode would serve as a pilot for a new series featuring McQueen as a bounty hunter. "After all the downtime you've had, the show will give you a chance to sharpen your acting skills," Marsh enthused.

"My skills don't need sharpening. I keep them honed," Steve replied with a pout.

Kamen went for his client's ego. "Your character, Steven, is a guy who people usually view as a heavy, but who played a pivotal role in frontier justice. The producers are convinced you have the qualities— innate integrity and quiet strength—to make Josh Randall come alive. And you'll be totally original on TV."

"Isn't Paladin in *Have Gun Will Travel* a similar character?" AJ interjected, referring to the role Richard Boone played as a hired gun in the Old West.

"See, guys, don't try to bullshit me when my buddy's around." Marsh and Kamen looked flustered. "I appreciate the offer, but I'm holding out for the big screen. That's where I'm meant to be."

"I think you should reconsider," Kamen pleaded.

AJ sensed what Stan *wasn't* saying—that no one in the film community had evinced the slightest interest in McQueen. Once Marsh and Kamen withdrew, McQueen made another beeline for the silver. "Some people actually pay for those rather than steal them," AJ said.

"Who stuck a pole up your butt?"

"No one, 'Steven.' "

McQueen blushed. "I used to call myself Steven, but Neile said I was more of a Steve. Let's split before Thor suffocates in the car."

"You're making a mistake." McQueen looked perplexed. "Not accepting the part is a major mistake."

"You said it yourself, the role's been done."

"That's what you *heard.* What I said was that it was similar to another hit show, which is good, not bad. It means the audience can accept a dark character like a bounty hunter." AJ began talking energetically. "I've read the script, and I think Kamen's right. You'd be terrific as Josh Randall. And there are tons of ways to distinguish you from all the other western stars."

"Name one."

"Your weapon. You need something unique."

"Like Bat Masterson's cane?"

"More lethal. I see a sawed-off shotgun."

"That's genius, man."

"But the reason to do this show isn't because you'll be great in it." AJ paused for effect. "The reason is to save your marriage."

"My marriage is none of your business."

"Maybe so. But you need to pull down a serious paycheck to feel good about yourself again. When I'm feeling useless, I get depressed. But you prove your manhood by bedding every skirt in sight." The veins in McQueen's neck bulged. "Did you think it was a secret? If Steph and I gossip about it, you can bet that Neile suspects. She can't ignore it forever."

AJ watched his friend circle the table toward him. He was ready for anything except a kiss. "You're the best fucking friend I ever had!" There were tears in McQueen's eyes. "I've lost so many people in my life. I can't lose her."

=

No one went from goat to hero faster in Stan Kamen's estimation than AJ Jastrow. Steve gave him full credit for his turnaround on the bounty-hunter pilot. While Marsh discussed shooting dates and salary with Steve, Kamen asked AJ what he did for a living. Rather than admit he was unemployed, he deflected. "I loaf, but in a decorative and charming manner."

"*Mildred Pierce*?"

The guy was impressive—no one else recognized AJ's obscure movie quotes. "I'm a producer," he replied, knowing Stan couldn't check a directory to verify, since anyone could hang out a shingle regardless of whether he'd ever produced a frame of film.

"Do you have any properties we might be interested in?"

"Yes. I've got a World War Two script set in New Guinea. It's not finished but—"

"We just screened *The Bridge on the River Kwai,* the new David Lean film. It's extraordinary, so it'll be hard to sell anything like it for a while. My advice is stow your project until memories fade."

Kamen started to say good-bye. Knowing that the Morris office always sought new scripts to feed TV's insatiable appetite, AJ gambled. "My hottest project is a television series."

"What's it about?"

It was a long shot, but . . . Months before, he had dutifully read Leon Ginsberg's screenplay about a wandering European rabbi. *Exile* was awful in the way of amateur scripts—misuse of technical jargon, clunky dialogue, and scant attention to logic. It was also so personal that criticizing Ginsberg's writing risked insulting him. So AJ had resorted to Hollywood etiquette and told the rabbi he loved it but that Mike Todd was too busy to consider another project. At the time, however, AJ had had an inkling that the idea behind the script might work on TV. "The main character is a young Presbyterian minister," he explained to Kamen. "He drives the back roads and each week helps new people with their spiritual problems."

"Have you got any of this worked out?"

"I'd be happy to come in and show you my ideas."

"How about Tuesday?"

AJ ceremoniously checked his pristine calendar. "I can make that work."

He was so drained he returned to his apartment rather than getting blitzed with Steve. In golf his biggest rush was to hit a recovery shot between trees, over a pond, and softly onto the green. That's what he'd accomplished at William Morris, but he couldn't enjoy the sensation. Although he had liberally altered Leon Ginsberg's idea—probably beyond the rabbi's recognition—AJ knew its origin. Plagiarism was out of the question. He retied his tie and dashed out to attend Friday night services.

CHAPTER 15

Stephanie was struggling to button her jeans when Dr. Ray Sturdivant reentered the examination room. Just yesterday she had seen the same hesitant expression on the guy from Deluxe before he'd told her the lab had detected a scratch on the negative of the *Gun-*

smoke dailies. There was no miraculous fix for that mistake—or for the one she and AJ had made. "The rabbit died, didn't it?"

"According to the lab results, you're due in August." He gently lifted her clammy hand and listened.

"You're going to have to count like a cash register to keep pace with my pulse."

"How do you feel?"

"Overwhelmed." That was honest, she thought, as far as it went. And safer than *robbed* or *cheated*. New mommies didn't direct an episode of next season's show, they didn't spend a year in Paris or ride wild horses on the beaches of Mexico. *Those* were her fantasies, not breast-feeding and diapering. But maybe she would change her mind over time. Most girls her age couldn't have babies fast enough. Screw it— she wasn't "most girls." The top button of her Levi's popped off. Don't cry—rip out the loose threads and sew it back on.

"What's the father like?"

"Adorable, brilliant, devoted to me, a bit young . . ." She didn't add that sometimes when she was with AJ, she already felt like a mom. "He's going to be a big star in Hollywood someday—I know it, even if he doesn't."

"And he's got excellent taste."

"Thank you."

The doctor strapped on a blood-pressure cuff. "Do you love him?"

Steph had asked herself that since their third date this past summer. Her answer was always "I think so." How could she be sure, since she'd never been in love before? Of course, that didn't stop AJ—he seemed certain of his feelings for her. And every day between them was better than the last, which was a positive sign.

Sturdivant studied the dial. "I guess that's a pressure-filled question."

"I love him very much." It sounded fine. It really did. "He and I need to talk this over, because if AJ flips out . . ."

The doctor completed his exam. "If you don't want the baby, Stephanie, I'll take care of the situation."

"Thank you." The prospect of a back-alley abortion by a guy with a wire hanger had already fueled her imagination. "But I'm also afraid if my boyfriend decides the baby is his responsibility, he could grin and still be miserable inside."

"Don't worry. *No* guy is that good an actor."

=

AJ hadn't squirmed in years. But he started again upon entering the rabbi's study, following services. After confessing his "overeagerness" at William Morris, AJ watched as a poker-faced Ginsberg poured himself a belt of Manischewitz. "Albert, are you familiar with the story of Joseph and his brothers?"

"Not intimately." Please, not another parable. In tonight's sermon AJ had already listened to a Bible story about Saul, son of Kish, who went off to look for his father's lost asses.

The rabbi described in excruciating detail how Joseph's brothers came to him because he possessed a unique ability to interpret their dreams. "Unfortunately, his insights were so personal they felt violated, as if he'd *stolen* their dreams."

"Sir, I've already agreed to cancel the meeting with Stan Kamen if you're uncomfortable." His words were respectful, his attitude defensive.

"Don't patronize me!" Ginsberg's burst of ungodly anger riveted AJ. "Whatever you actually think of the script that I gave you, it was the story of *my life*. But somehow 'Leon Ginsberg' has become 'Bret Tanner,' a goy minister preaching Christ's advice to the world."

"I saw Bret as more secular than religious," AJ offered lamely. "And with all due respect, no one is going to release a movie or air a television show in America today in which a rabbi is the lead."

Ginsberg scowled. "I'll get back to you when I've decided how I wish to handle this matter. Did it occur to you, even for a second, that the Jewish aspect of my story wasn't a *choice,* like soup or salad, but its essence?"

"I didn't murder anyone."

"The Germans who confiscated Jewish property in the 1930s, they also didn't murder anyone."

"That's bull!" AJ bolted, his apology over. "My action was premature, but it hardly makes me a monster!"

"It's a long way to a 'monster,' but the journey always starts with a baby step."

=

"We're lost."

"Don't be a defeatist, Steph." They had gone hiking in the hills north of downtown searching for Chavez Ravine, where, it was said, the new Los Angeles Dodgers would build their future stadium. But they hadn't found the site or signs of humanity in over an hour.

She wiped her forehead on her sleeve. "Why can't you admit that the vaunted Jastrow sense of direction has failed? They won't find our bones until the twenty-first century."

"They'll dig this place up to build a shopping center long before the millennium." Two footpaths lay ahead, both downhill but in opposite directions. He indicated the one to his right.

"Why?"

"What do you mean?"

"Why are you so damn sure we shouldn't go left?"

When Steph got ornery, it paid to deflect rather than argue. He pointed to the trails and recited:

> *Two roads diverged in a yellow wood,*
> *And sorry I could not travel both*
> *And be one traveler, long I stood*
> *And looked down one as far as I could*
> *To where it bent in the undergrowth.*

"We're past the poetry readings, AJ." She looked him directly in the eyes. "I'm pregnant."

From his girlfriend's behavior and bouts of nausea, he knew the answer even as he asked, "Officially?"

"Definitely."

"Are you okay? Is the baby okay?"

"*We're* healthy. What I need to know is how *you* are."

"Me? Me?" A ten-foot wave smacked into him. His mind churned and turned upside down, but when he broke the surface, it was all clear—Steph was going to marry him for sure. That was the good news. As for the bad news . . . there wasn't any. He smiled. "I'm . . . I'm . . . I'm fine. We intended to get married someday and have kids, so this is just a . . . refinement in our schedule."

"You're sure?"

"Officially and definitely. And you know what else? I'm going to be a great father. I come from world-class stock." He kissed her. "Jesus, Steph, you shouldn't be out here hiking."

They took the right fork. Climbing down the hill she stumbled a few times, so he held her protectively. Minutes later the city's skyline appeared like a mirage.

CHAPTER 16

In Hollywood the apology had become an art form. Because movie people compulsively hurled insults, then suffered stifling guilt, they had to find innovative and extravagant redress. Mike Todd's peace offering took the form of a five-foot Christmas present. When AJ slashed open the packing case, he discovered a suit of antique Spanish armor with a note taped to the visor: "Come on, Sancho, we belong together."

They lunched at Pink's, with AJ insisting on picking up the check. Guy Biondi had eventually admitted to screwing up with the Mummers. "He's a schnook," Mike explained, "but if I fire him he's got no place to go."

"You fired me."

"You quit. What are you doing these days?"

"Exploring possibilities." It was his newest euphemism.

"I start shooting in Spain this summer and I want you along." Todd shifted effortlessly into salesman mode, pitching the possibilities of their renewed relationship. How great would it be for AJ's reputation when the world found out that Mike Todd had asked him back?

" 'With enough courage, you can do without a reputation.' "

"I like that. It has a ring."

"Rhett Butler's advice to Scarlett O'Hara." If all decisions were this clear, AJ sensed, he would be as peaceful as a monk. "Mike, it wouldn't work. We're two hotheads and we'd walk on eggshells to avoid another blowup. But I'll be standing in line to see *Don Quixote* on opening day." Todd's quiet sadness left AJ feeling like the one who should apologize. They said good-bye awkwardly—a handshake interrupted with tentative hugs and mumbled promises about keeping in touch. Down the line . . . it was impossible to predict. Relationships in Hollywood continued after the end credits. It's what sequels were all about.

≡

The movie industry shuttered for Christmas, when even moguls left their phone lines unmanned. But they always picked pursuits and places—skiing in Davos, tanning in Acapulco—where they would encounter rivals to verify that they weren't missing the action. For AJ, va-

cations suggested golf, but his finances hardly suggested a vacation. Instead, he convinced the new pro at Riviera how intimately he knew the
course and was soon walking its fairways—albeit as a caddie, not a
player.

Two days before New Year's he carried a two-bagger for David O.
Selznick, the famed producer, and Harry Cohn, president of Columbia
Pictures. The nippy afternoon promised a lavish payday and valuable
contacts. Selznick was only in his mid-fifties, but a shortness of breath
and two packs of Camels kept him wheezing from the third hole to the
finish. It amazed AJ how long an ash the man could balance in the
midst of hitting a nine-iron. In his late fifties Cohn was in steep physical decline, worn out from tangling with the New York bankers to
maintain control of the company he'd founded thirty years ago. His
reputation as the meanest man in Hollywood, however, remained vigorous. He never conceded a putt, not even one inside the leather.
Selznick desperately pitched projects, but after four hours of hacking,
he failed to either sell Cohn or break a hundred.

As Steph massaged AJ's shoulders that evening, he mourned the turn
in Selznick's life. "The guy produced *Gone with the Wind* when he was
thirty-seven. To be washed up after his career, to have to dance like that
for a deal—I'd slit my throat."

"When he had power, he made Mike Todd look like Albert Schweit-
zer. My friend Mandy knows Selznick's son—even he can't stand the
guy."

"Still—"

She shrugged. "It's a die-with-your-boots-on business."

Her dispassion dismayed him. When he was growing up, Hollywood had been Camelot, but the knights of that glorious age were
dead, dying, or unemployed. He wondered if he could match their
achievements in his career—assuming he had a career. It was a year and
a half since that fateful telegram from Bing Crosby had started a sequence of events that had lured him into the movie business, and all he
had to show were stubs from unemployment checks.

AJ returned to his Remington and the letter he was composing to his
mother. Steph suggested that he call Maggie, but AJ feared he would
blow the conversation. Better that she learn their news in private. Now
he was in a quandary about whether to announce both marriage and fa-
therhood or only the former. The phone rang, sparing him the decision.

"Jastrow?"

AJ stiffened. He wasn't in the mood for another sermon. "Hello, Rabbi. Happy New Year."

"Same to you," Ginsberg grunted. "I've been mulling over my project, trying to find a suitable middle ground between what I desire and what you see as the commercial realities. Perhaps the answer lies with a King Solomon compromise. How about if it's a rabbi *and* a minister—co-leads?"

The man had been "mulling"? How desperately did Ginsberg long to get on the air that he was willing to be in business with a junior war criminal? Only one thing kept AJ from telling him to forget it—a hit series. "Your idea's got real promise. It could be a home run if you let me take it a step further."

"How big a step?"

"When you said 'a rabbi and a minister,' my initial reaction was to laugh. Not laugh *at* the notion, but *with* it. The combination sounds like the lead-in line of a joke. I know you envisioned this as a drama, and that's what I pitched to Kamen." AJ hoped Ginsberg wouldn't hang up. "But I think it would be ten times better as a comedy."

"A *comedy*?"

"Exactly. We should create a sitcom about a rabbi and a priest—a priest, not a minister, because a Catholic's a bigger contrast to a Jew than a Protestant. They'll live together. And though they're fond of each other, they argue constantly." The more he talked the more devout a believer AJ became. "It could be funny like *Lucy* and heartwarming like *Father Knows Best.*"

"Hmm. That puts rather a different light on things." AJ sensed that "different" was desirable. The rabbi was no longer bastardizing his personal experience because the project had traveled so far afield. "Perhaps it would be good for us to meet. Canter's Deli at noon?"

"If it's corned beef you're after, I suggest the Blarney Stone. You get the cabbage at no extra cost." AJ heard Ginsberg gag. "I'm kidding. They'd bust our schnozzes in that joint. But that's the fun of the show. Our characters can argue over where to eat. Noon it is, Rabbi."

"I would prefer that you call me Leon. Our relationship is commercial, not religious. I'm afraid you'll never be part of my flock."

$$=$$

Dear Mom,

    I hope things are well in Winnetka. I've had lots of part-time

work since quitting Mike Todd last fall. As you predicted, the
Hollywood economy stinks, and it makes finding the right job difficult. Still, I've got prospects and expect to land something soon.

Maggie closed her eyes after one paragraph. Her son sounded like
the thousands of pie-in-the-sky youth that flooded Tinseltown. But AJ
wasn't one of thousands—he was a young man of unlimited potential.

Mom, I've got something far more important to tell you about
than work. I have fallen in love with a wonderful girl. Her name
is Stephanie Salinger and we've decided to get married. The wedding is set for late March.

A day doesn't go by that I don't regret the gulf that's come
between us. I don't understand it. Perhaps I never will. But I'm
hoping that you'll come to California for the ceremony so that we
can put our differences behind us.

Love, AJ

A letter? A few crummy lines to announce he was getting married?
Maggie crumpled its single page into a tight ball. He *was* a coward. But
even as she contemplated her scathing RSVP, she feared that dialing
to deliver it would be as lethal as Russian roulette. Her gamble that
stonewalling AJ would quickly force him home had failed. He had built
a life—no matter how insignificant—over which she had no influence.
If she refused to attend his wedding, she risked losing him forever. And
where would that leave her?

Maggie was never going to remarry, her own mother would probably die of colon cancer within the year . . . then what? Growing old
without family by her side . . . Her legs weakened and she had to sit
down. Why hadn't the doctors been able to save Emily? She would be a
teenager now. A daughter would have been such a marvelous companion. Maybe they should have adopted a child. Harry had been willing,
but it had felt so much like a second choice. There was no use regret-
ting the past.

Her son was her gravest disappointment—and only hope.

=

Stan Kamen's announcement that the eminent Leon Ginsberg would
visit William Morris to pitch a television series drew disbelieving stares

from his colleagues but spiked attendance at the presentation. Although the rabbi had spoken in front of thousands of people, he grew cotton-mouthed at the prospect of describing the program to eight blue suits, so he muttered hello and introduced AJ, who took center stage as if he owned it. "Gentlemen, we'd like to introduce the two lead characters in our new half-hour comedy, *Kelly and Cohen*." He flipped the first page on an oversized sketch pad, revealing a cartoon of a rabbi and a priest cagily eyeing each other. Stephanie had stayed up all night drawing it to capture the irreverence of the idea. Two of the agents laughed out loud.

AJ described how Rabbi Meyer Cohen and Father Tim Kelly had both recently arrived in a working-class Chicago neighborhood, where their synagogue and church stood catty-corner. Since both clergymen received only small stipends, they decided to save money by sharing an apartment owned by Bessie, a cantankerous black landlady. AJ summarized the pilot and story lines he'd crafted for five future episodes.

When Kamen asked for a few moments to consult with his colleagues, Rabbi Ginsberg bowed out to prepare for evening services. "Anything you have to say, gentlemen, say it to my partner." In the lobby Ginsberg shook AJ's hand. "*Mazel tov.* You even made me laugh, which is not the easiest of tasks."

"Thank you, Rabbi—I mean Leon. I appreciate your confidence."

AJ fought against rising expectations, but there was reality to his grandiosity—that's why show business was so addictive. In five minutes he could be producing a television show for millions of people. He could have a staff of writers and be writing himself. Eight o'clock on Tuesdays would be a perfect slot for *Kelly & Cohen*. Maybe he could also work on McQueen's show, given that he'd helped make it happen. If he signed with Morris, they could figure it out. But suppose they passed?

That prospect was too crushing, so he paced the corridor until discovering a display of weathered photographs of the agency's earliest clients. He was no different from the vaudevillians, he decided, the guys with the magic acts, kazoos, and trained monkeys. They all had to sing for their supper, which wasn't so bad if all you really wanted to do was sing anyway. He was studying a picture of the Hilton Sisters, saxophone-playing Siamese twins, when the meeting broke up. There was something mysterious about the crook of Stan's finger as he motioned for AJ to join him in his office.

=

"I knew it! I knew you'd do it!" Steph's delight caught the attention of diners at Chasen's. "My fiancé sold a TV pilot to William Morris."

"Honey, come on. That's hardly big news in Hollywood. And all Kamen did was agree to represent the show and package it. The agency still has to convince the networks."

"With all its talent and clout? You should start thinking up ideas for movies, because the Morris office can help get those set up."

"What if I don't have any other ideas? *Kelly and Cohen* was Leon's notion . . . sort of. Maybe I'm a one-shot wonder."

"You've got a wonderful imagination. That guy we met last month who went to summer camp with you said you were famous for your stories and—"

"The competition's tougher in Hollywood." Sometimes her optimism grated on his nerves. Why couldn't she acknowledge that maybe, just maybe, he wasn't a creative genius? Was it because that's the kind of man she really wanted to marry? AJ's mouth was dry, but reaching for his water, he knocked over the glass.

"Take it easy."

He mopped up with his napkin. "The good news is, I don't have to worry about it. After Stan Kamen finished outlining the deal on the series, he offered me a job."

"What kind of job?"

"As his executive assistant. It's almost eight grand a year plus health insurance. Within two years I could become a junior agent in the motion picture division."

"What did you tell him?"

"That I wanted to talk to you and think about it. He gave me till Monday."

They nibbled at their dinners until Steph looked up and smiled. "You were so happy last week when you were working out the pitch."

"If *Kelly and Cohen* doesn't make it on air—and only one show in ten does—we wind up with nothing. I'll have to look for a job again, and as a family man, that's unacceptable."

"I could keep working until something turned up."

"Come on, Steph, that's not feasible. We have to behave like grown-ups."

She reached for the leftovers of his hanger steak. "I never thought you wanted to be an agent."

"It's not like I grew up thinking about it, like a fireman or a test pilot."

"Or a producer."

"On the plus side, you know how powerful the agencies have become in Hollywood."

"Does that matter?"

"It's a great foundation. I'll meet lots of people. And I like giving advice." AJ stoked his smoldering enthusiasm. "Convincing Steve to do the pilot made me feel useful. And when you told me we were having a baby, all I thought was how much fun it would be to guide our child."

"Split-level houses are fine, but in the family there's no room for split-level thinking."

He stared. "Where'd you come up with that one?"

"*Better Homes and Gardens.* There was a copy in the doctor's office. It sounds silly, but maybe it's true. In Elysian Park that day, you chose the 'right' fork and the wolves didn't eat us. We both need to trust your sense of direction." Steph smiled. "I'm having the lemon meringue pie. How about you?"

CHAPTER 17

"Stan Kamen's office . . . Yes, Mr. Sinatra, I'll get him for you right away." AJ connected his boss—for the sixtieth time that day. Although he had been on the job for a month, he remained starstruck by the procession of celebrities. Caller sixty-one was Red Skelton, a carrot-topped comedian whose fame in Hollywood had soared as a result of a whispered one-liner. At the funeral of Harry Cohn, who'd died two months after AJ had caddied for him, the crowd had exceeded expectations. "If you give people what they want, they'll come," Skelton had commented to a fellow mourner, who'd turned out to be a *Variety* columnist. AJ promised Red that his boss would call back. "Stan Kamen's office, how—"

"AJ, is that you?"

"Mom? Where are you?" It sounded like she was around the corner.

"In your apartment. The superintendent gave me the key."

"What are you talking about? You're not due until tomorrow."

"I came a day early so we could spend more time." AJ checked his watch. If he left now he could still beat Steph home. But Kamen aborted that plan, announcing that Sinatra and his pal Sammy Davis Jr.

were coming in for an impromptu meeting and AJ needed to run out to buy a cheesecake. Filling out the voucher, he flirted with the idea of using the petty cash for a getaway.

=

Maggie sat on the dilapidated corduroy sofa in AJ's studio apartment and stared at her future daughter-in-law with the spreading belly and plastered smile. It was clear what had transpired. AJ knew nothing about women. He had met a girl who'd trapped him. Anger cracked Maggie's resolve to be positive. "Is this your *first* pregnancy?"

"Yes, it is," Steph replied with exaggerated politeness. "I hope you're thrilled at becoming a grandmother."

Was that a sign of spunk? She'd determine soon enough. "I relished the idea from the first time I read AJ was getting married. Naively, I thought it might be *more* than nine months after the ceremony."

"Mrs. Jastrow, I can understand your shock. I had no idea that AJ hadn't said anything."

"I'm sure this is hardly his proudest moment."

"I love your son."

"So do I."

"I'm sure you do. He couldn't have become the terrific man he is without a great mother. Your approval would mean so much to him."

"Miss Salinger, the two of you are getting married in six days and having a baby in five months. No objection from me means much. But you have my congratulations. My son is a catch—though it would have been sporting of you to throw him back." The girl blinked back tears, which answered Maggie's question. "I'm wondering if you have any aspirin. I've got a headache."

Stephanie returned from checking the medicine cabinet. "My fiancé is so damn healthy, there's no Bayer. But there's a store on the corner. I'll be right back."

"Take your time." Maggie surveyed the surroundings. No two items matched. Had AJ picked up nothing of her taste over the years?

=

AJ motored up just as Steph was heading back into the lobby of the Ravenswood. "Honey!" He breathed a sigh of relief. "Am I glad I was able to catch you."

"You didn't *catch* me—and I certainly didn't *catch* you." She started to punch him with fists too small to do damage. "How could you do this? Do you know how cheap I felt when *I* had to tell her about the baby?"

"I'm sorry. When I didn't let Mom know in the letter, it got worse and worse . . . like an unreturned phone call."

"An 'unreturned phone call'?" Steph smacked him again. "Lying—"

"I didn't lie. I never told you I told her."

Steph shoved the bag from the pharmacy into his hands. "If you want to see me on Saturday, straighten out this mess!"

AJ opened the aspirin and swallowed two. Even as he unlocked the door, he hadn't a clue how to handle the situation.

"And Daddy makes three."

It was as nasty a welcome as their last good-bye. "I should have let you know we were expecting when I wrote about the wedding. I guess I wasn't prepared to deal with your criticism."

"But you're willing to deal with it now?"

"If it concerns *me,* yes, but don't take it out on Steph. She's fabulous, and you'll grow to love her like I do."

His mother laughed bitterly. "And suppose I don't? Suppose I don't even like her? Suppose I hate the idea that she's forced my son into a premature marriage?"

"No one *forced* me into anything! I'm becoming a husband and a father because it's what *I* want to do. Whether you approve or not!"

She said nothing but walked over to the window and stared at the Hollywood sign. He was breathing hard, ready to continue the fight if necessary.

"Hopefully my granddaughter will have more sense than you do."

She blinked. And was that a grin lurking behind her deadpan? He went for it, throwing his arms around her. "Did you say 'granddaughter'?"

"Yes. I feel it . . . in my bones."

CHAPTER 18

Mr. & Mrs. Theodore Salinger
request the pleasure of your company at the marriage of their daughter,
Stephanie Joan
to
Mr. AJ Jastrow

Saturday, March 29, 1958, at six o'clock P.M.
Ceremony and reception to follow at the home of Mr. & Mrs. Ray Stark

≡

A week before his wedding day, AJ's phone rang at six-thirty A.M. His Pavlovian response was "What's up, Mike?"

The voice *was* a Todd's, but not the one he expected. "AJ, my dad's not going to make the wedding," Junior announced.

His heart sank—he'd promised everyone they were going to meet Elizabeth Taylor. "Can't he stop by for an hour or so?"

"He's dead. His plane crashed in New Mexico last night. Art Cohn was with him. I'm leaving in an hour to identify the remains."

The words, the flat tone, the despair—AJ understood Junior's heart and mind. He knew how useless sympathy was, but that was all he could offer. "My God. I'm sorry."

"He read me the toast he wrote for you. It was so funny . . . and touching. He claimed you were more like him than I was."

What had Art said about Mike—"He never believes he'll fall, no matter how many times he's chewed concrete"? AJ pulled a blanket around his neck and stared mutely at the phone.

"What's wrong?" Sensing bad news, his mother emerged from the bedroom.

AJ recounted the tragedy. "I wish Dad were here." He instantly cursed himself for the admission.

"You can talk to me."

"I know I can." He couldn't—and from his tone of voice, he knew she knew.

≡

AJ was hiding in the Starks' library, perusing one of Ray's first editions, when a tap on his shoulder caused him to slam shut the book. It was his best man. McQueen appeared the old-fashioned movie star in the monkey suit he hadn't wanted to wear. "You look smart," AJ observed.

"Screw you." The actor was going to have to get used to prosperity, because CBS had announced his pilot on its fall schedule. Everyone who saw "The Bounty Hunter" concurred—Steve made the character a sympathetic enigma. Josh Randall did a necessary job in which he took little pleasure—precisely what McQueen was doing in playing the part.

"I'm looking for a few moments of privacy," AJ said defiantly.

"What for?" McQueen grabbed the book. "Shit, I thought you were jerking off to high-class porno. 'It is a far, far better thing that I do, than I have ever done.' " He read the ending so gracefully that AJ wondered if his friend might make a memorable Sydney Carton. He would surely look romantic marching to the guillotine. "Time to face the music, my friend."

Stepping under the *chuppah* at one end of the football field–sized living room, AJ shook hands with Leon Ginsberg, who would perform the ceremony. Last week ABC had ordered twenty-six episodes of *Kelly & Cohen,* making Ginsberg a unique Hollywood hyphenate—the rabbi-producer. The timing was ironic because under the conflict-of-interest rules at William Morris, AJ had already forsaken ownership in the project. His share of the producing fee would have earned him fifty thousand dollars—more than five times his current salary. When he'd learned the news, AJ had gotten roaring drunk. Now he only thought about it once a day. The saving grace was that the rabbi had generously given Steph and him five thousand dollars as a wedding gift.

He saw his new mother-in-law, Audrey Salinger, in the first row on the left. The woman was a dead ringer for Donna Reed, with a temperament to match the character in her TV show. Audrey's initial trip to Hollywood was proving Oz-like. In Cincinnati pregnant girls rarely married in white, never amid the grandeur of the Stark residence. She blinked as the photographer from the *Hollywood Reporter* clicked her picture. Ray had hired him to memorialize the occasion in the trades. AJ got along well with his new in-laws, although they couldn't grasp what he did for a living.

He waved to three of his new buddies from the training program at William Morris. Although he was only a rookie, AJ felt an integral part of the William Morris team, thanks to the man seated next to them. In Stan, AJ had found a sane and honorable mentor. For his part, Kamen bragged that his new assistant was destined to be a star at the agency.

As Neile Adams played the opening chords of "The Wedding March," Stephanie appeared at the end of the aisle, arm in arm with her father. The hair and makeup people from *Gunsmoke* had styled a regal look by creating a dramatic bouffant and highlighting her eyes with more shadow than she would have dared to use. With her empire gown con-cealing her pregnancy, she had a bride's radiance and the glow of an ex-pectant mom. "Grace Kelly" passed everyone's lips.

AJ nodded to his mother. Her smile seemed only slightly forced; that counted as a moral victory. She had behaved well after their showdown, graciously calling Steph and patching up their quarrel by agreeing that the fault lay with him. After all, what could one expect of a man? This morning she'd toured Brentwood with a real estate agent, scouting po-tential houses. Her decision to move back to Los Angeles rather than deal with another Chicago winter had surprised him. Though Steph was apprehensive at her living in the same state, he liked the idea of a baby-sitter they could afford.

Steph bade her father good-bye and arrived at the altar. AJ could tell she was as happy as he was. Lifting her veil, he kissed her before the rules allowed. "Leon, let's get this show on the road."

Moments later, Ginsberg pronounced them man and wife.

1965 – 1966

THE
REBEL

CHAPTER 19

In Hollywood, guilt was the last refuge of scoundrels desperate to close a deal. And no scoundrel was more conniving—or fatter— than Bernie Marcus. Paramount's chief of business affairs was all wagging chins, tumbling jowls, and puffing cheeks, but it was his eyes, anchored deep in their sockets, that menaced AJ. "If your father were here right now, he'd be sorely disappointed in you."

The more personal the attack, the more anxious the man. "Weren't you an office boy when Harry worked at the studio?"

"Well, I was . . . I was more than that—"

"Because people who actually *knew* my father said he respected an agent who championed his client's interests. Steve McQueen wants to do *Nevada Smith* but not for two seventy-five. That's only twenty-five grand more than you paid him on *Love with the Proper Stranger*—which made you guys a ton of money. Give me the four hundred I'm asking so we don't have to putz around until he's too old for the part."

"Suck my dick, Jastrow!"

"An attractive offer, but not what I'm looking for."

Marcus thumped his rosewood desk with a hand the size of a leg of lamb. "Anybody who pays your client four hundred is dumber than a post!"

"Then Lew Wasserman's an idiot."

"Mr. Wasserman . . . an idiot?" AJ had used the name of the Lord in vain. "How dare—"

"I'm not saying it—you are. The best agent in history, the shrewdest judge of talent, the guy who turned Universal into Hollywood's hottest studio, but now he's a dummy for offering McQueen five hundred thousand to do *The Plainsman*."

"He put a half mil on the table?"

"Forget it. Steve's star is rising too fast for Paramount. You guys are in the *alter kocker* business. That John Wayne movie you made last year—that was a snore. And those two bombs with Jerry Lewis."

"Get your uppity ass out of here." His nose flared. "But don't leave the building."

AJ paced the reception area like a boxer ordered to the neutral corner. He had fought his share of prelims, negotiating for directors and supporting actors, but this was his first solo shot at making a deal for a client at the top of the agency's bill. Normally, his boss would represent McQueen, but when Stan Kamen had been called out of town, he'd assigned AJ the task. That had raised eyebrows among the mafia at William Morris who thought AJ was moving too fast, even though they'd promoted him from assistant to agent five long years ago.

Marcus's secretary eyed him suspiciously. Sit down—quit telegraphing your anxiety. AJ flopped on the sofa, but as he thumbed through a crumpled copy of *Time* with Martin Luther King Jr. on the cover, his stomach chugged like his old Chevy. It was hairy to hang tough. He'd surprised himself with that riff about Wasserman. Universal hadn't even made an offer, much less half a million. But from the scuttlebutt around town, he was sure Paramount needed McQueen too much to walk away. God forbid he was wrong, because Steve was counting on the money from *Nevada Smith* to furnish his new Brentwood mansion. What if he had overplayed his hand? A blown deal and he'd have to slink back to El Camino and spend the rest of the decade booking personal appearances.

Hollywood was Vegas these days, with each negotiation a new hand of poker because few writers, directors, or actors were under long-term contracts to the studios. The corps of agents had tripled since the 1940s, matched by a phalanx of executives and lawyers at the majors—all of them striving to prove their added value. Even in the flush days trust had been rare, but now it had evaporated in a cloud of paranoia and reduced expectations. Television hadn't killed the movie business—just made it behave like a chronic invalid.

"We're going down the hall," Marcus ordered. AJ stuffed his hands into his pockets, hoping to dry his palms before reaching the double glass doors with Paul Herzog's name etched in gold. Inside stood the bespectacled, balding, middle-aged mogul who two years earlier had succeeded Barney Balaban as president of Paramount. His once-muscled frame had gone flabby. Herzog wore a six-inch-wide cushioned brace around his neck to keep it immobile. As they shook hands, AJ squeezed tightly, hoping to cause him pain from spine to toes. The statute of limitations on a murder never ran out.

"We'll pay three hundred and fifty thousand dollars and not a penny more." Studio chiefs spoke in fiats, even when they lacked leverage.

The only sound in the room was Bernie chomping M&M's from a canister on Herzog's coffee table. AJ responded with weighty consideration. But since his goal going into the meeting had only been three hundred thousand, his performance was pure sham. "I'll make three-fifty work."

Herzog nodded and prepared to dismiss AJ.

"One more point. We've got to do something about my client's motor home. Steve can't live with the 'toilet'—that's his word—that you guys provide. He's purchased a new Condor, which he'll rent to Paramount for his use during filming."

"What kind of money are you talking about?" Marcus asked cautiously.

The Condor cost ten thousand dollars—including the faux-marble bath in which the actor planned to couple with his leading ladies—so AJ had suggested to Steve that two thousand for the length of the shoot was aggressive but fair. McQueen had objected. He detested executives for not having recognized his talent earlier in his career and couldn't resist humiliating them. "Seven grand," AJ offered with more bravado than belief.

"Are you fucking nuts?" Marcus spouted like a whale. "A trailer costs us five hundred bucks. He'll be in profits on the Condor after two movies."

"I could close for six thousand."

AJ dodged Bernie's charge—but not fast enough—and wound up backed against a poster for *Sunset Boulevard*. "I'll close you, you little shit!" Marcus bounced his stomach into AJ to punctuate each threat. "Do you expect us to spread our legs while you rape like a Cossack? This business has gone to hell when a monosyllabic TV star can hold a gun to our heads."

"I'll handle this." Herzog wrestled his colleague away. "Paramount considers we have a deal with you on all points but this. You've overreached, young man. But we're not going to discuss it further. I want you off the premises and don't return unless you're invited."

In the parking lot AJ grimaced at the knife in his side. Suffering a bruised rib *and* getting thrown off the lot were a high price for a knock-out in his first main event, but Tubby's blood pressure must be 200/150 and the old man was probably rocking on the floor to unslip his disc. He did a shuffle dance around his Pontiac GTO, which drew the attention of a young woman wheeling a rack of evening gowns. " 'I float like a butterfly and sting like a bee,' " he proclaimed. She detoured to his left. Okay, maybe he wasn't Muhammad Ali, but he couldn't wait to tell everyone back at the office that he'd just booked his salary by bluffing McQueen's deal down Paramount's throat.

=

Ricky Jastrow dipped his hand into the back pocket of his khakis and removed a gold Zippo lighter that his dad had given Mommy for Valentine's Day. The wick was worn, but after a few snaps it flicked into flame. Crouched behind the oak card catalog of the Edgewood Elementary School library, the first grader glanced down the stacks to his classmates, who listened to Miss Zelinka explain how to borrow books. He had ducked the tour after she'd yelled at him for not paying attention. What difference did it make, since he could barely read a sentence? If there were no more books, Ricky reasoned, he wouldn't seem like such an idiot and the teachers would stop talking about leaving him back, which was the worst thing that could happen to anyone.

First, he made sure no snitches were spying on him. Standing on his tiptoes, he saw Melanie Broyden's pigtails headed his way. Her stupid Mary Janes passed inches to his left, but she was hurrying to the girls' room and didn't notice. Then he pulled out the drawer marked "Pi–Re" and set fire to the first entry. The flames singed the cards then spread. Maybe this wasn't such a good idea. The blaze could hurt people instead of just destroying the library. He tried to put it out by slamming the drawer, but a blister puckered his fingertips. Smoke wafted and the metal handles became branding irons. "Fire! Fire! Miss Zelinka! Somebody started a fire."

The librarian aimed the extinguisher while Ricky's teacher shepherded him and the class outside. Kids thanked him for saving their lives, and he was enjoying being hailed a hero for the first time when a fifth grader appeared with the principal and accused him of lighting the fire. Ricky tried to run. Despite his twisting and kicking, Mr. Shulman searched his pants and found the Zippo. He forced Ricky to take a seat between two steel filing cabinets outside his office while he called his mother. That didn't worry Ricky because all she was going to do was cry and call his dad.

≡

Stephanie was baking Toll House cookies with her four-year-old daughter, Jessica, in the kitchen of their Westwood home when the school notified her that Ricky was a budding arsonist. After years of irate calls from parents of other children, nursery school teachers, day-camp counselors, and neighbors, she skipped the "That can't be," "You have the wrong boy," and "Someone must have provoked him" and took down the details with the air of a toughened precinct cop.

None of her friends could baby-sit on short notice, which forced her to phone her mother-in-law, who was always available. But the quid pro quo was listening to Maggie criticize the school for not managing her spirited grandson. Steph immediately phoned AJ, to have him join her at school. He was headed to lunch with his co-agents Joe Wizan and David Geffen to celebrate his triumph at Paramount, and Steph cringed overhearing him alibi that he had to go home because Ricky was sick. AJ lived in such a competitive world that his son's disgrace was a chink in *his* armor. So why did his lie make *her* feel ashamed?

Stripping off her Bermudas, Steph rummaged for an outfit suitable for a court appearance. Her closet was a slum because she never discarded anything, even the size four slacks she'd bought before Ricky was born with the intent of fitting into them by Christmas. They still carried the price tag.

The first year of her son's life had been the strangest of Steph's. Her ambivalence about having a baby had ceased the moment she'd heard her son cry hello to the world. While she'd cradled him, AJ had hastily suggested names, because they'd been sure he was going to be a girl. They chose Ricky because Ricky Nelson was the cutest guy Steph knew. After a week in the hospital she'd headed home with a son who seemed so special, so endlessly alert that her husband had joked that he was already making lists of who had pissed him off. Maybe motherhood would be its own adventure, Steph had told herself.

Then, only two weeks later, she'd buckled like a bridge with a defective foundation.

Don't retreat. Don't retreat. Don't retreat.

She was late. Her hair was a fright wig. She couldn't find the car keys. Think. Right, the keys were exactly where Jess had put them—in the cookie batter.

=

AJ had spent years denying that his son was a problem child. Yes he was moody. And he had smacked a few kids in the sandbox. Maybe they'd deserved it. Ricky was prone to tantrums, but so were a lot of the successful stars AJ serviced. And in fairness, he had never pulled the wings off insects or tortured their cat. AJ had argued to Steph—and anyone who challenged him—that the boy would eventually grow out of whatever was bothering him and become a solid citizen. Then came first grade.

His son was like a sprinter nailed to the starting block. While his classmates gushed with the newly discovered power to read stories, signs, even milk cartons, Ricky struggled to decipher the alphabet. And forget arithmetic—the boy couldn't add a column of single-digit numbers. Every night AJ or Steph tutored him, but the sessions proved ugly and unproductive. Ricky's frustration made him meaner. A month ago he'd thrown a book that had almost decapitated a teacher. Then he'd bloodied the nose of a kid who'd answered a question he couldn't.

AJ didn't have a clue how to help, since the only subject he'd ever struggled with was Hebrew and his most heinous crime had been the theft of a package of Topps baseball cards. The vultures with Ph.D.s picked Ricky over, but half recommended stronger discipline, the other half more love and attention. AJ had dismissed the implication that they weren't good parents, but it drove Steph to distraction. She emerged from family sessions guilt-ridden, raw, her nails bitten to the cuticle, her psyche slipping back to the past.

One day Steph had been an upbeat, supportive woman, the next a quivering shell. He traced her descent to the first time they'd made love following Ricky's birth. After they'd cuddled each other to sleep, his wife had suffered a terrifying nightmare but wouldn't say what it was about. Instead, the next morning Steph had pleaded with him not to go to work. He should have called in sick, but Kamen had a crazy schedule. When AJ trooped home late, she was staring at their wedding pictures while Ricky whimpered in his soiled diaper.

His mother claimed it was a case of the "baby blues," but within six months Steph had gained thirty pounds, and she slept almost round the clock. AJ shopped and vacuumed till he developed the hollow eyes and slumped-over gait of a guy with a second job. Their fights grew illogical, ending only when Ricky cried like a banshee. As for sex, they didn't sleep together again until Ricky's first birthday.

Then, as if a tropical fever had run its course, Steph rallied. Her fears faded to doubts, her fourteen hours of sleep became eight, and life returned to a version of normal. And despite his trepidation, after Jessica was born, everything was Dr. Spock perfect.

"I didn't do it!" Ricky protested upon seeing his father enter the outer office.

AJ inspected his boy's hand, which was wrapped in gauze. "Are you okay?"

"It hurts something fierce."

"We'll put butter on it."

"Butter?"

"The oil in the butter reduces the burning. Maybe we'll bandage it with rye bread and have a Ricky finger sandwich." His son managed a tiny giggle, which was cut short when the principal beckoned AJ into his office.

As Shulman reconstructed the crime, waving the lighter like the sword of Damocles, AJ took his wife's trembling hand. "I'll pay for any damage." Shulman's estimate seemed high enough to finance the public library, but AJ resisted bargaining him down.

"This could easily have been a tragedy."

"We're doing our best to find out what's bothering Ricky," Steph apologized.

"Whatever you're doing isn't working. The next time a crime occurs, I'll insist you withdraw Ricky from school. Perhaps he would do better in an institution that takes an active parental role."

"Ricky doesn't need more parenting," AJ replied guardedly. "He's a good boy at heart. After all, he sounded the alarm, which shows his remorse."

While Steph picked up Jessica at Maggie's, AJ drove his son home. "You still expect me to believe you weren't responsible?"

"I hate that school! I hate everyone in it!"

"Why?"

"Are you and Mom going to punish me?"

"The next time you're allowed to watch TV, Opie will be my age and Lassie will have puppies. But this isn't about punishing you, it's about finding out why you do these things. Do the other kids pick on you or call you names?"

"They wouldn't dare."

"So what are you thinking?"

"Nothing."

Nothing meant everything. AJ made his living reading people's needs, manipulating their sensitivities, and sensing their bottom lines, but his son was a black box. "We're going to take you to a doctor who can help." Shulman had given them the name of a psychologist in Beverly Hills who treated the children of movie stars and industry heavyweights.

"Another shrink?" Ricky crossed his arms and stared straight through the windshield. "I'm not going."

"You've got to try."

"You can't make me!"

AJ drove home wondering how his life had turned into one testing negotiation.

≡

Turning thirty had troubled him for weeks. AJ assumed it was the passing of his youth, the disappearance forever of the "boy wonder." But with May 22 approaching he dreamed for the first time about dying and called his mother to ask if it were true, as Grandma Esther had once claimed, that every male in the Jastrow line had died before fifty. Maggie brushed off his fear, noting acidly that his grandmother couldn't count to ten, so how would she know? But when AJ checked with relatives, they verified the dying-young phenomenon. If his forefathers had lived abbreviated lives, then his might be more than half over.

Steph interrupted his reverie, halting her station wagon in front of an old oak gate. "We'll have a quick drink with Steve and Neile, then a romantic dinner." The wooden barrier swung open, creaking on its hinges.

That's weird, AJ thought. Steve was nuts about security.

Steph drove up the private road to "the Castle," McQueen's nickname for his eighteen-room mansion. "Is he happy with the deal you made on *Nevada Smith*?"

"It's still not finished, so I didn't tell him."

"He ought to be happy—*and* grateful. Without you and Stan, he'd have a bus ticket out of town instead of a chance for a star on Hollywood Boulevard."

Where had that hostility come from? Before he could ask, he noticed that the front door was also wide open. AJ rang the bell three times.

Not a single light was on inside. "Are you sure they said drinks to-night?"

"Maybe they're . . . you know . . . doing it upstairs."

"You stay here." AJ entered, tripping over a step and landing in the sunken living room. The air was thick enough with grass to give him a contact high. He was sure someone—or something—was watching. Getting up, AJ banged his head on an object suspended from the ceiling. He half-expected to find a body but stared instead at a garish piñata. Whatever McQueen was into, he didn't want to know.

"Surprise! Surprise!"

Spotlights flashed, blinding him and distorting the faces of fifty friends. Steve leaped from behind the sofa and whirled him around. On the second turn AJ caught Steph wearing the smile of the Cheshire Cat.

"Happy birthday, honey. I wasn't going to let you ride into your golden years without one last blowout."

People milled around, wishing him well. His mother, looking forty rather than fifty-two, kissed his cheek, while her companion, Leon Ginsberg, offered an enthusiastic *"Mazel tov."* Ray Stark patted his back. AJ had no idea why his mentor was arm in arm with Romy Schneider, an actress touted as the next European superstar, but he had to admire the man's taste.

McQueen shouted for quiet. "I've decided that we all need to know the birthday boy better than we do. He plays it a little too close to the vest. So I've written down some questions that AJ's close friends and family are going to answer." He closed his eyes and reached into a scarred Nazi infantry helmet and extracted a wadded ball of paper. "What was AJ's biggest adventure?" He paused. "Wandering through the Mojave frying on Teddy Bear acid with me last fall."

"Shit." AJ didn't fancy the world sharing his drug trials, even if mind-altering substances were increasingly common among their crowd. Steve's game felt too dangerous for a Hollywood party, whose success depended on maximum contact and minimum intimacy.

Steph rescued him. "My husband's a lot cooler than I thought."

McQueen whistled. "Since I can't describe *that* trip, I'll relate another. Back in sixty-two, I arrived on the set of *The Great Escape* and caused so much trouble that John Sturges fired my ass. When my agents arrived in Bavaria, Kamen begged the director to give me another chance, while AJ calmed me down—or tried to. The instant he walked into my chalet, I blasted him with complaints, the topper being that the fucking producers had given Jim Garner, who's one of my best friends, a white turtleneck as his wardrobe. 'So what?' AJ said. 'So what?' I said. 'So the audience is going to watch him, not me.' 'Can't they come up with something for you?' Wake up, AJ: there's not a god-damned thing in Germany for me to wear.

"While I screamed, he untied his tie, unbuttoned his shirt, and took off his undershirt, which stunk because he'd been wearing it for forty-eight hours, and threw it to me. 'I will not have my client go naked.' I didn't know what to do, so I started to laugh. When Stan returned, I agreed to meet with Sturges and we fixed the part, which sucked, and came up with the baseball mitt and ball as my props. Ask anyone—they don't know what the hell Garner wore." Steve hugged AJ. "That's my agent and friend—a guy who will give you the shirt off his back and keep you sane."

Barring a thank-you at the Academy Awards, it was the highest praise a representative could ask from his client.

His mother picked next. " 'What's my son's greatest need?' So many choices, but how about . . . a haircut."

AJ instinctively ran his hands through the longest hair at the party.

" 'What's AJ's secret desire?' " Steph smiled. "Few of you think of my husband as religious."

"He hasn't set foot in a synagogue since I bar mitzvahed him," Gins-berg yelled.

"No, Leon, he attends a different temple—Temple Riviera. Every Saturday and Sunday morning he tees off with his buddies. Don't hide, guys, I see you." The dentist, developer, and lawyer who formed AJ's foursome hid their faces like felons. "But no matter how well he plays, one triumph has eluded him: a hole in one. He'll mumble about it in his sleep. It's perfection, he tells me. But if you never get a hole in one, you're still perfect for me."

" 'Which historical figure does AJ admire most?' " While AJ was thinking Lincoln, Ray smiled. "That's easy: Harry Jastrow."

The last person to reach into the helmet was Joe Wizan, his next-door neighbor at William Morris. Joe looked like a beach boy but was sharp as coral. " 'What quality does AJ need more of?' " Wizan waited a beat. "Patience. My friend does not suffer fools, so in this town, he's al-ways steaming."

Enough—AJ took the floor. "Other than my eighteenth birthday, when I aced my calculus final, bought my first jalopy, and got laid, this is the most thrilling. I have a premonition that my fourth decade is going to be a hell of a ride, so I'm going to need all the help you can give."

"Let's get ripped." At McQueen's suggestion people poured out the French doors to the pool area. AJ's favorite band, the Rolling Stones, blasted from megawatt speakers. He rocked with Steph, but within minutes, Steve cut in and stole her away. Just like old times. Out of the corner of his eye, he saw Ray dancing Romy Schneider in his direction.

"I'm too old for this," Stark sighed. "You folks make a better couple."

They danced—or she did, because AJ could only stare. She wore leopard—and resembled one. Her angled eyebrows directed his focus to startling blue eyes. The woman had . . . secrets. "Ray says you're the future of the business." Add a sexy Austrian accent to the package.

"He must have meant the distant future," AJ replied. "What brings you to America?"

"I'm looking for an agent."

"You came to the right place."

The Dom Pérignon kicked in and, mixed with the turbulence of the occasion, produced a wicked cocktail. AJ couldn't remember how long he and Romy danced before Steph joined them. The Beatles replaced the Stones, seeking help in oh so many ways. But with the two most beautiful women at the party as his partners, he required none at all.

CHAPTER 20

On Monday morning AJ remained so hungover that he left his GTO in neutral after parking in the bowels of William Morris. Only when he heard metal grinding metal did he waken from his fog. His car had rolled back into a Bentley with a now-mangled license plate that read WM SW. Of all the cars in all the lots. . . . "I'm sorry, Mr. Weisbord."

The head of the agency's television department surveyed the damage, the red roots of his anger bleeding through a Palm Springs tan until he resembled a Jewish Indian. "You don't know how sorry, boy."

"I'll pay it myself—no need to hassle with insurance."

"It costs more than you make."

"You could change that at my next salary review." AJ's joke fell as flat as the Bentley's front tire.

"Pull yourself together, Jastrow. You look like a bum. Don't ever forget, you're a William Morris agent."

And an officer and a gentleman. Someone needed to lend Sammy a sense of humor. Trudging into the lobby, AJ hallucinated—was that Bernie Marcus smiling at him? His nemesis wore the same neck brace that Paul Herzog had sported last week, making it appear he had eaten Herzog whole, failing only to digest the collar. On closer inspection AJ saw that he wasn't hallucinating, but Bernie's smile was aimed at Abe Lastfogel, the president of William Morris. The two men shook hands, then glanced in his direction, whispering conspiratorially.

AJ shuffled into the weekly staff meeting conjuring dark scenarios, but his anxiety couldn't resist the energy in the room. It was part revival, part potluck breakfast, with every agent expected to donate a new piece of intelligence. AJ was plugged into the town's young executives, so he provided more than his share. What distinguished him, however, was his chemistry at compounding inside information on the studios with insight into the agency's clients. Yawns and snide asides greeted his announcement that MGM sought a director for *The Singing Nun*. Rising to his feet, AJ began singing "Dominique," the inane hit made famous by the Belgian nun. His colleagues finally paid attention—booing lustily—but he argued that though the movie wasn't chic, it would be perfect for Henry Koster.

Henry who? Half the agents consulted the client list to see that Morris still represented him. By a twist of fate AJ had accompanied his parents to the premiere of *The Bishop's Wife,* the 1947 tearjerker for which Koster had received an Academy nomination. AJ remembered the director sobbing at his own movie and knew Metro would love a sentimentalist.

"Bless you, my son," Dick Juria cried out. "An inspired idea . . . and not a bad job on the vocals." As Koster's longtime agent, Juria recognized that *The Singing Nun* could resuscitate the director after a string of flops. AJ glanced at Weisbord for a sign of vindication . . . or grudging acknowledgment. *Nada.*

Agents were bolting for their phone sheets when Abe Lastfogel, barely visible behind the forty-foot mahogany conference table, froze them in place. As short as he was, his deep voice seemed to emanate from his ankles. "Gentlemen, before we part, I must remind you of a threat we face every waking minute, a threat with names so evil I can barely speak them."

AJ wondered if Sacco and Vanzetti lurked in the corridor. Perhaps Leopold and Loeb had crashed the lobby.

"Fields and Begelman."

When they were the personal managers of Judy Garland and Barbra Streisand, David Begelman and Freddie Fields pocketed commissions from their clients *and* took fees from the studios to produce their movies. No one in Hollywood cared except Lastfogel, who'd complained to the talent guilds that the behavior was unethical. In response, the two men had abandoned management, established a new agency called Creative Management Associates, and targeted the filet mignon of the William Morris list.

"Their most recent treachery is unspeakable." But he spoke it nonetheless. "Last night at Begelman's house they tried to . . . steal Natalie Wood." Dead silence as people comprehended the atrocity. "Given half a chance, these ganefs will remove the fillings from your children's teeth. Swear you will stop them!"

While agents pledged death to the infidels, AJ felt odd man out. Why didn't anyone else realize that it was Abe's bitching that had spawned CMA in the first place?

"How about coming to my office for a seltzer?"

Seltzer with Lastfogel couldn't mean good news.

For ten minutes AJ listened to a torturous sermon about wisdom and compassion in business dealings—without a clue why he'd been summoned. His eyes roamed to a framed photo on the wall of Lastfogel in fatigues and helmet on a USO tour. Sandwiched between Ethel Merman and George Patton, he appeared to be standing in a foxhole. As AJ scanned more patriotic memorabilia, including pictures with three presidents and J. Edgar Hoover—*thwack!*—Lastfogel cut him off at the knees. "I have assured Paramount that McQueen will rent them his trailer for one thousand dollars."

"A thousand . . . no, no, you don't understand, sir—"

"Don't be so formal, we're colleagues. Mr. Lastfogel is fine."

"We can win this one."

"Perhaps, but Paul Herzog and Bernard Marcus have been good friends of the agency. Why punish them because they need our client? Ours is a 'live and let live' world."

"Steve made it clear he wanted us to remain firm. He's still furious that Paramount refused his family plane tickets to visit him on the last movie. How do I explain our caving in?"

"What do you think you might say?"

AJ bristled at the ersatz Socrates. "Nothing occurs to me."

"Sometimes I worry about you, son." Lastfogel squirted another hit of bubbly water. "You have the ingredients to make a fine agent—you're smart, intuitive, tough, and you've got impeccable taste. But you're cooking at too hot a temperature."

Get out of the office or boil over. "I'll dial my flame down."

"Good. And don't concern yourself about McQueen. I've asked Stan to handle it. Your client will respect *his* judgment."

AJ stormed into Wizan's office. "I can't take his patronizing bullshit! This was my deal. I should have punted the pecker out the window."

"Murder Abe? The chief's annoying, but—"

"He's a colossal old fart. The company's filled with them. So's the industry. Look at the guys who run the studios—they're nothing but survivors with cataracts who gum their lunch at Hillcrest, schmooze with producers who haven't had a hit in this decade, then pick old-fart directors who cast their old-fart friends. Does the audience care about Jimmy Stewart or Burt Lancaster anymore? No, we've seen all their moves. And have you visited a set lately? The crews take forever to light because half of them are arthritic. And we're supposed to wait for the walking dead to keel over before we can run the show—by which time *we'll* be the old farts."

Wizan laughed bitterly. "You're not the only one going nuts. Last Sunday while I was sitting by the pool thinking about my four-bedroom house, two cars, wife, and bank account, I realized I had everything in life I never wanted."

AJ's assistant, a cub named Bill Haber, dashed in frantically to announce that a pissed-off Steve McQueen was on the line. "Make him go away," AJ moaned.

"You got it, boss." Haber had the can-do spirit that time had robbed from AJ.

"No, never mind. I'll take it." So much for Stan Kamen "handling it."

=

"Your son is not retarded . . . at least technically."

"That's a comfort," Maggie snorted.

Steph shot her mother-in-law a nasty look as they sat in Dr. Mitt-man's office listening to his diagnosis of Ricky after two hours of evalua-tion. "I'm sorry, Doctor, could you explain?"

"Your son's scores on Stanford-Binet rank him low normal. On the Wechsler Intelligence Scale for Children, Ricky tests borderline dull, which means—"

"Are your tests infallible?"

"Maggie, let Dr. Mittman finish."

"They aren't *my* tests, Mrs. Jastrow. Developmental psychologists have used them for years." He returned his attention to Stephanie. "Your son is acting out in school because he's ashamed at being a slow learner. But it's not hopeless, depending on how you and your husband deal with the situation."

"Maybe they should get him a job pumping gas." Her mother-in-law waved in disgust. "If you'll excuse me, I need a breath of air."

Steph waited till the door clicked. "I apologize. You know grand-mothers."

He handed her a box of Kleenex. "I have one myself."

"She says whatever comes to her mind, regardless of how offensive."

"And she probably sleeps better than both of us."

Steph smiled feebly. "Do I look that tired?"

"Not tired . . . lost."

Lost—not precisely the word. Bypassed—that was it. As if she were stuck running a bed-and-breakfast on a two-lane and could see the cars zooming by on the interstate, headed to the real action. But her real ac-tion was being a mom, and if she didn't keep focus, her boy was going to end up roadkill. "Dr. Mittman, what do you recommend?"

"For you or your son?"

≡

Acting out? Give me a break. How about crying out?

Maggie bolted from the office. She had limited patience for psy-chiatrists and less for psychologists like this joker who hadn't been smart enough to get into medical school. How dare they sentence her grandson to second-class citizenship? As for her daughter-in-law, her miserable mothering was responsible.

The boy looked wide-eyed for news. "I'm hungry," Maggie an-nounced. "Let's go across the street for tacos."

"What did the doctor say?"

"It doesn't matter—he's a bum." She loved the way her grandson smiled; she wished he did it more often. "Why are you laughing?"

"You're not like most grandmas."

"Really? What are most grandmas like?"

"They have gray hair, fat butts, and stinky breath."

"And you're not like most six-year-olds—you're a rebel. You know what a rebel is?" Ricky shook his head. "It's someone who fights authority."

"Oh."

"When you set fire to the library, what were you rebelling against?"

He thought for a long time. "Books, I guess."

"But when I read you *Winnie-the-Pooh* and *The Jungle Book,* you loved them. You even said you wanted to write your own stories."

"I could never do that."

"I never use the word 'never.' Never, never, never." He giggled again. "Let's make up a story together. There once was a boy who . . . Now you go."

"A boy who could read minds."

Maggie thought for a beat. "So he always knew what people were thinking . . ."

"And one day he found out they were going to kill him because he was . . . he was—"

"Smarter than they were?"

"No, because he had three eyes and two noses and six chins." Ricky giggled. "So he took his dad's car and drove a thousand miles an hour and they couldn't catch him. But when they returned, he was waiting for them because he'd circled back. Then they realized . . ."

"He was smarter than them . . ."

Ricky jumped up in the air. "Because he had four brains!"

" 'The Boy with Four Brains.' That's a great story. The next time I come over we're going to write it down." Maggie shook hands to close the deal.

=

Romy Schneider was a half hour late for lunch at the Polo Lounge in the Beverly Hills Hotel. That was customary for an actress, and the reasons—traffic jams, wrong directions, a cat with a hairball—were as predictable and bullshit as the excuses for not doing your homework. Plain and simple, a tardy arrival guaranteed the actress attention, which was working for Romy as she garnered all eyes waltzing to the table.

Take control, AJ warned himself, take it now, or she'll toy with you like the other agents she's auditioned. While she sighed over the choices on the menu, he peremptorily ordered two McCarthy salads and a bottle of Sancerre, then sat back and stared.

"Do I have a piece of bread in my teeth?" she asked self-consciously.

It had taken a week of phone calls to arrange the luncheon, but rather than babble with pent-up enthusiasm, his strategy was to talk sparingly. "If you could model your career on any actress in the last decade, who would it be?"

"I don't understand why you're asking that."

A frown in those lethal eyebrows told AJ she was off guard. "If you said Ursula Andress, I'd suggest we get drunk and chat about the weather, because I wouldn't be the right agent for you. Bimbos don't interest me. But if you said Ingrid Bergman, for example, then I'm ready to help and the William Morris Agency should be your home."

"You think I'm that good?"

"You have Bergman's talent, her beauty, her sexuality—and her soul."

"Ah! And perhaps you saw my soul on display in *What's New Pussycat?* Or while we danced at your party? Or is it on display now over lunch?" Romy was cynical about all men, whether they wanted to make money off her, fuck her, or both.

"No, your English-language roles haven't showcased it, but it was evident in *Maedchen in Uniform* and *Die Halbzarte.*"

"You watched my German-language films?"

"I have a friend who's a refugee. We screened them and he translated. Frankly, you don't require much translation."

"Are you always this prepared?"

His expression questioned her question. "I want to manage your career, Romy. I *have* to be prepared. My plan is to link you with young filmmakers. The directors you've worked with—Orson Welles, Carl Foreman, and Otto Preminger—were great talents, but I don't think they have much left to say about the world we're inheriting.

"This script's a perfect example. The premise scares the hell out of me—in a good way." He handed her *Seconds* by Lew Carlino. "It's about a businessman who's so frustrated with his life he purchases a new identity but gets caught between his two worlds. The part of the second wife is terrific. And here's Freddy Raphael's new script, *Two for the Road.* The agency can get you together with the director, Stanley Donen. I also want you to meet a brilliant young director, Sydney Pollack. He's developed a story about the men and women who entered marathon dance contests during the Depression. The characters are desperate and hopeful at the same time. That's what the next decade will be about."

Romy barely budged until he finished his pitch. Then she arched her neck, shook her rich brown hair, and stared at the early-summer sky. "Most agents are smooth. They don't care, except about their commissions. I am surprised that you survive in Hollywood with your . . . intensity." She touched his hand. "You must be very lonely."

The pursuit of any client was a hunt, but from that moment AJ was no longer sure if he was the lion or the lamb.

=

After discovering *The French Chef* on National Educational Television, Steph launched a gourmet-cooking binge that left AJ craving meat loaf, mashed potatoes, and apple pie. But Sunday night family dinner was her showcase, so he gamely cut into an oval-shaped piece of fried chicken, only to have hot butter squirt from the center. It stung like a wasp. "Shit!"

"Daddy said the S-word," Jess giggled.

"It's called chicken Kiev," Steph explained while soothing his burnt lips with an ice cube. "I spent an hour getting the chilled fingers of butter inside the breaded chicken breasts so they wouldn't leak during the deep frying."

Leon Ginsberg prodded his with cautious respect. "I was in Kiev before the war, and I never saw a bird like this."

"That's because you hung with the wrong crowd," Maggie noted.

"Until you came along, it was always the wrong crowd."

Despite her rolling eyes, his mother relished Leon's puppy-dog attention. After years of rejecting his endless invitations, Maggie had finally accepted one because she was dying to hear Leonard Bernstein at the Hollywood Bowl. They had been a pair ever since. "AJ, since Ricky doesn't have school tomorrow, could you parole him so that we can all watch *Bonanza* tonight?"

It was another of his mother's low blows. By directing the question to him, she insulted Steph, who complained—with justification—that Maggie considered her an afterthought. There was no way out. "Honey, what do you think?"

"I think we shouldn't discuss this here," his wife replied coldly.

"Dad, Mom, please. I'm sorry about what happened at school, and I won't do it again," Ricky pleaded. "I really want to watch the show with you and Grandma and Uncle Leon."

Steph and AJ exchanged wary glances. It was the first remorse their son had shown, and its sincerity doubled the stakes. Holding firm to their two-week TV ban would make them cruel wardens, but if they showed compassion, they might appear indecisive. "Mom is right: we aren't going to discuss this now."

"That's not fair." Ricky jabbed his fork into his peas, scattering them on the table.

"Steph, why don't I help you clear?"

The door had barely swung shut before she hissed, "That woman is driving me crazy. Her interference has got to stop."

"I know."

"Then say something."

"I will."

"If you say it like that, she won't even notice."

"I'm sorry, Steph, but you know how close she and Ricky are. I can't tell her to get lost."

"They're too close."

AJ scraped the plates.

"Say something."

He sighed. "We've been through this before."

"And we'll go through it again until you *do* something. Just because she helped out when I was sick doesn't give her the right to act as if she's Ricky's mother."

Helped out? Maggie had bathed and dressed the boy, taken him for strolls, and carted him to the pediatrician for checkups. She'd seen him through teething, colic, gas, and sore throats. Steph had been too out of it to realize what a godsend Maggie had been. "I said I'll say something. Now what the hell do you want to do about *Bonanza*?"

≡

Ricky kept his bedroom door closed, unlike his sister, who welcomed the light and noises from the rest of the house. His son's penchant for privacy concerned AJ, but he chose to respect rather than fight it. He knocked and entered to find Ricky still in his jeans sitting cross-legged on his bed, the pieces of a complicated picture puzzle laid out in sorted piles. He fit two together and laid them into the mosaic. "That's great," AJ marveled. "I get so frustrated I force the pieces together."

"It's a picture of Goofy."

"So it is."

"I wish Hoss was my big brother."

In tonight's *Bonanza* Dan Blocker's character had saved Little Joe from outlaws. "I understand. Sometimes I wish I had an older brother. But you can be that for your sister."

"I suppose."

"As far as Mom and I are concerned, the past is past. But if things at school really bother you, please come to us before you do something silly again."

Ricky crossed his heart and hoped to die.

When AJ returned to their bedroom, Stephanie was asleep. He climbed gingerly into his side of the ring lest he wake her for round two. He had an early breakfast scheduled with a Canadian director named Sidney Furie, whose new film, *The Ipcress File,* was supposed to be a breakout hit. But you never knew whether the word of mouth from early screenings was real or hype. Turning his bedside lamp to low, he opened a perfect example—*The Sand Pebbles.* A friend at Fox had sneaked it to him for an early look, saying it was special.

After two pages his early-warning system kicked in—he sat up straighter, his mind cleared, his heart beat faster. A great script always trumped weariness or preoccupation. He finished at midnight and immediately began scheming how to get the part for his client. *The Sand Pebbles* was a shoo-in to win Steve McQueen the Academy Award.

═

Maggie was an insomniac, so Leon obliged by playing Scrabble with her till past his bedtime. "You should take the role." For weeks he had tried to convince her to star in *Miss Mayhem,* a new television series he was developing for ABC. Its lead was a woman who owned a private detective agency in Los Angeles.

"I already have a role. I'm Ricky and Jessica's grandmother."

"And you're overplaying it. What you did tonight was wrong—and you know it."

"Don't you have a home to go to?"

"I love you, Maggie, but that doesn't mean I have to agree with you."

She turned the board upside down looking for an opening. "They're lost as parents. AJ's going through delayed adolescence and she's a bowl of oatmeal that's been left out too long. I have to step in. Secretly, they're happy to have me."

Leon sighed. "I'll drop the family therapy. But in return, at least meet with the network people."

"You're only doing this to make sure you keep getting laid."

"It's an honest motivation."

Maggie laughed—louder when she spelled out *mystique*. "Let's see, with double-letter for *q* and triple-word . . . I get ninety-six points. Had enough?"

CHAPTER 21

AJ flew back to Chicago to drown in nostalgia and Schlitz. Jerry Roblin—the last single guy among his Zeta Beta Tau fraternity brothers—was finally getting hitched, and his bachelor party promised a blowout reunion. Sitting with the condemned man in a first-base box at Wrigley Field, AJ rejoiced in the trip's bonus: escape from the claustrophobia of a company town. His dentist raved about Doris Day's bridgework, his accountant bitched about Sam Fuller's gambling, and his barber gossiped about Gene Hackman's thinning hair. So what did they say about him? In refreshing contrast, Jerry was a product manager for Sara Lee Bakeries and more interested in pushing pound cake.

"What's marriage like, AJ?"

"Depends on your fiancée."

"Janie's a great girl. We're sitting in her seats—actually, her dad's. Mr. Drummond is chairman of Consolidated Foods."

The company owned Sara Lee. "I predict wedded bliss."

The party commenced postgame with T-bones at Eli's and segued to a dive in the Loop, where the guests tapped kegs, mauled hookers, and pissed on the rugs with impunity. To AJ's amazement—and dismay— even outside Hollywood a Hollywood insider couldn't remain anonymous. Guests peppered him with questions about which actresses he'd slept with, and his sly smiles and polite demurrals sent his stock soaring. He was refilling his drink when the profoundly endowed stripper cornered him. "I wondered what you thought of my performance?"

"Artistic . . . and truly committed."

"I could show you some other moves—in private."

"Angelica, I don't represent exotic dancers, even ones as talented as you."

"Oh. Does anyone at William Morris?"

"There's one guy, but you can't say I told you to call. His name's Sam Weisbord." AJ scribbled a number on a cocktail napkin.

Ben Drummond, the bride's brother, drunkenly sidled over. "So, Mr. Movie Business, you know the guy who runs Paramount Pictures . . . what's his name . . . Pete Hiller . . . or Hitzig . . . is it Hertzel?"

"Paul Herzog?"

"That's it!"

"Why do you ask?"

"I'm going to be his boss."

AJ reached for a bottle of Scotch and poured his new friend a nightcap.

The first part of Ben's story had headlined the trades two months ago. A businessman named Herb Siegel and his partner, Broadway producer Ernie Martin, had bought a sizable chunk of Paramount stock and proceeded to publicly accuse Herzog's management team of massive incompetence. To avoid airing their dirty linen, the studio's directors had awarded the dissidents two seats on the board as a peace offering. "I thought everyone was satisfied with the compromise," AJ commented.

"For a heartbeat," Drummond stage-whispered. "Siegel and Martin are sneaky bastards—they keep buying stock. So Paramount wants to find a white knight, which is where my father enters the picture. This investment banker came to him and asked if he'd like to be in the movies. Ha, ha, ha."

It sounded like a banker's joke. "And he said . . . ?"

Ben took another belt of Chivas. "Pop took me to the meeting because I go to lots of flicks. Herzog thought I was damn smart, even said so to Nate."

"Nate's your father?" Ben nodded. "And Nate said . . . ?"

Like the guy who gets shot as he's fingering the killer, Ben's head conked on the table.

AJ and Jerry carried his inert body outside. "My future brother-in-law can be a jerk," Roblin admitted. "Paramount pledged the family to secrecy, which is why I didn't say anything, but I almost told Herzog that I knew the smartest guy in Hollywood and he should hire you to make movies because the ones they're making bite."

"I'd appreciate it if you wouldn't say anything. I hate using influence to get ahead." AJ's skills as a liar were sharp, and his friend took him at his word. They shared a final drink in honor of Mopsy Moore, the girl they'd both screwed junior year.

But AJ had business to do before calling it a night. A colleague in New York had tipped him that a comedian named Richard Pryor, who was supposed to be the black Lenny Bruce, was performing in a nightclub off LaSalle. Pryor did solo stand-up, but his delivery packed the stage with characters. In one skit he played a husband soft-talking a broad into bed. Then he became the wife, catching her man flagrante. Finally, the comic flipped back to being the husband, bluffing to save his ass. "Who you gonna believe, woman—me or your lying eyes?"

After his scabrous act Richard's shy persona surprised AJ. "How you doing, Mr. Agent?" An instinct told AJ to low-key his pitch or find himself in a future Pryor skit. They sipped Jack Daniel's for half an hour, complaining about Mayor Daley and the sad state of American movies. Then Richard returned to the microphone for an even ruder second show.

Jazzed by the performance, AJ phoned Ray from his hotel room and repeated half the routines. "The guy's the future of comedy."

"They'll never let you sign him," Stark declared. "Those dinosaurs at Morris still think Sammy Davis Jr. is the hippest *schvartzer* in America."

"I'll convince them. I've got to represent him!"

"Even if you did, what would you do with him? The networks will swallow pabulum like Cosby, but they'll never order up a black man as belligerent as Pryor. And the studios . . . are you going to find him a role in *The Sound of Music* or *Cat Ballou*? Hollywood's idea of racial risk is *A Patch of Blue*."

"Poitier's a white man's black man. Pryor's the real deal."

"That's my point. We're a decade behind the rest of the country."

"Screw you. Anyway, it wasn't why I called. Is your deal at Paramount closed?"

"Next week."

"Don't bet on it."

The news that the fight for control of Paramount continued in back rooms and boardrooms sucker-punched Ray. After exiting Seven Arts to go it alone, he'd negotiated a lucrative deal with Paul Herzog to center his new production entity at Paramount. "It'll never get signed now," Stark mourned. "The whole company's going to stop in its tracks until this fight is over."

AJ didn't say "Serves you right." Ray's choice of Paramount had

offended him, but Stark was the ultimate pragmatist—Herzog had offered the most money and independence. "Who's Herb Siegel?" AJ inquired.

"He's a few years older than you, no experience with movies, but
he's a pro at taking over companies, then selling them for a profit."

"You can do that legally?"

"That's the future of corporate America."

After he'd ruined Stark's night, turnabout was fair play, so AJ called
Stephanie in Los Angeles. The good news on the home front was
Jessie's maiden ride on her tricycle. He loved hearing how his daughter
had squealed in delight navigating the driveway on her own. But despair transformed Steph's voice. "I helped Ricky with his homework.
He was reading aloud this story about a boy who gets lost in the forest,
but every time he hit that word, he read it as 'frost.' Then he confused
'mouse' with 'house.' "

AJ could imagine his son trying so hard that the veins in his face
turned blue. The fear that Ricky was stupid hovered over AJ like the
premonition of his premature death. "I bet you wanted to read it for
him."

"That's exactly what I did, which only made him angrier."

"Hang in, honey. I'll be home tomorrow."

Steph blew him a kiss, which sounded tinny over the long-distance
line.

=

"Tonight's the night," Stan Kamen declared, sticking his head into his
protégé's cubicle.

"If not, Miss Schneider's eaten her last dinner on a William Morris
expense account," AJ assured him. He had spent more time trying to
sign the actress than he had wooing his wife. "How do I look, boss?"

Kamen assessed, then straightened AJ's tie. "Irresistible."

They dined at Knoll's Black Forest Inn because Romy craved home
cooking. Dressed in tights covered by a checked silk half-dress, her hair
cut short, she affected the appearance of a tomboy—with only cosmetic
success. Unlike most actresses, the more he knew about her, the more
alluring she became. "Do you remember the war?" he asked.

"My parents were always behind stage lights or in front of the camera. That's the war I knew . . . except for the bombs. . . . They interrupted performances and annoyed my father."

"I never asked you why you retired."

"Ten movies before I turned eighteen—if I heard 'Action' one more time I was going to snap. But I could not figure out how to fill my days. That is sad, right?"

"No. You have awesome talent—it needs to breathe. But I won't let you overdo it, even if I have to chain you to your bed." He could see that his wife's old line touched Romy as it had once touched him. He leaned in for the kill. "Assuming I become your agent."

"You know I want to say yes . . . but I still can't."

He waved to the waiter for the check. "I think you should sign with Kursner." The rumor on the street said that Art Kursner, an older gay agent, was close to landing Romy. "Either I'm too aggressive or you don't like my taste or the Morris office is too big. You've had enough time to feel comfortable, and clearly you don't."

"Is this your idea of reverse psychology?"

"It's not reverse anything."

"You're hurt."

"Of course. I wanted you to recognize my value, but I'm too much of a pro to let that affect things. This is better for both of us."

"So I'm a bad girl who doesn't deserve dessert?"

"Order it from room service. I'm taking you back to the Marmont."

They drove from Santa Monica in self-imposed silence. As he made a left on La Cienega, Romy touched his hair, her fingers lingering on his neck. "This is all wrong," she said nervously. "We can't end this way."

Actress bullshit—they hadn't even begun.

She avoided eye contact by stubbing her cigarette into the ashtray. "God, these have no flavor. Do you have a Marlboro?"

"No and don't change the subject. What are you telling me?"

"Mr. Kursner represented Daddy years ago. Every time I visit America he is an uncle to me. When I met you, I had already promised him I would become his client."

AJ felt like the village idiot. "It's not that I didn't enjoy wining and dining you, Romy. Under different circumstances, I might have done it without a business incentive. But I don't enjoy being lied to, no matter how enchanting the liar."

"You're right." They pulled into the hotel's driveway and he opened the door. "Please help me figure out how to handle this," she pleaded. "I want you as my agent."

Get out with dignity—but get out now. "Don't mess with me again."

"I won't. Please come upstairs."

Her contrition intrigued him. He could imagine her on stage, trying desperately to please her parents. The next thing AJ knew he was in a suite that faced the Hollywood Hills. He sat on the sofa while she busied herself emptying ashtrays, picking up stray bras and half-finished highballs. "You smoke too much," he lectured.

"I know. No one ever made me stop."

"Stop avoiding me. Get over here and let's decide this now."

She approached the sofa, looking for guidance on where she should stand, as if the properly penitent position would appease him. "I am going to call Kursner tomorrow and tell him my decision."

"Should I simply take your word for that?"

"I swear it." She started to cry. "Why do I do things that make everyone I care about miserable?"

"Stop crying. Tears won't get you out of this one, young lady." His voice surprised him with its harsh authority. "At your age, apologies aren't enough. Don't forget, I know how good an actress you are."

She massaged the carpet with her toes. "I ought to be . . . punished . . . for what I did."

"Punished how?"

Romy spoke barely above a whisper. "The way all bad girls are punished."

"You mean sent to your room? Grounded? Extra chores?"

"No. I mean . . . sp . . . spanked." Romy unbuttoned her dress, letting it puddle at her ankles.

"Turn around," he ordered. Her face flushed as she executed an about-face. The muscles in her bottom clenched. "Bend over." He felt her land with a slight jolt on his lap. She tried to balance by grasping the floor. The sight of her submission kicked in a drive so primitive he lost any inhibition. As he yanked down her tights, she raised her hips. The crisp sound of his palm on her backside, her moan of discomfort, and the outline of his hand springing up on her cheek made him gasp. The more she wriggled, the more potent he felt.

"Please. It hurts. It really hurts!"

"It's supposed to. You're getting exactly what you deserve."

In trying to cover up, she revealed everything. He picked Romy up and deposited her butt on the bed, causing her to yelp. Entering her was the most exquisite sexual pleasure of his life.

Afterward, he asked how long she had fantasized about this evening.

"Since the Polo Lounge. At first you seemed too young. Most American men my age are. Then I saw how much you cared about my career—and about me."

"Do you want to know when I first thought about it?"

Romy got up to use the bathroom. "You're a man. I already know." She returned with a washcloth and gently cleaned him, explaining wistfully that she didn't want his wife to suspect. "For as long as we last, I only want us both to have joy."

They kissed for the first time.

CHAPTER 22

Southern California felt like a pizza oven when AJ stepped outside on the Saturday morning of Labor Day weekend. A sane member would be teeing off into Riviera's ocean breezes, but AJ had promised Ricky a "guys" vacation before school, so he stowed his clubs and rooted out the pup tent, and they headed north to the Ojai Valley. It was camp-counselor déjà vu, with him organizing fishing, riding, swimming, and a visit to Bob's Beehive, where the beekeeper put Ricky in a suit and helped him collect honey. Feasting on hot dogs and baked beans, they discussed the Dodgers' run for the pennant and AJ's upcoming visit with Uncle Steve, who would be shooting *The Sand Pebbles* in Taiwan, then capped the evening with a farting contest. Ricky won with a toot that lasted four seconds. AJ felt more sanguine about his son than he had in years.

But when he went to piss at two A.M., Ricky was still awake, mesmerized by the embers of the campfire. "Can't fall asleep?"

"I don't want to."

"Why not?"

"If I go to sleep, the next thing I'll know it'll be morning and we'll have to go home. But if I stay awake, time goes really slow."

"Makes sense to me. What are you thinking about?"

"Why do fish eat worms?"

"Hmm. Maybe they ask each other why we eat peanut butter and jelly."

"I'm serious."

AJ thought for a beat. " 'Why is the sky blue, Daddy?' "

"Huh?"

"There was a TV commercial when I was growing up where the son kept asking his father why the sky was blue, but the dad didn't have a clue, so he bought the family the *Encyclopaedia Britannica.* The answer to your question is that I don't know why fish eat worms."

That seemed to satisfy him. Ricky made a perfect cast with an imaginary rod into an imaginary stream. "Did I do it right?"

"Almost. Maybe a little more wrist." AJ sat down next to him and baited his make-believe rod. "I hope we get a bite soon."

A half hour later, they were both snoring softly.

≡

The hills were steep, and after a mile Ricky's throat felt like sandpaper. Somewhere in the night a colony of red ants had moved in to share his sleeping bag. Their bites stung, but he didn't say anything because his dad would have used it as an excuse to skip their hike and head home to play his dumb golf. Uncorking his canteen, Ricky drank greedily.

"Slow down, son."

Water dribbled down his chin. "Do you want me to die of thirst?"

"No, but if you finish it, you won't have any for the hike back."

"I don't want to go back."

"I never wanted summer vacation to end either. But school's going to be different this year."

That was easy for him to say. They walked to the top of a butte and looked west, to the beaches of Santa Barbara. "Daddy, you were an A student, weren't you?"

"I got some B's and a C once in chemistry."

"You can admit it, 'cause I saw one of your report cards."

"School was a lot easier in those days."

"What if I never learn to read the phone book? I won't know how to call anybody."

"Of course you will."

He knew his dad was lying. "I've been trying for a year."

"It's just a matter of time."

"I don't give a fuck."

"Hey, I didn't even *hear* that word until I was a teenager. I don't want you using it."

"Fuck you!" Ricky hurled the canteen, then watched in horror as it cut open his father's forehead. Nothing he did turned out right. He raced into the forest, hurtling over rocks and tree stumps in a blind dash to nowhere. He wasn't going back to Edgewood to look like a fool again. He was breathing hard, but his father was close on his trail. Why didn't he give up and have another son, one who was smart? Or just keep Jessica. She read better than he did. There was a clearing ahead, so Ricky swerved right to keep hidden. He saw a twisted stick, but couldn't avoid it and tumbled to the ground, his momentum carrying him onto the ledge below. Dusting himself off, Ricky saw that he had missed falling off a blind cliff by a few feet.

He peered above the lip and saw his father charging through the brush, blood and sweat pouring into his eyes as the tree branches whacked him. Ricky realized he wouldn't see the approaching cliff until he broke through the tree line—and that might be too late. His warning cry caught in his throat. But at the last instant Dad jammed on the brakes and skidded to a stop.

"Ricky! Ricky!"

His father's voice echoed through the canyon. He made weird sounds, like he was going to barf. That's what Ricky felt like every day in school. "Daddy, I'm here."

"Thank God!" His father's hug choked him. "I was sure you fell."

"I hit my head on a rock and I got sand in my eyes. I didn't see you coming."

"It's okay. You're safe."

He wasn't yelling about his curse word or the canteen. Ricky began to feel better. "Can we stop for ice cream on the way back?"

They started walking. There was enough sweat on Dad's hand to fill the canteen.

=

"It was the worst moment of my life."

Lying in bed that night, Stephanie wiped the perspiration from her husband's forehead. "You didn't do anything wrong."

"He hates me so much he almost killed himself. Do you have any idea what that feels like?"

She wanted to tell him she understood. But that meant confessing the mad dream that had plagued her when Ricky was an infant. It had recurred every night for months. She was warming his formula on the stove but it remained ice-cold, so she turned the heat higher and higher until the water boiled over, scalding, blistering, and drowning her baby. She buried Ricky in an unmarked grave in the backyard, next to her tomato vines. "Accidents happen." In the dream she suffered no twinge of regret. Her fear was that it revealed her soul. Steph felt AJ nestle close, searching for comfort, but she had no wisdom to impart or pep talk to give.

≡

Hollywood's social scene took a summer hiatus and didn't kick into high gear until after the Jewish holidays in the fall, when the premieres and charity events ran uninterrupted through Christmas. People courted AJ as a young man on the rise and Stephanie as the easy-mixing spouse, informed enough about the business to converse with the pros and still able to gab to the civilian wives. After so many gatherings they were blasé about getting dolled up, but tonight AJ struggled with his tuxedo studs and Steph practiced a curtsy till she was stiff in the knees.

The same scene played out in the homes of those lucky enough to have received an invitation to the party of the year. Bona fide royalty had arrived in Hollywood in the persons of England's Princess Margaret and her husband, Lord Snowdon. The "A" ticket in town was a dinner for the couple at the Bistro restaurant in Beverly Hills. Among the hosts were Mr. and Mrs. Ray Stark.

As Steph descended the stairs, AJ bowed deeply. From behind his back he produced a magnificent orchid. "For *my* princess."

"AJ, it's gorgeous. What's gotten into you?"

"What do you mean?" He pricked his fingers pinning it to her gown.

"Dinner at Scandia last week, the earrings, and now this?"

"I decided you deserve a more romantic hubby."

As they drove up to the restaurant, photographers snapped pictures of Steve and Neile McQueen. Directly ahead, AJ saw Paul Newman and Joanne Woodward exit their Volkswagen Beetle. "Paul works hard for that 'just folks' image, doesn't he?" Steph observed.

"There's a Porsche engine under that hood that cost more than the whole car."

Newman posed with Steve, both actors squeezing out smiles. They regularly competed for parts, but their supposedly friendly rivalry had shifted to another venue. McQueen was an avid race-car driver, and the pros had been quick to acknowledge his skill. His pet project was a racing movie called *Day of the Champions* that he planned to start next year with director John Sturges. Newman had recently taken up the sport, but Steve regarded him as an imitator. McQueen's envy of Newman was a pain in the butt for AJ. Not only did he have to sympathize with McQueen, he and Kamen also had to make sure that the actor saw every script offered to his rival.

Inside the restaurant even jaded old hands gaped at the glamour of the gathered stars: Frank Sinatra and Mia Farrow, Jack Lemmon, Roz Russell, Shirley MacLaine and her brother Warren Beatty, Judy Garland, Rock Hudson, Bob Mitchum, and more. Liz Taylor gave AJ a big kiss and introduced her new husband, Richard Burton. The Americans lined up eagerly to meet the princess while commenting on how dowdy she was.

Arm in arm with his wife, Gladys, David Begelman, dressed more Savile Row than the Brits, joined AJ and Steph. "Your husband is among the most talented—no, let me amend that—he is *the* most talented young agent in Hollywood."

"I agree."

"I keep asking him to come work with me, but I must not be a very good salesman." Begelman managed to make smarmy self-deprecation courtly and convincing.

An hour later AJ and Ray Stark relaxed in the courtyard. "Did you see Lastfogel eye you when Begelman did his number?"

"If it weren't for Stan, I might have switched to CMA."

"Forget it," Ray scoffed, "the agencies are all the same."

"Which is exactly why I have to talk my idea over with you." AJ's pause grew pregnant. "I want to buy Paramount Pictures."

Stark removed his wallet. "How much do you need?"

"I'm serious. I want us to do it together. Your connections and taste are a hell of a lot better than the duds running it now. And I can find the filmmakers who'll dominate the business in five years."

"Are you and your client dropping acid again?"

"Herb Siegel and Ernie Martin aren't Koufax and Drysdale. If they can try, why can't we?" Ray remained silent. "Hey, this is all your fault," AJ joked. "You whipped my butt in Monopoly and said I lacked balls."

"So you've developed elephantiasis? Okay, I'm too bored to go back in there. Let's explore your wet dream. How much?"

"We could buy it lock, stock, and shooting stages for one hundred million dollars."

"Assume your figure is correct and we go out to raise the money, the first question the investor asks is what's the EBITA."

"Huh?"

"Earnings before interest, taxes, and amortization. You should read that chapter. Okay, how much cash flow does Paramount throw off?"

"I'm not sure."

"What's the current debt-to-equity situation?" AJ studied the laces on his patent-leather shoes. "What will it be after the takeover? Do the corporation's voting regulations work in our favor? Are there any tax—"

"You've made your point!"

Stark shook his head. "No, I haven't. Elliot Hyman and I considered this two years ago. So have twenty *legitimate* players. You're way, way over your head. I know how much you dislike Herzog and Balaban—"

"It's more than that." How much, he wasn't certain.

"You need to think about the consequences. If you go sticking your cock into places it doesn't belong, somebody's liable to cut it off. Then you'll be worse than a eunuch." He started back to the party. "Come on, our wives will be getting antsy."

=

Ray's lecture embarrassed AJ. So he bought one share of Paramount stock at sixty-two dollars and, as a stockholder, requested every available piece of information on the company. Late at night he studied annual reports and 10-Ks. When he couldn't figure out how to interpret them, he audited a class at UCLA business school to learn more about finance.

The guinea pig for his final exam was Steph. If she could understand his presentation, so would investors. "The key is the enormous untapped value of Paramount's film library," he explained, pointing to a chart on an easel he'd carted into the bedroom.

"More than other studios?" she asked.

"Yes. In 1957 Herzog convinced Balaban to sell their pre-1948 films to Universal Pictures for fifty million dollars. Wasserman made a fabulous deal. He's already recouped his investment five times over—and owns those rights in perpetuity. When he realized his blunder, Herzog refused to sell the studio's post-1948 titles. So Paramount has two hundred virgin movies—never shown on the air—almost all in color, which is critical with color TV around the corner."

"Can you tell how much they might go for?"

"I can indeed." AJ flipped the page, delighted that his wife hadn't dozed off. "I used recent deals as a guide. Then I valued Paramount's other assets, like the Gower Street lot, the Famous Players theater chain in Canada, and the movies and television series in development."

She studied the bottom line. "So if you liquidated the company, the money you could get from selling all the assets would more than cover the cost of buying Paramount?"

"Exactly. Given the goodwill of Paramount's name, the place is a steal."

"Hmm."

"Why the long face? I thought it made sense."

"It does—a lot. Someone's going to pay attention, but if it's the wrong person, you'll lose your job."

"Is that such a terrible loss?"

"I think you've got so much going for you—remember what Begelman said."

"You think I can't do it."

"I'm worried about the kids—"

"Maybe you should worry about me."

Steph huffed out of bed. "Seven years ago I was the one who urged you to take a chance with your career. You didn't have the guts. If you'd stuck with Leon and *Kelly and Cohen,* we'd be rich. So don't try blaming me." She walked out.

Where the hell had that come from? Had she carried a grudge all that time because he'd opted for job security? Christ, he'd done it for her and for Ricky. Sometimes—no, too many times—he realized he didn't know who Steph was. Had he ever known, or just imagined?

CHAPTER 23

After a grueling fifteen-hour flight from L.A., AJ rubber-legged onto the tarmac at the Taiwan airport, gulped a breath of fresh air, and nearly threw up. A stiff breeze was blowing across a rice paddy fifty yards from where the Pan Am pilot parked his 707, and whatever they used to fertilize the crop had aged badly. Clap Clap Shapiro, Steve McQueen's local Chinese assistant, greeted him with a deep bow, then ordered three coolies to place his luggage into an ancient Mercedes. As they drove through the capital of Taipei, Clap Clap offered a chamber of commerce smile and pointed to a lonely palm tree shivering in the dying December day. "Just like home, Mr. AJ."

"Have you ever visited Los Angeles?"

"No, but I see movies."

The only familiar element was the acrid smog. "The air's a bit . . . pungent."

"No need to worry. Soon you not notice smell."

At a roundabout an unsmiling Chinese soldier blocked their progress with a locked and loaded M-1. Tanks, jeeps, and troop carriers roared by in an endless parade through the middle of the city. Although he had come of age during the Cold War, AJ had never approached its front lines, and the proximity of combat made Los Angeles seem more than an ocean away. Around him heroic posters of Chiang Kai-shek were plastered to the walls of buildings, exhorting citizens to defend themselves. "Is it always so martial?"

Clap Clap motioned across the Formosa Strait to Communist China. "Two day ago we fight big battle. Gunboats go bang-bang many hours."

"Who won?"

"No one ever win, just go bang-bang."

=

The chatter of coolies in the fields awakened AJ at six A.M. It was chilly enough in the McQueens' rented farmhouse to see his breath, so he dressed under the covers, then hurried downstairs to join Steve for his drive to the set. Neile produced a paper bag filled with cinnamon toast, explaining that her husband loved to eat it during the day. It was Clap Clap, however, who munched a slice while Steve drove. McQueen cheerfully confessed that he sold the toast to the crew for fifty cents a slice. His salary for *The Sand Pebbles* was $650,000, but no bank balance was fat enough to quell Steve's gnawing fear that the poverty of his youth would grip him again.

"Have you killed *Grand Prix* yet?" McQueen asked anxiously. MGM's film was the rival to *Day of the Champions*. Both productions had filmed footage at European tracks and were bumper-to-bumper in their race to start principal photography in the spring. Steve had pressured the Morris Agency to force Metro to abandon its project—a ludicrous demand to everyone but him.

"Bad news," AJ replied gingerly. "They told us to go to hell. Their movie's going ahead as scheduled."

"Fuck! Fuck! Fuck!" In his fury Steve hit a pothole the size of a bomb crater. The Mercedes launched into the air, bounced down, and skidded off the road toward a pond filled with green goo. McQueen re-gained control and halted inches from the edge. The wheels spun as he gunned the engine.

"I'll check the trunk," AJ volunteered. "There's got to be something to help with traction." He wedged himself out the passenger door—and immediately sank up to his shins. "Fuck! Fuck! Fuck!" Steve dissolved in laughter.

A truck carting winter melons stopped to tow them free. As he doubled his speed to make up for lost time, McQueen opened his window to let in the air. "You stink."

"I appreciate your candor."

"Personally, I love you, man." Steve reversed to dead serious. "But what the fuck am I paying Morris hundreds of thousands of dollars for?"

AJ knew that, like virtually every character he'd ever played, his friend was a distrusting loner who was incapable of acknowledging the help he'd received over the years. He also knew it was an agent's fate to suffer abuse. Still, the question hurt. "*Grand Prix* isn't cast yet," he told McQueen calmly. "And they're not going to land anyone at your level. As long as *Day of the Champions* starts when you're finished here, we're okay."

=

When he was locked in his office at William Morris, with a phone crooked in his neck till he looked like a listing ship, AJ felt so divorced from the actual filmmaking process that he might as well have been selling anvils. But that changed the second he spied the telltale signs of a movie in vivo—trucks and trailers, cranes and dolly tracks, assistants with walkie-talkies, and the crew noshing on snacks from craft service. His love affair with sets had begun in 1940 when his dad had taken him to see the filming of *The Road to Zanzibar*. Dorothy Lamour had bestowed lipstick on his cheek and Bing Crosby had helped him hit Bob Hope on the head with a rubber hammer. At the age of six, it didn't get much better.

Venturing onto the set of *The Sand Pebbles,* AJ felt conspicuous in his modern dress, so stunning was the re-creation of China in 1926. McQueen played Jake Holman, a disaffected American sailor who was the chief engineer on a gunboat patrolling the Yangtze River. The *San Pablo* (miscalled *Sand Pebble* by the film's locals) had been constructed at the staggering cost of a quarter of a million dollars because the director, Bob Wise, wanted all the details perfect. And after directing *The Sound of Music,* which had made Fox more than a hundred million dollars, Wise could have gotten the studio to build him Peking.

AJ had envisioned scenes from *The Sand Pebbles* the first time he'd read the script. Watching McQueen coach a Chinese coolie to box an American bully, AJ found himself grimacing with the blows, laughing at Steve's pained expressions, and cheering the knockout. This was what his negotiating, hand-holding, and bush-beating were all about. Beyond the thrill of shooting was the liberation of location. At home AJ's obligations to family, friends, and employer flattened *his* fantasies and desires. He needed the road to experience freedom. That's why his days at summer camp had been halcyon. A movie set was the adult version. The crew was oblivious to the world, focused only on their daily pursuit of two great minutes of film. Strangers bonded and fought and fell in love, then hugged and kissed good-bye—often never to meet again.

On the *Sand Pebbles* set Wise was king to everyone but Steve. Their power struggle was bound to explode, and the igniting incident was a two-hour delay while the cameraman lit a complex crane shot. AJ overheard Wise explaining the reasons to McQueen, who argued that the setup was unnecessary. "Steve, that's my call, not yours. And if you'd let me get to it, we'll be ready quickly."

"You don't want to talk to me, Bob?" Steve yelled. "Then I'm not talking to you!"

In frustration Wise beckoned to AJ. "I don't understand your client. Last week we couldn't get the boat started, so Steve went below and had it purring in ten minutes. The son of a bitch had learned *everything* about the engine because *Holman* would have known everything. He's the most dedicated actor I've met, but whenever he can't get his way, we become the enemy. Maybe you can calm him down."

McQueen was preparing to bolt from his trailer. Like a parent with a pacifier, AJ took out a deck of cards and suggested stud poker, then proceeded to lose twenty bucks, which wasn't easy because the actor was a lousy card player. AJ steered the conversation from Wise to women. "Candice is gorgeous. Can she act?"

Steve sneered at the mention of his costar. "She's as stiff as her father's puppet."

"Nineteen, her first big movie—"

"Bullshit. Candy Bergen needs to get laid."

"It doesn't seem that should be so difficult."

"You'd be surprised—sure she's beautiful, but she's colder than a witch's tit. Talk about getting laid, I see you signed Romy Schneider. There's a babe. Maybe you could introduce me."

AJ nearly spit up his beer. "She's got a boyfriend."

"So? I've got a wife." The assistant director knocked to announce that Wise was ready. Steve pinched AJ's cheek. "Never mind. I forgot what a prude you are."

=

A platoon of American soldiers on R&R from Vietnam packed the honky-tonk on Sun Yat-sen Road where AJ and Steve stopped for drinks on the way home. When two of them asked for autographs, McQueen offered to buy a round. "How long before you whip those gooks?"

The one with the heavy beard laughed bitterly. "We got to find them before we can whip them." His eyes displayed the haunted look of someone who had watched his house destroyed by a raging fire.

"The papers at home claim we're making progress," AJ commented.

"Assholes. They're listening to Westmoreland." The second G.I. was high on something other than enthusiasm. "The light at the end of the tunnel? The only thing at the end of the tunnel's another fucking tunnel."

After they left, AJ knocked back a shot of rice wine. "That was uplifting."

"Every one of them is like that," Steve observed.

"The parallels are eerie."

"What parallels?"

"Richard McKenna wrote *The Sand Pebbles* a decade ago—about a world four decades ago. But the way the Chinese despise your character as a foreign devil, I'll bet it's exactly how the Vietnamese view a marine patrolling the Mekong Delta."

McQueen nodded. "I suppose, but if we don't halt the VC, Hong Kong will be next."

"You think so?"

"You don't?"

AJ shrugged. "I've been trying to sign a young writer named Dan Cohen, and he gave me a pamphlet by a group called Students for a

Democratic Society. It argues that Vietnam's a civil war and we've got no right to get involved."

"We can be involved in whatever the fuck we want if it kills Reds."

Given Steve's politics, this was one fight AJ didn't need. "Relax. I'm just keeping an open mind. Are you buying the next round or am I?"

The phone was ringing as they reached the farmhouse. Neile shouted that James Garner, who was caring for their dogs, was on the line from Los Angeles. Steve grabbed the receiver. AJ and Neile assumed that one of the animals was hurt, but as color drained from Steve's cheeks, they wondered . . . earthquake?

"Hey, Jim, you've got to do what you've got to do. . . . Of course there are no hard feelings." Steve then screamed at the dead receiver, "Die, you motherfucker!"

"What's wrong, honey?"

"MGM offered Garner the part in *Grand Prix*. He took it and didn't want me to read it in the papers." McQueen mimicked AJ. " 'The part's not cast.' Uh-uh. The part is cast with my next-door neighbor."

Why the hell hadn't the office cabled a warning? He would ream Haber a new asshole for this screwup. "It must have just happened. I still think that—"

"Who the fuck cares? It's your fault I'm stuck here, not back home prepping *Champions*."

What about "You're my hero"? That's what Steve had proclaimed after AJ delivered *The Sand Pebbles*. "If you'll let me finish—"

"Tell Kamen I expect William Morris to keep Warners from canceling us. And don't forget my papers are up in a few months. This would never have happened if Freddie Fields was representing me."

AJ walked the perimeter of the farmhouse, formulating a strategy. He would make sure Stan got on a plane. They would beg the studio to hang in. Somehow McQueen would stay put. But where was the light at the end of AJ's tunnel? He had fallen for the illusion of representation. For eight years he'd considered Steve a friend first and then a client, but reality was the reverse. Cynical agents understood this, but AJ was a romantic. The realization left him certain that he needed a new line of work.

=

AJ fingered the gold Chinese characters embroidered on his royal blue silk robe. According to the butler who'd toured him through his suite at Hong Kong's Peninsula Hotel, the letters signified inner peace. For the first time in his short-term memory he knew what that meant. The Peninsula was a haven of class and elegance in the gaudiest, most electric city he'd ever visited. AJ gazed across a congested harbor, where modern cargo ships threatened to swamp ageless Chinese junks, to Hong Kong Island, whose skyline rivaled Manhattan's. But the best view was reflected *on* the windows from *inside* the suite.

Romy Schneider sat at an inlaid-ivory desk composing postcards to her friends in Vienna. This assignation had been her idea, but he'd planned every detail. Now that she was his client, they talked daily, but because of her prior commitment to a film in Hamburg, they had seen each other only once since the affair at the Chateau Marmont. Romy had flown in yesterday to shop, entirely, it seemed, for alluring lingerie. She fingered the lacy edge of her gray gossamer teddy, wet the pen with her tongue, and closed with a line that pleased her.

Romy departed to the bathroom and AJ returned to bed. The sheets and blanket formed a mountain range of peaks where they had kicked and rolled for hours. He heard her heels tap the marble floor. Damn it—the woman had left the door open. In the full-length mirror he saw the teddy slip off her shoulders as she sat gently on the commode. Did she forget or was she teasing him? He glanced over as the toilet flushed. Romy was astride the bidet, beckoning him to join her. He entered, timidly at first, then ran the tub at her request. Where was his former dominance? Frankly, he didn't give a damn.

L.A. Chinese food consisted of wonton soup, spareribs, and chow mein, so the menu at Qua Ling's presented a new sensation. His favorite dish was called drunken shrimp. The waiter selected live prawns, woozy from swimming in a bowl of rice wine, and submerged them in a silver samovar filled with boiling broth. "If your time is up, it's definitely the way to go." AJ sliced off a shrimp's head and swallowed it, shell and all.

"I believe he's coming back." Romy was straight-faced. "In some other form, but he'll be back."

Horror crossed AJ's face. "You think he'll be pissed?"

"Go ahead, make fun. I believe in reincarnation. I was a doe in one life and an African slave in another. There are dozens of existences I haven't discovered yet. What do you believe in?"

"After my dad died, I tried to believe in an afterlife because then I could see him again. But I'm not spiritual. No one born in Brooklyn is.

These days I don't think about it. If there's nothing out there, then I didn't waste my time in idle speculation."

"You're so pragmatic."

"Is that a bad thing?"

"An American thing." Romy stared at him enigmatically. "Do you think about what will happen to *us,* or is that also 'idle speculation'?"

It was the first time either of them had discussed their nascent relationship outside the present tense. He affected nonchalance. "I thought after this trip you would get bored and dump me."

"I thought the same thing—now . . . who knows? But the idea that my agent can drive me crazy with his cock . . . that could be a problem."

Great—he risked being fired by friend *and* paramour within forty-eight hours. While picking the red peppers out of his Hunan beef, he asked, "Do you know a really rich guy?"

"Several. Why?"

"Since we're not breaking up, I may have to quit being an agent."

Romy laughed. "I appreciate the devotion."

"I'm actually contemplating another opportunity, but it requires a major investor."

"I know a man who is a multimillionaire and a gambler." Her rich man's name was Charles Bluhdorn, a fellow Austrian whom she'd met at a party a year ago. "He's taken me to dinner at Lutèce and still calls frequently."

"Old guy?"

"Late thirties. Fascinating. And I think he might like you. He owns a company that makes bumpers for automobiles."

"Hardly a résumé that relates to movies."

"Charlie doesn't care about what a business does, only if it can make him money." Romy added a worldly-wise smile. "But he does care about beautiful women, and the movies have lots of those."

"Will you set up an introduction?"

"If you behave yourself. Now let us hope the next course is vegetarian."

=

Steph and the kids waved American flags at LAX when his plane touched down. He gave Jess a Chinese doll, Ricky a carved puzzle box, and his wife a breathtaking string of freshwater pearls. At home *his* present was a carton from work. While divvying the fifteen new scripts into "must read," "someday," and "no way," he recounted his debacle with McQueen.

"Steve's a different person since he made it big in films," she sympathized from the dressing room. "I didn't tell you at the time, but after volunteering to host your surprise party, he sent me a bill for the food and wine."

"I hope you ripped it up."

"Neile did when she found out." Steph emerged wearing a black cocktail dress and her new pearls. "I missed you so much, AJ. Any chance you missed me?"

He threw his wife down on their bed, determined to make spontaneous, crazy love, to find the passion he longed for here on the home front. But when he started to talk sexy tough and kiss her where she wasn't used to being kissed, Steph looked . . . confused, as if a disc jockey had slipped a Jimi Hendrix release on the turntable of a folk station. It was back to basics. The only unusual development was that she fell asleep first.

A victim of jet lag, AJ trudged downstairs. Overspiced by Chinese food, he wanted nothing so much as a Tab and a corned-beef sandwich. His marital reunion had proved a disquieting blah. On the kitchen table a magazine was dog-eared to an article about a doctor in Texas who helped kids with learning problems. His mother strikes again. This kook was probably recommending leeches. The first few paragraphs were more potent than a sleeping pill, and the next thing he heard was his daughter's giggle.

"Daddy, it's time to go to work."

AJ raised his head from his deli plate, his chin stained with crusty mustard. It was six-thirty A.M. and Jess was happily feeding Dimples, the cat. Back to reality.

CHAPTER 24

Thank you, Adidas. AJ had purchased a pair of their new luxury sneakers after arriving in New York to confront chaos from a New Year's Day strike that shut down bus and subway service in the five boroughs. Now, hiking past honking traffic and leaking garbage in lower Manhattan, he recognized in Mayor John Lindsay's struggle against the transit union a harbinger of his generation's death match with the archaic powers in Hollywood. This trip was his chance to strike a blow for the good guys. In the next forty-eight hours AJ planned to meet with two investors who had the resources to finance his proposed takeover of Paramount.

By chance, his presentations coincided with a showdown in the lawsuit that the studio had instigated to kick Herb Siegel and Ernie Martin off the board of directors. Entering the federal courthouse, AJ slipped into a seat at the back of the gallery, immediately identifying the key players. The guy with the curling iron hair was Louis Nizer, Paramount's pit-bull attorney. Yesterday Nizer had pressured Siegel into acknowledging that his part ownership of a talent agency created a conflict of interest because the studio was a potential buyer of his clients. From the annual report AJ recognized the steely patrician peppering Nizer with advice as Ed Weisl, chairman of Paramount's executive committee. Weisl was a senior partner in a prestigious law firm and virtually ran the Democratic Party in the state. And there was Paul Herzog supporting a stoop-shouldered old man. . . . God, was that . . . ? It was. After Barney Balaban had given the green light to *The Fall of the Roman Empire*—one of the sorriest financial flops in movie history— Weisl had stripped him of his power and forced him into the figurehead role of chairman.

The clerk called Balaban for his cross-examination. It took forever for him to reach the stand. The defense counsel, Paul Connelly, approached within inches because the witness was nearly deaf but too vain to wear an aid. "Sir, you love Paramount Pictures, don't you?"

"Like my firstborn."

"And you'd do whatever is necessary to protect it?"

Balaban nodded. "I would."

Connelly backed away like a camera on a slow dolly shot. "When you saw Mr. Siegel and Mr. Martin in your boardroom, you feared for the well-being of your company, did you not?"

"Yes, sir."

AJ noticed Weisl and Herzog shifting nervously as Connelly continued his faux-friendly cross-examination. He enticed Balaban to admit that the board had been less outraged by conflict of interest than by meddling and criticism. And with each question, he roamed further afield, forcing the chairman to lean off balance to hear him. Nizer objected, but Barney insisted he was fine. "They called Paul Herzog and me incompetents," he snarled. "They complained we were giving away the store."

"So the real reason you came to court was to have Judge Palmieri do what the Paramount board couldn't—get the foxes out of your chicken coop?"

"You're damn right! I don't have to kowtow. Who the hell do those bastards think they are?"

Connelly charged. "I'll tell you who they are. They're stockholders. Mr. Siegel and Mr. Martin own eight percent of Paramount." The lawyer was instantly in the witness's face. "And your attempt to strip away their legitimate votes is a disgrace!"

AJ pumped his fist. The admission had damned Paramount's case. Judge Palmieri excused Balaban, but as he stood up, the gallery gasped. A stain spread from the crotch of his brown tweed suit down the right leg, spotting his brown oxford shoe with piss. In the movie business there was no dignity to the downfall of the mighty: David O. Selznick, Harry Cohn, and now his dad's old boss. AJ determined that when he finally achieved power, no one would dispatch him in disgrace.

=

A table at the '21' Club meant you had arrived among the city's power brokers. The booth commanded by the famed investment banker Charlie Allen announced that you were here to stay. Ray Stark had arranged the lunch after Paul Herzog had reneged on Stark's Paramount deal. AJ summarized his plan while Allen attacked his blood-rare hamburger with the precision and dispassion of a feeding shark. "After we assume control, Ray would be chairman. We've drawn up a list of possible heads of production, including Stan Kamen, John Calley, and David Begelman, any of whom would be a monumental improvement over the guy there now." His nervous energy expended, AJ grabbed for the rolls and butter.

"Fascinating." Allen suppressed a belch. "But I'm afraid backing your play would be an inefficient use of our money."

A bread stick froze in AJ's mouth like an exploded cigar.

"The movie business is too risky and the returns on investment are minuscule at best. The creative assets walk off the lot at night. And, frankly, I'm not sure there'll even *be* a business twenty years from now, given the growth in cable television."

AJ glanced at Ray, who became a silent partner. "Sir, you're underestimating how strongly demographics favor us. The baby boomers are hitting prime moviegoing age. They've been raised on TV dinners, but they want more."

"I think he's right." Those were Herbert Allen Jr.'s first words since ordering the three-pound lobster. And they earned the recent Williams College graduate a glare from his uncle.

"As for filmmakers, sure they're fickle," AJ acknowledged, "but if you manage them properly, they'll stick by you."

A commotion at a nearby table aborted the debate. "You're a miserable pig, Lazar." The man shouting was Otto Preminger, a director better known as the Nazi prison camp commandant in *Stalag 17*. He towered over a bald sixty-year-old whose Coke-bottle-thick oversized black glasses made him look like he'd tripped out of *Mr. Magoo*.

"Oh shit," Ray murmured.

"Who are they?" Herb Jr. asked.

"The short guy's 'Swifty' Lazar."

"A literary agent," AJ added. "He reps Nabokov, Gore Vidal, guys like that."

Swifty was on his feet, which brought him face-to-face with Preminger's belt buckle. "You would have botched the material."

"Otto tried buying the film rights for Truman Capote's *In Cold Blood*," Ray explained as he edged out of the booth. "Lazar sold them to another director."

Preminger turned his attention to a woman seated at the table. "I feel sorry for anyone who has to go to bed with this crook."

Ray closed in . . . too late. Mary Lazar slapped the director, and her husband smashed a water glass into his temple. Preminger crumpled while the couple fled the scene.

"Waiter, my bill." Charles Allen shook his head. "Mr. Jastrow, I don't believe anyone can manage these kind of ruffians."

Outside the restaurant Ray waxed philosophical, dabbing at the blood on his suit with a wet napkin. "Charles is a tough nut, but that contretemps didn't help matters."

"My only ally was the kid," AJ remarked testily. "What gives?"

"You need to experience the hardball they play in the big leagues."

"The only lesson you just taught me was how to duck and run. Are you giving up?"

"I want to reflect on that before our next meeting." Ray hoofed it to the Theater District to pester Neil Simon for his next play.

But AJ had no place to go. A cop came over to question him because

Preminger was pressing charges. "Can't help you," he lied. "I was having too much fun to notice."

=

The more her husband traveled, the more Stephanie inhabited the kitchen. It was packed with her gadgets, secondhand cookbooks, and scraps of paper with new recipes she'd scribbled down in the night. For lunch with her mother-in-law, Steph experimented on a quiche Lorraine using shrimp instead of bacon. Opening the oven, she noted that the quiche jiggled like the one they'd sampled in Brittany on their fifth anniversary, but the piecrust seemed a bit sad. Had it gotten soggy swimming under the eggs and cream? Prebaking was probably the key.

"I don't understand why you spend all that time preparing something that will be tomorrow's bowel movement," Maggie commented.

Steph ignored the crudeness since the woman cleaned her plate. "Mom, we talked with the psychologist about your idea of Ricky going to that clinic in Texas. Dr. Mittman thinks it could prove damaging, so let's forget about it, okay?"

"Not okay. What could be more damaging than allowing him to rot in that school, listening to children call him a retard?"

"Letting him fail in some untested program, that's what. I've indulged your harebrained schemes for too long. You suggested vitamins, I bought out the drugstore. Try hypnosis, you said, so I carted him to that quack downtown. He's had two sets of reading glasses even though his vision's twenty-twenty."

"Better to try things than sit around. We'll discuss this with AJ."

"No, we won't!" Steph was damned if she was going to be dismissed. "We won't discuss it again."

"Why are you so touchy?"

Because you're an insensitive cow! "Because what we do with our son—*our* son—is none of your business."

"Since when did I become an outsider?"

"Since now! I'm his mother."

"And a splendid job you've done. He's the unhappiest child I've ever seen."

"The subject is closed."

Maggie sighed. "Very well. Your husband's under enough pressure." She gathered her purse to leave. "The quiche was delicious. But be careful—you're enjoying ten pounds too much of your own cooking."

Steph raced upstairs, where the scale confirmed her mother-in-law's cattiness. After all the jokes AJ made about monster butts, there was no way that she was becoming his next target.

≡

The day after the debacle at '21,' AJ encountered his second Charlie. Charlie Bluhdorn was cut from a wholly different cloth, but he shared Allen's insatiable drive to make money and his grim view of AJ's idea. "You're fucking crazy," Bluhdorn barked in heavily accented English.

AJ was beginning to agree. He was in the living room of a man he'd met through his lover, an investor Wall Street had labeled the Mad Austrian, who'd made his fortune in the auto-parts business and whose last conquest had been a zinc-mining company. Bluhdorn and his conglomerate, Gulf + Western, seemed so unlikely a contender that Ray had skipped the trip to Connecticut.

"First, I only buy companies that want me to buy them," he lectured. "The other way's too big a pain in the ass. Second, I like well-managed businesses, and the guys at Paramount sound like circus clowns." Before he could get to "third," the phone rang again and Bluhdorn got involved in a heated conversation about buying some sugar company in Puerto Rico.

When he finally hung up, AJ dived back in. "I'm telling you, Mr. Bluhdorn—"

"Charlie."

"The movie business is in need of a kick in the ass—the kind you could provide. The men running it haven't a clue about the future." He was Mike Todd born again. "Paramount's the worst offender. Barney Balaban and Paul Herzog squandered a franchise. But as bad as they performed, the breakup value of Paramount is *still* worth more than the market cap." He was yelling from frustration.

Bluhdorn grabbed AJ's analysis out of his hand. "Dupee!" Out of nowhere stepped a young man with the kind of lean, hungry eyes that caught rounding errors in the fourth decimal. "Take a look at these numbers. See if they're as full of shit as our visitor."

It was the skimpiest of victories, but it enabled AJ to catch his breath.

"What the fuck does an agent do?"

"Think of me as a pimp for actors and directors."

Bluhdorn guffawed. "You're screwing Romy Schneider, aren't you?" His emphasis on verbs made him sound particularly aggressive.

"She's my client. It would be highly unethical . . . and dumb."

Bluhdorn looked him up and down. "She fucks *you,* but she won't fuck me. Tell me how that makes sense."

The question provided AJ's last chance. "Romy thinks the world of you. But you're in the wrong business. Ladies like her don't fall for guys who manufacture widgets, even if they have all the money in the world." For once, the man had no response. "Call me if you like the numbers. Otherwise, thanks for your time." AJ waved good-bye without waiting to be excused and headed back to the city.

His bravado cracked before he reached White Plains. The trip had been worse than useless. He'd lied to Kamen that he had a lead on signing a stage actor named Dustin Hoffman. Now he would have to lie again that he'd failed. His play for Paramount was a washout. If a stranger had guessed he was having an affair, the rumor was sure to reach Stephanie. In his downward spiral he missed the turnoff to the Major Deegan and backed up on the highway, only to be flagged down by a state trooper, who wrote him a fifty-dollar ticket. AJ banged his steering wheel. These risks were insane. The only way he could calm down was to make a solemn vow to go straight.

=

For two weeks AJ kept his religion. He accepted defeat graciously when his bosses denied his request to sign Richard Pryor. At his yearly performance review he thanked Lastfogel and Weisbord for his two-thousand-dollar raise, even as he fumed at its unfairness. In his conversations with Romy he doggedly stuck to business, despite her whispering how much she longed to be with him.

His anxiety abated, but it was replaced with a headache so pounding and persistent that he swallowed bottles of Excedrin until one morning he discovered blood when he used the bathroom. The doctor assured him that it was only a reaction to the painkillers. To celebrate not having cancer, AJ drove Steph, Ricky, and Jess to visit Sea World and the San Diego Zoo. Seeing the pleasure his children took in the vacation, AJ decided his life was fine, just fine.

But when they returned home on Sunday, a long-distance phone call from the Dominican Republic set his world spinning anew. Despite the lousy connection, Bluhdorn's gruff accent was unmistakable. "How the fuck are you?"

"Good. And you?"

"I've been thinking about your crazy idea. You know what—I *love* it!

I'm coming to L.A. next week, so don't go nowhere. And take whatever money you got and buy Paramount stock."

"Why?"

"So I can make you rich."

=

AJ usually avoided the artistic funk of Laurel Canyon, with its shanty bungalows, one-horse lanes, jackknife turns, and London-fog lighting, so it wasn't surprising he got lost trying to find Dan Cohen's house. The writer had invited him to hear a speech by his friend Tom Hayden, who had just returned from a visit behind enemy lines to Hanoi. The more attention he'd paid, the more uncomfortable AJ had felt about the war in Vietnam. He'd even written his congressman to urge hearings on America's involvement, but the guy hadn't bothered to write back.

A neighbor with the dead-eyed daze of a stoner finally directed him to a wood-and-glass cottage on Hermit's Glen. There were no Cadillacs and Lincolns, de rigueur at most Hollywood affairs. Parking his Pontiac between a Harley and a Dodge Dart, AJ approached the house, which hung precariously over a ravine. Skunk was in the air. Forty people showed up, and sat around listening to Phil Ochs on the stereo and smoking grass. Cohen welcomed his guests and introduced the Diggers, a group of mimes from the Bay Area, who performed a short play about the atrocities of the South Vietnamese army.

A young man came over with a jug of wine and poured AJ a glass. With his pudgy cheeks, blond curls, and full mouth, he looked like a Raphaelesque angel who'd rebelled by growing a beard. "I know what you're thinking, but the mimes were a lot better than last week's entertainment."

"Really?"

"I'm serious. Dan showed a documentary about teenagers in Da Nang who make puppets out of bombshells from B-52s."

"Point taken. I'm AJ Jastrow."

"Pete Leventhal. Nice to meet you." He studied AJ's Brooks Brothers button-down. "Let me guess. Dan's mother sent you to bring him back to the fold?"

"Worse. I'm a William Morris agent hoping to sign him. But I'm also trying to learn what's going on in Southeast Asia."

"A royal fucking. Wait till you hear Hayden. He, Dan, and I all went to school up in Berkeley. I'm the lawyer for Get Out Now."

Cohen tapped the microphone and introduced the intellectual guru of the New Left. With his tousled hair, coffeehouse pallor, jeans, and work shirt, Tom Hayden embodied the generation that distrusted anyone over thirty. AJ hoped no one noticed that he'd passed the cutoff. Hayden denounced the idiocy of the domino theory and the American leaders who believed in it. All that drove Lyndon Johnson and the old guard, Hayden insisted, was "Don't Tread on Me," the machismo ethic that America could never tolerate disrespect. But in this war, military might wouldn't make right.

AJ distrusted proselytizers, but he burst into applause and raised his hand when Hayden asked for questions. "I just got back from Taiwan, where I had the chance to see the low morale of our troops. Do the North Vietnamese suspect we're vulnerable?"

"Their defeat of the French convinced them they'll prevail, but I'm interested in hearing your observations, since the only part of Vietnam I could get into—or out of—alive was the North."

AJ held the spotlight—uncomfortably at first, then with burgeoning enthusiasm. Afterward, Pete Leventhal walked him to his car. "We need people like you, people who can influence the media to get our message out."

"Don't overestimate what I can do."

"AJ, you've got charisma. If you tell your clients and friends, they'll listen. We all listened to you tonight."

"That's flattering—"

"Come on up to Berkeley next month for our Vietnam teach-in. Learn more."

AJ accepted eagerly. On the way home he imagined what he might be doing in Washington if Mike Todd hadn't seduced him to Hollywood. Shit! The date of the teach-in conflicted with a William Morris staff meeting. Of course, he couldn't miss *that*.

CHAPTER 25

The instant the *Los Angeles Times* smacked against the pavement, AJ darted onto the driveway, clad only in pajamas. He hadn't been this anxious for news since his college acceptance letters had arrived. Steph's investment ideas began and ended with United States Savings Bonds, so she'd labeled him a lunatic for risking *double* their savings by buying two thousand shares of Paramount stock on margin. Executives in Hollywood rarely invested in their companies. His father had never owned a share, and Barney Balaban—after nearly four decades on the job—owned barely ten thousand.

So far he was beating the game. The stock had risen to sixty-eight, three dollars a share more than he'd paid. Under "P-Q-R" in the stock tables he located the ticker symbol for Paramount. Next to it the price was . . . no, it couldn't be fifty? He was ruined. Inside the house the phone rang—probably his broker calling his margin loan. But as his panic deepened, he realized he'd read the line for Paragon Petroleum. Paramount had skyrocketed to seventy-one, the biggest gainer on the New York Stock Exchange. An article credited the rise to speculation in the wake of the Siegel-Martin proxy fight. AJ kissed the page and danced into the kitchen. Twelve grand in profit went down smoothly with his orange juice. In less than a hundred hours he had earned a third of his annual salary—without hard work or kissing ass.

=

Charlie Bluhdorn had transformed his pink poolside cabana at the Beverly Hills Hotel into a Gulf + Western annex, complete with a secretary, multiple phone lines, reams of computer printouts, and . . . a chipper Paul Dupee? My analysis must have checked out, AJ thought. Charlie paid the ultimate compliment of dismissing his entourage and yanking out the phone jacks. The haphazard way he rubbed lotion over his milky white body suggested a man with limited sunbathing experience.

"Thanks for the stock advice."

"Only the beginning, my friend. Did I miss a spot?" AJ applied a dollop in the middle of the thicket that was Charlie's back.

"Call for Mr. DeWitt. Call for Mr. Dick DeWitt." Joey, the midget-sized pager who'd played a Munchkin in *The Wizard of Oz,* pranced around the pool area until he spotted a man whose toupee had been dyed green by the chlorine.

"This DeWitt's a big shot?"

"Nope," AJ replied. "A journeyman producer whose last two movies flopped."

"He's gotten more calls than me."

"Dick has himself paged so that people will *think* he's important."

"Fuck me."

When agents perceived a producer as "cold," AJ explained, they avoided him like smallpox and steered their scripts and talent to guys who were "hot." To heat up his image, DeWitt had hired a publicist to get him invited to premieres and mentioned in *Variety*. AJ could see Bluhdorn salivating at the prospect of capitalizing on the town's insecurity. But first he had to buy a ticket in.

Herb Siegel had given Bluhdorn an earful. He and his partner were a couple of poor bastards who'd wandered into a back room where a gang was planning a bank robbery; they couldn't get out but were too honest to join the crooks. According to Siegel, Paramount was sinking under Herzog's mismanagement. He'd blown a chance to make a whopping profit by selling the studio's annex, believing they would need it for increased production that never occurred. After purchasing David Susskind's company, Talent Associates, Herzog had sold it back to Susskind for a multimillion-dollar loss. The studio faced a dozen lawsuits from actors and directors alleging breach of contract.

"It's worse than I imagined."

"That's why Weisl's shitting himself," Charlie confided. "Herzog's his guy. If these stories leak, he'll look like a fucking idiot."

"Doesn't he already, after what happened at the trial?"

"Nah, he spread the word that Balaban went senile. Here's the drill. I need eight hundred thousand shares to control Paramount, but there's so little outstanding stock it's hard to acquire. Drummond at Sara Lee owns a huge block. Lester Crown of General Dynamics has ninety thousand shares, and a guy named Dan Rottenberg holds several thousand more. Right now those guys are *all* in Weisl's pocket. I called to say I might be interested in taking a stake in Paramount, but Weisl treated me as if I was too dumb to realize I'd never get into his club."

"So we're screwed?"

"If we were, I wouldn't be here. Eventually I'm buying Siegel's and Martin's shares. They can't win a proxy fight—there's already too much bad blood. When I offer Herb the right price, he'll pocket the profit. So the next step is to shake loose one of the pro-management groups. The minute Weisl believes he could actually lose—and be publicly embarrassed—he'll get out, especially when I come along as the savior."

"But if he finds out you're trying to dislodge his backers, won't he see Gulf + Western as the black hats?"

Bluhdorn grinned mischievously. "He'll never know, because *you're* the one who's going to do the dirty work. You've got to use your relationship with your chum in Chicago to sour Drummond on Paramount."

AJ turned ashen. "That's a suicide mission."

"We're flying under the radar to drop a hydrogen bomb—that's the fucking fun!"

Why should he bet his professional life on Bluhdorn? What if he turned out to be another Mike Todd? Like Todd, Bluhdorn had reckless faith in his own ideas and was a charismatic salesman. But Bluhdorn was a businessman, not a "showman." In other words, he wasn't full of shit. At least AJ hoped so—because he was hooked. "Suppose we succeed. Where do I fit in the long run?"

"If we get control of Paramount, you name your job at the studio."

"Vice president of production."

"You got it. By the way, what's a vice president of production do?"

They laughed together. AJ liked this guy, more so when Bluhdorn offered to loan his new VP money to buy another two thousand shares of Paramount stock. They schemed together, with Charlie giving him inside information that he could use to convince Drummond. AJ was curious how he knew so much, but the raider refused to reveal his sources.

Shaking hands, Bluhdorn inquired if AJ knew anybody who might be "good company" for dinner. No translation was needed. He called Gail Suchinsky, a casting director who kept track of which young actresses were on the make, and booked a scrumptious blonde with a continuing role in *Get Smart*. Bluhdorn exploded into the shallow end of the pool. The girl would have a good time because, despite his piggy features, Charlie's bravura energy made him seem dashing. Disappearing into the lobby, he heard Dick DeWitt paging himself again. It made AJ feel marginally less of a pimp.

≡

On Monday AJ arrived to find a pall over William Morris reminiscent of the morning of JFK's assassination. Agents slumped at their desks, whispering to each other rather than answering phones. The mailroom guys steadied their eyes on the new shag carpeting. Even visiting clients seemed dispirited. The reason, AJ learned from agent Benny Gelvin, was that Natalie Wood had fired the agency to sign with CMA. Fields and Begelman had wooed her with the siren song that if she was to be *the* movie star of the future, she needed modern agents, not fossils. "Are you certain?"

Gelvin nodded glumly. "Mr. Lastfogel heard it from his wife, who heard it from her hairdresser, who also tints Natalie's hair. The letter from her lawyer confirmed it."

Because of their self-absorption and fragility, clients rarely demonstrated the compassion or courage to deliver bad news personally. Instead, they worked themselves into a frenzied anger at their former agent—recalling every past slight—so that they could say that it was better *for the agent* if they avoided a direct confrontation. The self-deception worked for the client, but the lack of closure was maddening for the agent.

"How's the boss taking it?" AJ asked.

"The rumor is . . . he tried hanging himself."

Come on—the man couldn't reach a scaffold. AJ embraced Benny with a hug and a chuck on the chin. Secretly, he couldn't help smiling at his home team's defeat.

Stan gave him the real skinny as they drove to Fox to discuss the latest delays on *The Sand Pebbles.* "I spoke to Abe," Kamen reported. "He feels like Ralph Branca in 1951."

"After Bobby Thompson hit that home run for the pennant, Branca never pitched a decent game for the Dodgers," AJ reminded him.

Stan parked in the VIP lot. "Lastfogel will hang in. *He's* not the guy I'm worried about. Your body may be showing up for work, but your head's somewhere else."

AJ was immediately defensive. "Who's complaining about me?"

"Me. I'm complaining." His pique caught AJ unawares. "Dustin Hoffman called me—"

"Stan—"

"I know what you were doing on the trip to New York."

Word of his upcoming meeting with Nate Drummond in Palm Springs must have leaked. Suddenly the job he hated seemed like the best in the business. "Let me explain."

"Cut the shit, AJ. You're having an affair with Romy Schneider, aren't you?"

Plead guilty to the lesser charge. "How did you know?"

"Never mind. I know what a great girl Stephanie is. Why don't you?"

AJ hated seeming an adulterer in Stan's eyes, but he also resented his friend's lecture. What the hell did Kamen know about love and marriage? Homosexuals didn't have to face the wife and kids every day. They could move on whenever the affair they were in bored them. "There's a line from *The Philadelphia Story*—'A husband's philandering has nothing to do with his wife.' " He offered an ironic smile. "That's me, I guess."

"Can the movie quotes and clean up your act, okay?" Without waiting for an answer, Stan slammed the door.

C H A P T E R   2 6

AJ lane-hopped through the orange traffic cones that reduced Interstate 10 to a parking lot. The holdup was a battalion of bulldozers gouging access roads to the chocolate hills of El Monte and Pomona, where hundreds of hard hats constructed variations of the identical model home. The last time he'd traveled east of downtown there hadn't been a Covina, much less a *West* Covina. Blame the Beach Boys, the Dodgers, and tourists with motor mouths—the city was spreading as fast as the good word on the sybaritic life in southern California.

Beyond Riverside, where L.A.'s sprawl faded into the bleached vastness of the Mojave, he floored the accelerator and powered down the windows to let the wind ward off his anxiety. All he managed was a cinder in his eye. Through tears and blinks he spotted a lonesome sign saying, WE'RE HALF-NUTS—THE OTHER HALF IS FRUITS and pulled off the highway at Hadley's Orchard, the mecca for figs and pistachios. He remembered his first visit with his parents on a trip to Palm Springs in the days before air-conditioning, when the resort town had been a hideaway for publicity-shy celebrities. Hadley's still made a great date shake, all foam and bits of silky brown fruit. It coated the butterflies in his stomach, but by the time he checked into his bungalow at the La Quinta resort, they were fluttering again.

At the squeal of burning rubber, AJ stepped outside to greet his fraternity brother. Jerry Roblin was as juiced as his golf cart. "When I told my father-in-law you were a scratch golfer at Northwestern, he thought we should play to get acquainted, so we're meeting on the first tee."

"*Hello,* Jerry."

"Hello to you." Roblin looked chagrined. "Sorry, man, but I'm feeling a *lot* of pressure."

"All you did was arrange the meeting. I'll take it from here."

"Nate's suspicious. He keeps pressing to know what you want."

"Then let's go tell him." AJ jauntily grabbed his clubs from the trunk, but his mouth was drier than the dunes.

=

In his Lacoste shirt and plaid Sansabelt slacks, Nate Drummond looked like a fleshy midwestern burgher rather than a multimillionaire business-man. He was so remote that AJ worried he would be impossible to approach—until "Mr. Sara Lee" hit his first three golf shots in as many directions. The way to a duffer's heart was to help him break ninety. But AJ withheld advice, choosing to let the grace and rhythm of his own swing function like a letter of recommendation. After hitting a bullet within a foot of the pin on the fifth hole, he noticed Drummond staring in awe. "What I'd give to be able to do that even once."

"You can, but not until you stop swaying."

"Swaying?"

"Yes, sir. You think you're turning your hips and shoulders, but you're just swaying your body. All your weight is shifting to the outside of your right foot, and from there it's impossible to hit with force or ac-curacy."

"Can you help me?" A visitor to Lourdes couldn't have been need-ier.

AJ took a golf ball and placed it under the right side of the man's right foot, then held him gently while he took a practice swing. "See how that forces your weight to stay on the inside of the foot, which then requires you to make a real turn."

"That feels completely different."

AJ's hands moved confidently as they swung the club with his pupil in a pseudodance. "You've picked it up fast. That means you're a natu-ral athlete."

Drummond beamed. "I played varsity football for Iowa." He laced a six-iron down the middle and followed its progress with pure delight. "Amazing." His next swing was equally impressive. "I've never hit two in a row like that." AJ thought the man might kiss him. Cruising down the fairway, Nate looked contented. "Now that you've solved the tough problem, you want to tell me how to fix Paramount?"

"Let's concentrate on making pars. We'll talk later."

Back in the clubhouse, AJ found Drummond unexpectedly savvy about the movie business. "All the studios hit these cold spells, don't they?"

"Yes, but Paramount's reminds me of our Chicago winters. The films they released in 1965 lost five million dollars."

"Paul Herzog believes that his head of production will turn things around."

"Howard Koch? No one in Hollywood buys that—not Herzog, not even Howard. Remember *The Magnificent Seven*?" Drummond nodded. "Paul's the Mexican mayor who hires gunfighters to protect his town. He's sucked up to high-profile producers like Joe Levine and Ingo Preminger, praying they can make the hits that his people can't."

"Maybe they can."

AJ laughed cynically. "It won't matter. Their deals are so obscenely rich the studio can't possibly make money. He's paid fortunes for scripts that have no commercial value. Case in point: Herzog bought *Reflections in a Golden Eye* from a friend of mine, a producer named Ray Stark, but Paul was so preoccupied saving his corporate ass that he didn't bother to read it. According to Ray, the guy assumed the movie was a James Bond clone when it's actually a kinky drama about a homosexual Army officer in the South. On page eighty there's a scene in which a woman's nipple is sliced off." Drummond gulped. "I've got a copy in my room. By the way, it cost a bundle to kill the picture."

"Why are you trying to help me?" Nate glanced to the practice putting green, where Jerry had waited to give them privacy. "And don't yank my chain that you and my son-in-law share a secret handshake."

AJ leaned forward. "Paul Herzog and my father worked at Paramount twenty years ago. I've watched him systematically destroy the company I grew up loving. When I learned about your investment, I debated whether to say anything." AJ paused as if he were making his agonizing decision at this moment. "Herzog's an incompetent who shouldn't be allowed to run a studio. You deserve to know that. But he's also a bad guy, and to be brutally honest, seeing him in power offends my sense of justice."

" 'Revenge is mine, saith the Lord.' "

"Something like that."

"Enough. Let's go work on my grip."

An hour later, showered and shaved, AJ waited at the Palm Springs airport. As a turboprop circled the field for its final approach, he deposited change into a pay phone and dialed Gulf + Western in New York. For a man controlling a far-flung empire, Bluhdorn was fast to pick up the call and the situation. "I'm not sure if I made any impact," AJ admitted sourly.

"The fish doesn't bite when you bait the hook. He swims a bit. That story about the nipple, believe me, Drummond didn't like the taste of that with his Sara Lee Danish. We're going all the way, my friend."

"We better be. How'd the stock do today?"

"Down a point and a half. It's just under seventy."

AJ perspired, even though the desert at dusk had turned cool. "Maybe it's time for me to sell and take a profit?"

"Don't touch it."

It was easier for a shark to smile than an overextended family man to follow that advice. AJ bid Bluhdorn good-bye, then turned to confront a more devilish test of his willpower—the beauty in black jeans descending the ramp from the Air California commuter.

=

AJ knew he had to end the affair. Beyond fear of exposure, the double life made him feel schizophrenic. During sex with Steph he superimposed Romy's face or breasts—once he'd even mumbled her name into a pillow.

"Hi. How was your flight?"

"AJ, I missed you so much."

"I have something I need to say."

"Later."

They kissed . . . away his resolve. Tire tracks from the highway trailed to a rock formation. Parked behind it, they tore at each other's clothes while semis and sports cars roared by. AJ barely made it back to the bungalow before the games began again.

Dinner was now or never. The Mexican joint he found for his declaration was blessedly dark and served margaritas the size of swimming pools. Romy wiped hot sauce from her lips and leaned across the table till the heat of the chilies on her breath dried his lips. "I want you to leave your wife."

He nearly bit through his tongue. "Oh, jeez . . ."

"We've made love in three cities. I thought that would satisfy me, but now I want to *fall* in love, and we cannot do that while you are married."

Her lines weren't in his script, so he improvised with the truth. "I don't want to get divorced."

Romy sat back stunned. "You love her . . . but you prefer to fuck me?"

"Yes. And yes."

"And you're willing to give up the passion we have—for what?"

Aphorisms about loyalty, commitment, and kids convinced neither of them. "I can't explain what my marriage means to me."

"Whatever it means, it doesn't satisfy you—otherwise you wouldn't be here."

"I'm here because you're—"

"The 'Sexiest Woman in Europe.'" Romy pushed aside a half-eaten taco. "But you don't believe I could be a good wife."

She would be awful. "It's not you. I'm sorry."

Romy reacted with Germanic steel. "You probably assume I'm going to fire you, but I insist we continue working together, so you *have* to see me. Every time you fuck your wife—if you do—you'll think of me. I need twenty minutes to clear my things out of the bungalow." When he protested that she shouldn't leave tonight, Romy silenced him. "The only advice I want from you is about my career."

AJ paid the check and took a walk in the desert. All he could think of was never seeing her naked again.

———

Room 342 reeked so much of sex, perfume, and cigarettes that Steph was sure the idiot at the front desk had misdirected her. But the sight of AJ's Dopp kit on the sink doubled her heartbeat. Perhaps the maid had enjoyed a quickie with someone while turning down the bed. Then Steph spotted a pair of bikini panties in the crack between the headboard and the mattress. The lacy Oriental silk seemed an unlikely choice for the cleaning staff. Touching them triggered a sickening, psychic flash of what had recently transpired in the room.

Goddamn *Redbook*. Their article "100 Ways to Spark Your Marriage" had inspired her to surprise AJ by driving down to spend the night. Steph slumped on the bed, only to jump up in horror upon hearing the creak of the springs. In the mirror she looked for any freshness or fun. Reflected back was a has-been. She'd always feared that she was cold in bed. What if it was more . . . what if her husband realized how boring she'd become? The romantic cooing of a couple returning from dinner ended her self-pity. Storming out the door, Steph smacked headlong into AJ. In a different situation his sudden palsy might have been comical.

"You miserable, cheating piece of shit!"

"Steph?"

Bastard—he was trying to peer over her shoulder into the room. "No, AJ, she's not there. Too bad, we could have compared notes."

"You don't understand."

"Are you going to pull a Richard Pryor? 'I should believe you, not my lying eyes'? That's right, you did his routine for me. Who is she?"

"She's no one—I swear. Bluhdorn arranged a hooker—his idea of a surprise. I don't even know her name. Before I could say no, she was giving me a blow job. That's it. I swear."

Stephanie glared. "Your hooker stripped off her panties to give a blow job?" She hurled the offending underwear into his face. "It stinks like you."

"The woman was naked when I walked in. I'm sorry, Steph. It was nothing."

When he tried to take her in his arms, she slapped his face, her wedding band leaving a welt on his cheek. "I never should have married you. I didn't want to. But I did—because of how much you said you loved me."

"I did love you. I still do."

"What an idiot I was."

"Don't talk like that."

She felt a break in her panic, which gave her just enough time to get away. "I left Ricky and Jess with your mother. Go take care of them. I don't know when—or if—I'll be back." She hurried to her car but couldn't get the damn door open.

"Let me help."

"Don't you dare touch me! Not now or ever again!"

Steph peeled out of the parking lot, her brain too fried to form a coherent thought. The next thing she noticed was a road sign welcoming her to Barstow, a couple of hours to the north. Steph pulled into a diner with a fritzing neon sign that promised "Home Cooking." The ladies' room smelled of mildew and dime-store perfume. A mild sandstorm was rattling off the glass. Better not to drive in these conditions—or hers.

Over coffee the consistency of sludge, Steph tried to believe her husband. The alternative was that Fancy Pants was his mistress and AJ was in love with another woman. Steph shivered. The hooker scenario was more palatable—and more likely. If AJ did have a lover, where was she when they'd run into each other? And a stunt like Bluhdorn's was exactly the kind of boys' club bullshit Hollywood encouraged. But just as Steph got comfortable with the lesser of two evils, she remembered the lie in AJ's eyes.

She was hungry after not eating for hours, so she ordered an omelette, then made an unusual request. Since there was no one around, the waitress agreed. Steph stepped behind the industrial stove and drowned her woes cracking eggs and sautéing onions.

=

AJ stared at the cottage-cheese ceiling, counting contradictions. The affair was wrong, he was wrong to hurt Steph. But it was a miserable, intractable reality that his wife couldn't provide the passion he needed. What was he supposed to do—spend his one lifetime whacking off in the bathroom to pictures of Romy? Even now, even as he held the panties that convicted him, he became hard. Like a career criminal, he was more frustrated about being caught than contrite about what he'd done.

He drove home at dawn, intent on showering, getting under the covers, and sleeping till tomorrow. The garage was empty—no sign of his wife's station wagon or Maggie's Chrysler. He called the kids in vain, then spied an envelope propped up on the kitchen table. He trembled, certain that Steph had taken Ricky and Jess and was suing for divorce. But the scribbled message announced a defection on a second front.

=

Ricky nervously traced the stitching on the cowboy hat Grandma Maggie had bought for him as soon as they'd landed in Austin. The salesman hadn't had one in his sister's size, so Jess had gotten a rawhide vest. The trip was a surprise. Only minutes after his mom had dropped him and his sister off, Grandma had whisked them to the airport to board a Braniff Airlines plane. On the way they'd played tic-tac-toe and he'd won every time.

They arrived by cab at a school that looked like UCLA and went straight to the office of a man who had shaggier hair than Ringo Starr. He called himself Dr. Doug, even though he must have had a last name. His grandmother said the doctor would help him learn to read, but Ricky didn't see why coming to Texas would make a difference. After she left, Dr. Doug asked him to read a story, but he got mixed up, like always, so the man read it to him. The story was about an elephant named Eric who enjoyed playing with the other elephants, but they didn't like him. "I thought it was boring," Ricky answered when asked for his opinion.

"Doesn't do much for me either. I like stories with more pow!" Ricky giggled. "Why do you think the other elephants teased Eric?"

"Because his trunk was pink. Only girls have pink trunks."

"How would you have rewritten it?"

Ricky thought that was a good question. "Eric's father takes him to a class where he learns judo and kicks the other elephants on their big backsides. Then he hits them with his trunk to prove that pink ones can also be strong."

Dr. Doug removed cards from his desk and flashed the first. "What letter is this?"

"I think it's a *d*." From the doctor's expression he knew his answer was wrong. He grabbed the card and ripped it up.

"You're a young man with strong feelings—that's good. How about this one?"

"Maybe a *b*?" Maybe a *b*—he was seven years old, what was the use? "I don't want to do this."

"Do you like skywriting?"

"Like at the beach?"

"Exactly. I want you to write some of the letters you're not sure of in the sky, as if you were the pilot of the plane."

It sounded silly, but Ricky let the doctor guide his index finger, slowly tracing a *b* in the air.

"Now feel how the line goes down and then up halfway to form the circle to the right. That's *b*," Dr. Doug said firmly. "Now we're going to make a *d* and touch it."

Ricky felt the letter even though it wasn't there.

"Now I want you to do it by yourself."

His hand weighed a million pounds, but he managed to raise it.

=

Maggie watched her granddaughter curl up on the couch in Dr. Ger- lich's waiting room and cry herself to sleep pleading for her mommy. Jessica was sweet but lacked firepower and feistiness—she was the un- lucky beneficiary of too many of her mother's genes. Ricky was deter- mined and special, although AJ couldn't see it—he was too blinded by his career to see anything. The doctor stepped out to invite her into his office, but there was no wink of assurance.

Ricky was pacing, practicing a karate chop he'd seen on *I Spy*. The doctor held up a card with the word *bed* on it. "I'm going to read it,

Grandma." Ricky slowly traced the letters, retraced them in the sky, then back on the card. He spoke the word *bed* with as much hesitance as hope.

"Oh my God." Maggie hugged her grandson.

"Why don't you try one, Mrs. Jastrow. Make it tough."

Maggie chose *was* because Ricky had difficulty with *w*'s and *s*'s. It took a moment, but he read it correctly, celebrating by snatching all his imaginary letters from the air. His cheer woke Jess, who came in rubbing her eyes. Ricky rushed to brag about his success.

"Your grandson's extremely intelligent," Gerlich whispered. "There's no problem with comprehension—Ricky surpasses grade level. His difficulty lies in *decoding* the written word. The way he transposes letters indicates a condition called dyslexia."

"How come they don't know this in Los Angeles?"

"Most professionals in my field think they already have the answers. And the public school establishment brands these children as being slow or having behavioral problems because it's easier. With your permission I'm going to write up Ricky's case, because his impatience, aggressive touching of objects, and impulsiveness fit the profile perfectly." Gerlich handed her a business card with the name of one of his former students who taught in San Diego. "I'm afraid that's the closest help available."

"What causes this?"

"Shake your family tree, a dyslexic relative will probably fall out."

"I'll bet it's my husband's mother. Everyone said the old bat couldn't read because she came from Russia."

On the way to the airport Maggie noticed that Ricky's sense of triumph had waned, replaced by melancholy. "Do you think that Mom and Dad will really believe I was able to read?"

The question made her sad as well. "I'll swear to it."

"Why didn't they come on this trip?"

Maggie swallowed her actual thoughts. "Your mom and dad love you very much, but they're busy with their own lives. Parents are like that. That's why God made grandmas—to make sure that children's problems always come first."

CHAPTER 27

AJ fashioned his phone cord into a noose. Should he risk Lastfogel's wrath by being late to the staff meeting or cut off McQueen's trans-Pacific bitching? The client always got the nod—especially when he had a legitimate gripe. After four months of shooting, Steve faced seven more grueling weeks on *The Sand Pebbles*. AJ glanced at his desk calendar, which starred a July 1 start for *Day of the Champions*. "I'll call John Sturges and tell him we have to delay principal photography."

"Thanks but no thanks. You've got to kill it."

"Kill what?"

"The movie."

AJ assumed Steve was teasing. "Yeah, right."

"I'm dead serious, man. Five films in two years—you guys have overscheduled me. I'm too fucked up to face another production."

"You can still beat out *Grand Prix*, even with another delay."

"I don't care."

"I don't care"—but how about everyone else, asshole? How about all the chits and favors we called in to keep the project alive? How about the million dollars Warners has already spent? How about your friend Sturges—he passed on five other gigs. "Steve, are you absolutely sure?"

"Yeah," he yawned. "But I can't look like the heavy. Find somebody to blame."

AJ slumped in his chair. It was impossible to reason with his client and useless to tell him to go to hell. That left the depression of accommodation. "Finessing these things is our job."

"What would I do without you, man?"

You'll find out, AJ consoled himself, sooner than you think.

=

Abe Lastfogel was even later than AJ to the Monday meeting, which provided agents a chance to spread gossip over their bagels and lox. Topic one was a story in *Variety* under the headline G + W TO SCALE PAR MOUNTAIN? Over the weekend Charles Bluhdorn—a mysterious stranger to movie executives—had purchased the Paramount stock owned by dissidents Siegel and Martin and was in negotiation for the shares owned by Chicago businessman Nate Drummond. The article speculated that Gulf + Western targeted total control of the studio.

AJ played dumb. He and Bluhdorn had spoken briefly yesterday, with Charlie assuring him that everything was on schedule. After their golf outing Drummond had indeed called Weisl to announce his lack of confidence in Paramount's management team. And as hoped, Ed had panicked and asked Bluhdorn if Gulf + Western was still interested in stepping in. But AJ wished it were official, because something in Charlie's voice had given him pause. Or maybe he had read too many thrillers where the guy with the axe came out of the closet at the last possible moment.

A squadron of agents, including Kamen, listened to Sammy Weisbord whine. "I hope this Bluhdorn rumor is bullshit, because if it's not, you're seeing the beginning of the end of Hollywood as we know it. A guy like him doesn't even know what a director or a producer or, God forbid, an agent *does.*"

Stan couldn't mistake the fear on the faces of his troops. He needed to rally them. "Then we'll teach Bluhdorn. He's probably so bored with the auto-parts business he'll love joining our world."

"You're assuming he *cares* about movies and TV," Sam replied grimly. "Don't kid yourself. Our only value is to make him a buck."

AJ fired from the outer circle. "Maybe Bluhdorn can help *us* make a buck."

Agents backed away so that Weisbord could spot the sniper. "You don't know squat about this, Jastrow."

"I know that the people who ran the film business for the last twenty years failed to regain the audience they lost." That's *your* generation, Weisbord. "Time's run out on them."

AJ readied for a counterattack, but Weisbord snorted and returned to Kamen. "This won't stop with Paramount. Corporate types are ants in the kitchen—there's never just one. A year from now Procter & Gamble or some insurance company will snag U.A., Warners, or Fox. Wasserman's the only guy tough enough to take them on. Nobody will ever own Universal but him."

"You're right about that, Sammy." Lastfogel barged in, all smiles. "But take it from me, none of us has to worry about Bluhdorn."

Weisbord turned puppy dog. "Good news, Mr. Lastfogel?"

"I just got off the phone with my contact in New York. Ed Weisl and

Paul Herzog met Bluhdorn last night—it turned into a lovefest, Chinese food and all. Charlie admitted that outsiders had bad-mouthed their performance but confided that he'd discounted those statements as sour grapes. The more he investigated, the better he liked Paramount's prospects—otherwise he wouldn't have gotten involved. Paul Herzog is in like Flynn. Now, can we get down to business?"

AJ shook, but no one seemed to notice. They were too busy pumping their clients' careers. He could barely sit still when Lastfogel and Kamen asked him to remain behind at the end of the meeting. This time there was no offer of seltzer.

"A mistake was made at your salary review."

They want their money back—tough luck.

"We're going to rectify it by awarding you a bonus of five thousand dollars."

"What?"

Kamen chimed in. "You've done a great job servicing Steve McQueen and several of our clients."

This was the kind of gesture the partners made only to those selected players who would someday own a piece of William Morris. AJ knew that beyond the gratitude, Lastfogel expected to hear "I want to be here forever." He didn't want to be there another minute, but suppose Bluhdorn *had* lied to him? He was defenseless. Ray had been correct way back when—AJ didn't have guts. Capitulate gracefully. "Mr. Lastfogel, Stan, I'm really pleased that you—"

"One other thing, Jastrow." Abe slid a file across the table. "Cut out this extracurricular garbage."

AJ had never seen an FBI file—much less one with his name on it. Inside were memos, marked "Confidential—Eyes Only," that reported his participation at the antiwar meetings at Dan Cohen's house in Laurel Canyon. "What is . . . I don't understand. . . . How did they get the letter to my congressman? Cohen's people couldn't hurt a fly."

"The Bureau is the best judge of that," Lastfogel replied abruptly. "Special Agent Banks, who's in charge of the L.A. office, has concluded that cells like his are undermining the war effort and risking the lives of our troops."

AJ told himself he wasn't part of this ridiculous discussion. "Sir, I voted for Barry Goldwater."

"We won't hold that against you . . . just kidding."

"This isn't fair. You can't silence my political views—"

"Jastrow, this Commie stuff ends here."

AJ stared at the wisps of hair growing out of the man's ears. The tendrils grew longer and longer, till they reached across and under the table, ensnaring him in a net. He flailed helplessly, weakened by too many pragmatic concessions, swallowed objections, and self-serving rationalizations. But just before Lastfogel reeled him in and pickled him in the William Morris barrel, AJ broke free. "Thanks for the offer, but save your money. It's time for me to move on. I'm resigning."

Kamen's elbows slipped off the table.

"It's Begelman, isn't it?" Lastfogel thundered. "You bought his bullshit."

"I'm not going to CMA. I don't have another job right now, but—"

"You ungrateful snotnose . . . you . . . you Benedict Arnold . . . you Alger Hiss. Get out! I want you out of this building before lunch." He stormed over. "And if you try taking your Rolodex, I'll call the cops."

"Abe, a Rolodex theft is a federal offense, isn't it?" AJ rose from that table one last time. "Call the FBI instead."

Stan followed him out, spinning him around by the shoulder. "You want to explain what that was about?"

"Survival." AJ flushed from his daring. "I don't know how you've taken this shit for so many years."

"Low expectations."

"I can't live that way . . . not yet."

Bill Haber helped pack his personal possessions. "I'm going to miss you, boss. Any room for me where you're going?"

"I don't know if there's room for *me*. But I've recommended to Kamen that he make you an agent immediately."

His assistant blushed. "I already got three calls saying you were fired. What do I say?"

"Tell them they should be so lucky."

=

Steph popped the lid on a cold Coors. Her weekly drives to the reading specialist in La Jolla, combined with the fallout from AJ's infidelity, were taking a toll in crow's-feet and back spasms. Now she could add her husband's rash independence to the mix. Speak of the devil . . .

AJ stepped into the kitchen. "Ricky's doing great," he ventured. "I actually understood the story he read me. And he seems . . . easier to be with."

"Try four hours in the car twice a week before you say that."

"Okay. I'll drive him next week."

"We'll see." Her husband promised anything and everything to get back on her good side, but she refused to believe a word. "You still think Bluhdorn will come through?"

"I do."

"I hope you're a better judge of character than I am," she remarked snidely.

"The FBI bullshit was a blessing in disguise. I'm too free-spirited for Morris, and bottom line, I don't want to be an agent. You know how crazy it's made me."

"Don't blame Palm Springs on a lousy career choice."

"Christ, how many times do I have to say I'm sorry?"

Are you kidding, buster?

AJ recognized that mistake and took a different tack. "Let's use some of the money we made on the stock to take a vacation . . . just you and me." He nuzzled her neck. "I love you."

Her body stiffened. "I've got to mash the potatoes."

"This won't work if I'm the only one."

"Is that a threat?" Anger was a relief, so she seized every pretense for it. "Are you telling me you want a divorce if I don't screw you?"

"Hey, I'm leaving before you charge me with rape."

She heard him in the garage revving the engine of his car. Divorce was all she thought about—how much alimony she might get, how it would affect the kids, where they could afford to live.

Jessie trotted in. "Read me a story."

Steph suggested *A Little Princess* or the Bobbsey Twins, but her daughter insisted on Nancy Drew. "Are you sure? That's for girls a little older than you."

"Grandma gave it to me. She's gonna be a defective."

Out of the mouths of babes. "You mean a detective?"

"Uh-huh."

When they came to the part where Nancy discovered the dead body, Steph made a note to tell her mother-in-law to keep her literary choices to herself.

=

AJ's extended summer vacation ended on October 8, when stockholders voted final approval of the merger of Paramount Pictures into Gulf +

Western Industries. A limousine honked from the curb. He grabbed an attaché case with nothing in it and set off—fighting a case of the jitters worthy of the first day of school. Bluhdorn sat ensconced in the back, surrounded by scripts and files. "This is a total piece of shit," he sneered. "What do you think?"

Its title was *The Psychopath*. "Cut-rate Hitchcock. But, Charlie, it would be better if you asked the opinion of others *before* you gave your own. Most Hollywood people won't contradict the big *macher*, regardless of what they really think."

"Fuck that. I don't want no yes-men around me." He studied AJ suspiciously. "You got too good a tan. Next time I come out, you better be pale from making me money."

"Are you excited?"

"Nah. Just another business to me."

Not according to Gail Suchinsky, Paramount's new head of casting; she'd confided to AJ that Bluhdorn was having a wild time with Hollywood's under-twenty-five-year-old blondes. Sam Weisbord had been wrong when he'd predicted that this Attila would pillage for riches— Charlie had bought in to get laid.

"I'm excited enough for both of us."

"It's still not too late to change your mind." For the past month Bluhdorn had badgered AJ to forget about working in production and become one of his top staff men, involved with Paramount and the conglomerate's other businesses. "You'll learn everything and wield more fucking power than you ever dreamed of."

"The only power I want is to make movies. I'm a film guy, plain and simple."

Bluhdorn looked disgruntled. "You're a fool. But Evans likes you."

"I like Evans. When you announce him as head of production, the town's going to go nuts."

"Fuck the town."

And fuck Paul Herzog—especially Paul Herzog. "It might go smoother today without me in the meeting," AJ suggested tentatively.

"He's got the right to meet his accuser face-to-face. It's in the Constitution."

When they reached the main gate, a guard stepped forward and saluted. "Welcome to Paramount, Mr. Bluhdorn."

Charlie saluted back. "Hey, my own fucking army."

=

"What's *he* doing here?" Herzog croaked.

"Jastrow? I don't make a move without him," Bluhdorn replied matter-of-factly.

"We're on the same side now, sir." AJ extended his hand, and the studio's president couldn't think fast enough to avoid shaking it. AJ figured his presence must be disconcerting, because Paul had told friends he was confident of keeping his post under the new owner.

"You and the mutt close?" Bluhdorn gestured to the wall, where a candid shot showed Rin Tin Tin licking Herzog.

"He made Paramount a lot of money."

"A long time ago. All our production is for shit, Paulie. You want to tell me why?"

The bold gambit shocked even AJ.

Herzog looked appalled. "I don't understand. We've got excellent projects—"

"*Hurry Sundown* is a disaster. Only an idiot sends a crew to Louisiana. Right, AJ?"

The locals had persecuted the black actors, especially Diahann Carroll. "We think that you might have anticipated the racism in the state and filmed in Florida instead, where you'd get more help from the officials."

Herzog glared. "Preminger is an experienced producer and he assured—"

"How could you trust Preminger?" AJ shook his head. "He's certifiable."

"And the dailies—they're awful! That's also right, isn't it?"

AJ nodded. "The scene in which Jane Fonda seduces Michael Caine with a saxophone, that's pretty rank, Paul."

Herzog attempted to defend the movie, but Bluhdorn interrupted to savage *The Busy Body*. "It's going to lose me more fucking money!"

"Sid Caesar's a major star and—"

"*Was.* Was a major star," AJ corrected. "And only on TV. We don't think movie audiences will pay to see him."

"I don't care what *you* think!" Herzog bellowed. "I've been a senior executive in this business for thirty years. I will not be patronized by the likes of you." He whipped around to Bluhdorn. "I'm willing to answer any of your questions. But I want this punk to leave immediately."

The silence must have lasted ten seconds. "Jastrow doesn't leave until we're finished."

Herzog steadied himself against his desk.

"Now, I've got some news. I'm firing Howard Koch and naming Bob Evans as my new production chief."

"Robert Evans, the actor?"

"Yeah."

Herzog was aghast. "He's . . . he's a failed leading man with virtually no experience."

"So?"

"Don't you think you should have consulted me? I'm president."

"Nah." Charlie waved him off. "You don't talk to Evans—he'll report directly to me. You're no longer involved in the movies we make. I can't afford your mistakes."

Cut out of the loop—Hollywood's version of stoning. Paul tried salvaging his dignity. "Abuse someone else. I'll have my resignation on your desk by close of business."

"As you wish." Bluhdorn departed, signaling for AJ to follow.

But Herzog grabbed him by the arm, pulling him so close that AJ could see the hatred in the man's soul. "There's something I wanted to say. It's about your father. Everybody liked good old Harry. But you know the truth? Your old man was a putz."

Charlie was yelling impatiently from the outer office, but AJ broke the man's iron grip. "Your opinion of my father is as irrelevant as you are. " He turned and walked out.

Hiking down the hall together, Bluhdorn seemed untouched. "I thought that went better than I expected."

"Jastrow? Is that you?" Bernie Marcus wedged through the doorway of his office and enveloped AJ in a hug. AJ disappeared into the fat man's flesh. "Thank God you're here. We've needed some new energy." Marcus shook Bluhdorn's hand. "Hiring this guy, Mr. Bluhdorn, is a stroke of genius. He was a motherfucker of an adversary, so it's great to have him on our side."

AJ was confused. "You guys know each other?"

Charlie laughed. "As smart as you are, kid, you'll never be smarter than me. Remember when you asked how I knew what was going on at the studio, and I said I had 'sources'?" AJ nodded dumbly. "Bernie here is fat enough to qualify as plural."

At that instant AJ lost any illusions that Paramount would be a cozy place to work.

"I like that guy." Charlie waved back at Bernie's office as they continued through the halls. "Maybe we should send him to one of those places that sew your stomach shut. So, what's next?"

"I need an office and a phone. I've got scripts to read and phone calls to make."

"Good. Get down to business," Charlie urged. "I've only got two pieces of advice—make hit movies and make them fast."

AJ supplied the "or else."

THE
CHAIR
SHOT
FIRST

AJ jived to "Jailhouse Rock" on an ice floe in Hudson Bay. The glare from the midnight sun obscured the identity of his partner, so he angled to the left for a better look but . . . no, the woman remained in the shadows. Then a serrated knife the size of a shark's fin slashed up through the ice. Quick cuts left him dancing on a cube. A polar bear extended a paw, but was it rescue or was he dinner? "Take it," Phil Kaufman screamed. Why were the director and crew of *The White Dawn* filming *him* instead of their movie? With the frigid water lapping his ankles, AJ leaped . . .

He awoke with the covers cocooned around him. It must be minus ten outside, with a wind that could blow you backward. But rising to dress for the day's shooting, AJ's toes sank into cozy wool pile rather than curling on the freezing concrete of the Admiral Byrd Hotel. Sun peeked through the windows, not fresh snow. It took him a moment to reorient—he was back home in California, not visiting a set fifty miles from the Arctic Circle. His unconscious was becoming an incorrigible pain in the ass.

At six A.M. he grabbed a head start on the day by making a crisis call to Europe. The dailies on *Mandingo,* a blaxploitation film about miscegenation in the Deep South, had drawn blood in the Paramount screening room. The movie needed a dexterous touch, but the early footage was purple and violent. He caught the legendary Dino De Laurentiis in Rome returning from lunch. While listening to the producer's rapturous description of his *rigatoni al verdi,* AJ scraped crusty scrambled eggs into the garbage disposal—three years as a bachelor and his cooking still stank. He ordered Dino to reduce the whippings, splayed flesh, and contorted faces, and refused to wilt when the producer screamed that he was a "poossie" who lacked the vision to see that *Mandingo* was a black *"Gun wid da Win."*

Lacing up his sneakers, he mused over how people could be so blind. Couldn't they tell the difference between good film and bad? Or were they too scared to own their failures? There wasn't enough time to conduct seminars in taste or coddle sensitivities. Fix the problem or get out of the way. The tide rolled in as he ran the beach in Malibu. AJ had rented a cottage on the ocean because the Pacific promised a new start. He zigged and zagged around pools of water, stones, and jellyfish, leaving him saltwater soaked by the time he flopped on his deck. Squeezing his incipient love handles, AJ vowed to add a fourth mile tomorrow.

Dressed in a black turtleneck and tan cords, he eased his Mercedes 450SL onto Pacific Coast Highway for the forty-five-minute commute to Paramount. Normally he used the time to prepare for the day, but today he made the mistake of turning on the radio. Every station was reporting the gap in the Watergate tapes, an event that rendered movie plots conventional. No writer could create a character like Richard Nixon. The president was such a bucket of slime it was a wonder that he'd wound up in politics instead of the film business.

Ronda Gomez-Quinones waited at the office wearing the necklace of dominoes he'd given her to celebrate his former assistant's promotion to West Coast story editor. Her predilection for kooky jewelry belied a speed-reader with an eye for compelling scripts. Two of the five she'd covered yesterday merited his consideration, which spelled four hours of homework for him.

Mornings like this, AJ required an air-traffic controller more than a secretary as writers and producers pitched stories they wanted Paramount to commission and agents pitched talent for projects the studio already owned. Yes two times out of fifty rated a positive week. AJ had earned the town's respect for being definitive, unlike studio execs who cowered behind "Let me think about it." He emerged from his meetings to a spate of urgent messages, putting out the worst of the wildfires before double-timing it to the commissary for lunch with Peter Bogdanovich.

They had become friendly during the making of *Paper Moon*—the movie that encapsulated the long-running soap opera of Paramount's production process. Two years ago Peter Bart, a *New York Times* reporter recruited to the production team at the same time as AJ, had shown him a novel about a precocious girl and a con man who crossed Kansas in the 1930s selling Bibles. Together they'd hooked Bob Evans on the project. But Bluhdorn, who monitored every decision made at the studio, had called from New York to complain that period pictures were the plague. Evans had held him at bay until Bogdanovich had evinced an interest. If the director of *The Last Picture Show* liked *Paper Moon*, Charlie conceded, maybe his executives weren't total idiots.

AJ had then undertaken the mission of getting Peter to commit, which had proved an exercise in mud wrestling because the director couldn't articulate what he needed to feel comfortable. Then Polly Platt, Bogdanovich's ex-wife but continuing collaborator, had suggested casting Tatum O'Neal, which had given AJ the idea of hiring Ryan and marketing a real-life father-daughter team. Bogdanovich had loved the notion. But when AJ had broken the good news, Evans had bellowed that he was a traitor. Was he the only one who hadn't heard the rumors that Ryan had slept with Bob's wife, Ali MacGraw, during the making of *Love Story*? Chagrined, AJ had volunteered to kill the deal, but Evans had ordered him to let it stand—Paramount couldn't give up a potential hit.

Paper Moon opened to smash box office and lavish reviews. Unfortunately, the demon of success swallowed its filmmaker. At lunch, after interrogating the waiter to ensure that his cold poached salmon had been spawned in Alaska, Peter obsessed on whether the credits for his next film, *Daisy Miller*, should read "A Peter Bogdanovich Film of Henry James's Novella" or "Henry James's *Daisy Miller*, a Film by Peter Bogdanovich." But a more serious crisis loomed. Should he walk ahead of Cybill Shepherd—the film's leading lady and Peter's girlfriend—at the New York premiere or be on her arm? Perhaps he should be the last to enter?

Forget the last to enter—he might be the only one. The movie was stillborn two months before its opening, as turgid and stiff as *Paper Moon* was tart and witty. AJ longed to wring the polka-dot ascot around the demon's neck until it coughed up the old Peter—the one more concerned about on-screen images than his own.

Back at the office, a three-hour story meeting on *The Hephaestus Plague* proved a welcome relief. The studio owned a novel about scientists fighting a colony of fire-breathing insects, but the challenge was to anthropomorphize the creatures into interesting villains. Brainstorming even absurd premises was AJ's favorite part of his job. His least favorite was goosing Paramount's business-affairs people. The kid making the deal to option *North Dallas Forty* whined that the agent wouldn't agree to a reasonable price. Bernie Marcus would have squashed him. "Alas, poor Bernie"—he'd weighed less than 150 pounds by the time he'd died of pancreatic cancer.

AJ knew he was entering a minefield as he hiked across the lot at four o'clock to join his boss in the editing room of *Chinatown*. Not only was Evans the studio's chief, he was also the producer of the film. Bluhdorn had awarded him this unprecedented perk rather than raise his salary. But the dual roles meant Bob had to be both good cop and bad cop in a raging dispute between writer Robert Towne and director Roman Polanski over the ending. Neither was present while Evans ran Polanski's version.

"Tell me the truth," Evans ordered.

It was the last thing anyone in Hollywood really wanted, but Bob had an indefatigable dedication to perfection—and a flawless bullshit detector. AJ watched the scene in which Faye Dunaway's character died and her father stole the daughter born of their incestuous relationship, while Jack Nicholson's Jake Gittes watched impotently. "That's dark."

"Depressing dark or memorable dark?"

"Both."

"You think it's too dark—you do, don't you?"

Eight years and still testing. Was it because AJ was Bluhdorn's boy? Perhaps their skills overlapped, or maybe Bob, who had the sleek look of a tango dancer, resented that AJ was almost as good-looking. The guy deserved a lot of credit. When AJ expressed a passion, Bob backed it, and when AJ failed, Evans took responsibility. Their relationship generated profits for Paramount—but also thunderclouds. "It depends on what you want to say to the audience."

"Towne's a mess." Bob spoke like a telegram. "Weeping it's 'ruinous and immoral.' My sense—he's scared. Can't see the genius. Afraid audiences won't like it."

AJ shook his head. "Robert's seen *Midnight Cowboy, Easy Rider,* and *Rosemary's Baby.* The movie doesn't need a happy ending to succeed. He probably hates Polanski telling the audience that evil triumphs."

"Look at the successful assholes we deal with. Tell me evil doesn't triumph."

AJ took a different tack. "It might be novel to respect the writer's vision instead of the director's."

"That gets us Towne's next script, my way gets us Polanski's next *movie.* Sorry, AJ, but you'd suck as head of production."

It was the muted trumpet call of the elephant in the editing room—any room the two inhabited. Persistent rumors predicted AJ replacing Evans within the year. No one in New York had spoken to him, and he and Bob never discussed it directly, but Hollywood was a "where there's smoke, there's fire" town. AJ smiled thinly at Evans. "Compared to you, anyone would suck."

His dinner guest was Michael Douglas "the producer," who was flogging a movie version of Ken Kesey's novel *One Flew Over the Cuckoo's Nest*. AJ found the project off center enough to be intriguing. By dessert, he was more interested in Michael Douglas "the actor." Although the rap was that Michael had reached his potential with *The Streets of San Francisco,* AJ saw a dangerous, mischievous quality reminiscent of Kirk in his prime. Then again, he was so bushed by the time he paid the check, maybe he couldn't see clearly.

Mercifully, the first of Ronda's recommends resembled *Shampoo,* which was in production at Columbia, so AJ discarded it after forty pages. He fought through the second, a drama about a California lifeguard. The writer had too much talent to ignore, but his main character lacked ambition. After a couple of hits off a joint, AJ reevaluated. Did the lifeguard know more than he did? If he was happy soaking up rays and rescuing lame swimmers, so be it. Look how ambition had twisted Nixon. Maybe AJ had too much, spewing in too many directions. Then again, lifeguards probably didn't pay child support. He decided to show the script to Evans.

At eleven P.M., AJ cast off his day job, slipping into his den, drawing down the shades, and removing a sheaf of neatly stacked paper from the right-hand drawer. A goosenecked desk lamp shadowed him and a typewriter. Had his dad followed a similar routine? AJ had begun his screenplay in the midst of the bitter funk that had trailed his divorce. Some nights he wrote an entire scene, more often a few paragraphs of action or a single speech. The next evening he'd read that work aloud, playing each part and envisioning the staging. If it didn't scan true, he ripped it up and started again. But when it worked—he was a child again, playing with words instead of blocks.

Tonight wasn't an ordinary night. Screenwriters no longer penned "The End" on the final page of a screenplay, which was a shame, because AJ wanted the closure. He read the last line aloud. "Do you think anybody in the hamlet knows how the Yankees did last night?" Maybe it was too cute. Tomorrow would tell. Heading off to bed, he offered a silent prayer: no more polar bears for the next six hours.

"Ladies and gentlemen, the Academy of Motion Picture Arts and Sciences welcomes you to the Dorothy Chandler Pavilion for the forty-sixth annual Academy Awards. Your host for the evening . . . Mr. . . . David . . . Niven!"

AJ had sat on the fifty-yard line at the Super Bowl, in the pit at Indy, and ringside for the heavyweight championship of the world. But attending those events hadn't diminished the honor or dulled the rush of joining nominees and neighbors in the orchestra at the Oscars. This year his anticipation soared because Paramount had fourteen nominations, trailing only Universal. Although it was the hottest April day on record, Niven stood at the podium as cool as a Tanqueray and tonic. "Tonight I'm reminded that those of us in the movie business are the luckiest people in the world. Can you imagine being wonderfully overpaid for dressing up and playing games?"

"Amen," AJ whispered.

Bob Evans, who was sitting two rows ahead, next to Charlie Bluhdorn and his wife, Yvette, turned around—his fingers crossed—and mouthed, "Good luck." The first category, Best Performance by a Supporting Actress, would provide an early indication of the voters' predilections. The nominees were Candy Clark for *American Graffiti*, Sylvia Sidney for *Summer Wishes, Winter Dreams*, Linda Blair for *The Exorcist*, and Madeline Kahn and Tatum O'Neal, both for *Paper Moon*.

Tatum jabbed AJ's ribs. "I bet I didn't get any votes."

During his frequent set visits he had struck up an easy friendship with the actress, who was a year younger than his daughter. AJ had chosen to sit next to her because Ryan was shooting *Barry Lyndon* in England. "I voted for you, so you're going to win."

"Nope. I'm washed up at the age of ten."

Not washed up but maybe a little screwed up. His hand enveloped hers.

"And the winner is . . . Tatum O'Neal for *Paper Moon*."

For one instant Tatum had the only thing she wanted in the world—a career. As she skipped to the stage, AJ noticed his mother's old friend Sylvia Sidney applauding like a generous runner-up. It wasn't her most convincing performance—after four decades trying to capture an Oscar, Sylvia knew she'd die without one.

Three hours later AJ exited the men's room and spotted Julia Phillips clumping toward him across the lobby in giant platform shoes bedecked with rhinestones. She had sharp, fierce features, and the feathery boa around her black Halston made her appear a wild child dressed in adult clothing. She and her husband, Michael, and their partner, Tony Bill, were the producers of *The Sting,* which was in a horse race with *The Exorcist* for Best Picture. "Don't jinx me," she warned before he'd even managed a hello. If she won, Julia would become the first woman to receive that coveted Oscar.

"You look beautiful." AJ adjusted her boa so that her pearl necklace was visible. It was an intimate gesture for such a public setting.

"I want to win so badly, Jastrow. Kiss me good luck."

He did so, and instantly her tongue darted into his mouth. AJ refused to break first, but when she pushed him behind a column, biting his lip and grinding her body, he came up for air. She had certainly grown up since the day he'd first met her, a year out of Mount Holyoke, slaving as David Begelman's assistant. Although it would make a grand story, this wasn't the time to consummate their long-standing flirtation. "Go make history."

"I'll try."

It was past midnight in the East when David Niven introduced the final presenter of the evening. Elizabeth Taylor reacted like a deer caught in headlights when a figure leaped from the wings. He was pencil thin, hairy—and stark naked. AJ gasped, then giggled and booed with the crowd. When the security guards finally corralled the streaker, Niven deadpanned, "The only laugh that man will ever get is stripping and showing off his shortcomings."

With order restored, Taylor announced the nominated films: *The Sting, The Exorcist, American Graffiti, Cries and Whispers, A Touch of Class,* and. . . . "The winner is . . . *The Sting.*" Julia jumped up, only to snag her string of pearls on the arm of her chair. An instant before they garroted her, Michael untangled the strands. Tony Bill hustled to reach the microphone first. It was too late for Julia to catch him, but fate favored the trailer—his standard speech served as the lead-in to her spontaneity. "You can't imagine what a trip it is for a nice Jewish girl from Great Neck to win an Academy Award and meet Elizabeth Taylor all in the same night!"

Millions of men around the world fell a little bit in love.

In a flash AJ recognized his mysterious ice-dancing partner.

=

At the Governor's Ball he skipped the celebration of the winners and their entourages because the participants were so drunk with their immortality they wouldn't remember he'd stopped by. The losers were a shrewder investment. Ten minutes spent listening to Bill Blatty bitch at how *The Exorcist* had been robbed won AJ a comrade in arms. It also gave him a headache, so by the time he arrived at the studio table, he needed the champagne Bluhdorn was pouring for Jack Lemmon. The actor had won an Oscar for his performance in Paramount's *Save the Tiger.* "Lemmon's fucking award cost me two million bucks," Charlie whispered hoarsely to AJ. Despite critical acclaim, the film had bombed at the box office.

AJ smiled at Yvette. "Your husband's shedding crocodile tears."

"What's a handsome man like you doing without a date?" she asked. "I like that girl you were with last year, what was her name? Kate something . . . ?"

"Katharine Ross. We went our separate ways."

"Hey, Samson—or is it Delilah these days?" Short and bald, Frank Yablans never missed an opportunity to needle AJ about his shoulder-length hair. Bluhdorn had appointed Yablans president of the movie division—over Evans—so that Bob could concentrate on production rather than worry about marketing, administration, and legal matters. "I'm putting a clause in your next contract that keeps you from walking around like a pansy."

It was the typical defensiveness of guys who'd started their careers on the sales side of the business. AJ dealt with bullies by ducking under their jabs to land an uppercut. He stepped forward and kissed Frank full on the lips. "I love it when you talk tough."

Yablans was either homophobic or bacillophobic, because he backed away, spitting and wiping. "That's disgusting."

"Gentlemen, a toast." Bob Evans raised a champagne flute. "One year from tonight we're going to have forty nominations—and God knows how many Oscars. We'll own this ballroom, and everyone in it will be hailing us as the reincarnation of Mayer and Thalberg." Their rousing "Hear! Hear!" narrowed the envious eyes of executives at bordering tables. With *Chinatown, The Conversation,* and *The Godfather, Part 2* slated for release in 1974, Bob's was no brazen boast.

=

It was midnight by the time AJ directed his driver to a house on a cliff. Frank Konigsberg, the new head of the International Famous Agency, was the geek in high school—a TV agent trying to curry favor with the movie crowd by throwing a wild party. Unfortunately, his effort was wasted because no one knew who he was, even though he was the host.

Socializing on automatic pilot, AJ navigated among the agents, attorneys, and executives, who outnumbered the actors and directors ten to one. From too chummy greetings he guessed the rumors of his promotion had intensified. To avoid the limelight he edged over to the terrace, gazing down a thousand feet to the Sunset Strip. On a night like this, a guy with the right job on the right lot could imagine he ruled the world.

But even a prince's stomach rumbled, and the buffet looked more appealing than anything in the room. He dunked a slice of French bread into an enamel pot and promptly singed the roof of his mouth with fondue. It was past time to go home, but AJ had a final congratulation to offer. Taking the stairs in twos, he left behind the chattering exuberance, finding in its place . . . near silence. The upstairs crowd was smaller and more artistic, and the drugs they were doing drove them into their psyches. No one looked as if they were enjoying the trip.

AJ located Julia in the master bedroom. White powder dripped from the edge of one nostril. Her companion ranted about his Mexican gardener. Don Simpson worked in publicity at Warners. He was street-smart and a coke freak. AJ ignored him. "Hey, Jule, I'm really proud of you. Your speech was great."

She hugged him as if he were a life preserver. When Simpson offered AJ a hand mirror striped with lines, Julia gave Don a dirty look and pulled AJ into the hall. "I know this isn't your scene."

"I was wondering . . . I have this favor . . . could I stop by in the afternoon—"

"Michael and I are leaving for Mexico in the morning. When I get back?"

"Absolutely. There's no pressure. Have a great time." They kissed good-bye, this time chastely.

AJ detoured to the kitchen. A woman in a chef's toque sliced and diced vegetables into crudités with amazing dexterity. "Excuse me, could I bother you for some ice water?"

"Sure." She handed him a glass, which he almost dropped.

"Steph?" Although they talked whenever he picked up Ricky and Jess for weekend visits, this chance encounter with his ex-wife spooked him. He couldn't think of anything to say. "Your fondue's fabulous."

Reflexively, Steph smoothed her apron and pushed aside a stray hair. "Thanks. The Gruyère's imported from Switzerland."

"But I'm always burning myself on your cooking." Her back stiffened. "What are you doing here?"

"I cater IFA's staff luncheons. Frank gave me a shot."

"I didn't know you were expanding your business."

"If I get successful enough, I won't need your alimony."

Now it was his turn to take offense—he'd never begrudged her a dime. "If you don't have enough money, we should discuss it."

"I have all I need."

Count to five, then go anyplace but the past. "Have the kids made a decision about the summer?"

"They've both decided to go back to Raquette."

"Great." Ricky and Jess attended his old camp in the Adirondacks, which meant he'd get one last visit to his favorite place.

"And for your birthday, Jessie wanted to know if we could celebrate together."

"I'd like that."

He was thirstier than ever as his limousine sped west on Sunset, the only car headed toward the beach. He couldn't remember the last time Steph's body had looked so tight. The only reason she was in such good shape . . . shit, she must have met a guy.

CHAPTER 29

Kierkegaard was cool, cooler than anyone Ricky knew. The nineteenth-century Dane was this tortured genius who'd dumped his fiancée, even though he was desperately in love, because he feared revealing his despair and lust. Kierkegaard's "dread" wasn't fixed to an external danger, like a hit man or a wild dog; it lived inside him. But the dread was also positive, because it drove him to sin, and once he'd sinned, he was free to figure out how to assuage his guilt. People who were innocents weren't free—or alive.

Ricky pondered this heavy philosophical shit until his father interrupted to say they were late for a barbecue at Joe Wizan's. That was so lame. He'd be bored, sandy, and sunburned inside an hour. The old man called him selfish and left with his sister. Screw barbecues. If Kierkegaard lived in L.A., they'd make him write lyrics for Jan and Dean.

"Life can only be understood backward; but it must be lived forward." Ricky unfolded his lanky body from the overstuffed sofa to search for a Magic Marker to underline the passage. His scruffy bell-bottoms dragged the floor from room to room. He preferred home to Malibu. His mother wasn't scintillating company—unless you wanted to discuss braising versus roasting—but at least he knew where his things were. The custody game was bullshit. Saturdays and every other Tuesday he and his father were supposed to become pals . . . chaps . . . buddies . . . amigos—not in this lifetime.

Rummaging through the desk in the den, Ricky spotted the title page of a screenplay. *Don't Tread on Me.* Sounded intense. But the name of the author—whoa! Talk about lame ideas—his father writing a screenplay had to be a howl and a half. The only sure thing was a gooey ending, like that pappy *Paper Moon.* The barbecue had an hour to go. If he skimmed, he could get all the way through the script.

But after a few pages, skimming wasn't an option, and by the end of the second act, he paused to read a scene twice:

EXT. JUNGLE—PHAT LAO—DAY.
Farber and his platoon slog through heavy vegetation. Ahead lies an abandoned Buddhist shrine. The roots of huge banyan trees have tumbled the statues and cracked the walls. Light and shadow create an eerie mood. Farber signals to Cpl. Oman to take two men and scout ahead. Oman moves forward. Farber consults a topographical map with Sgt. Deeves.

FARBER
Either the chopper dropped us too far east or the
map is wrong, because this pit stop's not on
here.

DEEVES
You check all the tourist sites in Phat Lao?

FARBER
Yep. Amusement parks, museums . . . but no
"ghost temple." (*refolds map*) You ever see one of
those Triple-A TripTiks?

DEEVES
With the route marked in yellow? Yeah.

>   FARBER
>
> If the auto club had mapped this hellhole, we'd
> have already won the war.

Without warning, MONKEYS and BIRDS start to chatter. Farber
barely has time to look up before MACHINE-GUN FIRE explodes.
He sees Oman and his team exiting the temple on the run. They're too
terrified to shout. Farber whips around to his men.

>   FARBER
>
> GET DOWN!!

As he turns, Deeves's HAND SMACKS him across his face. He can't
believe his sergeant hit him. But it wasn't Deeves's fault—he stepped on a
LANDMINE that BLEW OFF his arm. The arm hit Farber on the
fly. Both men look shocked. Then Deeves's HEAD falls off his neck and
rolls to a stop in front of Specialist Covey.

Ricky heard Jess and his dad singing summer camp songs. He shoved
the screenplay back into the drawer and dived back onto the sofa.
Kierkegaard was calling Hegel a jerk, but all Ricky could think about
was what a sick fuck his father was—in the best sense of sick fucks.

※

Turnabout was fair play. As a production executive, AJ pissed judg-
ments on hundreds of scripts, but after finishing his own, he em-
pathized with the writer. Rereading his screenplay revealed massive
inadequacy. Who the hell was Farber? How could AJ have written a
character with no back story? Sure, the script started with a bang, but
then it bogged down. Condense the first thirty pages into ten. As for the
title, how many readers would know what *Don't Tread on Me* meant—
unless they were a friend of Tom Hayden's? Overpunctuation and
commas killed the rhythm of the speeches. Oh, yeah, the margins were
too fat and he'd left too little space at the bottom, destroying the symmetry of the page layout. And . . . just give up.

He chose as his initial reader someone smart and vicious enough to
end his misery in one fell critique. AJ entered Alice's Restaurant and
asked the maître d' to take him to Julia Phillips's booth. She sat on the
patio wearing a sombrero that shaded her reaction. The script shared
the table with a butt-filled ashtray and a bottle of tequila. "Lousy, huh?"

"Shut up." She poured him the drink he needed. "When you asked me to read your screenplay, I assumed a romantic comedy, maybe an earnest drama if I got unlucky. But a violent, kick-ass war movie—no way, not from AJ Jastrow. I can't believe *you* did this. You did do it, right? This isn't Schrader or Milius?"

"Mea culpa."

"It's fucking fabulous!"

"You're not just saying that?"

"I'm not that kind of girl." She leaned close. "No one's seen this movie. It's what Peckinpah did for westerns with *The Wild Bunch*. Farber's a fantastic character. The dialogue's too grand in places and the descriptions too gruesome, but it's small stuff. For Christ's sake, where did this come from?"

"*Catch-22.*"

"Huh?"

"Heller's book. I fought for Paramount to make the movie. War with an attitude—Mike Nichols directing—it had to succeed. The day it opened I hung around the Bruin, but no one came, so I crossed the street to the Village, where *The Out-of-Towners* was playing, and asked the people in line if they had any interest in *Catch-22*. Nope. To boomers who'd lived through moonwalks, assassinations, ghetto riots, Kent State, and Agnew, World War Two was ancient history."

"The film was a self-conscious piece of shit."

"Yeah, Mike tried too hard to be ironic. But I loved the idea. Men in combat surrounded by lunacy. Only it needed a war relevant to today's moviegoers. That night I reread an unfinished screenplay my father had written about his experiences in the Pacific. Adapting it for Vietnam seemed a cinch, so I tried. In the end I scrapped almost everything except the heart."

"You have to offer it to Paramount first?"

"Contractually."

"In case they're too dumb to appreciate it, I'll figure out where you should go next and come up with a list of directors."

"Julia, thanks. What you said meant so—"

"It's a great script and you should be really proud. Now I've got to get home. Michael and I decided to call it quits last week, and we're trying to settle without lawyers."

"Jesus! I'm sorry—"

"Hey, it's open season on marriage. Save the condolences and find me a new guy. Preferably a twisted writer."

≡

Gulf + Western ruled a Caribbean nation. The South Puerto Rican Sugar Company, a G + W subsidiary, was the dominant employer and landholder in the Dominican Republic, so "Emperor" Bluhdorn had bullied the government into ceding him hundreds of prime acres on the northern shore of the island, where he built a lavish resort. When AJ first visited Casa de Campo, he observed that the location was perfect for a tropical Pebble Beach, so Charlie hired a young golf architect named Pete Dye, who proved as consummate an artist as the best directors AJ had worked with in Hollywood. His construction crew chiseled, pickaxed, and dynamited eighteen memorable holes out of the violent terrain by the ocean.

At Bluhdorn's behest AJ's golfing partner today was Joachim Balaguer, the president of the country. The way the man cheated, AJ despaired for the national treasury. On the par-three seventeenth, Balaguer's iron shot plopped into the slate gray sand, but when they reached the ball, it had magically ricocheted onto the green—via his armed bodyguard's left instep. Balaguer sank his putt and declared himself the winner. AJ reluctantly forked over a hundred dollars, since El Presidente wouldn't accept the local currency, and made a note to submit his loss as a business expense.

The round was a useful diversion before the meeting in which he would learn the fate of *Don't Tread on Me* at Paramount. With its CinemaScope windows overlooking a darkening sea, Bluhdorn's living room reminded him of Gibson's Gulch. Charlie entered and hurled the script against a wall. A charming naïf painting clattered to the floor. "You're a fucking Communist!"

"But do you like it?"

"Yablans thinks it's amateur night."

"Frank's the son of a chicken plucker. He got his education on the street, so no offense, but his literary credentials are suspect."

"I don't know why I still like you."

"Because I make you money."

"*Death Wish* is shit."

"A big hit, you'll see this summer. Trust me."

"I do." His answer abbreviated their banter. "I don't want you to leave. Evans isn't going to stay around Paramount forever. When he quits—"

"I'll be on Social Security."

"When he quits, I name you head of production."

Finally, confirmation of the rumors. "I'm not looking to leave," AJ said sincerely. "I can produce my script and continue as an executive, like Bob did on *Chinatown*. If and when he departs, we'll discuss my next move."

"I can't do it. Letting Evans produce *Chinatown* was a huge mistake. The other producers and directors on the lot bitch that he's favoring his film. I do it with you, it's a revolution. You got to choose."

"Will Paramount make my film?"

Bluhdorn shook his head. "Evans likes it but doesn't think it works commercial. I agree."

"So I either forget it and stay an exec or quit and shop the script?"

"That's it. We can't have you out there selling to another studio while we're paying your salary. Don't be a schmuck. There are hundreds of producers and writers but only seven heads of production. The whole town will be sucking your toes."

Charlie had a point. In Hollywood, the power to green-light movies meant control over people's lives, as well as the creative right to tell the stories he wanted to tell. "Let me think about it."

"Executive vice president in charge of worldwide production. With that title even you could probably get a date." Bluhdorn enveloped AJ in a corporate security hug. "You're my boy. You're family."

CHAPTER 30

ASE CLOSED. *MISS MAYHEM* CALLS IT QUITS AFTER SIX SEASONS. The headline atop the Calendar section of the *Los Angeles Times* served as a fitting tombstone for a series that had consistently ranked in the top ten and had catapulted Maggie Jastrow to number two, behind Mary Tyler Moore, among favorite female TV personalities. America mourned the May 20 final episode, but AJ breathed a sigh of relief. Complete strangers had besieged his mother with requests to help with their real-life mysteries, and she'd responded by establishing an institute to investigate unsolved crimes.

To celebrate, Leon Ginsberg hosted a gala wrap party at his Holmby Hills palace, inspired by the châteaux of the Loire Valley. He'd paid the

construction bill out of pocket change; his estimated syndication profits from *Miss Mayhem* topped fifty million dollars—ten of which fun-
neled to Maggie. Jessica craned her head past a nineteenth-century
Baccarat crystal chandelier hanging three flights above the Carrara marble entry. "I don't understand why Uncle Leon needs fourteen bed-
rooms."

"Because Aaron Spelling has thirteen," her brother replied. "Residuals
are a very good thing."

"What are you going to do with yours?"

Ricky's proudest possession was his SAG card, earned with appearances in four episodes of *Miss Mayhem*. "I'm buying a Harley."

AJ had overheard. "Be my guest." He'd refused his son's request a
dozen times, but static was their normal communication. "Just wait till
you're twenty-one and living too far away for me to visit you in the hospital."

" 'Physical space and time are the absolute stupidity of the universe.' "

"In your humble opinion?"

"No, José Ortega y Gasset's."

"Then ask Señor Ortega to pay your insurance premiums."

"Hello there." Leon interrupted with a smile as wide as he could
muster in the aftermath of a too ambitious face-lift. "The Jastrows must
be very proud."

"We are, but you should take credit," AJ reminded. "I know how
many times my mother said no to the part."

On cue Maggie swept down the spiral staircase, modestly acknowledging the applause even as she was milking it. Then she beelined to
the only people who interested her—her grandchildren. After hugs and
kisses, she asked about Ricky's acting classes and Jess's election as president of the Laurie Partridge fan club. Maggie doted on them until Leon
shepherded everyone into the living room, where four television sets
provided the crowd a perfect view of his leading lady. At the first note
of Burt Bacharach's jazzy theme, AJ slipped away. He'd seen a cut of
tonight's finale, in which Miss Mayhem sold her agency to her deputy
and married Detective Halloran, her longtime suitor. If he couldn't win
in real life, Leon was determined to fulfill his fantasy on the tube.

His mother paced in the foyer, ripping the cellophane off a package
of Tareytons. "Mom—"

"I know, they'll kill me." She took a deep drag and offered him one.

"Don't you want to watch the final moments?"

"I could never watch my work. That's how I met your father. I was hanging out in the lobby at a premiere of that awful sailor movie."

"He'd be proud."

"Ha. Harry hated the idea of me acting, which was why I quit."

"It was a different time for women. I'm sure he only wanted the best for you."

"He wanted his dinner on time."

This wasn't the place to debate history. "Are you sad the show's over?"

"Sad that I'm through with killer schedules? Mediocre scripts? Hack directors? A producer who can't keep his hands off me between takes? I'm miserable. But I won't be for long, not with him behind me." She motioned for a young man, who emerged from the living room to join them. Maggie kissed Mike Ovitz on the cheek, then introduced him as her new agent.

The guy packaged television variety shows for William Morris, but Bill Haber had bragged to AJ that his twenty-eight-year-old colleague possessed a genius vision of the entertainment business. Mike's eyes—the only distinguishing feature in a tapioca face—darted from one Jastrow to the other. He wrested AJ by the arm, drew him close, and spoke sotto voce—although no one was within earshot. "Your mother's going to revolutionize daytime television."

AJ waited, but Ovitz provided no follow-up.

"Mike's negotiating for me to host a talk show," Maggie added, "like Johnny Carson's, for broadcast in the afternoon."

The notion was inspired. Phil Donahue and Mike Douglas dominated daytime talk, even though their audiences were heavily female. With Maggie's TVQ and uncensored mouth, those doughboys faced trouble. "Would you start production right away?"

"Absolutely."

"Which network?"

Mike grimaced, as if AJ's question had put them in harm's way. "Serious players, you wouldn't even recognize their names. It's levels beyond the networks."

AJ stiffened as the agent cast a knowing glance to *his* client. She's *my* mother, asshole. Who needs this high-school shit? He excused himself to watch the last act of the show. On-screen the detectives were saying farewell, and Miss Mayhem shared a personal connection with each. So where was his?

AJ used the excuse that it was a school night to make an early exit. When they arrived at Steph's shortly after eleven, Jess bolted from the car to describe the menu to her mom, but Ricky remained—probably to talk about the damn motorcycle. "I read your screenplay."

AJ accidentally hit the horn. "When?"

"Last week at the beach, while you were at Joe's. Are you doing it? I mean, are you going to produce it?"

"I'm not sure. Should I?"

Ricky shrugged. "Why not? It was okay. You know, not faggy."

His first quote. "Thanks."

"Russ Matovich should direct it."

"*Buried Alive?*"

"He'll make it real."

"I'll keep that in mind."

"Right." Ricky cracked open the car door. "Yeah, Dad, I think you should do it."

=

Julia Phillips was searing some poor soul's flesh when AJ arrived at her home one beach below his in Malibu. As best he could tell, the victim was a publisher who'd slipped the galleys of his hot novel to a rival producer. Julia twirled the phone cord like a bullwhip. "You know what I've got on my mantel? . . . That's right, a fucking Oscar! You know what's on the table—the script of my next movie, *Taxi Driver.* And beside it, *Close Encounters of the Third Kind,* it's going to be the biggest film of all time. I own Hollywood, Eberhart, but you hand your book to a guy whose last credit was in black and white? He's a dead man, you moron. . . . Who cares if you've known him twenty years . . . ? I'm warning every writer I know that you're a limp-dick weasel! Only fucking illiterates will publish with you. . . . Yeah, sue me for slander. The truth's a defense!" She smashed the phone into its cradle.

"Dick Eberhart in New York?" AJ ventured.

"He betrayed me."

"It's four A.M. there. You couldn't have waited till morning?"

Julia breathed heavily, aroused from combat and itching for more. "You don't understand how hard it is to be a woman in this business."

She was hell on wheels, but a lost soul at the same time. "Poor baby." Playing doctor, he touched her heart. "It's beating a mile a minute."

"Fuck you, Jastrow."

He took her face in his hands and kissed her. "No, I'd like to fuck you—more than you can imagine."

She stripped off her threadbare T-shirt as if to say "What have you been waiting for?" After months of flirtation—bam! The ensuing sex was definitely a "Julia Phillips Production"—forget the intros, get to it, and don't relent until the audience is spent. She straddled him with her legs, guided him inside, and settled into her own jolting rhythm. He didn't consider coming until she'd climaxed twice.

Afterward, they cooed and touched and savored skin on skin long enough for his arm to fall asleep under her body—long enough for AJ to fantasize a side of her he could hang with. Then sadly but inexorably, the business refueled a mind that couldn't idle in neutral.

"What are you doing about Paramount and the script?"

"Until a couple of hours ago I wasn't sure. On one hand, Evans's job looks like the 'come true' of a dream I've had for a decade. Head of production—the guy who calls the shots."

"Don't forget Yablans. He'll make your dream a nightmare."

"I know that. Guys like him, Paul Herzog, Barney Balaban—they're in the walls at Paramount. I'd spend half my time making movies and the rest watching my back."

"And eventually wind up with a shiv in it."

"But until then it could be sweet. Wherever Bob travels, a guy unpacks his luggage, another makes sure the hotel's got soft enough toilet paper."

"Screw that. I don't want anyone knowing what I use to wipe my ass."

AJ laughed out loud, then sat up and pushed back his covers. "I envied you at the Awards. You'd done your own thing, and your accomplishment would live forever. But in spite of all your assurances, I wasn't convinced my script was worth doing. Then tonight I found out my son had read it. Nothing I do ever pleases him, but I could tell he loved *Don't Tread on Me*. It spoke to him. That means that it could speak to millions of young people. I can create something of value, and feel like you do about *The Sting*. I'm going for it."

"Thank God. I'd have looked like an asshole otherwise."

"What are you talking about?"

"I gave your screenplay to Begelman, confidentially. It 'spoke' to him too—big time. He wants to meet immediately."

"Jesus!"

"I know I shouldn't have, but your Hamlet impersonation was making me antsy."

How irritated could he get in the face of good news? When he pressed for details, Julia nibbled on his earlobe, whispering that he needed to get his priorities in order.

=

Like her sisters in the sorority of secretary-guardians, Constance Danielson was adept at welcoming the favored while barring the hordes. "Mr. Begelman will be with you in a few minutes," she told AJ. "Would you like some coffee? A soft drink? How about an apple juice?"

How about a Valium? "No, I'm fine."

AJ gazed out the windows of the chrome-and-glass Columbia Pictures headquarters to a row of squat, nondescript brown buildings just across the lot. They housed the offices of Rastar. Begelman might be the studio's king, but Ray Stark was the power behind the throne. Hell—without him, there wouldn't be a kingdom.

In 1973, when Columbia was verging on bankruptcy, Ray's movies with Barbra Streisand, especially *Funny Girl* and *The Way We Were,* had kept the place afloat. Seizing the opportunity he had blown at Paramount, he'd convinced Herb Allen Jr., who'd come of age at his family's firm, to buy the studio in a fire sale. Stark had negotiated the richest production deal in Hollywood and the right to anoint Columbia's new chief. It still rankled AJ that his old friend had never discussed the job with him. Maybe it was a case of "knew you when." How could you give the top slot to a kid you'd once used as a beard? And Begelman was certainly qualified. To Wall Street, an Überagent was the best choice to run a studio.

David emerged, as affable and elegant as ever. In response to AJ's compliment about his cashmere sport jacket, Begelman explained that he'd commissioned an English tailor to custom-make a dozen in all the classic patterns. "If you give me your size, I'll have him make up a houndstooth for you." AJ trailed David inside, now fixated on the man's loafers, as glove soft as the seats in a Lamborghini.

"Our world is full of surprises. Who could have predicted that beyond his other talents, AJ Jastrow would be an immensely talented writer?"

"My English teachers." He jettisoned the persona of humble writer to make sure he didn't get screwed on the deal.

"Your script is unique, it's emotional, it's provocative. It's also a gamble."

"Then it's perfect for you." Begelman was one of the heaviest sports bettors in Hollywood, risking twenty thousand dollars on NFL action on any given Sunday.

"I like a smart bet. So if we were to make *Don't Tread on Me,* the budget should protect the downside."

AJ was way ahead. "We can do it below the line in Thailand for four million."

"John Veitch, our head of physical production, thinks three and a half is possible."

"Anything is possible, depending on who directs and whether we try to cast a name as Farber." AJ fished to find out if Columbia felt comfortable only with high-end talent, which was notoriously difficult to attract.

"A name isn't a prerequisite, but the script's a natural for your old friend."

AJ and McQueen had remained friendly by *not* working together after AJ left William Morris. "Steve feels a decade too old for the part. Farber's in his twenties."

"It's the movies. The audience will imagine Steve younger. Do you think you can get a quick read?"

"I can try."

"Who do you see directing this?"

"Friedkin before *The French Connection.* If we want to do this at a price, David, we can't afford Billy or Rafelson or Nichols. Let's find a young director with style and energy. Lucas?"

Begelman shook his head. "George is writing a Vietnam project for Francis."

"Russ Matovich."

"Hmm. I'm not sure he's experienced enough. Draw up a list of candidates. We'll find the right man."

As always, it came down to money. Begelman proposed optioning the script for fifty thousand dollars, with a bonus of an additional fifty when the movie was made, plus a producer's fee of two hundred thousand dollars. The total package of three hundred thousand seemed fair to AJ, since his annual Paramount salary was only a hundred thousand. But what would happen if he resigned and then Columbia *didn't* make *Don't Tread on Me*? He had family obligations. "I need you to go pay or play with me before I quit my job." That meant Columbia owed him his producer's fee, in addition to the option money, whether or not the studio ultimately made the movie.

"I'm not prepared to reach that far."

His fantasies—casting, supervising the set, screening dailies—dimmed. He rose, hoping he'd be told to sit. "David, I understand, but I can't go forward for fifty thousand."

He had his hand on the doorknob when Begelman weakened. "We'll option the script for fifty thousand and guarantee you another hundred thousand dollars as an *advance* against your producing fees, regardless of our decision to go forward."

It wasn't the security AJ sought, but . . . "I can live with that."

He was pumped by the time he reached his car but detoured across the lot to tell Ray the news.

"Good for you." Stark sulked away.

"What's wrong?"

"Nothing."

Did anybody simply say what was bothering him without being begged? "You're upset, and I don't know why."

"It's personally insulting that as my protégé you didn't give me your script to read or ask my opinion on becoming a producer."

AJ was almost forty—he could make up his own mind about what to do with his life. But *because* he was almost forty, he was smart enough not to bait Stark or remind him that he hadn't considered his "protégé" a worthy candidate for production chief. "I'm sorry. I *know* how you feel about producing—it's your life."

That should have defused the situation, but Stark simmered. "How could you let that bitch bring it here . . . I won't forget that."

Vintage Ray: despise anyone who might topple you. At least Stark remained consistent. "That's not my fault," AJ explained. "Julia acted totally without my knowledge. She's not making a penny on my film."

"Forget it, Mr. Big Shot. You want the credit, get ready for the headaches!"

═

"I'm so fucking proud of you, AJ." McQueen riffled through the pages of the script. The two men were knocking back beers in Steve's trailer on the set of *The Towering Inferno*. Through the screen door the assistant director announced that director Irwin Allen was ready, then skulked off when the actor bellowed to be left alone.

Just like old times. The idea of taking Steve to Thailand—far from home, close to drugs—terrified AJ. But he'd promised Begelman a full-court press. "I wrote it for you."

"I can't wait to read it."

A pair of perfectly polite lies.

AJ marveled at how together McQueen looked for a man who'd gone way over the deep end. His career had almost ended after the disaster of *Le Mans,* the race-car movie he'd waited too long to make. But just as Hollywood was writing him off as over the hill, Steve responded with *Papillon,* his most successful film to date. His marriage to Neile had died after he'd put a gun to her head, forcing her to admit to a brief fling with actor John Gavin. He couldn't accept or forgive her infidelity, he announced—forgetting that he'd fucked hundreds of girls. But just when he'd hit the bachelor market, he'd fallen in love with Ali MacGraw filming *The Getaway.* How small was the town? Their torrid affair had begun while Bob Evans lived in the cutting room of *The Godfather.*

"You look great in fireman's gear, Steve."

"I do, don't I?" He broke into an ear-to-ear grin. "Freddie got me top billing over Newman." McQueen had turned down Redford's role in *Butch Cassidy and the Sundance Kid* because Kamen couldn't get him first position in the ads. He'd eventually fired the agent who'd created him—in a three-line telegram—and hired Begelman's former partner, Freddie Fields. "He's the kind of son of a bastard you want on your side. Now that you're a writer, I'll get him to represent you. And I've got a hot broad for you. She's my masseuse—the most incredible hands."

The last woman Steve had matched him with was an actress who trained wolves for a hobby. "I better get out of here or they'll blame me for making you late. Give me a call as soon as you finish it."

"Absolutely." Steve skimmed a few scenes. "My character's a lieutenant, huh? I'm a little old for that, so maybe we could promote him to major."

Farber's inexperience was crucial to making the story work. "No problem," AJ assured him. "We can figure it out."

=

Bluhdorn cursed AJ's stupidity for leaving—and never offered anything as gracious as "good luck"—but the sentence was exile rather than execution. Although he refused to attend, Charlie authorized a thousand dollars for AJ's going-away party. At the bash's peak, the fire department threatened to close down Lucy's El Adobe Café for overcrowding. AJ's studio colleagues and friends from the movies he'd supervised were sloshed by the time Bob Evans, whose trust in AJ had been restored by his decision to leave, called for a speech by the guest of honor.

"Last night my years at Paramount played on a loop in my mind, AJ began. "The amazing thing was . . . they were all bad." People laughed nervously. "Actually, they were awful, devastating, and catastrophic. Reading the reviews on *Darling Lili,* I recall worrying that I'd have to default on my mortgage when they closed the studio. Or that night on the set of *Waterloo* when Sergei Bondarchuk was cursing in Russian, while five thousand extras stood around with nothing to do. Or trying to understand the dailies on *Harold and Maude,* then rushing to the set to find Hal Ashby so stoned he didn't recognize Bob or me."

AJ studied the sea of faces. Maybe he was drunk or emotional—but friendship was alive and well in Hollywood.

"Now I see that those terrible times were my best times—because I was able to share them with you. We're in the same lifeboat and I wouldn't have it any other way."

CHAPTER 31

Russ Matovich had a pogo stick for a spine. From the moment he arrived at AJ's house—his motorcycle spraying gravel against the white stucco walls, his hair blown into unfathomable clumps—he bounced his way from room to room and subject to subject in a dizzying plea to direct *Don't Tread on Me.* "If you want to be sure that I'm the right guy, look into my soul."

At least AJ hadn't heard that one before. "That's exactly what I'll get to do, *if* we make the movie together."

"I've got a shortcut." Russ thrust out his hand, featuring an oversized ring he might have picked from a box of Cracker Jack. "The guy in New York who invented it said the color of the crystal reveals your mood. Blue means I'm happy. You try it." When it slipped into the groove where AJ's wedding band had once rested, the quartz darkened to a rainstorm gray. "Whoa! That means you're *mucho* tense."

AJ removed the ring before it faded to black—but didn't argue with its diagnosis. Under prodding from Begelman he had spent weeks searching for an experienced director. Typecast candidates, like Frank Schaffner, who'd won the Oscar for *Patton,* didn't wish to retread old territory, while pros like Fred Zinnemann and Sydney Pollack evinced no interest in a war movie. Peter Yates, the director of *Bullitt,* loved the script but was prepping *Mother, Jugs & Speed.* Frank Perry wouldn't travel to Southeast Asia. As the rejections mounted, AJ sensed that David was second-guessing his decision to go forward. In his dad's day, Frank Freeman would have ordered one of Paramount's contract directors to the set. But in the wake of free agency, the new breed indulged their passions, which too often mismatched their talents.

Fortunately, Matovich loved the script, and Begelman grudgingly agreed to approve him if AJ felt strongly after their meeting. In conducting due diligence AJ had spoken with Russ's first producer, Roger Corman, who'd cited the director's ingenuity and energy but warned that the guy needed slapping around from time to time. Matovich's professors from USC Film School had graded him at the top of his class. Art Pratt, his last cameraman, had praised his sharp eye for shot making. And Ricky had never quit lobbying.

"I think producers are mostly bullshit," Russ offered breezily.

Give him credit for honesty. "Really."

"It's the writer and the director who make the difference. The fact that you wrote the script is cool."

"You're what . . . twenty-eight?"

"Twenty-six."

"How'd you beat the draft?"

"I had my mom get her shrink to write a letter that I was gay. At my medical exam I came on to the colonel like a flaming faggot, then went home and balled my girlfriend."

"God bless America."

"I'd have done worse to avoid that cluster fuck. Your screenplay catches it—the sense of being totally out of control. I've got to make the audience feel that Nam was free-falling without a chute."

"But in the end Farber *regains* control. His decision to determine if Tet Vanh is clear of VCs rather than simply annihilate it, that's the moment we say that a person can maintain his humanity, cut through the chaos, and save innocent lives."

"I suppose."

"You suppose?" Supposing was unacceptable when it came to the core of what he and his father had created.

"Don't shit a brick. What Farber does is great. I wouldn't have risked

it, but I respected him. Maybe it just worries me that the end is anticli-
mactic when Tet Vanh turns out to be clean. But it's my job to figure
out how to deal with that." Matovich reached into his portfolio and
withdrew detailed storyboards. "I know I don't have the job yet, but
I've started planning shots for the key scenes."

AJ studied the first action sequence, in which VCs ambushed Farber's squad. Palpable tension suffused the crude sketches. Something
mysterious—perhaps the enemy or only a potbellied pig—remained
slightly beyond the frame line. Tantalized, AJ turned the storyboards on
their sides to catch a peek. Matovich seemed oblivious to his opinion,
too busy bouncing around the garden, fingering the viewfinder that
hung around his neck like a talisman. Directors used the device to vi-
sualize what the camera would see with different lenses. "Russ, this
represents a lot of work on spec."

"I only sleep three hours a night, so I've got plenty of time to think.
I've already shot half your script in my head."

"How is it?"

"Ballsy. Tough. Scary. I heard you're out to McQueen."

Sore point. "Yeah, but he's been working crazy hours on *Towering Inferno* and still hasn't read it."

"No big deal," Russ replied nonchalantly. "He'd be primo for box office, but I'm not sure he'll take the chances we need an actor to take. I'd
go with a newcomer. Shit, we're the stars of this film!"

An hour later AJ reported to Begelman, "The good news is he's brilliant. The bad news . . . let's just say modesty isn't his strong suit."

"You think he's our man?"

"Unquestionably." In the prolonged silence AJ worried that he was
too ebullient.

Finally, Begelman spoke. "I think you should book a trip to the Far
East."

"Is this an official green light?"

"Blinking yellow. Turning green when you're cast."

Alone—but anxious to share his elation—AJ dialed the Sherry-
Netherland Hotel in New York and asked for Julia Phillips's suite. A
man growled hello in a voice husky with illegal substances. AJ flinched.
"May I speak to Julia?"

"She can't talk now, she's giving me head. Call back in an hour."

Every single man and woman in Hollywood slept around—hell, so
did half the married couples—and he and Julia weren't remotely exclu-

sive. So why was he jealous enough to think about prowling some bar to find an ingenue sipping a Harvey Wallbanger and seeking quick romance? Instead, AJ flipped on the TV, where his mom—already in reruns—pointed her Beretta at a quivering criminal. He poured a brandy, hunted up *Breakfast of Champions,* and crawled into bed.

=

Stephanie jolted awake from her nap, disoriented to find herself riding shotgun next to her ex-husband. The sign on the shoulder of Interstate 87—ENTERING THE ADIRONDACK STATE PARK—reminded her why they were together. "How much longer?"

"Another hour." AJ exited onto two-lane Route 28. "Having second thoughts?"

Her ex-husband could always read her mind—when he bothered to do so. "I'm worried about Jessie. Any time we do something as a team, she assumes that we're going to reconcile."

"I explained we were visiting camp on the same weekend so we could both see Ricky in his big show."

She laughed at his naïveté. "Rational explanations don't cut it with thirteen-year-old romantics."

They drove in silence through forests of pine trees thick enough to blot out the sun, past lakes that shimmered as if the winter ice had just melted. A put-put, or even a canoe or sailboat, was rare. The few towns they passed had soda parlors, general stores, and barbershops. To Steph, this enclave of upstate New York seemed "the land that time forgot," but it was Brigadoon to her ex. Proximity put a goofy smile on his face. That's what he must have looked like from ages eight to eighteen. AJ returned to the car from a road stand carrying a handful of . . . muddy brown shoelaces?

"Have a strip. It's the best beef jerky in America. Based on an old Algonquin recipe."

The first bite almost cracked her molar. "Which is why the tribe disappeared."

"I used to make my parents stop and get a pound when they came up." A quizzical expression crossed his face. "I never looked forward to those visits."

"I wouldn't have either, if it meant seeing your mother."

"I miss how you used to snipe at her—it saved me the trouble."

Her giggle jolted both of them. Giggling—and every other joyful act between them—had ceased years ago, after Steph had learned through the grapevine the identity of AJ's former mistress. How the hell was an Ohio girl supposed to compete with the memory of Romy Schneider?

Still, they might have survived the affair if it weren't for his job. Being a studio executive was hazardous to your soul. She couldn't decide if she liked her husband less when he was arrogant or when he was scared—he seemed to flip-flop on alternate days. But in these last six months since he'd quit Paramount, she'd sensed a tectonic shift. AJ remained anxious, but his passion for his movie touched her, and his renewed ability to think about things other than film—the kids and the world—was refreshing. Steph actually found herself missing his . . . energy. That spirit had been the prevailing breeze in their marriage. Her reminiscences, however, were fraught, so she changed the subject. "How's it going with your director?"

"I get a kick out of Russ. One out of every three ideas he comes up with is brilliant. We're trying to convince Begelman to let us hire Michael Douglas for Farber."

"Steve turned you down?"

"Would you believe he never read it? You can't approach an actor while he's shooting."

"Please, he's an ass."

A slice of blue flashed between the trees, then another, like skip frames in a film. Finally, the trees gave way and Raquette Lake, swelling with whitecaps, came into full view. "God, I could dive in right here," he sighed.

"Fight the impulse."

They parked and walked—AJ practically skipped the last few yards— to the *Antlers.* Modeled on the *African Queen,* it transported them two miles to the island camp. Fifty other parents joined them, their purses and bags weighed down by junk-food contraband, including enough jerky to keep the area dentists in business.

Bernie Halperin, who had owned Raquette since AJ was a camper, understood that a mom and dad on the move couldn't complain about their child's soiled underwear or earwax, so he scheduled ninety minutes into every visiting hour. After rooting for Jess in volleyball, Steph panted hiking over to the soccer field. Meanwhile, AJ followed his daughter to the tennis courts.

Could two children be less alike? Steph wondered. Ricky was tall for his age, with muscles filling out his pale frame and the hint of a beard. The way he played spoke volumes. Her son was focused, fast, and capable of breathtaking saves in the goal, but despite the high fives of his teammates, he responded with the deep blue stare of an ascetic who couldn't be bothered with the kudos of the masses. But Jess was so tanned she might have summered in a different clime than her brother. She was more than part of the team; she was its captain—and soul— never ceasing to chatter encouragement and advice. No wonder the two of them co-existed rather than loved.

By the time morning activities ended and everyone assembled for lunch, the bedraggled parents looked like they needed a summer vacation. Steph could no longer eat a meal without reviewing it in her mind. The barbecue sauce for the steak was too sweet, the corn waterlogged, and the salad overdressed, but only she seemed to mind. A forty-minute rest period normally followed lunch, but today Bernie had announced a surprise. From underneath the cool shade of an evergreen, Steph and Ricky watched AJ in the center of the campfire circle telling a new generation of campers "The Coney Island Maniac." Apparently, the tale of horror he'd first concocted as a counselor was a legend.

"Ahhhh! Noooo!"

Steph smiled at the screams, including Jessie's. "Your father can be a spellbinder."

"It's a good thing, because Sis bragged to all the kids," Ricky reported. "She's heard him tell this ten times and still gets scared."

"How about you—are you nervous about tonight?" Her son was the lead in the camp's production of *Jesus Christ Superstar.*

"I don't get nervous. It's negative energy. A half hour before I go on I disappear into my part. It's cool, especially when—"

Another shriek from the crowd startled them.

"I hope Dad doesn't wear them out."

"You want to see something funny?" From her purse she removed a photo of AJ as Raquette's youngest camper, in 1942. Ricky studied the fading picture as if it were an artifact from an Egyptian tomb. "Can you believe how small he was?"

"I bet he had the neatest cubbies in camp."

Steph laughed. "Right. His underwear probably saluted."

A bugle blasted over the loudspeaker, then the disembodied voice of the head counselor urged his troops to the next activity. Jess obeyed, while Ricky loafed off. Steph saw AJ hustle toward her and signaled that she was through running around. He already had an alternative.

As AJ paddled a canoe into a quiet cove off the lake, Steph broke the silence. A tremor in her voice betrayed her message. "AJ, I want to tell you something that you—"

"You're going to marry François Volk."

His mind reading was eerie. "How . . . how did you—"

"The same 'friends' who told you about Romy."

Steph had met her Frenchman when he'd opened a bistro in Santa Monica. "We're going to live together. I'm not sure I'll ever remarry. But I'd like François to move into our house."

"It's your house, the state of California says so."

This was hard for him. When they'd divorced, everyone had predicted that he'd find a new wife quickly, but she was the one in a committed relationship. "If it's too weird, I could sell it and buy another place."

"I appreciate that, but stay. You deserve more happiness there than I gave you."

Turning to thank him, Steph slipped on the damp wicker seat and went for her first actual swim in Raquette Lake. How the kids hadn't come down with pneumonia or hypothermia every summer was a mystery.

Four hours later Steph was still shivering as she and AJ stood at the back of the social hall, which was packed with campers and parents. The mimeographed program listed Ricky as Jesus, Jane Cohen as Mary Magdalene, and Neil Hirshfield as Judas. "Kind of an odd choice for a Jewish summer camp," she whispered as the lights dimmed.

"Hey, all the characters *were* Jews."

The curtain parted and the cast appeared costumed in white robes and sandals, everyone's hair so naturally long that no wigs were required. Their rendition of "What's the Buzz?" promised that this wouldn't be one of those amateur productions that made entertainment professionals cringe. It was well rehearsed, and nobody's voice cracked. Ricky's performance elevated the evening. He commanded the tiny stage, his voice echoing off the log walls. The pain and passion he mustered in his final plea to God amazed Steph. The audience rose as one for its ovation.

Steph and AJ hurried backstage to congratulate their son but couldn't find him. Morris and Minnie Cohen, the father and mother of Mary Magdalene, also searched in vain. By the time the leads arrived, flushed with excitement, the parents had to board the boat to return to the mainland. AJ raised a cup of punch in a toast. "You were phenomenal. I

THE CHAIR SHOT FIRST ||| 217

saw the show on Broadway, and I swear the guy playing it wasn't as be-
lievable."

"Really?"

"Really."

"That's great, because I want the chance to audition for the part of
Private Morgan in your movie."

"Come on. There's a small matter called school."

"Morgan gets killed in that first firefight, so I could do it and only
miss a week."

Clever timing, Steph thought—go for it when parental pride was
burgeoning. AJ jumped her attempt to postpone the discussion.

"We agreed you could visit the set over Christmas. That's it."

Ricky turned stage left and walked off without saying good-bye. A
wonderful visit ended in another meltdown.

The lake was a mirror as the *Antlers* powered back to the mainland.
"When we couldn't find Ricky after the show, you know what he was
doing?" she asked.

"Figuring out how to make me a villain," AJ remarked glumly.

"No." Steph smiled. "Trying to get laid."

"Please!"

"I saw a stain on his jeans and the girl's cheeks were flushed."

"Boffing Mary Magdalene?"

"Precisely."

"I need a drink!"

AJ drove to his old hangout in Raquette Lake Village. The bartender
remembered him from past years and provided a pitcher of Utica Club
on the house. While they played pinball and shelled peanuts, Steph
brought the subject back to their son's career dreams. "Acting's a tough
life, with so much rejection. I understand why you're fighting it."

"That's only part of what bothers me. Actors are from another
planet."

"Some—I grant you not many—are very nice people."

"There's where you're wrong. They do great impressions of human
beings, but they're really Martians. The idea that we conceived one . . ."
He grabbed her hand theatrically. "You don't think . . . Jess?"

AJ was too drunk to drive, so she took the wheel. It was almost midnight when she ran over the geraniums at Deer Meadows Motel. A
Paul Bunyan apparition named Mrs. Mulcahy emerged in a billowing
plaid dressing gown. "Mr. Jastrow, a man's called five times, saying it's

an emergency." Suddenly sober, AJ studied the message slip. "I don't mean to pry, but is that *the* Steve McQueen?"

"Did he say anything?"

Mrs. Mulcahy turned as red as the beefsteak tomatoes ripening on a nearby vine. "I can't hardly repeat it, but he said, 'Tell that son of a bitch Jastrow that his script is . . . effing great. I'm in!' "

=

Within a week the negotiations for McQueen to star in *Don't Tread on Me* turned into a debacle that threatened to scuttle the movie. Freddie Fields demanded three million dollars, 15 percent of the profits, a dozen first-class round-trip airfares to location, ten bodyguards, two chefs, and a motorcycle. Sins of the past returned to haunt AJ and Begelman. As agents they'd ravaged buyers, but as producer and studio *they* now had to choke down the numbers. One point, however, proved a hopeless stumbling block: Steve's refusal to approve Russ Matovich as the director.

In order not to overshadow Russ, AJ had deliberately skipped the initial meeting between the two men. It was a mistake, because Steve immediately called to bitch that Russ's take on the character of Farber was too dark. AJ guessed that creative differences had been less problematic than the director's failure to acknowledge McQueen's stature. But the battle of egos grew more complicated than their *mano a mano*. By forcing AJ and Columbia to fire Russ, Steve was declaring himself the boss. Screw pragmatism—that move offended AJ.

For advice he consulted the master of talent relations. Ray Stark recovered from his pique the instant AJ needed him. "If you start searching for a director who McQueen will approve, who knows what will happen. Even if you find someone else, Steve's crazy enough to drop out anyway. Kiss him off."

"It's not that easy. Columbia's salivating at the marquee. If I lose Steve, it's going to prick the balloon. I'm worried Begelman will kill the film."

"You can't allow yourself to appear vulnerable. A weak producer is like the president of Poland. The studio, the director, the actors, and the crew are all waiting to march over you. You'll live a lot longer as a son-of-a-bitch dictator."

But without his studio stripes, AJ evolved a different slant on the geopolitics of production. He saw himself as a diplomat whose job was to forge an alliance among the talent, who distrusted—and often despised— one another, an alliance that would last long enough to get the film signed, sealed, and delivered. So he leaned on McQueen to give Mato- vich a second chance, then drilled Russ on how to behave.

The site of the summit was his beach cottage. Filling a cooler with beer, he fretted that both his guests were late. To kill time he picked up yesterday's *Hollywood Reporter*. The lead story covered the turmoil at Paramount following the firing of Frank Yablans. An axe was hanging inches above Evans's neck. Had AJ remained, Charlie Bluhdorn would probably have honored his promise rather than turning to Barry Diller, who was rumored to be on his way to Paramount from his post at ABC.

Matovich's arrival cut short the what-ifs. The director turned sullen when he didn't see McQueen. "At USC we only waited ten minutes, and that was for a full professor."

"For the number one movie star in the world, you toss your watch."

Geographically, Hollywood was built on a fault line. Emotionally, so was the film business. And at the epicenter of most local temblors was a movie star in a foul mood. Was that a rumble? AJ wandered out onto his deck. Sure enough, across the sand he spied Steve marching toward him. AJ hopped the railing. McQueen's body language announced a cocaine breakfast, which was reason enough to call it a day right here. The actor had a snub-nosed Smith & Wesson stuffed into the waist of his jeans. "Loaded for bear, huh?"

"I got too many nuts trying to prove they're tougher than me. I don't go anywhere without it."

"Thanks for coming."

"You had no fucking right pushing me into this. Matovich is a punk."

"Come on. Let's discuss it calmly."

McQueen followed him into the house, but politeness didn't survive the handshakes. When AJ suggested they talk about Farber's dilemma, Steve cut him off. "Spare me the bullshit. I like the script. I get the char- acter. If John Ford here wants to tell me where to stand, that's fine. But if he thinks he's going to tell me how to act, you're both living in a dreamworld."

"I'm no traffic cop," Matovich shot back.

"Russ!"

"I'm not." He rose from his chair and paced the room.

AJ tried his last gambit. "Listen, Steve, we all respect your talent. Russ was only offering his thoughts. You make the final choices."

"He wants me to play an antihero. That's not Farber."

"You misunderstood," Matovich interjected. "I said Farber was complex. More than other parts you've played."

"You think my performances are one-note?"

"If the shoe fits . . ."

AJ thanked God Matovich had said it under his breath.

"Hey, asshole, I asked you a question." Steve turned purple as Russ continued to pace. "Sit down, you cocksucker, and tell me what you really think."

"You already know everything."

"I said sit down!"

"Are you going to make me?"

AJ saw the black menace of Steve's gun spotlighted by the sun. The actor's finger poised on the safety.

"SIT THE FUCK DOWN!"

Matovich glanced back. He screamed too late.

An explosion rocked the room. The chair wobbled. One leg crumpled. Another shot splintered the second leg. Impossibly, the chair remained upright for a few agonizing seconds before pitching forward to the floor.

The acrid stench of gunpowder rushed to AJ's brain, clearing any illusions. If he didn't get McQueen's attention quickly, God knows. "Hey, hey . . . no problem." He raised his hands in mock surrender.

Steve stared at him. "What?"

"If the police ask, I'll swear the chair shot first."

"Fuck both of you." The actor spit swill and stormed out.

Matovich collapsed on the sofa. It was the first time AJ had seen him in repose.

CHAPTER 32

The Oriental Hotel in Bangkok served a breakfast banana that made the Chiquitas AJ usually ate taste like wax. Diaphanous skin, silky saffron flesh, and sweetness . . . he joked that it was sex for breakfast. His passion and imagination had blossomed once he'd arrived to survey locations for *Don't Tread on Me*. After the long winter of script development, scouting was the spring of moviemaking, when anything was possible and everything came alive.

Their Thai production manager, Jimmy Chitapoorn, waited in the lobby with a map and a smile. He claimed to have found the perfect location near the Burmese border. Two hours later AJ wished only for a safe place to land. Brutish thunderclouds enveloped them at two thousand feet. The pilot cinched his harness, but before AJ could follow, turbulence knocked him into the bulkhead. Russ focused his viewfinder on the lightning strikes. Their destination was supposedly just over the horizon, but the only thing AJ could see out the grimy window was a dead beetle trapped in the double glass. How the poor bastard wound up there was a mystery for which there'd never be an explanation.

A sunburst worthy of DeMille unveiled a jagged valley cut deeply into the terrain of northern Thailand. The verdant hills, teeming jungles, and Buddhist shrines eerily matched the Vietnam in his screenplay—and all stood within a two-mile sweep of the village of Lo An. AJ flashed thumbs-up to Russ and yelled for the pilot to land. On the ground the two men splashed around the rice paddies like kids in a mud puddle, planning shots and blocking action. From beneath his conical hat a suspicious farmer tried to figure out why these strangers were so excited about his home. For AJ it was the promised land.

=

A month later—too late—he realized that his euphoria was an arrogant rookie's blunder and the choice of base camp a mistake from which there was no recovery, only survival. Lo An delivered all the conditions that had made war in Asia a tropical hell. The ground slithered with poisonous snakes. The heat sapped the crew's energy. Because the locals were neither friendly nor skilled, the company imported every worker who hammered a nail. As for nails, Lo An lacked them—and everything from sixty-watt bulbs to Q-Tips. A truck convoy arrived daily with its deliveries jarred or broken by the potholed roads. And the graft . . . forget the expense, AJ couldn't determine whom to bribe. An endless procession of Thai officials held out their hands. "A few baht smooth the way," Jimmy advised. AJ smoothed and smoothed, but the production still encountered friction.

With principal photography ten days away, dysentery ranked as their most urgent problem. Eric Masters, the production designer, shuffled in late to a meeting. Forty pounds thinner than the day he'd arrived, the man could have doubled for a POW. While describing the ghost temple, Eric gagged and vomited over the blueprints.

In their tiny community, however, news was contagion, and Russ cut short a camera test to contest AJ's decision to send the designer home. "Isn't there a drug that will make him feel better?" The subtext was, Who's going to build the temple and the tunnels I intend to blow up?

"Eric has malaria."

"It's war, right?"

"No, it's a war *movie*."

Matovich assessed the potential replacements. "A bunch of hacks."

"Wake up! Dick Sylbert and Dean Tavoularis are too expensive. We're hemorrhaging in construction and set design."

"Don't go bean counter on me. Coppola and Altman make movies, not budgets."

"The only thing you've got in common with those guys is your DGA card. I'll have someone here by Thursday." Matovich sulked off, leaving AJ wondering if the dissonant winds from the Vietnam War, still raging among the Vietnamese two hundred miles to the east, had blown paranoia and disaffection in their direction.

Walking through the lobby of the Sao Mai Hotel, the site of their production offices, he fielded twenty questions before reaching the men's room. AJ hoped for a moment's solitude, but found instead a naked male butt stuck high in the air. A stunning Oriental woman prepared to jab the left cheek with a syringe.

"Hey, AJ, how's it going?" Michael Douglas grinned through his legs.

"Are you okay?"

"I'm great." The actor had dedicated the past four weeks to mastering infantry techniques under the tutelage of their military adviser, Colonel Mack Goodwin, a Green Beret hero. "Doc's giving me a B_{12} shot. It wards off every local disease."

Dr. Sung Si Pak, the company's physician, waved the needle at AJ. She was lithe, with a doll's straight black hair, and spoke fractured English with a French accent. "You would enjoy one too?"

"I'll take a rain check."

Sung Si shook her head. "I do not think it rain."

"No, you see—"

"I make joke."

Her laughter charmed him. Unlike most liberated American women, Sung Si seemed content with her lot. After Michael left, AJ decided to take her up on the offer. "Be gentle." She struck at the instant his walkie-talkie crackled. "AJ, channel four, please."

It was Jack Sobel, the assistant director. "Boss, a few of us need to speak to you."

AJ might bitch about having no time or place to relax, but he loved living at the center of the action. "On my way." He smiled at Sung Si. "How about dinner tonight, assuming I can sit down?"

"I would like that."

AJ shut the door to his office, noting that the men in attendance averted their eyes. No one wanted to squeal on Matovich because they respected his zeal and ambition. But the director's demands were squeezing schedule and budget past the breaking point. Sobel kicked off the confessions. "The way he plans to shoot the ambush can't be done in three days."

"Is this Bo's bullshit?" AJ asked. With his stringy hair and disdain for soap and authority, Bo Alpert, their cameraman, was pure counterculture. At thirty he was already infamous for waiting half a day for the precise light to shine, but Russ had pleaded that he and Bo were so in sync they'd get the job done on schedule.

"I don't know who's goosing who, but his setups definitely mean two more days."

Merle Wrightwood, the stunt coordinator, reported that Matovich had doubled the dynamite and M-16 rounds for the firefights and ordered ten additional stuntmen. Then Dana Dorey, the casting director, asked if he should hire three hundred extras rather than the one hundred previously agreed upon. Staring at his sandals, he whispered, "Russ wants a few of the Thai girls to . . . well . . . work personally for him. Do I bill it to the company or ask him to pay?"

"Him—and make sure he doesn't wind up with a case of the clap. Guys, I appreciate this heads-up. Russ is going to make a great movie, but I need to protect him from his own appetite. He could eat our whole budget by the third week." They trooped out relieved that he'd be the one to say no.

=

AJ's head throbbed at the prospect of tonight's first full-table reading of *Don't Tread on Me*. Would the dialogue reveal the complex characters living in his mind, or would it sound arch and false? And did the first act establish the core conflict sharply enough? Suppose he couldn't make the necessary changes? If Russ pushed for a new writer, he faced the humiliation of firing himself. The next two hours would tell. Jack Sobel read the stage directions. The actors, swilling coffee and puffing cigarettes, performed their lines 10 percent below full throttle. Russ scribbled on a pad. AJ held his breath.

During a routine search-and-destroy mission, an American squad commanded by Lieutenant Ken Farber and his key men, Sergeant Deeves, Corporal Oman, and Specialist Covey, survived a fierce ambush by the VCs. Upon their return to base, Major Hanley ordered the squad to reconnoiter Tet Vanh, a hamlet suspected of serving as a supply junction on the Ho Chi Minh Trail.

AJ exhaled. The first ten pages ripped along.

The team considered their mission virtual suicide, but Farber kept them from splitting into factions. After they unearthed documents showing that Tet Vanh was clean of VCs, the major insisted they enter the village to verify the finding nevertheless. The second act ended with the heroes in imminent danger only two miles from the target. During a skirmish at the ghost temple at Phat Lao, the enemy killed Deeves, the squad's father figure. Morale sank. When Farber radioed a second request to abort, his C.O. agreed but announced he would arrange for B-52s to carpet-bomb Tet Vanh as a precaution. Farber knew that would mean the incineration of hundreds of innocent civilians. His choice was either to let it happen or take his men deeper into danger by personally inspecting Tet Vanh.

His father had posed this ethical dilemma in his screenplay, and though he'd died before Farber chose, AJ knew his intentions. Half the squad remained behind, but Farber, Oman, and Covey pushed forward and radioed an all clear. Their action saved the village.

The actors and crew broke into applause and besieged AJ with congratulations. He was too giddy to notice that the only person who hadn't said a word was his director. He caught up with Russ on the teak deck outside the hotel. "That was a relief, huh?"

Matovich fixed him with a deadly stare. "If you weren't so in love with your fucking dialogue and the praise of assholes who don't know shit from Shinola, you'd see we have a huge problem."

"I don't understand."

"The ending of my movie sucks! When they walk into the village, nothing happens. The movie doesn't climax, it stops. People are going to leave the theater saying, 'What the hell was that all about?' "

"It's about a man having the courage to avoid a slaughter. It's about the sanctity of life."

"We're not conducting a philosophy seminar."

This wasn't their usual haggle over budget. Still, AJ's first instinct was to cajole. "Come on, Russ. The ending can be hugely dramatic. If you shoot the grateful reactions from the women and children in the village, the audience will feel proud of our guys."

"Now you're telling me how to shoot it?"

"I'm suggesting, not telling."

"And why should the villagers look grateful? They haven't seen the movie, they don't know that Farber saved their asses."

The question was legitimate—and AJ was pissed he'd never asked it. "You're right, we need to—"

"It's irrelevant, because even if we figure a way to let them know, the audience is waiting for an explosion. We need a topper when the squad enters Tet Vanh. Hear me out on this—the VC should be hiding in the village. Then we could end with a massive firefight."

They lived in opposing universes. "That would make Farber's decision meaningless. It would make him look stupid and undercut his courage."

"No, it wouldn't."

"Yes, it would."

Russ rolled his eyes. "Then let's have Covey go berserk and try to kill Farber."

"If Covey was crazy, why did he go with Farber instead of staying with the mutineers? You're not making sense."

"How about if someone in the village makes a false move and Farber goes wacko and starts a shoot-out?"

AJ experienced intense déjà vu. Hadn't he conducted this debate a thousand times? "Your curfew is eleven." "You will go to college." "You cannot buy a motorcycle." Did he possess radar that identified a director who could play his son? The collective frustration of years of parenting raised the stakes. "Let me make this clear. There'll be no VCs in the village and no firefight. If you felt strongly about the end, you should have said it in L.A. Now you have to try to make it work."

"I don't have to do shit!"

"You have to do your job." AJ shouted his last line at Russ's back and two raised middle fingers. The son of a bitch was probably headed to the local bar to scheme with Bo Alpert, then fuck the girls that Dana Dorey had found.

AJ glanced at his watch. It was Thanksgiving Day in Los Angeles. He could be home watching the Cowboys play the Packers, eating himself into a stupor. Instead, he kicked a chair over the deck's railing.

=

"Camera's rolling," Jack Sobel called.

"Action!" Russ Matovich sent his actors marching through the jungle in full battle gear. Fearful, pissed, stoned.

AJ bought it.

Twenty seconds later Russ called, "Cut." The first take on the first scene of AJ's first movie was history. But the director didn't yell his first "Print" until the fifteenth take, then repeated the same shot ten more times before yelling "Print" again and moving on. AJ fumed as the hours slipped by. At this rate, they should buy homes rather than rent hotel rooms. Later that morning Matovich ordered Michael Douglas to dive into the mud eleven times before he felt the actor looked sufficiently splattered. A torrential rainstorm washed out shooting for three hours, and when the skies cleared, Bo informed them that the fading light wouldn't match the earlier work. Reluctantly, AJ called it a day. They'd finished a quarter of their scheduled work.

AJ pulled Russ aside, but the director launched into a spirited defense. "On those early takes they were marching like a band in the St. Paddy's Day parade. I had to wear them down so you could see their despair."

"I'm the one in despair, Russell."

"Hey, I wish it had been quicker, but this is art."

"No, art is brushing twenty bucks' worth of paint on a ten-buck canvas in your attic. When you're spending fifty thousand dollars a day, it's also business."

"I know you're quaking because the studio's going to bust your butt. But the only real job you have now is to get me what I need to make this movie. It'll be tiresome to have this conversation every night."

"If we have this conversation one more time, you'll be on a plane home." AJ stalked off. His eyes were focused dead ahead, but he couldn't miss the crew's astonishment. A few snickered. Behind his back Russ made some insulting remark AJ couldn't make out. It drew stifled laughs. He should have known from his Paramount days—once the show was going, the balance of power shifted to the director, even one as young as Matovich. The cost of replacing him was catastrophic.

AJ phoned John Veitch, Columbia's head of physical production, who took the news with surprising calm. He suggested asking Russ to print the earlier marching footage so Columbia could make an independent judgment about whether he was being too precise. AJ kicked himself that he hadn't thought of that. It took him hours to fall asleep. When he awoke to go to the john, he felt light-headed and sick to his stomach. Waiting for the nausea to pass, he determined to get control of himself—and retain control of his movie.

CHAPTER 33

No one achieved stardom without a first lucky break. Ricky's arrived ten minutes after his flight from L.A. landed in Bangkok. Medics carried Larry Detmer, who played Specialist Covey, off a plane from Lo An, his patella shattered in an on-set accident, his eyes dazed, and his jaw slack from morphine. "What happens to the movie now?" Ricky asked the assistant director who accompanied the actor.

"We shoot around him, but Covey's in most of the scenes."

"Who will replace him?"

The guy shrugged. "That's up to Russ and your father."

Maybe Ricky could save them the hassle and downtime of shipping in a substitute from the States. Technically he was too young for the part, but everyone said he looked older. College girls hit on him, and with the right makeup it might work. Then again, he had no time to prepare an audition. And a friend who'd acted in Russ's first film said the director took no prisoners when it came to performance. In his overnight bag, between his underwear and a bathing suit, Ricky located a squashed copy of the script. Go with Goethe: "One lives but once in the world."

=

"Why do we have to have this conversation?" Five minutes on the ground and his son was already testing AJ's patience.

"Just give me a chance."

"This isn't about chances." Ricky refused to hear that he was too young, that he would miss too much school, that it was nepotistic for the producer to hire his son. And AJ couldn't say what he feared most—that his boy would fail and look stupid, as he had in those early days at school.

Ricky kicked dirt and stalked off.

AJ tried to maintain his dignity with the members of the crew who'd observed their argument. Why did they assume he was the villain? Maybe they didn't, maybe he was too sensitive—they had kids too.

Matovich ambled over. "Look, I don't want to spoil your family reunion—"

"Russ, stay out of this."

"I'll read Ricky, reject him, and take you off the hook."

Why was Matovich offering to help?

Russ must have guessed his cynicism. "I need you paying attention to me and the movie, not a sullen sixteen-year-old."

=

Fuck you, Dad.

It helped to hate in this situation. Ricky was facedown in a circular length of pipe three feet in diameter. Despite the chilled metal beneath his belly, sweat dripped into his eyes, obscuring a pinpoint of light fifty feet down the pitch-black cylinder. Insects crawled over him as if he were a freeway. He couldn't track time but guessed he had ten more minutes to prove he could survive the combat scenes in the Vietcong tunnels. He would last as long as he had to. How pissed had his old man been when Russ had loved his performance in the scenes he'd read with Michael Douglas? So pissed that he'd concocted this torture in hopes of getting Ricky to chicken out.

"Time's up. Give him a hand."

Russ's voice was welcome relief. The light blinded him, his legs wobbled, and pain shot down his arms. How did anyone survive solitary confinement? Remember the weakness and use it. "That was great," Ricky bragged.

"We lucked out," Matovich announced. "Your kid's tougher than Detmer—and better. Now we've got two Jastrows on the call sheet." Russ yelled for Peter Jeffries, the costume designer, to outfit him in military garb.

Ricky could see his dad trying to be a good loser—emphasis on *loser.*

AJ awoke to the sound of tiptoeing on the floor. It was five A.M. and inky black in the jungle outside. A week ago, after he'd almost slugged Russ in a fight over the director's unbudgeted redesign of the ghost temple, Sung Si had come to his room with an herbal drink that tasted of jasmine. He'd sipped, she'd massaged his temples . . . then they'd made love. Just like that. Neither of them had talked of a future beyond the last day of production. The promise of her narrow hips had kept him going late in the day, when they were losing light and Matovich was concocting a new crane shot. It had seemed so simple. But tonight her silhouette was sad. AJ stumbled out of bed to kiss her goodbye, lost his balance, and tripped. "I'm fine," he assured her, "but you're not."

She checked for broken bones, never looking up. "People are saying I'm your whore."

"I'm sorry."

"How did they find out? We have been so careful."

Gossip about affairs ranked with complaints over catering as the staple of set conversations. "The crew notices everything." He kissed her forehead. "I shouldn't have risked your reputation." Or made myself look foolish and fallible. She disappeared into the night, along with his absurd assumption of no consequences.

Today's work involved Ricky's pivotal scene—Covey reacting to the death of Sergeant Deeves. Casting his son had worked out better than he'd anticipated. Ricky was acting brilliantly—and studying harder with his on-set tutor than he did back in school. Steph had argued that the experience of working together might strengthen their relationship. Although that hadn't happened—Ricky chose to spend his time with the other actors—father and son managed to avoid further fights.

Arriving on the set at seven A.M., AJ wished him good luck. "How's the man of the moment?"

"Go to hell!"

"What's wrong?" The boy was close to tears.

"Russ told me you guys were going to fire me and get someone else. Why didn't you say something?"

Ricky stalked off. No such discussion had occurred. AJ ran over to Matovich.

"I've been here for an hour undermining your kid's confidence," the director confirmed. "He's too much of a rock. When I go in for the close-up, I've got to see his guts pouring out."

"Fucking with the head of a sixteen-year-old is your idea of motivation?"

"Grow up, man. It's good for him." He pushed the viewfinder inches from AJ. "I'm going in so tight you'll see every zit."

"Put that thing down!"

"Oooh, whatever you say, master. I should have trusted my mood ring back in L.A.," he snorted. "You have *got* to chill, man."

For once Russ was right. AJ watched the rehearsal from a discreet distance, lest his presence inhibit Ricky.

The sight of Deeves's rubber and plastic head gave AJ the chills. It was supposed to roll toward Ricky, who would pick it up, scream in horror, and attack Michael Douglas. One camera equipped with a forty-millimeter lens covered all his actions, while a second camera, with a hundred-millimeter lens, focused tight on his face. On the first take, the head stopped a yard short. People laughed nervously. But on take two it bounced into his hands on a short hop. Ricky hoisted it off the ground, then impulsively put it next to his cheek and caressed it like a mother with a newborn infant. An agonized howl distorted his features. He threw the head so ferociously it struck a light stand, splitting into smithereens.

Matovich forgot to call "Cut." Sobel nudged him, and Russ quickly ordered, "Print it. Let's move on." Bo Alpert suggested another take for protection against a technical glitch, but the director iced the set. "If anyone scratches that piece of film, I'll hurl *him*—farther and harder."

"That was fabulous," AJ gushed. "Where'd you get the idea of comforting it?"

Ricky shrugged. "Just came to me."

"How about dinner tonight, you and me, to celebrate?"

"Maybe. I'll probably be pretty tired."

The rest of the crew rushed over to laud Ricky. No one noticed AJ heading back to the production office, head down.

═

The citizens of Lo An wandered freely onto the set, ruining shots by popping into the background and toying with the equipment. After Ricky passed on their dinner to stay in for the evening, AJ met with the village elders to encourage them to keep the looky-loos away. He gave the international signal for "How much is it going to cost?" Mayor Kim demanded fifty thousand baht and a milk cow. Before AJ could tell him to forget it, an assistant announced that a David Begelman was on the line from Los Angeles.

The studio chief was apoplectic. Russ had sent a confidential memo arguing that the scripted ending of the movie was disastrous and complaining that he couldn't get an alternative because Jastrow was both writer *and* producer. So Russ had penned his own. AJ downplayed the drama—Russ's desire for a slam-bang finale reflected a lack of confidence in the audience rather than a genuine problem. Begelman wasn't interested in a long-distance script conference. Studio chiefs regarded the producer, director, and actors on location like children horsing around upstairs. They could scuffle, but God help them if Dad had to come up to stop the ruckus. AJ promised he and Matovich would resolve their conflict.

Incensed, he searched the compound. Finally, one of the assistants said Russ had headed down to the set, which made no sense. The path was dark. So was AJ's mood. He heard the music of the Kinks over the screeching of the gibbons. Another of his penetrating headaches clamped down and he half-imagined he was hallucinating. Or maybe he was suffering some weird Asian flu, since swallowing was difficult. The closer he got, the clearer the music. Someone had lit the set for a night shoot. Through the dense foliage AJ saw a 10K light positioned in front of Russ's trailer, illuminating a Felliniesque picnic. Blankets covered the ground, but sex replaced the hot dogs and potato salad.

Bo Alpert had mounted one of the wardrobe girls doggie style. As he pumped like a piston, she squirmed so frantically that his cock slipped out. Bo was too stoned to notice that he was fucking air. Meanwhile, Matovich was lying naked on his back, his viewfinder focused on the crotch of a Thai girl who squatted over him. He masturbated furiously. Ricky stood to Russ's right, his jeans at his ankles. A village girl no older than eleven sucked his prick, which barely fit in her lollipop mouth. Drugs and pleasure fogged his eyes.

A bullet shattered AJ's brain. The fragments flew like shards of crystal. One must have severed his optic nerve, because black paint splashed over his left eye. AJ lunged toward Matovich, but his throat was so constricted that all that emerged from his mouth was "Rrrrr!"

The girl atop Matovich pissed in terror. He knocked her on her butt, then looked at AJ. "Get away from me, you motherfucker!"

Ricky grabbed for him, but he backhanded his son, splitting his lip. "You littttt ssss . . ." He screamed for the "little shit to stay out of this," but words refused to form. AJ seized the tripod supporting the camera—its pointed end a makeshift bayonet—and raised the weapon over Russ. But the fingertips of his left hand numbed. The sensation shot up his arm and shoulder until his entire left side evaporated. All his weight balanced on his right leg as the tripod dropped harmlessly to the ground. He teetered, then collapsed. Matovich pushed his dead-weight aside and yelled something to Bo Alpert. They hightailed it into the jungle.

His son crawled to his side. "Dad!"

"Gggg Suuuu nimm . . . !" AJ spoke as if underwater.

"What's wrong? I'll get help." Ricky raced to the hotel.

AJ passed out, sure that he'd become the final American casualty of Vietnam.

CHAPTER 34

AJ's view of the world narrowed to a few square inches. Lying supine, strapped into a stretcher in the rear of the company's scout plane, he focused on the blackness outside the passenger window. Muted purple crept through, creating a rectangular bruise. Dawn. After last night he hadn't expected to see another. As the light brightened, he spotted his comrade in arms—the beetle— still ensnared in the double glass. Behind him AJ heard the metallic clack of a seat belt and the sound of muffled voices as Sung Si briefed the pilot. Gunning his engines for takeoff, the man glanced warily at AJ. "You folks have a higher body count than the Marines at Nha Trang."

"Please fly low—do not go over mountains."

"Forget it, lady. There's fog in the valleys between here and Chiang Mai. We'd wind up hitting something a whole lot bigger than us."

"If you go high, the air too thin and he will die."

Their debate was irrelevant to AJ, since he counted his life expectancy in hours. He wanted to tell them that death in a fiery plane crash might elevate his obit to the front page of *Variety,* but it was useless because he sounded like Peter Sellers mocking an eastern European dialect. Whatever Sung Si had injected had doused the inferno in his head, creating a swampy dullness. A razor blade seemed to be lodged across his esophagus, which made swallowing impossible, so he breathed through his nose and ignored the drool leaking from his mouth. The muscles on his right side contracted spasmodically, as if a rodent was scrambling from biceps to calf in an effort to escape a sinking ship. He preferred that discomfort to the paralysis on his left side, where he couldn't move a single extremity. His left eye was totally blind, though the vision in his right remained sharp.

As the plane lurched into the air, he began the dreaded test. With his working hand he reached to his crotch. It was damp. Great, he'd pissed himself. But that wasn't his primary concern. AJ fondled his penis—nothing. Forget a hard-on under the circumstances, but he could always generate a little action. He squeezed harder—flaccid. Rubbing the shaft, slapping, pinching—dead meat. His hair tingled, his stomach vomited up last night's peanut chicken, and his working eye twitched SOS. He screamed at himself to relax—why worry when he was going to die imminently? But suppose he didn't; what if he lived a half life, buried only from the waist down? AJ prayed for the stroke to immobilize his imagination. Instead, it stampeded. He gagged and clawed at his body until something sharp pierced his upper arm and his mind went as inert as his cock.

=

In Ricky's twisted dreams the head that kept rolling into his hands wasn't Deeves's and it wasn't rubber and plastic—it was his father's flesh and bone. Was he responsible for what had happened? Jack Sobel had explained that Dad had suffered a stroke. If Ricky had gone to dinner with him, maybe it would have been different. He'd lied about being tired because he wanted to celebrate with Russ and Bo. They were allies, they believed in him. The girl they'd arranged for him looked younger than his sister, but she claimed to be sixteen and he was desperate to break his cherry. The orgy must have totally grossed the old man out.

A knock on the door. "It's me, Russ."

Ricky jumped to let Matovich in. "Is he dead?"

"Just the opposite. They landed in Chiang Mai and he's headed to the hospital. Production's shut down for today. The studio's sending an executive. Until then I'm in charge."

"We fucked up, didn't we?" Ricky asked tentatively.

"If that's what you think, we *need* to talk." Russ reversed the desk chair and sat facing him. "Your dad's been weird for a while. Shit, the way he paraded around, some guys had nicknamed him Ho Chi Minh. I told them to keep their mouths shut, but the word was out. Who knows why he couldn't cope? This is a fucked-up place. But you can be certain that it had nothing to do with you or last night."

"You really think so?"

"I *know* so. But it's my job—and your job as his son—to circle the wagons. I'm not going to tell anyone he tried to kill me with the tripod. He'd look like such a lunatic that no studio would hire him again. Hell, the Thai police might even prosecute."

That possibility had never occurred to Ricky. "Are they going to question us?"

"I'm going to make sure they don't. But you, Bo, and I have to make a pact to protect him."

"Okay, if you think it's best."

Matovich shook his hand. "When we first met, I wasn't sure whether you had guts. That's why I tested you in that tunnel. You're a pro. I don't mean to make lemonade out of lemons, but I'm betting these events will actually *help* your performance."

After the director left Ricky listened to music, then read philosophy. "What does not destroy me makes me stronger." Maybe Nietzsche's advice made sense—for both him and his father.

=

After a night and day of travel Steph and Ray arrived at the Chiang Mai hospital, where they located AJ at the end of a long ward that housed a dozen patients with ailments from rickets to cancer. The smells of lemongrass and curry clashed with those of bedpans and antiseptics. AJ sipped water through a straw, but the liquid ran back out of his mouth. Four feet away, Steph realized, and he doesn't know we're here.

"Move to his right," Sung Si suggested gently. "He has blind spot to left."

Steph shifted. "Hello, AJ." His smile was ghoulish since only half his mouth turned upward. Her tears must have freaked him out because in frustration AJ knocked the IV stand to the floor. "Isn't there a private room available?"

Sung Si shook her head, reinserting the needle. "This most private room in hospital."

"Let me handle it," Ray whispered.

Steph decided to relate news from the home front to calm AJ down. Joe Wizan was going to join them until he'd had a violent reaction to his typhoid injection. *The Godfather, Part II* grosses continued to set records. Jess's class had elected her president, and Maggie's show had debuted two weeks ago, which was why she hadn't made the trip. Steph felt her act growing old. She felt herself growing old. The victim in the bed was not the man she'd known for nearly eighteen years. Thankfully, Stark returned with a troop of orderlies, and within thirty minutes the staff had cleared a room used to store extra bedding. It was cramped, but AJ was the only patient in it.

"How did—"

"You're now looking at the Fran Stark wing of the Chiang Mai hospital. Come on, the chief surgeon's ready for us."

Dr. Patpong explained that AJ's stroke had damaged his middle cerebral artery. A blood vessel had burst, leaking blood into the firm tissue of the brain. Pressure from the bleeding had pinched surrounding vessels, shutting off more blood flow and producing further stroke effects. The doctor believed that the patient would die unless the bleeding in the brain slowed dramatically. The lasting damage couldn't be assessed until the swelling subsided.

"But he understands what's going on?" Steph asked quietly.

"He has understood from beginning," Sung Si noted. "Being not able to speak make him very anxious."

"I bet," Ray noted dryly. "How quickly can he begin rehabilitation?"

"That is not a good idea," Dr. Patpong advised. "He must not be moved until his condition has stabilized."

After the conference, however, Sung Si pulled them aside. "You are right to ask," she whispered. "In my country doctors are not modern. They only wait. But journals I read from the West say it better to start soon." Before Steph could press for a risk assessment, a nurse rushed over waving a piece of paper. In scrawled capital letters—still unmistakably AJ's—was the single word HOME.

=

When AJ's Thai nurse asked him if he could get her tickets to Disneyland when she visited the United States next year, he assumed he was no longer on the critical list. Swallowing proved less painful, and he forced down saliva for the first time. But danger lurked. Every time someone stuck him with a needle, he worried that it hadn't been sterilized. Were the drinking straws being reused? And the drugs—hell, they'd probably been made in Communist China by workers with filthy fingernails. Thank God for John Veitch. The Columbia executive had chartered a plane to fly him out tomorrow. In a crisis, Hollywood took care of its own.

That was more than he could say about his mother. She could have ignored the network's pressure to remain on the air, but apparently her audience came first. The one time she had called to wish him well had caused a stir among the hospital staff because *Miss Mayhem* was a big hit in Thailand.

"Hey, man, you look like shit."

The voice startled AJ. He sensed a figure emerging to his left. Even though it was only a shadow, it was the first image to register in his blind eye. He banged the bed in frustration because he hadn't been able to tell anyone he never wanted to see Russ Matovich again.

"I'm sorry this happened." The director was maddeningly matter-of-fact. "When the guy from Columbia arrived, I told him that you'd been under tremendous pressure. It didn't surprise Veitch—he mentioned that you'd seemed unstable over the phone. If the local police learn about the girls, the booze, and the Thai stick, this could be a real mess for everyone. So I covered, explaining that we were blocking a scene when you dropped by. The stroke just hit . . . wham!"

The only one Russ gave a shit about covering for was Russ. Even in Hollywood his blossoming reputation would suffer when people learned he used hard drugs and had pimped for a minor. Telling the truth and exposing the bastard's bullshit was reason enough for AJ to get his voice back.

Matovich read his mind. "Bo . . . and Ricky completely backed up my story."

A tremor sent AJ's right arm bouncing up and down on the mattress.

"So if you say anything different . . . well, that's up to you."

His son's lie created a new kind of paralysis. In order to make his case AJ would have to get his voice back, which was iffy at best. Assuming that he did, would anyone believe him, or would they view his explanation as a paranoid fantasy resulting from the brain injury? Finally, suppose he could convince them. People would regard him as a villain and a failed father. To punish Matovich, Columbia might shut the movie down. Scandal would ruin all of them. AJ squeezed Matovich's hand to signify agreement.

"The picture's going to be great," Russ added cheerfully. "So concentrate on getting better. I'll look for you at the premiere."

CHAPTER 35

AJ conducted a mental witch-hunt to determine why him, why a stroke. Rule out the "Jastrow curse" or a genetic predisposition to high blood pressure, even a sin in a past life, as the monk in the Chiang Mai hospital had proposed—those explanations rendered him a comfy victim. Although he ranked a player in Hollywood, it had always been on someone else's team. Mike Todd, Stan Kamen, and Charlie Bluhdorn had shielded him, so he'd never developed the thick skin and steel backbone to master a monster like Matovich. Paralysis was harsh, but poetically just punishment.

As a cripple in the land of the radiant smile, hearty handshake, and vigorous gait, AJ needed a hideout to recuperate from his shame and pain. None promised more privacy than Cedars-Sinai Medical Center. Its studio-studded board of directors had dedicated the secure eighth floor—more Hilton than hospital—to Hollywood's disabled VIPs. The premium package included cutting-edge doctors, discreet nurses, edible food, and Lichtensteins and Stellas on the walls.

Once the swelling in his brain subsided, AJ could make sense again, but his voice slurred and it took him a minute to stumble out a complete sentence. The perverse side effect of the stroke was enduring visitors who mistook his sluggish speech for mental deficiency and projected onto his prolonged silences their insecurity that a stroke could fell them. He blocked their maddening babble by imagining himself the healthy one in the room and observing *their* neurotic styles.

The town's powerful executives treated him as contagious. David Begelman broke eye contact and Bob Evans deposited his muffin basket and vanished. Most of his friends anxiously prattled about whatever interested them, whether it was Julia Phillips gossiping about her latest lover or Stan Kamen complaining about his clients. AJ's devastation muted gentler spirits, like Stephanie, but encouraged others to revisit their tragic pasts. Leon Ginsberg recounted horrors of family members gassed by the Nazis, while Ray Stark talked openly for the first time about the suicide of his son Peter. Maggie compensated for skipping

Thailand by pressuring the staff at Cedars for better care. Only Jess avoided monologues, waiting patiently for his responses and joining a conversation. His daughter soon topped his wish list of visitors.

This afternoon's guest intrigued AJ because he was the ultimate survivor. In 1973 Adolph Zukor had celebrated his one hundredth birthday at a televised party at Radio City Music Hall. He had the permanently stooped shoulders and bowed head of a man who'd delivered eulogies for almost everyone he knew. "I remember your bar mitzvah as if it were yesterday," he intoned. "It was a magnificent haftorah reading. Your father was so proud, then he drops dead."

Did Zukor think it helpful to remind him of the second worst day of his life? Maybe Promethean insensitivity led to longevity.

"You look like I feel—useless. Ever since that ungrateful bastard Barney Balaban replaced me, I've been stuck in the desert. I know what Moses went through. If you're going to wind up a vegetable, get out of Hollywood. All they eat here is meat."

How could Zukor be this angry after all his good fortune? "Thhankss fff the advice."

AJ turned to his mail. Opening each envelope took five minutes and was hardly worth the inevitable Hallmark card with its brief "thinking of you." Infinitely more rewarding were the occasional handwritten notes, like the one from the pro at Riviera suggesting an early date for their next round. The return address on a large manila envelope chilled him. Despite the Gunfight at the Malibu Corral, Steve's failure to visit shocked and hurt. But AJ couldn't accept the contents—a standard eight-by-ten publicity shot of the actor in his *Towering Inferno* gear with a scribbled "Best wishes for a speedy recovery." He knew McQueen's signature; an assistant had forged this one. Securing the picture in his teeth, AJ ripped off a strip with his right hand. He rotated it and ripped again. By dinner it was in shreds.

But he preferred the stress of activity to the isolation after the nurses cleared away his flank steak and mashed potatoes. The January nights felt glacial in their darkness and endurance. The polar bear dream recurred with ghoulish variations. His mother wielded the knife; he was dancing with Russ; a team of huskies came to the rescue, but on closer inspection the sled dogs were William Morris agents. At first he watched television from the set mounted divinely above his bed, but the studios had recently started running commercials for their movies. Maybe it worked for marketing, but every spot stabbed him with the realization that someone else did what he might never do again. Shutting off the TV with the remote, AJ closed his eyes, but couldn't beat the rush of fear.

What if he didn't get better? He'd heard the innuendo of the doctors and had evaluated the grim resolve of his nurses. Suppose the best he could manage was to talk like a dim-witted alcoholic? Suppose someone always had to escort him to the toilet? For weeks he had cooled his panic with the prospect of suicide. But tonight even that illusion evaporated—he lacked the nerve. His heart hammered and a migraine clutched his head like a vise. Certain he was suffering another stroke, AJ jammed the button on his night table. The simple act calmed him and by the time the orderly arrived, he claimed his call was a mistake. The nurse changed his pajamas and sheets, which were soaked in sweat, and gave him a pill, which he swallowed greedily. Its gift was dreamless sleep.

═

"Three, two, one . . . you're on the air."

Maggie ignored the self-important young man with the headset. She'd paid too damn much attention to the advice of others when her afternoon talk show had debuted four months ago. Fawn over guests and moderate her opinions—in other words, copy the competition. But the audience had rejected a defanged Miss Mayhem, and even reruns of I Love Lucy had beaten Maggie's World in the ratings sweeps. Her producers had panicked, whispering cancellation, so she'd informed Mike Ovitz that she wanted control of the show and a new format—a no-holds-barred interview with a single guest. Mike no longer carried the clout of William Morris because he and four other agents had defected to form a new agency called Creative Artists, but he'd somehow convinced the show's syndicators to grant both demands.

On the downbeat of her new Helen Reddy theme song, Maggie parted the curtains to the applause of her live studio audience. "Today's guest was supposed to be my friend Ronnie Reagan, but he called a few hours ago to say he was stuck in Sacramento and asked to come tomorrow. Even I can't refuse a governor. That left my staff phoning everyone to find a substitute. But none interested me, so I'll use our time to share a crisis that's affected my family."

People leaned forward, anxious for her well-being and titillated by what disaster might touch the mighty.

"My son—his name is AJ—recently suffered a terrible stroke while producing a film in Thailand. Every time I visit and see his palsied body, I feel like screaming. My guest today was an eyewitness. He's one of the stars of the film. Please welcome my grandson, Ricky Jastrow."

Maggie saw how scared he was. Was her inspiration a blunder? Ricky hadn't wanted to come, but since returning from location he'd remained withdrawn, even from her. He needed to talk. And AJ needed help. Despite their august reputations, her son's doctors did *bupkis* but reduce his expectations of recovery. Publicizing his case could shake things up.

"Tell me, what was it like to see your father in such pain?"

She hadn't prepped him—that rule stood for all guests. Ricky couldn't make it through a sentence. Only after racking sobs did he describe his feelings that night. He was afraid, terribly afraid that when he touched his dad, he'd feel stone-cold death.

Maggie knew the show was a success when a production assistant slipped her a note from the control booth during a commercial break. Phone calls from viewers around the country had overwhelmed the station with suggestions for AJ's rehabilitation. Ricky hugged her in thanks just as the light flashed that they were back on the air.

=

AJ grimaced as the venetian blinds snapped open, highlighting his pasty complexion and backlighting his tormentor. "Laterrr . . ."

"Rise and shine, amigo!" With his bandanna, accent, and ponytail, Oscar de la Cuadre looked more like Carlos Santana than a physical therapist. Not any physical therapist, but the best in the business. "You look like Casper the Ghost after a bender."

"Fuck you."

"Easy for you to say."

"Bastard." Cursing was an "automatic"—the only speech AJ could utter without impediment because it required no complex thought.

"Let me hear you do 'Peter Piper picked a pepper,' then I'll be impressed."

No one bullied Oscar. His medical career had started at the age of ten caring for peyote-addled Indians in an old-age home in Monterey. A decade ago he'd sneaked across the border, then worked double shifts as a janitor in a San Diego veterans' hospital until a doctor had noticed his natural skill with patients. Giving paraplegic soldiers back their lives was his specialty. One of those soldiers had tracked Maggie down after watching her show to say no one could get AJ back on his feet faster than this Mexican kid. Officials at Cedars had huffed and puffed, claiming their own people were the best, but had finally agreed to bring him on board if Maggie paid his salary.

Oscar was the only reason AJ forgave his mother for making him the poster child for stroke victims. He suspected that her pitch was a last-ditch attempt to improve ratings, which was exactly what had happened after the festival of tears. "The end justifies the means," his mother had replied. That had always been her philosophy, in contrast to Dad's. But Harry was long gone, while Maggie graced the cover of that drippy new magazine *People*.

For ninety days Oscar encouraged, cajoled, and bluffed AJ into accomplishing the Herculean exercises designed to restore his self-sufficiency. As feeling incrementally returned to his left side, AJ assumed that all the normal functions would click into gear. But Oscar explained his muscles had "gone *loco*," and he needed to relearn the simplest of moves. Putting one foot in front of the other required as much effort as a normal person expended climbing three flights of stairs. The ten steps to the bathroom felt like ascending a thirty-story high-rise. He gasped following five repetitions.

Rousing his paralyzed hand and arm, which seemed to weigh as much as a sack of charcoal, required the same kind of energy. To keep from boring his charge, Oscar gave AJ a mission not mentioned in the manuals—picking his nose with left hand. When he succeeded, the two men celebrated with shots of tequila. Immediately after the stroke, male nurses had supervised and assisted in all AJ's transitions—from bed to wheelchair to toilet and back. But this morning he rose alone, strapped an L-shaped orthotic brace on his left leg, and with the support of a four-pronged cane struggled to the bathroom. Once upgraded to the "contact-guard assist level," he needed hands-on help only for potentially dangerous activities.

Oscar wheeled him to the lobby and announced, "You take it from here."

"Excuse me?"

"You need to pick up some forms at the front desk." When Oscar refused to drive, AJ pushed the chair, but his therapist held it in place. "The free ride's over. Walk there and get them."

Walk—into a sea of people, all in a rush, none aware of his plight?

The prospect reduced AJ to a five-year-old crossing his first busy inter-section alone.

Oscar massaged his shoulder. "When I swam the Rio Grande, I knew the INS was out gunning for me. They'd shot a wetback two nights be-fore. You know what made me run?" AJ shook his head. "The place I was running *from* really sucked."

AJ mapped the traffic patterns, then inched forward, almost tripping with his first step. Halfway across, no one had passed within ten feet, and his confidence built. He put less pressure on the cane and even swiveled to smile at Oscar. But he turned back to see a fat family of five racing to the candy machine behind him. AJ pivoted, and the littlest boy brushed his robe like a matador's cape. The whole drama took five sec-onds, but in its aftermath his strength flooded back. His body per-formed. The final thirty feet were a Sousa march. When he gave his name, the clerk at the desk pulled out his file and handed him a sheet of paper headed "Instructions for Leaving the Hospital and Aftercare." Oscar materialized by his side. "Yyyou ttth . . . you think I'm ready?"

"The doctors believe you've hit the wall. Their books say stroke vic-tims get back ninety percent of all the functions they'll ever get back in the first three months. No disrespect, but I think they're full of shit."

"You're ssssaying I cccan be hundred ppercent?"

"With a percent or two for wear and tear? Yeah. But it's going to re-quire the *cojones* of a bull, 'cause now your progress is going to be tor-ture. Most people quit and settle for being alive. If you want more, I'll be there for you."

Snapping off the light by his bedside that night, AJ imagined the pos-sibilities rather than the limitations in his life.

=

A close-up of an ant—otherworldly, implacable, and ugly—filled the opening frames of *Don't Tread on Me*. A column marched across a de-caying palm frond, their destination a squashed mango. But before feasting the colony mired in a pool of congealed blood. A title appeared on-screen: "Produced by AJ Jastrow." It faded away as a military boot crushed the ants. The boot belonged to a weary, unshaven Michael Douglas as Lieutenant Farber, leading his men on patrol. Superim-posed over Farber's footprint was "Directed by Russell Matovich." Gunfire erupted and the VC launched their ambush. The symbolism might be a touch heavy-handed, but AJ couldn't criticize Matovich's eye.

Like producers from the nickelodeon days, he'd let his fantasies flourish in advance of viewing the first cut of his movie. It lived as a classic in his mind, even though AJ knew his fantasies would surely be dashed by the first changeover of reels. After an hour, however, *Don't Tread on Me* commanded him. He ceased being the writer-producer and became an ordinary moviegoer. The visual highlight was the shoot-out in the Vietcong tunnels, so intensely disorienting that the only other person in the screening room at Columbia—a prematurely balding marketing executive named Andy Faddiman—lay down on the floor to regain his equilibrium.

Douglas captured Farber's determination to remain in control. As Sergeant Deeves a young actor named Paul Michael Glaser instilled the standard wise guy with an endearing edge, which promised to make his upcoming decapitation devastating. And Ricky . . . he was so genuine that AJ stowed his ambivalence. The battle at the ghost temple played more violently than in his script—and more effectively. By the end he'd dug his nails into the upholstered seat.

But then . . . what the hell was this? In a new scene Corporal Oman raped a Vietnamese girl after interrogating her, while two other soldiers watched. Then came a rewritten version of the squad arguing over whether or not to enter the village. In AJ's scene Farber *convinced* Covey and Oman to join him. Russ had Farber *force* them to accompany him by aiming his M-16 at their heads and cursing them as cowards. As for AJ's ending . . . it played only in his imagination. Farber, Oman, and Covey patrolled the village to verify the absence of Vietcong. A B-52 roared overhead. The three soldiers waved it off, then watched in horror as the plane dropped its napalm bombs, sucking the oxygen out of the air, incinerating the village—and reducing the heroes to ash.

It amazed AJ how instantaneously tears could form. His script had proclaimed the triumph of courage and reason over fear and fury. Russ had corrupted it—no, he'd obliterated it. The message in Farber's death and his failure to save the innocent civilians of Tet Vanh was that insanity reigned.

From Andy Faddiman's concealed grimace, it was apparent that Matovich's ending also slashed the commercial prospects of *Don't Tread on Me.* The marketing executive searched for a politic phrase. "It's like nothing I've ever seen."

"Be honest," AJ ordered.

"The last reel was like watching baby seals being clubbed to death . . . but not as much fun."

AJ hobbled down the hall to David Begelman's office, where he practiced deep-breathing exercises while the studio chief begged Julia Phillips, who was scouting locations in North Dakota, to control the spiraling costs on *Close Encounters*. When he finally hung up, David regained his aplomb. "You must be very proud of your film. We certainly are."

"What happened tto the otthherr ending?"

"Where the three soldiers stop the massacre? Russ never shot it." AJ gasped. "As you know, the production was a month behind schedule."

"Wwwe have to gooo bback and shoot it."

"I understand that your script was different, but as you know, AJ, film is a living organism. We agreed with Russ that his ending was more in keeping with the way the footage evolved. It's also closer to the attitude of the country toward the war."

"Then ttake my nnnn . . . nname off it."

"Do me a favor—let me amend that, do *both* of us a favor. Think about it and let's talk next week."

The temperature in Burbank shot past one hundred degrees. Sweat poured from AJ like a fountain, and he tripped on the broad, flat stone steps outside the executive building. An assistant carrying the cans of film containing *Don't Tread on Me* back to the editing room paused by his side. "Pops, are you okay?"

"Pppops?" He knocked aside the helping hand.

"Hey, I was just trying to help."

Out of the corner of his eye AJ spotted his driver. The man was engrossed in a newspaper. Fifty yards away—the car might as well have been parked in Ventura. Was Begelman smirking at him from his office window? He turned to tell him to fuck off, but he lacked the voice or the control to point his middle finger in the right direction. He had to prove to those bastards that they couldn't run him out of Hollywood. His legs ached, but he marched to the car.

CHAPTER 36

"Do you take this woman to be your lawfully wedded wife?"

This time around, AJ had a seat and no lines. Perhaps that explained his foreboding as he sat dry-eyed among the guests at his ex-wife's wedding. François Volk was imperially slim. Didn't he like his own cooking? Prematurely gray hair and a Gallic nose gave him the appearance of a swaying silver birch. Like most French émigrés, Volk detested the slick impermanence and parochialism of Los Angeles but preferred stardom here to his desultory career as a chef in Lyon. The guy overcooked with an arrogant attitude that promised to make him a son of a bitch as a spouse.

"*Oui.*"

François's response struck AJ as a petty attempt to maintain his identity, but it drew indulgent smiles from those packed into the trellised garden of his Bistro Gamin by the ocean in Santa Monica. They delighted in associating with the man responsible for the town's dining renaissance. If a chef could become a celebrity, who was next? The justice of the peace turned his attention to the bride. At their wedding Steph's beauty had stunned, whereas now it soothed, time having transformed the ingenue to leading lady. Did her bright smile conceal an underlying melancholy upon hearing ". . . in sickness and in health, till death do us part?" No, his imagination suffered a case of male-pattern jealousy.

AJ had dreaded this last Sunday in September since receiving his invitation, but Steph had wanted him to attend, and her support during his recuperation made declining impossible. He nervously straightened his green-and-blue paisley tie. Two hours ago he'd realized in horror that he couldn't make the knot. On his tenth attempt he'd poked his eye with his thumb, and blinded by tears of frustration, he phoned Oscar for help. That setback aside, today was his "coming out." The California summer sun camouflaged his pallor, and a dogged regimen of exercise had enabled him to regain most of his gross muscular functions. And while fine motor skills, such as signing his name and flossing, remained erratic, AJ was no longer a cripple. His world needed to know.

"I now pronounce you man and wife."

The restaurateur's kiss was so French that AJ averted his eyes to Ricky, who was seated next to him in the third row. The boy maintained a straight-ahead stare. "You okay?"

"Why shouldn't I be?"

"That kiss made me uncomfortable," AJ whispered.

"It's a free country. She can fuck who she wants."

An impenetrable wall existed between them, and AJ lacked the energy or desire to knock it down. Seventeen years ago, when he'd first seen his infant son resting on Stephanie's breasts, he could not have imagined disliking Ricky. "Watch your mouth. Your mom deserves to enjoy today."

"Fine." It took an actor to pack so sullen a snarl into a single word.

AJ took his daughter's hand up the aisle. After he'd checked out of Cedars, Jessie had regularly stayed at his beach house to help care for him. To his amazement—and dismay—he'd realized how little he knew about her. The daughter he'd discovered reminded him of her mother in younger days. Jess possessed a spirit that embraced the world, missing even the hint of entitlement born into most Hollywood kids. The physical resemblance extended beyond their blue eyes and freckles, because his daughter dressed like Steph had in the Eisenhower years. Her passion for Sha Na Na and infatuation with the Fonz spoke of a yearning for the imagined innocence of an earlier era.

Nibbling on foie gras, Jess shook her head in wonder. "François's cooking is amazing. We have roast duck and crème brûlée in the refrigerator for snacks."

So that's why she was pudgy. Jess had accepted the remarriage more easily than her brother. It was probably her trusting spirit, which could take a hell of a beating if her new stepfather—Christ, even the word pissed AJ off—turned out to be a jerk. "That's great. Get his recipes and cook them for me."

"Dad, do you think you'll get remarried?"

"No, I think those days are over."

"It would be okay. Most of my friends' folks are splitting, so I could try and find you someone."

"No need to do that."

"My math teacher is single . . . and kind of cute if you don't mind the chalk in her hair."

AJ hugged her fiercely. How could he explain why matchmaking wouldn't work? "I'll take a look at the next parent-teacher conference."

Pot filled the air and the dancing started in earnest, with Van McCoy's

"The Hustle" blasting from the speakers. AJ hated the synthesizer-dominated sound and used his stroke as an excuse for an early exit.

"Are you okay?" Steph asked.

"Fine, just tired." He hugged her gently. "Be happy."

"I will, but, AJ, I want you to find the same kind of happiness." She smiled. "Maybe not quite as much, but you know what I mean."

Fat fucking chance. Unless he found a frigid woman who loved him, AJ planned to remain single for the rest of his life. He couldn't even consider dating, because if he cared about someone and found her sexy, how was he supposed to demonstrate it—a box of chocolates? Sure, the urologist had given him a clean bill of health, but the guy didn't have to get it up. AJ had had no success, even with the help of Oscar's porno magazines.

On his way to the car he spotted a phone booth, then extracted from his wallet a piece of paper whose folds suggested it had long been hidden there. He lifted and put down the receiver a half dozen times before dialing. A woman answered, and he gave his name, then listened.

"Home, Mr. Jastrow?" his driver inquired.

"Yeah . . . no. Take me to 12075 Wonderland Avenue . . . the long way."

His destination was a funky Spanish bungalow on a side street off Outpost in the heart of the Hollywood Hills. Thick stucco walls and narrow recessed windows assured privacy. Linda Moreno greeted AJ by swinging open a door heavy enough for a dungeon. He fought the urge to run away by remembering that he couldn't run anywhere. Linda was exotically beautiful. Her shiny brown hair cascaded over the back of a white terry-cloth bathrobe. Though she was in her early forties, her olive skin remained unblemished. She extended a hand with graceful fingers that reminded him of a classical guitarist. "Oscar told me all about you. I'm pleased that you took his suggestion and called."

Her business card said "Sexual Healer," but her price for the night suggested top-of-the-line call girl. Linda's every move was sensual and unhurried. Unbuttoning his shirt, she ran her hands over his upper body, complimenting him on his physique. He felt less like a freak. As she massaged Tiger Balm gently into his shoulders, AJ fumbled with the belt of her robe. She wore nothing underneath. He gasped and his hands began to shake. "I don't think I can please you," he whispered.

Linda gently put a finger to his lips. "That's not what's bothering you, is it?"

AJ shook his head, a child caught in a fib.

"You're afraid you'll have another stroke if you get excited, even though the doctors have controlled your blood pressure. I want you to trust me."

Did he have a choice? Standing naked, a desirable woman touching him, arousing him . . . sex meant too much, he would wither without it. They fell back on her king-sized bed and made love as hard as he dared. After fifteen minutes she churned her hips and pelvis, trapped him inside her, then clutched tightly with her inner thighs. AJ worried that his orgasm would drown her. His body vibrated, and for a moment he waited for . . . nothing.

"What are you thinking?"

"You know those cults that predict the end of the world at a specific time? I always wondered if their members were disappointed when the sun came up the next day." He jumped up with a smile from an earlier time. "Now I know."

=

As the last of the crowd filed into the premiere of *Don't Tread on Me* at the Coronet in Manhattan, AJ started across Third Avenue and Fifty-ninth Street in the opposite direction. "Get your ass back here," Ray shouted.

"I'm going to kill an hour at Bloomingdale's."

"That's nuts, AJ." Stark came over and yanked him back onto the curb. "You've been around long enough to know that no one can guarantee how these things turn out. But it's still a movie!"

"It's just not *my* movie."

Stark shook his head. "You're the only producer I know who doesn't grab all the credit for success he can."

"We're not looking at success."

"You don't know that."

"Come on. You heard what Levy said." On the flight east aboard Columbia's private jet, Norman Levy, the head of marketing for Columbia, had complained that exhibitors in the South and Midwest had refused to book *Don't Tread on Me,* arguing that moviegoers needed a break from years of coverage of Vietnam on television.

"Is this what I should expect working with you?" Ray asked facetiously.

Stark's offer of head of production under him at Rastar was AJ's best job option. "I promise, I'll be a barrel of laughs." When the light changed, he again headed off to Bloomie's.

After the movie the line of limousines idling in front of the theater reminded him of a funeral procession, so AJ hailed a cab to Tavern on the Green for the party. His driver spoke only Pashtu and could barely find Central Park. Where were the wonderful Checker cabs from his youth? Crammed behind a bulletproof partition in the backseat of a Chrysler without a suspension, AJ rubbed his left leg to maintain circulation.

Gauging an honest reaction to a film from an industry audience required a fluency in Hollywoodese. The operative word tonight was *intense.* Julia Phillips had modified it with "unbearably," Peter Bart had added "unbelievably," and Stan Kamen had used "unflinchingly." Combined with one too many slaps on the back, this meant that his friends found the film as grim and empty as he did. Hang in, he told himself, until eleven o'clock, then escape with dignity.

It was a fine plan . . . until AJ caught the reflection of Russ Matovich in the picture windows that fronted Central Park. "What did you think?" the director asked with feigned casualness.

AJ hadn't called after screening the movie in L.A. "It's ugly."

"Ugly? That's all you've got to say?"

"You don't want me to go on."

Russ tried regaining his balance. "You're the only one who sees it that way, except for those idiots in the test screening."

"Those idiots are the public."

"What kind of a producer bad-mouths his own film?"

"The kind that can't tolerate a sick, lying, egomaniacal director."

Matovich laughed savagely. "If you weren't already a cripple, I'd make you one."

AJ lowered his head and butted the director in his chest, knocking him to the floor. The first referee to the scene was Matovich's new agent, Mike Ovitz, who yanked his client away. "Cool down, Russell. You're the star tonight." Matovich shook off Ovitz's grasp and stalked away. Mike soothingly put his arm around AJ. "I know you two didn't get along during shooting. Russ is hotheaded, but he's a brilliant talent who's going to direct great movies. And we both know directors make movies happen. There's no reason why some of them shouldn't be for the producer who gave him his first break."

"Mike, let me be crystal clear—your client will never work with me again."

The agent smiled wanly and patted AJ's hand. "This isn't the time to discuss the future. Let's just enjoy the moment."

AJ sat sipping a Courvoisier when he heard a familiar voice over his shoulder.

"Are you all right?"

"Fine, Mom. Just tired from standing on my feet."

"You did well to get the movie made," she volunteered. "It's much better than you think."

"Dad would have hated it."

"Harry's been gone almost thirty years. Give him—and it—a rest."

"I wanted him to rest in peace." They never talked on the same wavelength about the most important man in either of their lives. "I'm sorry Leon couldn't make it. "

"He sends his regrets, but *The Newlyweds* is taking all his time these days."

"Another jewel in the crown." Ginsberg's latest series about a husband-and-wife spy team was his third show in the top ten this season.

"He's amazing, isn't he? Right from *Kelly and Cohen* he's had an incredible eye for what people want." She spoke in an uncharacteristically soft voice. "Leon's asked me to marry him . . . this time I said yes. He's getting old and I want us to spend what's left of his life together."

AJ toasted with his snifter. "Relax. I've had fifteen years to get used to the idea."

At the sound of laughter they turned their gaze to a table across the room, where a television reporter interviewed Ricky. Maggie reached for the bottle of brandy. "Here's another idea to get used to. Your son's not going to college."

"Of course he is. He's applying to Carnegie-Mellon and Northwestern."

"He was only going for their drama programs, but now he's decided he can act without a B.A."

"He'll never earn a living."

"Mike Ovitz is the shrewdest man I've met in a lifetime in the business. He's agreed to represent Ricky."

How many times could he fight the same fight? "Was this your idea?"

"No. Frankly, I'd rather see him do something more significant, but he asked if I thought he was talented and I said he had the makings of a star."

"Everyone, come on over." Ovitz hefted a stack of newspapers.

"Four stars from the *Daily News*. A rave in *Newsday*." He held *The New York Times* aloft, open to Vincent Canby's review. " 'During the Vietnam War our generals claimed there was light at the end of the tunnel. Their boasts proved hollow lies. But with the arrival of *Don't Tread on Me,* the light finally shines with this dark, deeply disturbing and brilliant film, the first to look at the war without John Wayne's rose-colored glasses.' "

Ovitz smiled to the audience that circled around him. "Let's skip to the really good parts. 'Russell Matovich has directed a war movie in which the final scenes are as shocking and brave a statement about the idiocy of combat as those in *The Bridge on the River Kwai*. Michael Douglas leads a convincing cast highlighted by the indelible performance of newcomer Ricky Jastrow.' "

The *Don't Tread on Me* team might as well have won the World Series. Cheers, hugs, tears—even the requisite champagne poured over the heads of the cast by a jubilant Matovich. AJ experienced not a scintilla of joy but knew that showing anything less than public delight would mark him a spoilsport. His grin hurt. The party found a gusty second wind, but none puffed his sails. A torturous hour later he grabbed his coat and slipped out of Tavern. Thank God the only person he encountered was Paul Glaser, who was reclining in a horse-drawn cab, stoned on weed. AJ took a couple of deep hits that made Central Park look greener. On the walk back to the Plaza he mused as to how long it would take anyone at the party to realize he was gone.

The stroke had made him invisible, irrelevant, and a pain in the ass. Despite everyone's elation over the reviews, the film would prosper only in the artsy sections of Manhattan and in upmarket, intellectual enclaves. That salesguy from Columbia had called it right. *Don't Tread on Me* would hit middle America with a thud, knocking AJ back to square one as a producer. Remaining independent was suicide. Tomorrow morning he would accept Stark's offer. Nobody fucked with Ray, and starting now, that made him AJ's role model.

MANIAC

CHAPTER 37

For a man with a plan at a price tag of fifty million dollars, Tokyo was the place to be. After forty-eight hours in town, AJ understood how the country had launched itself on a trajectory to rule the world and why "Made in Japan," once synonymous with cheap and shoddy, now announced quality and innovation. People on the Ginza didn't stroll, window-shop, relax on benches, or sip cappuccinos in sidewalk cafés. They *hustled* to their destination, heads down, feet churning. But try flagging them over to get directions. For the past half hour AJ and Pete Leventhal had searched in vain for the Nippon Maritime Building.

"I'm going to have a heart attack," Pete grumped.

"Catch your breath." His lawyer was alarmingly out of shape—not just fat, but soft, buttery fat. Pete's curls had gone gray, making him look a decade older than AJ, even though their birthdays were only days apart. "Where's your sense of adventure?"

"They confiscated it in customs. Maybe you find it fun sleeping on a tatami mat, but to me it's like camping in the backyard. And I hate sushi."

AJ handed him a Snickers bar. "Don't eat it all at once. It cost me twelve bucks."

Leventhal stared at the incomprehensible street signs. "These are not our kind of people. When Commodore Perry first visited, he said the Japanese were the most xenophobic race he'd ever met."

AJ smiled. "That was 1850." Middle age, a mortgage, and marriage to a Jewish princess had subdued the spirit of the passionate activist AJ had met at Dan Cohen's antiwar symposium. As a lawyer, however, he remained sharp and challenging. "Pete, has even one person been rude to us?"

"The bowing and nodding is their aggressively passive-aggressive way of telling the gaijin to go home."

AJ clapped an arm around his friend's shoulder. "Maybe, but for us, that's not an option."

≡

Their journey had started improbably six months ago, at the premiere of *The Answer Man,* the first movie AJ made for Twentieth Century–Fox under his J² production banner. It was a comedy about a depressed failure, played by Steve Guttenberg, who discovers one morning that he's able to answer *every question* anyone asks. A young Japanese man with a ponytail, dressed head to toe in Versace, had pumped AJ's hand, saying he loved the film because he identified with the main character. Sensing a psycho, AJ had smiled and escaped to work the crowd.

But after *The Answer Man* opened at number one, Koji Keiku had tracked him down. For months AJ had been seeking a wealthy financial partner to fund a new studio. He'd talked to pension-fund managers, venture capitalists, self-made millionaires, and heirs of fortunes great and small—any investor, domestic or foreign, who evinced a twinkling of interest in Hollywood. He'd even met a character who'd turned out to be a Mob ambassador—all to no avail. Koji had explained that his father was a wealthy entrepreneur. They had secured a copy of AJ's prospectus from a banker at Nomura Securities, and its possibilities intrigued them.

An over-the-transom solicitation was too good to be true, even in a business where producers discovered stars at soda fountains. But when AJ did his homework, he learned that Seiji Keiku controlled the largest whaling fleet in Japan. Capitalizing on his countrymen's insatiable appetite for whale flesh, he'd built a fortune in excess of a half billion dollars. As for Koji, he eschewed becoming a mini-Ahab. By investing in J², he hoped to transform his principal joy—he was the ultimate movie geek—into a profession, at once impressing his father and declaring independence.

The Japanese were an unsettling choice for a partner for AJ. He still remembered the awesome image of his father hobbling off a troop transport from Tarawa. But he had no use for racial prejudice. So AJ had courted Koji assiduously, introducing him to Michael Douglas at the premiere of *Romancing the Stone* and Paul Glaser, whom Koji idolized from *Starsky and Hutch.* But when his mark had suddenly stopped returning calls, AJ had crossed his name off a dwindling list. Then on New Year's Day 1985, Koji had phoned to say his father would give him an audience in Tokyo.

=

While Pete trailed behind in a cab, AJ jogged the four blocks to Keiku Enterprises. It was no sweat for him, since he had never abandoned the vigorous regimen that had enabled him to overcome his stroke. Gone were any vestiges of limp, stutter, or twitch, and he'd even regained the eye-hand coordination required to break par at Riviera. As final proof of his recovery, he imagined that the stroke had happened to someone else.

A dentist's office displayed more character than the reception area. AJ leafed through pictures in an old whaling magazine until a photograph on the wall caught his attention. "You have to see this."

Leventhal rose from the vinyl sofa to examine the picture of a young Seiji in a World War II naval uniform. "He came from a whaling family, so it makes sense."

"But it's on the flight deck of the *Akagi*. See the date."

"October 1941."

"The *Akagi* launched the attack on Pearl Harbor." AJ shook his head in wonder. "Can you imagine what he must have felt like the morning the Zeros took off? And when they returned, dipping their wings in homage to the emperor, he probably believed his country had conquered America."

"So he was wrong . . . by forty years."

AJ glanced nervously at his watch. "I wish they'd call us. Otherwise we're not going to have enough time for our presentation."

Time always seemed to be running out. Not just any time, but the most precious kind—time to succeed. In a business dominated by youth, an almost fifty-year-old couldn't squander so much as a minute. He'd enjoyed numerous triumphs in his five years at Rastar. *Murder by Death, California Suite, The Electric Horseman,* and *The Goodbye Girl* were good movies, but they were Ray's, not his. No matter how hard he worked, he remained the guy people called when they couldn't reach Stark. When he'd quit, the gossip in town said that he'd fizzled and would never achieve the illustrious station predicted for someone with his head start in Hollywood. Compared to Barry Diller at Fox, Sid Sheinberg at Universal, and a dozen others, AJ was an overripe second banana.

And then there was money—or the absence of it. In the 1980s
Hollywood had raised the bar of financial success, making him feel like
a high jumper among pole-vaulters. Eddie Murphy had earned ten million on *Beverly Hills Cop.* Jim Brooks could make three million for directing the phone book. Terry Semel's salary for running Warners
exceeded four million, and Mike Ovitz had accumulated a personal art
collection worthy of a small museum. Although AJ earned three hundred thousand dollars, drove a Jaguar, and wore Armani, he spent every
cent he had to keep up.

Koji bounced out to greet them. "Hey, Jastrow, good to see you.
Really good, good, good."

The man's manic manner struck AJ as anything but. "Is your dad
ready?"

"Absolutely ready. Totally, totally ready." AJ made a sniffing gesture to
Pete. "Just remember, he's not an upbeat guy, so don't expect a lot of
enthusiasm. But that doesn't mean he isn't interested. So let's get
going, okay? Okay? Okay?" The guy bounced down a bleak corridor
with low ceilings to a cramped conference room.

Around a table of inlaid wood with designs of sea serpents sat a
dozen Japanese businessmen, none under sixty. Their eyes had two positions: cast down at their documents or up in obeisance to their boss.
As for the elder Keiku, *his* eyes were impassive, tiny marbles resting in
pouches of flesh. After polite introductions Seiji barked something in
Japanese that flustered Koji. "He wants you to start because they've got
another meeting after this one."

AJ signaled Pete.

The crowd soured Leventhal even more. He rushed through the key
points in the proposed deal, making it difficult for Koji to translate.
Keiku Enterprises would invest fifty million dollars of equity, in return
for owning 40 percent of J^2. As managing partner, AJ would retain
60 percent and control all business decisions. In lieu of putting up his
own money, AJ would take no salary until there were profits. Wells
Fargo Bank had agreed to loan one hundred million dollars, and HBO
had contributed an additional twenty-five million in return for the
cable and videocassette rights to J^2 films.

AJ would use the funds to green-light four movies per year through
1990. According to the plan, the output would then rise to ten films annually, but revenues generated by the earlier releases would fund the
new production. The initial working capital would also cover the com-

pany's overhead. Leventhal was slated to serve as chief financial officer and second in command, while Andy Faddiman would head marketing, choose release dates, book theaters, and advertise the movies to the public.

AJ tried gauging Seiji's reaction but might as well have studied the dregs in his teacup. The only evidence the man was alive was that he periodically sipped from a tumbler filled with fifty-year-old Glenlivet. Pete didn't so much finish as wind down. When he turned the podium over, he sighed, "That's the toughest jury I ever faced."

AJ stared into the abyss. No, it wasn't a jury; it was an audience. And he was in show business. *"Tora! Tora! Tora!"*

No one expected to hear an American scream the code for the attack on Pearl Harbor. One of the functionaries shouted a reflexive *"Hai! Hai!"* Another knocked a saucer to the floor. Koji's mouth dropped open. His father sparked.

"Gentlemen, no one understood an opportunity better than your military did in 1941. Their intelligence and instincts told them America was a complacent foe. They dared to steal the moment—and almost won the war. Today Hollywood is the same soft target.

"In 1982 the Coca-Cola Company purchased Columbia Pictures and created a sister company called Tristar in order to double the output of movies. They offered me the job of president, but when I flew to Coke's headquarters in Atlanta, I found arrogant men who assumed movies were carbonated beverages. They told me to use marketing research to test the concepts of films. When I counseled that such techniques wouldn't be automatically transferable, they smugly said I'd learn. Then my hosts escorted me to a secret facility where the company had changed the formula for Coca-Cola—the best-loved franchise in industrial history. When I tasted 'New Coke,' I found it too sweet and flat, but they told me that research proved that consumers favored it. I shook hands and passed on the job."

Koji's translation brought nods of approval and knowing smiles.

"I began to wonder . . . if this was the quality of the competition in Hollywood, maybe it was time to start a new studio, because the movie business—as a business—is a gold mine. Attendance rose last year, as it has every year since the middle of the 1970s. The procession of blockbusters that started with *Jaws* continues with *Star Wars, Raiders of the Lost Ark,* and *E.T.* And a technological innovation—a Japanese innovation—makes my idea truly viable. The availability of movies on videocassettes has fundamentally altered the economics of the business. Most film executives issued dire warnings saying 'home entertainment centers' would kill theaters. This whining reminded me of the first reactions to television. But cannibalization hasn't occurred. A movie now earns as much from videocassette rentals and pay TV as it does in its theatrical release."

Seiji put his Scotch on the table. "I have studied your career and read your business plan." The man's crisply accented English shocked AJ. "But until now I was doing it more for my son's benefit than my own. You are familiar with a man named William Goldman?"

"I am." Why, AJ wondered, should Seiji reference the writer of *Butch Cassidy and the Sundance Kid*?

"In his book *Adventures in the Screen Trade,* he says that 'nobody in Hollywood knows anything.' He says it is all a gamble. Do you not think that thirteen billion yen is too much to invest in a game of craps?"

Koji jabbered something in Japanese, then sulked when his father curtly cut him off. Pete's grimace said "Forget about it." But AJ smiled. An accomplished sixty-five-year-old Japanese industrialist wouldn't struggle through a smart-aleck book about the movie business unless he was genuinely interested in joining it. "Goldman is a wonderful writer, but he hates the authority of the studio chiefs who pay for his handsome lifestyle. To ridicule them, he argues that they are all frauds."

"You do not agree?"

"Keiku-san, are you a baseball fan?"

Everyone in the room bobbed their heads knowingly. Koji interjected, "He loves the Tokyo Giants more than me."

"Think about two players, one who gets thirty-three hits in a hundred at bats, the other twenty-five. They both fail far more often than they succeed. Only eight hits out of one hundred separate them. But if that pattern continues over their careers, the former will enter the Hall of Fame while the latter disappears from the sports pages. It's the same situation in the movie business. Executives strike out a lot. In that sense Goldman is correct. But the great producers make a *higher percentage* of right decisions, they create more than enough memorable movies to cover their failures. The companies they manage become legendary assets for all time."

"You think you are destined for your Cooperstown?"

"Yes."

"And you do not secretly say to yourself that a Japanese whaler will be as dumb a partner as Coca-Cola?"

AJ laughed. "By asking that question, you have answered it. I trust you will let me manage our affairs while I teach your son about the film business. Over time he will become more involved; then we can marry the strengths of our cultures."

Seiji Keiku took a final draw on his whiskey. "Why is your company called J-Squared?"

"My father and I had a dream to be in business together. He died long before that was possible. But I believe he would approve of our venture."

=

The negotiations proved arduous, but only one point threatened to derail them. Seiji insisted on a fail-safe mechanism specifying that Keiku Enterprises could assume control of J^2 if the company suffered losses in excess of fifteen million dollars. "We'll operate with a samurai sword over our heads," Leventhal complained as he suffered through an almost raw hamburger drenched in wasabi mayonnaise. "If we have an expensive failure early in the program, you'll lose control."

"I'll be supercareful, keep budgets down."

"I say we tell them we're sorry but it won't work."

"Just blow it off?"

"Believe me, they won't let us get on a plane to L.A."

"And suppose you're wrong?" AJ shook his head.

Pete threw down his napkin. "You've made me believe in J-Squared as much as you do. I'm bored being a full-time lawyer. I want to build the company with you. But you have to hear me. Signing an agreement with this clause is dumb. You never listen to me, but on this point, you have to."

The issue was no longer logic. "Maybe you're right—"

"I *am* right."

"I've come too far to go back empty-handed. But, Pete, I can't operate without the support of my colleagues. It's too easy to lose my way in a fog of second guesses. I want you on board. But that means *all* the way on board."

Leventhal ran his hand through his curls. "They're all I've got left of my youth."

"I won't let you down."

"I'll close it tomorrow."

=

For AJ's final night in Japan, Seiji organized a celebration at a hole-in-the-wall dive called Kyubei that purveyed the finest sushi in the city. Rather than offend his host, AJ anesthetized himself with sake to sample fugu, the infamous blowfish that was poisonous if improperly prepared. He survived—but carried the sake strategy a tumbler too far, which explained why he was standing at midnight in front of a microphone at a nightclub in the Roppongi district. The joint specialized in a weird new form of entertainment called karaoke. Seiji was a freak for it, and after AJ's performance of John Cougar Mellencamp's "Jack and Diane," he led the crowd in cheers of *"Ankooru."*

"Hello, Tokyo!" AJ shouted into the microphone. "Are you ready to rock 'n' roll?" They were. "Are you really ready?" He grooved on the rock-star fantasy. "Because for my next number I've decided to be . . . the Boss. I don't mean Keiku-san. He's a big boss, but he's not *the* Boss. Do you guys know who the real Boss is?"

"Bruuuce! Bruuuce!"

"That's right! But Springsteen needs his E Street Band, so gimme some backup. Pete, come on up. And Koji. Keiku-san, get up here too." It didn't take coaxing. AJ wailed away on air guitar as the bass and sax of "Hungry Heart" pulsed over the sound system. He and Seiji went nose to nose for the chorus, banging away on their imaginary instruments. The banzai spirit lived in the old man's eyes.

Together—J and K—they'd deliver Hollywood a swift kick in its flabby butt.

CHAPTER 38

On the bulletin board at Riviera a wise guy with handicap envy had posted a caricature of AJ hanging from the flame tree beside the ninth green. He wore a noose fashioned from a twisted putter around his neck. After failing in the finals of the club's match-play championship a record ten times, his pursuit of the Hogan Cup had reached the status of a standing joke. His eleventh attempt stood "all square" with Jeff Danna, the top-seeded player in the field.

As he teed up his ball on the thirty-sixth and final hole, AJ knew exactly what he had to do, which was not think—just swing. But in the next two seconds he warned himself to slow his take-away, extend his left arm, keep his right elbow tucked, drop the club into the slot, and, above all, avoid casting over the top. That he made contact was miraculous, that the ball duck-hooked to the left inevitable. He always made the same mistake under pressure.

"You goddamn idiot! Forty years of practice and that's the best you can do?" A self-loathing, two-hundred-yard uphill hike wore out his rage. The result was even worse than the shot. The ball was buried on a down slope in a spongy nest of Kikuyu grass, nature's Velcro. AJ repeated his mantra, "Play it as it lies."

"Lays."

AJ stared at his caddie. "What'd you say?"

"It's 'play it as it lays,' isn't it?"

"No, you lay your club down, but the ball lies."

"You're so clever." A smile stole across Megan O'Connor's face.

"Why do you torture me like this?"

"So you won't torture yourself." Megan unsheathed a seven-iron from the bag she was humping. "*Lay* up short of the green."

"I can reach with a five-wood if I hit it perfectly."

"If you hit it at all. There's a good chance you'll pop it up and stay in the rough."

"Danna's in perfect shape. Ben Hogan—"

"Wouldn't have hit it here in the first place. Lay up, then put your third shot close and sink your putt. It will demoralize the Golden Boy." Megan gestured toward their opponent, whose UCLA team visor couldn't hide his smirk. Danna had ogled Megan's butt since the first hole. At fourteen AJ had overheard him ask her how an old man like Jastrow could have a girlfriend half his age who was a total babe, a ten-handicap golfer, and a willing caddie to boot. But as he'd prepared to tell Danna to fuck off, Megan had jabbed a pitching wedge into the guy's crotch, which had produced the desired effect.

AJ executed his orders and laid three on the green, with a twenty-foot putt for par. Meanwhile, Danna's second shot sailed wide right but luckily rebounded off a eucalyptus. He chipped onto the green, where he faced a five-foot putt for par on the same line.

Megan leaned over AJ's shoulder, both of them trying to read the break. They had lived together for the past six months, but he still found her closeness exhilarating. "How can you smell so good after six hours?"

"Concentrate. I think it'll swing left to right about a ball."

"I'm following my own instincts here." AJ approached the putt but was distracted by the sun glinting off the quarter that Danna had used to mark his ball. At his request Jeff shifted the coin four inches to the left. AJ exhaled and shook his arms to rid them of tension, then swung his putter like the pendulum of a grandfather clock. The ball rolled downhill, gathering speed. Just when it seemed destined to run past the hole to the right, the Titleist detoured left, rimmed the circumference, and plopped in. The small gallery applauded, while AJ smiled at Megan.

Her kiss tasted of Gatorade. "How'd you see right to left?"

"Hogan had the same putt in the '48 Open."

"God, you're old."

Now Danna had to sink his putt to force a sudden-death play-off. But in the shock of the shifting fortunes, he forgot to replace the ball in its original location and was about to putt from the spot he'd marked *after* AJ had asked him to move his quarter. Doing so meant a one-stroke penalty. AJ was sure he was the only person who spotted the imminent mistake. If he remained silent—and nothing in the rules of golf required him to speak—the match was over and the championship his, regardless of the outcome of Danna's putt.

The sportsman in him—the guy who'd learned to play by the side of the fairest of the fair—cursed the idea of winning on a technicality. But how fair was it that he'd lost two of his prime golf years to a stroke or that his opponent got to play six times a week to his two? What did fair even mean anymore? It was a "look out for yourself" world. Sign an ironclad contract; negotiate a tight prenup; gate your home; bank your "fuck you" money. Today's Good Samaritan was the schmuck who got sued tomorrow. AJ stared at the carpet of green beneath his steel spikes, his lips sealed.

When his putt fell in, Danna shook his fist in the air and headed gleefully toward the first extra hole. AJ remained by the eighteenth green and called quietly after him, "Jeff, I think we have a problem."

"What?" As soon as he saw AJ's cool expression, he understood his error. "You knew, didn't you? You knew all the time."

"On twelve I called a penalty on myself for hitting a tree on my backswing, which you didn't even see. Those are the rules."

"Congratulations, asshole." Danna left before the awards ceremony.

AJ bought rounds for everyone in the Grill. This time when he kissed Megan, she tasted of Dom Pérignon. "You were fantastic, AJ."

His mouth was stale with beer. "I couldn't have done it without you." Her advice, her belief, and her energy rallied him.

"You know what frightened me?" Megan asked, caressing the Hogan Cup between her thighs.

"That I'd run out of gas?"

She shook her head. "That you'd chicken out and warn that privileged piece of shit that he was putting from the wrong place." She nibbled on his ear. "I was scared you didn't want to win enough."

=

The prospect of sex with Megan had stirred him before they'd even met.

Ronda Gomez, the Paramount story editor turned literary agent, had slipped him *The Scholarship,* the first screenplay by a young reporter for the *The Philadelphia Inquirer.* AJ had taken it along for a holiday weekend with his girlfriend, Carrie McDougal, at the San Ysidro Ranch, near Santa Barbara. Carrie was a gutsy lady with powerful ambitions and hair to match. As an executive at Columbia, however, she competed with AJ, who produced his movies for Fox. Predictably, Carrie had peeked at the title page the moment she saw him engrossed in the script. He'd put it aside, made love to her, then sneaked it into the toilet to finish it.

The Scholarship was a drama about a coed who paid her tuition at Princeton by moonlighting as a call girl for high rollers in Atlantic City. The character was as daring as she was self-destructive. When AJ finished he wondered if the script was autobiographical. Monday morning he shopped Melrose until he found a Bakelite brooch as a gift for Ronda and delivered it with a card thanking her. Carrie had already requested a copy, so AJ made a peremptory bid.

But Megan O'Connor feared allowing a razor-cut Hollywood producer to turn her lead character into a movie prostitute with the clichéd heart of gold. She wouldn't close the deal until they met. When she entered his office, AJ decided the woman had the looks to charge a thousand bucks a night. Megan was black Irish, who, according to legend, were descendants of sailors from the Spanish Armada. After their ships had broken up in a gale off the coast of Ireland, the Spaniards had swum ashore and coupled with the local women, producing an exotic combination of black hair, blue eyes, and pale skin.

Her mother had died when she was ten, and she'd raised her two younger brothers while her father took care of the greens at the famed Merion Golf Club. At the University of Pennsylvania she'd worked multiple part-time jobs to finance her college degree. Just as she'd emerged as a star on the *Inquirer*'s city desk, she'd smashed her car into a lamppost rushing to cover a plane crash at the airport. Megan had written the first draft of *The Scholarship* in a body cast.

At twenty-four, Megan was as suspicious and pointed a questioner as Mike Wallace. To allay her anxiety, AJ offered to work together on the script so she could see the kind of changes he wanted *before* she agreed to sell. Megan defended every scene to the barricades, then returned with brilliant improvements. Was it her challenge that turned him on? Or her passionate commitment to what she believed? Or that heartfelt thank-you she offered for his help? After wandering through meaningless relationships for too many years, the promise of Megan was like the return of his sight after the stroke.

=

"Jessie Jastrow. How can I help you?"

It was her philosophy of life as well as a phone greeting. As the youngest in a family obsessively pursuing their own agendas, Jess had gracefully adapted her personality to the service sector. She found satisfaction solving the problems of others, so much so that her mom fretted that she'd become a doormat. Some doormat—a year out of UCLA, Jess already had a dream job reading scripts and meeting writers, her own cool apartment in one of those kitschy Hollywood buildings on Fountain—and the best boss in the world.

"You're sure?" Concern clouded her face as she listened to the caller. "Thanks." She bit hard on her lip, then picked up the intercom. "Dad, can I stop down?"

"Son of a bitch!" Her father heaved a script across the room. "I should know by now that people in this town would murder their mothers for an extra buck. I should have protected us. Pete should have."

He stomped around the office in a fury, his neck stiffening as if a puppeteer yanked on his strings. Jess worried about him having another stroke but had given up asking him to calm down once he'd made the J² deal. Dad was determined to prove wrong those people who considered his effort to create a new studio an act of arrogance. In Hollywood, envy was as common as a cold, but it hurt Jess to discover that even his supposed friends hoped he would fail.

"Mike Ovitz, please. It's AJ Jastrow." Waiting to be connected, he signaled her to pick up the extension next to the sofa in his office.

"How are you, AJ?"

"Lousy. I thought we'd signed Debra Winger to do *The Scholarship.* But now I hear that you're backing her out."

"We had discussions about Debra doing your movie. We had interest."

"We had a deal."

Jessie cringed. They had aimed their first-year production slate at the youth market, so the actors in their films were mostly young unknowns rather than established movie stars. Winger was their biggest name, she was perfect for the part, and Mr. Keiku was excited that the star of *An Officer and a Gentleman* and *Terms of Endearment* would appear in J²'s first feature.

"Debra likes your project, she enjoyed meeting you and the writer. Maybe if you're willing to wait . . ."

"So you can tell me she's found another movie for the fall."

"AJ, I thought Rick informed you there were competing projects."

Rick was Rick Nicita, the actress's personal agent. "This isn't Rick's issue. You guys represent Redford and Ivan Reitman and you packaged Winger into *Legal Eagles* because Universal's paying through the nose."

"Frank Price made an aggressive offer."

"How can you do this, Mike? You know how important getting her is to what I'm building."

"AJ, you must believe I'd never do anything to hurt you intentionally." It was the "must" of "you have no choice," not the "must" of "you know how much I care." Ovitz was transparent and unflappable in the same breath. For the next three minutes he blamed everybody but the KGB for the misunderstanding. Finally, in a faux attempt to be conciliatory he suggested Sally Field as an alternative. Rather than remind him that the part called for a college senior, not an actress in her late thirties, AJ hung up.

Jess stared at the receiver. "I don't believe that."

"A vintage performance, even for Mike."

"My friend at Universal said Winger hated *Legal Eagles* and wanted to do our movie, but Mike convinced her that an 'art-house' movie like *The Scholarship* would hurt her career."

"Mike does what *he* thinks is in the best interests of his clients. Regardless of how good they are, he doesn't believe actors and directors can manage their own careers. Hell, he's probably right. The talent, the studios, producers like us—we're pawns in his chess game. But go argue with results."

Ovitz hired the best young agents and taught them to function as a team rather than compete as rivals. Their savage loyalty to their mentor and their "CAA-speak" inspired bad jokes about Jonestown West. But despite criticism, they swarmed Hollywood seeking new talent and raiding established stars from William Morris and ICM. Everyone said CAA would soon become the most powerful organization in the movie business. But Jess didn't care—Mike's betrayal sucked. "Did he forget all the packaging fees from Grandma's talk show? That money kept the agency alive in the early years."

"Yeah, but he can't commission her now. It's always been a 'What have you done for me lately?' town. Now the question is, 'What have you done for me *this week*?'"

"Sue his butt."

"All that does is lose us Kinison from *General Assembly*." The next J² film slated for production was a comedy about a New York cabdriver who impersonated the head of state of a fictional country at the United Nations. Her father had chosen a young shock comic named Sam Kinison to play the lead, but CAA represented him as well.

"Okay. How about Diane Lane?" Jess offered. "Before we landed Winger, I thought she'd be great."

"The writer doesn't think she's sympathetic."

She tensed. The "writer"—Dad's girlfriend—was not her favorite person. Megan's coolness was more annoying than her age. "Cheryl Davis would be fabulous, but everyone's after her."

"I'll lean on Stan." AJ's former boss ran William Morris and represented Davis. "In a crisis like this, Jess, a twenty-year relationship is invaluable."

She took a long sip of a Diet Coke, building up the courage for a more delicate question. "Have you decided what to do about casting *Water, Water Everywhere*?" The third film on the J² slate was a thriller about a young forensic physician at the Centers for Disease Control assigned to track down a terrorist who is poisoning the water supply of major cities.

"We've offered it to Dennis Quaid."

"Dennis isn't available when you want to start." She noted his suspicious look. "Dad, I know you don't think Ricky's right for the part—"

"Jess! Ricky hasn't asked about it. Don't put the idea in his head."

"He's a terrific actor."

"I know. I know a hell of a lot more about him than you do."

Dad frequently alluded to some secret, but every time she probed, he ducked. Her brother was the same. Their feud had started in Thailand, then got worse after Ricky's drug bust. Her mission was to get them speaking again. And personal grumps aside, her brother was right for the part. "I gave him the script."

"You did what?"

"I think he likes it."

"Keep out of this!"

During his recuperation, Jess had heard her father yell every day when he couldn't tie his shoelaces or scratch a mosquito bite. He couldn't bully her. "You're wrong."

He reached her before she reached the door. "I'm sorry . . . for yelling."

She hugged back—no sense being bitchy. "Dad, remember that time you came to camp when Ricky starred in *Jesus Christ Superstar*?"

"Yeah."

"I hoped that if he did *Water, Water* it would be like that camp visit again."

"Don't forget, that visit ended badly." Her father looked sad. "Things happen. Things that can't be undone."

=

"My ass is getting wet," Megan complained.

"I sympathize," AJ replied. "But I can't tell this story in a comfortable living room." So he'd built a campfire in the backyard and put down blankets, but a cold March rain had soaked the grass. AJ stripped off his Navy pea jacket and draped it around her shoulders. He had to be chivalrous because his girlfriend was in a hostile mood. The news about Winger infuriated her. It infuriated him too, but that was the movie business. Maybe her replacement would turn out better. Hell, Warners had hired Clint Eastwood as Dirty Harry only after Frank Sinatra refused the part.

He'd experienced that kind of serendipity a few hours ago. In order to establish J^2 as a factor in Hollywood, he was determined to start four movies in the company's first year, only none of the other projects in development was ready. But when his daughter mentioned Raquette Lake, AJ flashed on the idea that would round out their schedule. All he needed was a terrific writer to put it down on paper.

"The story begins at an amusement park in Brooklyn called Coney

Island on a summer night in 1948. Thousands of people queue up for rides, munching cotton candy and hanging out. Everyone sweats in the humid heat. Over the ocean thunder booms and lightning flashes."

Megan fell under his spell like another kid at camp.

"A ten-year-old boy heads to Nathan's, the world-famous hot-dog stand. He holds his dog—his real dog—on a leash, but the mutt catches a whiff of charred beef and breaks free. The boy chases, yelling, 'Corky, come back!' They disappear into the Hall of Mirrors. Suddenly, a bolt of electricity strikes the Ferris wheel at its highest point. *Bzzzzz!* The sound is people being fried in midair."

"That's gross!"

"No, grotesque. The distinction separates a B movie from a classic. The lightning strikes again in the exact same place, which violates the laws of nature. The Ferris wheel crashes down. A fire breaks out, and the crowd rushes toward the exits in panic. But inside the Hall of Mirrors, disoriented by the reflections and unaware of the fire, the young boy searches for Corky . . ." For the next half hour AJ mesmerized Megan with the story of how the boy died in the fire but returned years later as a grown-up ghost with a mission to haunt visitors to the park.

"So that's how you spent your time at that expensive summer camp?" Megan looked quizzical. "It's such a natural movie idea and you know it so well—why don't you write it?"

"I don't have the time. And you're a lot more talented. Please."

"It's going to cost you."

No doubt of that. His girlfriend was a practical woman.

CHAPTER 39

"Five, four, three, two, one . . ." AJ silently counted down until 4:18 A.M. flashed on the alarm clock by his bedside. He'd turned officially fifty—the only male Jastrow to make it. So why wasn't he celebrating like those nuts in Times Square when the ball rings in the New Year? He put his head on the pillow, but sleep was history.

In the spare bedroom converted into a gym, AJ extended each stretch until he felt an inch taller, then picked up a pair of free weights and did ten reps to exercise his pectorals. In his youth he'd never cared about the definition of his muscles, but now . . . there was no way he was letting his waist outstrip his chest. Or getting the lard ass of an old man. His legs could carry him to level eight on the StairMaster, although his right knee creaked like an antique rocking chair. In the mirror he gratefully noted a full head of hair, even if it was salt-and-pepper. Battle lines creased his forehead, but all in all, not too shabby for a half century of wear and tear.

Returning to the bedroom, he listened to Megan murmuring in her sleep. She kicked off the duvet. A tattered Penn crew shirt served as her nightdress. He adored that alabaster body—flashes of it interrupted his train of thought at script meetings. They rarely discussed their age difference, though last night, while watching Johnny Carson, she kidded that if they got married, he'd be seventy when their kids left for college. Her legs scissored, revealing a tuft of black hair. Wake her and start the family now.

Maybe the reason he wasn't celebrating fifty was how much game he had left.

Reaching into his night table, AJ removed a yellowed envelope. It bore the address "Master AJ Jastrow, RLBC, Raquette Lake, New York." The postmark was August 8, 1945. His father's handwriting was so big he couldn't fit many words to a page. "Dear AJ, it's only been a few weeks since I saw you, but I already can't wait for camp to end and for you to come home. Mom's off visiting Grandma in Chicago and I'm just lazing around and playing golf. We're all waiting for news that the war in Japan is over. Did you hear about the atomic bomb we dropped . . ."

That was it. The second page was lost. Dad had been in his late thirties when he'd penned the letter—probably sitting at the oak rolltop desk in the den. Less than three years later he would be dead. But in his short years he'd accomplished so much and touched so many. Witness the throngs who'd packed Forest Lawn for his funeral. AJ wondered how many would mourn if he died tomorrow. His father was a loving husband, a dedicated parent, and a war hero who'd nobly served his country. AJ served no one but the people who paid him. As for family, he'd screwed up his marriage and rarely spoke to his son.

Maybe the reason he wasn't celebrating fifty was how little he had to show.

The bedroom window framed a square of night sky. AJ hadn't prayed on the flight from Lo An when he'd thought he was dying, but now . . .

age caused him to hedge his bets. He considered mentioning the environment or world peace—like the Almighty wouldn't recognize pandering. "Thank you, God, for letting me live this long so I'd appreciate a few more years to get it right. Amen." Just like in a script—less is more. The rosebushes in the front yard rustled briefly in the wind. Otherwise, his world remained the same.

=

It wasn't an overdose of butter and garlic but François Volk's affair with a *Vogue* cover girl that had prompted Steph to escape on an extended tour of Southeast Asia ten months ago. She'd returned with an inspiration for a new restaurant whose cuisine blended the recipes and culinary techniques of Southeast Asia with the flavors and produce of California. The Siamese Cat was decorated in the colonial style of Saigon under the French. After only four months it had emerged as a trendy L.A. spot.

AJ and his girlfriend were regulars from the start. Megan looked a bit too Morticia Addams for Steph's tastes, but her personality was . . . *formidable.* AJ hung on her every word, but he seemed happy. Thinking back, she remembered that it had been Megan's idea to hold his fiftieth birthday party at the Cat. The woman was either remarkably secure or slightly perverse to celebrate with her boyfriend's first wife.

At Steph's request, AJ arrived an hour early. They settled into a table beneath a black-and-white photograph of Ho Chi Minh. The waiter served Hanoi hummers—her original cocktail of vodka, lemonade, and cassis. "What's wrong with me that makes a man leap into bed with another woman?"

AJ's head slumped. "Volk . . . again? That fucking frog—"

"Literally. Please answer my question. Before I divorce him, I need to know if the cheating is his fault. After all, you did the same thing. So did almost every other creep I was serious about. Am I that lousy in bed?"

"Jesus, Steph. Don't think that for a second." He paused, searching for some way to lift her mood. "McQueen had the hots for you. That qualifies you as stone-cold sexy. And you're the nicest person I know."

"But that's my problem, isn't it? I'm 'nice' in a world where that quality's gotten the same rap as rice pudding."

"Nah. Flashy women walk into your husband's restaurants, they make no demands, just offers . . . it happens. You have to decide whether to stay with him, but you deserve better."

His "Dear Abby" worked. "I've got to put my personal touch on your feast, but thank you. You're a good guy."

"I wish."

"You can be—when you want to."

≡

Ricky stared at a red light on Sunset and Vine, hoping it wouldn't turn green.

"What's he like?"

The voice surprised him—he'd forgotten there was another person in the car. His date for the evening, a young woman with the solitary name of Rix, had dabbed on enough makeup for it to qualify as clown paint. "Who?"

"Your dad."

"Take the sense of humor of Cliff Huxtable, the moral fiber of Ben Cartwright, and the cardigans of Mr. Rogers . . ."

"Are you serious?"

Ricky grunted.

"So he's an asshole?"

"Let's just say he's not my favorite parent—and he doesn't have tough competition."

"So why are we going to his party?"

"My sister and grandmother bugged me. Kind of a powwow."

"We can split early to the Palladium. I used to drum for the band that's playing tonight."

Ricky glanced longingly at his glove compartment. In the good old days—was it only a year ago?—he'd kept enough pills in there to get him past the party and through Rix. Someone honked. The light had changed.

≡

During the past decade AJ had made countless acquaintances but counted few of them as friends. His Rolodex groaned with the names and numbers of a new generation of Hollywood executives, agents, and producers, men and women who were smart and ambitious but seemed more motivated by wealth and fame than passion for film. Because the old black-and-white movies rarely played on TV, few of them had viewed the classics like *The Philadelphia Story, All About Eve,* or *Mr. Smith Goes to Washington* that were AJ's vocabulary. No one recognized the names of Harry Cohn and Adolph Zukor or knew that the studios had once owned theaters. In their minds the film business was born with the release of *Star Wars* and the founding of CAA.

Socializing in Hollywood mirrored the modern action movie—loud and relentless. To raise the profile of J², AJ dutifully trekked to cocktail parties, charity events, and premieres. He made small talk, gathered information, closed deals, and headed home feeling like he needed a shower.

To keep his fiftieth birthday from descending into a thinly disguised business event, he restricted the guest list to close friends and family. Other than the aggressive videographer, who shot enough tape of people arriving to make a documentary, the evening promised to be intimate. Steph had coordinated the menu and seating arrangements so that he could eat a different course at each of the five guest tables.

AJ began with crispy California vegetable sushi with a Thai peanut dipping sauce in the company of three mentors, one colleague, and an ex-lover. The babe on Bob Evans's left arm was proof that he retained the bravado of a studio chief and the looks of a movie star, even though he was merely a struggling producer. *The Cotton Club,* his bloody, over-budget reunion with Francis Ford Coppola, had flopped at Christmas. "I have a script Mark Canton's begging me to bring to Warners," he confided to AJ. "But I'm making it your birthday present." It was cheaper than a tie or a sweater, but Jessica had covertly read the "gift" last week and judged it dreck. Like Selznick pitching and putting his guts out to Harry Cohn back at Riviera, Evans was fifty-five, broke, and battling. AJ shivered. Producers displayed an alarming tendency to wind up like palooka boxers, tin cups in hand, sporting cauliflower ears from too many hours on the phone.

To his right sat the exception. Ray Stark was the Machiavelli of the movie business. After AJ's departure from Rastar, however, the Rabbit had failed to find a replacement he could respect and chose instead to tend his sculpture garden and advise AJ on how to run J². "I did God's work today—I gave Mike Ovitz a migraine," Ray announced. "At lunch Redford told me what a miserable time everyone was having making *Legal Eagles.* I mentioned I'd seen dailies from *The Scholarship* and Cheryl Davis was so great he should work with her. Bob told Winger, who screamed at Ovitz that he'd screwed her career. The lady's yours for the stealing, Stan. It would even things up for his poaching Stallone and Fonda."

Stan Kamen stood at the peak of the pyramid he'd scaled stone by stone for thirty-five years. He was the soul of William Morris and represented the biggest divas in the business, including Barbra Streisand and his beard for tonight, Diane Keaton. But Hollywood's pyramid was slick, and Stan was slipping—or being shoved—from his perch by Ovitz and his CAA hordes. "Mike's a winner. We had him and lost him."

"There's no one from *Variety* here," AJ interjected. "Tell it like it is." Joe Wizan and Julia Phillips joined the chorus. Not by coincidence, each had once been an agent.

Stan remained politic. "You have to applaud how he's made it happen on his own."

Evans gave the universal symbol for "jerk off." Kamen joined the laughter, but when his hiccups degenerated into a coughing fit, AJ and Joe helped him to the men's room. Reports from William Morris headquarters claimed Stan was cracking under the pressure, screaming at assistants and colleagues. There was no justice. Just when his generation should be waltzing gracefully, someone sped up the music and forced it to disco. Wizan wiped the sweat from his old boss's brow with a dampened towel. The agent had suffered health problems during the past year—a cut that wouldn't heal, nasty blisters on his back, and now this hacking cough.

"I don't know what's wrong with me," Stan sputtered. "Give me a minute."

Reluctantly, they headed back to the dining room. "He looks like hell," AJ said sadly.

Wizan thrust himself within inches of his face. "Stan's killing himself. I don't want to see that happen to you."

"This is my time. I've got to push it."

Burning in Joe's eyes was the passion he kept hidden from Hollywood, where people regarded him as a loner living a spartan life. Six months after quitting the presidency of Fox, Joe was a producer again, listening to the pounding surf outside his Malibu condo rather than the bitching of his bosses. "After a year in that cockamamie job I couldn't sleep for more than an hour at a time. I lived on Mylanta. Building J-Squared could destroy you. You're too good for that." Wizan embraced him so tightly AJ thought he broke a rib.

Something about the occasion encouraged people to unburden themselves. And there were four courses to go.

"Were you guys doing drugs?" Julia asked upon their return. Her hair was cut short and spiked, she wore a dress of studded leather and puffed cigarettes like Joan Crawford.

"Drugs without you? No way," AJ replied. "What did we miss?"

"She was nailing Marilyn Bergman and Paula Weinstein," Ray offered.

"I founded the Hollywood Women's Political Committee with them. And they had the nerve to drum me out of my own organization. It's un-fucking-American. I hate Ronald Reagan as much as those cunts do!" A decade after winning the Academy Award, Julia had lost none of her feistiness but all of her clout. She hadn't made a movie in five years and scrounged deals from studio chiefs, who avoided her calls like a voice from the grave. Maybe Don Simpson, the hottest producer in town, could survive drug-related transgressions, but the men in power refused to forgive a woman who'd stripped the gears getting to the top.

AJ did a quick computation. Take all the success, fame, and fortune achieved by the guests at that table, divide it by all their dreams . . . it was a fraction of the contentment they deserved.

For the next course, AJ savored Stephanie's Gulf of Tonkin seafood chowder and pesto crostini with the Keikus, who were seated between Michael Douglas and Steve Guttenberg. "Our venture goes well?" Seiji inquired of AJ.

Koji jumped in. "Super. We got one movie started, another begins next month and a third goes in August. J-Squared is happening."

"We're on schedule, Keiku-san," AJ declared modestly. "But it will be the first quarter of '86 before we can measure results."

"All my advisers predicted problems from the start."

"Your advisers are old farts." His son giggled, then blew his nose in a napkin.

Seiji ignored him. "I have brought you a gift from my homeland."

Tearing open an elegantly wrapped package, AJ discovered the sharpened head of an ornamental harpoon etched with Japanese characters.

"Thank you so much. The words say . . ."

" 'Do not seek to follow in the footsteps of men of old. Instead, seek the essence of what they sought.' "

At the J^2 table everyone applauded as their boss joined them for Vietnamese chicken calzone. "Damn, now I have to return the harpoon *I* got you," Andy Faddiman quipped. AJ patted the receding hairline of his marketing chief, hugged Pete and Paula Leventhal, and Shelly Nelton.

The former Grambling University homecoming queen was the company's vice president of physical production. This was the joy of owning his own company—picking the people with whom he had dinner.

"How are you doing?" Jess asked.

"I'm surviving." He looked adoringly at his daughter. Her hair was upswept, and she wore her mom's string of pearls. "Did I mention that you remind me of Leslie Caron in *Gigi*?" AJ turned to her escort. "Doesn't she, Gary?" Or was it Larry? Jessie's guys melded into one overly eager prom date.

Barry nodded agreement.

"Thanks for the reprieve," she whispered, indicating a table diagonally across the room. AJ had placed his daughter with her colleagues rather than her family, where she would have run interference all night.

He left the J² crew talking shop to share papaya sorbet with old friends and golf buddies. Jerry Roblin had flown in from Chicago on his father-in-law's private jet and Oscar de la Cuadre had arrived—legally, he reminded everyone—from Mexico, where he now ran his own clinic. Among people without Hollywood agendas, he felt free, but civilians were an intermezzo in his life. The waiters entered with the main course in flaming pots, and AJ crossed the makeshift dance floor to the head table.

The peppers in the Laotian crispy beef weren't hot enough to stifle Ambassador Maggie Jastrow Ginsberg. At seventy-two she was more monument than mom. As a reward for her hefty campaign contributions, President Reagan had posted her to Mexico, whose government she denounced for its collusion with South American drug lords. "The local police supplement their salaries with monthly bribes from the Medellín cartel. They'll never curtail the cocaine smuggling because *they* are the smugglers."

"Maggie, calm down." Leon was still spry at seventy-seven—and still failing to rein in his wife.

"Don't complain to us," Steph baited. "Tell your bosses at the State Department."

"I'm sure she has," Megan interjected. "They're afraid to spoil our relationship with the PRI."

"A smart girl—finally."

His mother's pointed insult, his ex-wife's scarlet anger—for AJ it was a rerun of home movies of a disastrous family vacation. "All the women in my life are smart."

"Jesus. You should be the diplomat," Maggie groaned.

He noticed that Ricky didn't look up, picking away at his food while his bored girlfriend beat out "Material Girl" with her chopsticks. "You've lost weight, haven't you, Rick?"

"I'm working out."

"Looks great. And, Rix, you're an actress?"

"When I get a part I will be."

"I know it's difficult to get your career started."

"And to keep it going." His mother transformed a declarative sentence into an accusation. "But I understand that there are more parts in Hollywood these days for actors under thirty."

"That's right, Mom. You made a good decision to get out of the business."

"That trend should be perfect for your son's career." Her words rang like a klaxon on a submarine, but he didn't have time to dive. "I understand you've got a part for Ricky in one of your upcoming films."

Depth charge. He shot a look across the room, where Jess was laughing at one of Andy's stories—so much for her bonus.

"I read *Water, Water Everywhere*," Ricky noted casually. "It's a decent script. Maybe I should do it."

"Wouldn't that be wonderful!" Maggie beamed like an overeager yenta. "The last time you two worked together you both got nominations. And God knows, AJ, you need to produce another good movie. *Don't Tread on Me* is the only film of yours anyone will remember."

"Let's dance," Megan interjected.

The small combo covered some plaintive melody—Foreigner or Journey? These eighties bands sounded too manufactured to distinguish. She lifted her head off his shoulder. "Your mom's comment bummed you out?"

"I'm used to it. The last time she complimented me was after my bar mitzvah. But this pincer movement to cast Ricky could be a nightmare."

"He's a good actor."

"It's not his talent that troubles me."

She bit his lip slyly. "After we've finished celebrating, you might want to look next to your pillow."

AJ ran his hand down the small of her back till it rested just above her jutting bottom. He could feel that she was naked under her raw-silk dress. Why couldn't this be a fraternity party? "Another present?"

"The Coney Island Maniac. I finished my first draft this afternoon."

They danced until the toasts and roasts began. The video guy covered the action so AJ could savor the one-liners of his gifted guests for years to come. As people spoke, he half-listened, his attention drawn to an empty table shoved into the corner. Maybe it was there for those who could attend only in spirit.

Mike Todd would award his assistant a passing grade on showmanship, with extra credit for the chutzpah of starting J². No one had championed the producer more passionately. Charlie Bluhdorn outshouted Mike. "I don't get heart attacks, I give them," he'd once shouted at AJ. Charlie had been right about most things, but not that. Seated next to the Mad Austrian was the woman he could never have—now no one could. Romy had committed suicide following two bad marriages, the death of her child, and a faltering career. Steve McQueen had also died alone, in a quack clinic in Mexico. But tonight he looked as good as he had at AJ's wedding. It would be more fun with his best man here.

All of them had passed from his life without warning, without closure. There was so much left to say—especially to the man at the head of the table. AJ remembered how fine a figure his father had cut, how resonant his voice and how deeply satisfying and contagious his laugh. This was his kind of evening. AJ was poised to go over to hug him when the strains of "Happy Birthday" cut through his reverie. It was a good thing he'd made notes; otherwise he wouldn't have anything to say.

CHAPTER 40

There was a dark but telling paradox in Hollywood: the only thing worse than not making a movie was the heartache of making one. Yesterday Sam Kinison had charged onto the set of *General Assembly* carrying a chain saw, with the avowed intent to cut the balls off Ted Barkley. Unwilling to risk his manhood for art, the film's director had fled back to his suite at the Regency. When AJ learned that production had shut down for the third time in as many weeks, he canceled his plans for the Fourth of July weekend and boarded the next flight for New York.

He'd first concocted the idea of *General Assembly* in 1978, as a vehicle for Richard Pryor, with whom he'd become reacquainted during the filming of Rastar's *California Suite*. After Pryor nearly self-immolated while freebasing cocaine, he'd signed John Belushi, but four months prior to production, Bernie Brillstein, John's manager, had called to say Belushi was dead from a drug overdose. AJ had hunted for a comedian with their scathing intensity and inventiveness, refusing to compromise by casting an ordinary actor in a tour de force role.

Then, at midnight in some forgettable comedy club in Van Nuys, he'd watched a short, fat man with stringy unwashed hair convulsing the Valley crowd. "I like Ethiopians as much as the next guy," Sam Kinison bellowed. "But I'm sick of sending them money. Sure they're starving, but what the hell do they expect—they keep trying to grow crops in the desert. Hello! You don't see us farming in Palm Springs, do you? My idea is that they pack up all their shit—after all, how much shit do Ethiopians have—and hike someplace where there's a lot less sand."

AJ had instructed Leventhal to make the deal, but in the process Pete discovered that Kinison had a history of drug and alcohol abuse to rival the deadest of comics. AJ reacted to the news like a frustrated four-year-old, warning his lawyer "to mind his goddamn business," which was exactly what Pete was trying to do.

Over dinner at the Hamburger Hamlet, Kinison disarmed AJ by acknowledging the rumors. His parents were revivalist preachers in the Midwest, but when the Kinisons passed the hat, they rarely collected more than four dollars in change. Growing up among failures had made him insecure, but he had put his fears behind him. Sam's excitement about *General Assembly* was palpable, and as far as AJ could tell, chocolate was the man's only current addiction. He inhaled two malts and a slice of seven-layer cake that slopped over a dinner plate. Five fans—all under twenty-five and terminally hip—asked Kinison for his autograph. The upside of breaking a unique talent was too massive for AJ to pass up.

He assigned Shelly Nelton to monitor the production. She reported that during rehearsals Kinison made valuable contributions, arrived punctually, and accepted direction from Barkley. Koji, in New York dating rejects from the Ford modeling agency, adopted Sam as his new buddy. He phoned to read AJ an item in the *Post* describing how Kinison had won over the crew by wiping his ass with a slice of bologna. The game changed, however, the morning the cameras rolled.

As Prime Minister Slobo Boboggian of Kamackastan, Sam negoti-

ated peace between two warring countries by getting their foreign min-
isters too drunk to realize they'd signed a treaty. In L.A. the J² team
laughed out loud at the first day of dailies. Perversely, Kinison hated his
work. Although Barkley reshot the scene, Sam's improvs made it
worse. The next day the actor was three hours late, which pushed the
movie two days behind schedule after a week. Then Kinison told his
costar, Marcello Mastroianni, to ram a salami up his ass and stormed
off, leaving two hundred extras at the United Nations Plaza with stories
for the tabloids. Upon his return to work, he wore earmuffs to block
Barkley's direction—proving he hadn't bent to authority. Ted accused
the actor of behaving unprofessionally, which prompted Kinison's
chain-saw threat.

In the lobby of the Lowell Hotel, Shelly and Ted pounced on AJ with
their recommendation: fire Kinison and recast the picture. God, how he
wanted to oblige, but the part *required* a crazy personality and all the Bill
Murrays and Rodney Dangerfields had already turned down the project.
The options were to stick with Kinison or close down the movie—at a
cost of three million dollars.

"You know what we're fighting?" Barkley asked cynically.

The answer was the bane of the eighties—pure Colombian gold.
"No way to keep it from him?"

"The guy cruises Synanon to pick up addicts when he wants to get
laid," Shelly replied. "He's got an entourage with gram bags stashed in
every pocket. Can't CAA do something about this?"

The days when AJ had flown to the set of *The Great Escape* and convinced McQueen to stop acting like a baby were history. Today's young
actors responded only to pistol-whippings. "In the morning I'll inform
Kinison that his career's on the line. If he doesn't get his act together,
we'll sue his ass for every penny he's made or ever will make. What's his
call?"

"Seven A.M.," Barkley grunted. "There's not a snowball's chance in
hell."

"Believe me, Ted, he'll be there on time." AJ's bravado disappeared
as soon as his visitors left.

Armed and dangerous with two hours of fitful sleep, he arrived at
Kinison's loft in the East Village at six A.M. A mammoth, tattooed bodyguard was passed out by the front door. With a set of keys provided by
Sam's teamster driver, AJ impatiently unlocked four dead bolts but met
resistance as he pushed against the door. What he saw and smelled in-

side made him gag. The least of it was the detritus of a bizarre party that must have ended shortly before dawn, because cigarette butts still smoked and vomit soaked the rug. AJ counted fifteen empty bottles of gin and vodka. The glass coffee table had five lines of unsnorted cocaine, but every other table, lamp, and chair was smashed to bits.

The object blocking the door turned out to be a naked woman. A muddy brown substance covered her broad buttocks. To his surprise, the overpowering scent was cheap chocolate. Then he noticed a nearby cache of Hostess cupcakes. From the tooth marks up and down her crack, he deduced that a chocoholic had smeared the snack on the girl and eaten it off her ass. Flipping her over, AJ discovered a Devil Dog in her vagina. Fortunately, Cupcake was alive and none the worse for wear. A staccato bleating emanated from the bedroom. AJ couldn't exclude bestiality.

The sound was Kinison's ripsaw snore. Sprawled across a king-sized bed, Sam swamped two young women with his blubber. One of them had garish henna hair and looked like a witch. The bad dye job reminded him of the time Jess had poured a bottle of peroxide on her head and let the sun bleach her hair white. Anger and disgust overwhelmed any thought he had harbored about salvaging the situation. "Get the fuck up!" His bellow got no response, so he pushed Kinison off the side of the bed. The floor shook when he landed.

"What? What's wrong?" Sam stood up unsteadily. "Who the fuck are you?"

"I'm the guy paying your salary. The guy paying for your fuck pad, your blow, your liquor, and your girls." The witch chanted a spell to make him disappear. AJ didn't budge. "Aren't you due on the set?" he asked Kinison facetiously.

"I'm not doing your fucking movie. I got script approval and I don't approve anymore." He struggled toward his dresser to ingest a line of cocaine AJ had mistaken for a piece of chalk.

"You don't have script approval. You don't have jack shit!" AJ tripped him. "Put some clothes on and get to work!"

Gasping for air, Kinison rolled like a beached whale toward a canister of oxygen and drew huge gulps. AJ observed the pathetic performance in desolate silence. The comic was too far gone to answer the bell. How the hell was AJ going to explain to Seiji Keiku that he was in the red before a single movie had appeared on-screen?

Sam mumbled a piteous plea for water, so AJ slammed into the bathroom looking for a glass and found—shit!—Koji Keiku asleep in the Jacuzzi bathtub, dirty water bubbling over his chin. It was a miracle he hadn't drowned. AJ had no sympathy for poor little rich kids and pushed his head underwater to wake him up. That was when he spotted a hypodermic needle and heroin on the ledge of the tub.

He moved swiftly into damage control, and within an hour doctors had treated everyone. Sam was more belligerent than ever, screaming long-distance that CAA should pay him in full. The agent hung up in his ear. After Koji promised to seek immediate help for his drug habit, AJ agreed not to report the incident. An industrial cleaning crew fumigated the apartment, while the transportation captain drove Sam's groupies home. That afternoon Shelly announced to the crew that production on *General Assembly* was officially terminated.

=

The Kinison debacle increased the pressure to cast *Water, Water Everywhere* properly. AJ enticed Richard Dreyfuss with the novelty of playing a villain, but no one wanted the role of hero. Kevin Bacon and Sean Penn both turned it down, as did Tim Hutton, even though AJ offered to double his last quote. The director, Donnie Kornberg, was excited about a newcomer named D. B. Sweeney who'd auditioned brilliantly. AJ liked the kid, but he wouldn't do squat for the marquee. The only viable alternative, his family reminded him, was his son.

Personal animus aside, the professional question that plagued AJ was why Ricky had failed to become a movie star. After his debut in *Don't Tread on Me* he'd appeared in a half dozen art-house films, and critics had raved about his ability to embody the soul of assorted losers and psychos. Among his mainstream movies, however, he was unrecognizable in his only success—as the creature Igloid in *Catch a Falling Star,* the sci-fi hit that catapulted Russ Matovich to Spielbergian status. A year ago he'd lost out to Emilio Estevez for a part in *The Breakfast Club* and director Joel Schumacher had passed him over for the coveted role of the preppy leader in *St. Elmo's Fire.* The result was that Ricky's name disappeared from A-lists as if written in invisible ink.

His response to rejection was to get zoned and stoned one night, high and wired the next, until he ran his Porsche 911 over the edge of Mulholland Drive at three A.M. The first person the LAPD notified was AJ. He made bail and, after dodging reporters, bundled Ricky into his Jag. They barely spoke during the two hours it took to reach the Betty

Ford Center near Palm Springs. After drying out and joining AA, Ricky refocused on acting, not acting out. The only offers, however, were for TV movies, which he refused to read.

"Roll film."

AJ had decided to test both Sweeney and his son. As the lights dimmed in the screening room, both actors played a four-minute scene in which their young doctor-detective character accused Dreyfuss of being the madman poisoning the water supply. After the lights came up, AJ studied the silent, poker faces of Andy, Jessica, and Kornberg. Film rarely lied, but it always required interpretation. "You first, Donnie."

"D.B.'s not your classic leading man, but he's got rough charm and integrity. Ricky clearly looks like a star and I found his performance . . . edgy."

"Thanks for not mincing words."

Kornberg looked sheepish. After his years of making millions of dollars cutting trailers, *Water, Water Everywhere* was his directorial debut, and he was reluctant to offend the man who'd given him his big chance. "This is too weird, knowing Ricky's your son. But honestly, I can go either way."

AJ turned to Faddiman. "What's your sense?"

"Neither one of them is Tom Cruise. Nobody knows this B.D."

"D.B."

"Exactly. And nobody cares about Ricky. We'll have to sell Dreyfuss and the concept. From a marketing perspective, it's a wash."

This kind of mealymouthed input was no help. "Folks, you have to—"

"I vote for my brother," Jessica piped up.

"Good. Because . . . ?"

"I've always worried about the believability of our premise. Would an urban terrorist really do something so heinous? Ricky did a better job of convincing me."

"I know I'm not a creative guy," Pete interjected from the back row. "But if they're so close, aren't we better off with Ricky, who's proven his acting chops, rather than Sweeney, who's inexperienced?"

AJ deliberated for a seeming eternity. "I'm going to make a statement. If any of you disagrees, it's critical that you speak up."

The four nodded solemnly.

"Sweeney's performance was interesting and I rooted for him to nail

Dreyfuss. Ricky's acting was *riveting,* but I found myself rooting for Dreyfuss to escape."

No one said a word.

After they departed, AJ paced the room alone. He was confident of two things. First, no matter how cleverly written and directed, thrillers like *Water, Water* worked commercially only if moviegoers cared about the hero. Equally critical, the camera captured some ineffable quality in Ricky that kept an audience at arm's length. It was the same in his prior films, which made it unlikely that a director—especially a rookie— could eliminate it. AJ circled the essence of the problem with adjectives like *dark* and *cold.* But they described the surface, whereas Ricky's problem resided deep within. From his earliest days his son had despised his own inadequacies. Acting was his attempt to escape, but the audience had caught him. How could they embrace someone who so obviously hated himself?

=

Silver Lake sucked. The neighborhood west of downtown had slipped from funk to grunge in the three years since Ricky had put a down payment on a two-bedroom Craftsman with his paycheck from *Evil on My Mind.* One of his next-door neighbors was an abstract artist with a hundred unsold canvases in her garage, the other a sound engineer laid off by Capitol Records. Low expectations choked the place, like the everyday smog. He had to move—and move on in life—but first he needed to earn some bucks and he wouldn't take a handout from his grandmother. That's why he'd gotten so charged when his father had called to ask if he could drop by. It had to be good news about the part; otherwise the old man would have sent an emissary, probably his dutiful sister.

The premise of *Water, Water Everywhere* was sufficiently sick to make it a fun read. Ricky's immediate instinct, of course, had been to play the terrorist, but it was an instinct he had to deny to keep his career from going deeper into the toilet. Hell, he'd be making a million dollars a picture now if he had accepted the lead in *Risky Business,* but he'd been afraid it was going to be another dumb comedy. It was time to go commercial—without sacrificing quality.

Paying the devil his due, his father had a knack for producing that kind of film. And the role of the CDC investigator had potential. Ricky had gone without water for a day to see how it felt. Shit—anyone who wanted to see thousands of people dying of thirst was seriously sick. To track him down, he had to adopt that mind-set, and that's how he'd played the screen test. He'd almost skipped it because he was so pissed at the idea of having to compete with an unknown like Sweeney. But what could he expect—his father was a walking, talking power trip. At first he worried that his anger might have seeped into his performance, but apparently not.

The doorbell rang twice while he reminded himself of his promise to his grandma to make an honest effort at getting along. "Hey, Dad. How you doing? Want something to drink?"

"No thanks."

Small talk was a dry hole. "So, how'd I do? Did that suit I wore in the test make me look too corporate?"

"You looked good . . . very convincing."

His father sounded like he had gravel in his throat. "I've decided that casting you would be a mistake—for all of us."

The words made no more sense than the gibberish the old man had spouted the night of his stroke. "I don't understand."

"Son, you're great when you play unconventional. But the role of the doctor straitjackets you into the standard Hollywood hero."

"Are you saying that you're giving the part to someone else for *my* own good?"

"It doesn't showcase your talent. I'm worried that if the movie fails, it will ruin your career."

It was all clear now. His father had baited him by having Jess slip him the script, and now he was snapping the bear trap. What better way to humiliate him—and Grandma—than to make his son beg for a chance, watch him sweat through a trial he couldn't win, then reject him? Ricky tried controlling his emotions, but . . . shit, he was crying. "I . . . was . . . I was great."

"But not in the way I need."

The bastard tried to put his arm around him. "Get your hands off me!"

"I didn't think you'd want to get the part out of guilt or charity."

"You jealous fuck! It's just like *Don't Tread on Me*. You can't live with the idea that I'd be great in the movie and get the credit. So you cast some bum and disgrace me."

"That's totally untrue."

"Are you insane? How will I ever get another job in this town when people learn my own father won't hire me? Get the hell out of here!"

He slammed the door and closed his eyes but still imagined his father's triumphant march back to his car. "Fuckerrrrrr!" Ricky hurled a beer bottle against the wall, then collapsed on his sofa, sending puffs of dust into the air.

=

The phone was ringing off the hook when AJ returned home from the scene of the crime. A voice with a military cadence announced, "Madam Ambassador Ginsberg calling."

He'd figured he had until tomorrow before the fallout.

"What were you thinking? Do you have any idea how vulnerable Ricky is?"

"Would you like to hear my side of the story?"

"Your side? There are no sides—you're his father."

AJ squeezed the plastic receiver till it almost cracked. "I have a hundred people depending on me. I can't fail them just because Ricky needs a gig."

"Doesn't family mean anything to you?"

"How about me, Mom? I'm family too."

"But you don't have a drug habit. If Ricky falls off the wagon, there's no telling where he'll land. It could be his grave."

"Was he high when you spoke to him?"

"No, AJ, he was low—as low as it's possible to go. Let's not have a ridiculous argument. The simple fact is that you have to be there for him. If you handle it properly, I believe he'll still take the part."

Wishing for his mother to change was wasted energy. A half century of bullying had to stop. But it wouldn't—unless he stopped it. Like he'd stopped Paul Herzog. "Casting Ricky was a bad idea. I should have cut it off at the start. But I allowed you to steamroller me. I'm not a fucking moron or a coward, I'm not selfish or irresponsible. I loved you, but that's not enough. I don't know what is, and I'm tired of trying to figure it out."

He felt his mother swallow his assault. But she could never digest it. "Stop trying. As long as I live, I will never see or speak to you again."

CHAPTER 41

T he coffin resting before the altar was mute proof of the incalcula- bility of life. Sixty hours ago AJ and Leon Ginsberg had shared steak and onion rings at the Palm. They'd reminisced over the blind turns in their kinship, then segued to discussing how Gins- berg could help J² enter the television business. As they hugged good- bye, Leon promised to broker peace in the family, whether anyone wanted him to or not.

When AJ flipped on CNN the next morning, the last person he ex- pected to see was the woman who linked them in a triangle. But there was his mother amid the rubble-strewn streets of Mexico City. An 8.1 earthquake had devastated downtown in the early hours of Septem- ber 19. Racing toward a collapsed building, the ambassador shouted to a trailing reporter that thousands of victims were buried alive, while Mexican government officials "took a siesta." Then she stumbled and disappeared.

Leon jetted down in his G-3, tracking her to an emergency room where she'd been taken after breaking her ankle. They'd barely said hello when an aftershock hit. When the lights came on, Ginsberg lay facedown on the peeling linoleum, dead of a massive coronary.

AJ shivered. Although the official name was now Mount Sinai Me- morial Park, the chapel was the same one they'd used for his dad's ser- vice. It was equally jam-packed. The difference was that his son stood at the pulpit. "Wherever my uncle Leon is," Ricky began, "I'm sure it's a good place, but I'm also sure the person he's missing most is Gram." Maggie—her ankle in a cast, her eyes puffy, and her cheek cut by flying debris—ignored AJ. No, she disdained him. The mourners in the con- gregation rose for the Kaddish. He had long ago memorized the prayer for the dead. But that didn't make chanting it easier.

=

The scene by the grave site reminded Ricky of a funeral for an interna- tional leader attended by representatives from hostile countries. He nodded hello to his father, but Grandma refused to acknowledge him. The Starks looked twitchy. The family's schism was public enough to embarrass even the neutrals. As he leaned against the limousine smoking a cigarette, he spied his dad's girlfriend approaching. He'd been shocked by how much he'd enjoyed talking to her at his father's birthday party. Among the throng of Jews, she looked aggressively goyish.

"I was afraid nobody in this city smoked anymore," she complained.

He lit one for her. "They're too busy trying to live forever."

"That's a fucking bore."

Ricky laughed. "I never figured my father to choose a hedonist."

"I chose him."

"Touché."

"You spoke beautifully."

"It's easy when you believe what you're saying. For Uncle Leon's seventieth birthday, my grandma gave him a scrapbook. It had pictures and articles going back to his childhood in Berlin. When he was our age he'd graduated rabbinical seminary and been appointed to a pulpit in a town ten miles from Bergen-Belsen. Then came the war."

Megan inhaled deeply. "Today was the first I knew that he was anything but a legendary TV producer. What a fantastic opportunity to live two lives."

"It must have taken a lot of guts for Leon to make the shift—even to realize that his first choice was wrong." The crowd dispersed. "You probably shouldn't be consorting with the enemy. But even under the circumstances, it's good to see you again."

She ignored his offer to escape. "I'm sorry about what happened with the part. You were clearly better."

"You saw the screen test?"

"I asked your father so I could educate myself. When I gave my opinion, he grunted that I had a lot to learn."

"I appreciate your telling me." He studied her. "Why are you here?"

"I thought AJ would want support today—"

"No, I mean here in Hollywood. You don't belong—I say that as a compliment."

"Biding my time . . . and getting rich."

"If you're so rich, how about buying me lunch?"

=

Maggie gazed at a framed picture of her and Leon atop the Eiffel Tower. "Thank you, my dear. I know the world gossiped that I took you for granted, but I didn't. Your love was a precious gift. Beyond all the riches, that's what I'll remember." She kissed his face. The glass was cold. Maggie forced a brush through her hair, touched up her makeup, and walked downstairs.

"We went through thirty pounds of lox," she reported to her grandson after the final condolence caller disappeared into the night. "That's a true measure of how much Hollywood loved your Uncle Leon."

"At twelve bucks a pound, I hope so."

"Believe me, I can afford it." Yesterday Gary Hirsch, their lawyer, had announced that Leon's estate exceeded one hundred million dollars. She was the sole beneficiary and, since she was his wife, it passed to her without taxes. The number was double what she'd expected—the result of the steep escalation in the syndication prices paid by local TV stations for his six successful series.

"I'm more concerned about your health than your wealth," he replied.

"Don't worry about me. I want to talk about you—about your future."

Ricky sounded upbeat. "I'm close to getting a part in the new Simpson-Bruckheimer movie. It's about these aircraft carrier pilots, and I'd play Tom Cruise's rival."

She didn't reveal how hard she had pressured CAA to procure him the job or that at the funeral Ovitz had reported that the nod was going to Val Kilmer. If Hollywood preferred that punk to her grandson, the place was hopeless. "If you continue to act, of course I'll support you. But you'll be making a huge mistake."

Ricky was stung. "Don't you think I'm good?"

"*You're* wonderful. It's the job that stinks. As an actor you'll always be at the mercy of fools like your father. Even if you succeed, you're no better than your next movie. After Christmas I'm resigning my ambassadorship. When I return to L.A. I intend to build on your Uncle Leon's legacy. A month ago Mike Ovitz introduced us to Mike Milken. He's a financial genius on Wall Street and he described how we could multiply our net worth. It involves these things called "junk bonds," which have unbelievably high rates of interest. They're used to finance hostile takeovers."

Maggie realized that her grandson didn't understand what she was talking about—or why—but she kept selling. "Leon was impressed, so I'm moving forward. When we have hundreds of millions, we're going to march back into the entertainment business and buy something big. Don't ask me what because I'm not sure. But I've lived long enough to know there are incredible changes on the horizon. Maybe it will be a new way of seeing movies or new ways of making them. The opportunity will occur before I'm pushing up daisies. And when it does, I want you to head it."

"I don't know, Gram." He looked embarrassed. "The closest I've come to business was playing Biff in *Death of a Salesman* at the Taper."

"In which you were fabulous, and after which those idiots at Fox turned you down for a part in *Revenge of the Nerds.*"

"And I tried to kill myself."

"Exactly. Ricky, you can play any part you want in life. Just promise me you'll consider it."

"I promise, although I don't think I'd make much of a tycoon."

"Let me be the judge of that."

≡

Why, Jessica wanted to know, had Danny Hilman sent her an invitation to his famous Halloween bash? Hilman was an elegant producer, a few years older than her dad, and his friends were the most chic people in Hollywood—no one's description of her. Maybe it was a mistake? Maybe there was another Jessie Jastrow? No, he had the address correct, and his office had confirmed her on the list. Checking with her friends, she discovered an unnerving explanation: her host's penchant for seducing smart young women into erotic, twisted trysts.

While shopping with Shelly Nolton, Jess confided how much Hilman's reputation worried her, then chose a Cleopatra outfit that would have backed up barge traffic on the Nile. A straight black wig masked her auburn curls. A tiara in the shape of a cobra head reared up on her forehead. She wore a bustier of beaten gold, a flowing gown of turquoise blue chiffon, and a jeweled asp on her breast.

A Chinese butler dressed as Fu Manchu ushered her into Danny's domain. A Ming vase was the only item gracing the endless white entry. The guy had taken minimalism to the max. At the bar Jess recognized the Roaring Twenties' flapper to her left—her idol, Sherry Lansing, the first female head of a studio. "Ow!" A bloodcurdling Dracula bit her neck from behind.

"I can never resist young blood." Her dad's old nemesis Russ Matovich swept away with a flourish.

Several women her age attended. Polly Newcomb, a lawyer at Ziffren, Brittenham, snapped her Catwoman whip. In her E.T. outfit

Leslie Kemp, a story editor at Amblin, chatted with ICM's Milly Vance, dressed as Joan of Arc. Jess felt better—and worse—knowing she wasn't alone in Hilman's lineup.

" 'Age cannot wither her, nor custom stale her infinite variety: other women cloy the appetites they feed, but she makes hungry where most she satisfies.' "

"Huh?" Jessie stared at the Mad Hatter, who quoted *Antony and Cleopatra* as gloriously as a Cambridge don.

"I'm Sean Devine, an agent at CAA." His name, rank, and serial number were impressive. Sean had once served as Mike Ovitz's assistant and was irresistible in courting hot young talent.

With CAA on her shit list, however, Jess remained distant. "I didn't think agents recited Shakespeare—or knew who he was."

"That's presumptuous." Sean removed his mask, revealing the kind of all-American good looks she fancied. He was tall, with a dreamy body that featured narrow hips, unlike the last two guys she'd dated, who were wide enough to give birth.

"The truth hurts."

He sighed theatrically. "I guess Cleopatra's attitude came with the asp."

Sean was cute and clever . . . and a little outrageous. "I'll forgive your insult because *Alice in Wonderland* happens to be my favorite book. Anyone who comes as one of its characters can't be all bad." She stuck out her hand. "I'm not really Queen of the Nile, just Jessie Jastrow."

They partied together and went for drinks afterward. As soon as she got back to her apartment, Jessica called Shelly. It was one A.M., but she had to tell someone that Sean had picked *her* out of *that* crowd! When her friend interrupted to ask if Hilman had also hit on her, Jess realized she had never actually met the host of the party.

=

The first preview of *The Scholarship* took place in early November in the trendy beach community of Marina del Rey. The National Research Group, the firm that dominated market testing in the industry, recruited four hundred moviegoers ages sixteen to forty. After NRG's founder, Joe Farrell, requested that the audience stay at the end to fill out questionnaires, the house lights dimmed and people settled into their seats—except the J² team. They stood in abject terror at the back of the house.

AJ had seen *The Scholarship* twice in the screening room. He respected it more than he liked it. The director, Paul Hovening, had coaxed the actors to performances that were honest rather than "movie cute." The resulting film was edgy, sexy, and uncomfortable. Playing the Phi Beta Kappa prostitute, Cheryl Davis didn't *ask* the audience to like her. Whether they would or not was the evening's multimillion-dollar question.

AJ leaned forward on liquid knees at the scene in which Cheryl first took money for sex. It was the Hail Mary touchdown pass, the jury foreman reading the verdict, the envelope with the notification from the college admissions office, the doctor with the biopsy results. It was every one of those events, profound and trivial, in which people feel that their fate rests in the hands of the gods. AJ felt totally alive and wished he were dead in the same instant.

When they realized that the winsome Princeton coed hooked for her tuition, people's hands froze in their vats of popcorn and they ceased slurping their soft drinks. Within a few frames they'd forgotten the day at work or the upcoming exam or the cost of the baby-sitter. A collective "Ooh!" filled the theater.

Jessie elbowed Andy Faddiman, who was a pro at reading audience reactions. "Was that a good 'ooh'?"

"That was a *great* 'ooh.' "

AJ paced the back of the theater as if his hockey team had scored the first goal. Every laugh, plot twist, and emotional moment played as designed. Ninety minutes later, as the credits rolled, he embraced Hovening. "You did it, Paul. You trusted the material. That took guts."

Next in line were Andy, Jessica, and Shelly, with a special hug reserved for Megan. The audience sat quietly, rating the movie on a five-point scale. NRG staff members tabulated the cards while Farrell conducted a focus-group interview in the front of the theater with twenty moviegoers. Joe combined the authority of a Harvard professor with the glitz of a Mercedes salesman. His job was easy tonight because the audience bought the movie. People praised *The Scholarship* as original, honest, sexy, and provocative and appreciated the nonschmaltzy ending, even though the heroine wound up alone.

After the group filed out, the J^2 contingent converged on Farrell as if he'd just been handed the Ten Commandments. The preliminary tabulation of the comment cards showed that 41 percent of the audience rated the movie "excellent," 40 percent "very good," 7 percent "good," 8 percent "fair," and 4 percent "poor."

"Yes!" AJ pumped his fist in the air.

Above 80 percent in the top two boxes was outstanding, suggesting highly positive word-of-mouth on *The Scholarship*. Joe noted that the ratings were stronger among younger moviegoers, while those over thirty expressed ambivalence about the character's moral choice. Tonight's audience was more sophisticated, more liberal, and better educated than average, he cautioned. No one cared—they had a hit.

Outside the theater the salty air from the Pacific provided an intoxicating nightcap. Too jubilant to drive home, AJ grabbed Megan's hand and set off for the boardwalk. Only then did he realize how subdued her reaction during the postscreening celebration had been. By her choice, tonight was her first viewing of *The Scholarship*. Did she hate it? They'd hiked almost to Venice Beach before he found out. "You've probably wondered if my script was autobiographical."

"Megan, I never—"

"AJ, come on! You're my lover. How could you not?" She slipped from his arms and faced the surf. "I did it once—took money to sleep with a man."

He'd expected her admission—but not the fact it turned him on.

"I needed money, I don't remember for what." She whirled around wearing a sardonic smile. "That's bullshit. It was for a Ralph Lauren camel-hair coat, which cost as much as my room and board. One of my jobs was to escort alumni around campus for ten bucks a tour. This billionaire from Dallas wanted to relive his football glory in Franklin Field. At midfield—with fifty thousand empty seats surrounding us— he offered me five hundred dollars to spend the night at the Bellevue Stratford. I was horny, he was distinguished, and the coat had my name on it."

"Megan, it's okay, it—"

"It's not! Let me finish! I never repeated it with him or any other man. But watching the film tonight . . . it was like taking off my clothes again. I felt really dirty."

"I don't care, Megan. I've done things I'm ashamed of—we all have."

She kissed him—more salt than sweet. The wind whipped her hair against his face. He couldn't get enough. "Will you marry me?"

Megan didn't say yes—but she didn't say no.

On their way to the car, he noticed a motel with a flashing vacancy sign. AJ checked them in as "Mr. and Mrs. AJ Jastrow."

CHAPTER 42

It was as predictable and nauseating as morning sickness. Six weeks to the day before *The Scholarship* opened in malls across America, AJ awoke with acid reflux. His burning, curdling burp was not a human sound. When he explained to Megan that it was the first symptom in the prerelease panic he'd suffered since his Paramount days, her concern shifted from his health to the film's. He assured her that his anxiety was neurotic, not predictive. Producers and studio executives experienced perverse comfort in the role of Sisyphus. On the way up the mountain they and the boulder were one. But after it crested, the rock was on its own. Nothing was more sickening than standing helplessly on the heights and watching its downhill run.

The only reliable remedy AJ had discovered was working brain-numbing eighty-hour weeks in the company of colleagues with as much at stake. Throughout Christmas, J^2 remained as hectic as Santa's workshop. Obsessively, he triple-checked the selection of theaters, shipping of trailers, and cutting of TV spots until Andy threw a tantrum at his interference. Then he turned his focus to fighting fires on *The Coney Island Maniac.*

There hadn't been a promising moment on the movie since Megan had handed in her draft. Koji had initiated the downward spiral. To revenge AJ for forcing him into rehab, he'd warned his father that the movie would be a disaster. AJ had reassured Seiji that he would keep a tight rein on *Maniac,* so he'd hired Gordo Slaughter, a veteran Australian director of low-budget movies. Gordo was ruthless, but his compromises produced complications.

AJ reclined in his desk chair, trying to make sense of the latest crisis. Bobby Manelo, the actor playing the Maniac, talked like one. "Calm down," AJ urged.

"I can't calm down. I'm going to explode."

AJ heard Slaughter yell, "Do it for me," then a door slammed. "Bobby, where are you?"

"In my dressing room. I told you it wouldn't work. . . . I've tried to be a good guy but this suit's a disaster. I won't split my gut for a goddamn movie."

The fire in which the Maniac died fused molten steel over his body till he looked like a metallic man. Each morning it took three hours to apply the metal full-body suit and one to remove it, which left little time for shooting. Gordo had chosen a low bidder to design it, but the guy was so inexperienced he'd forgotten to give the actor a way to shit without removing the suit completely. AJ grimaced, anticipating the specifics.

"I've been trying to make sure I used the bathroom before makeup," Manelo explained. "Maybe it was that three-bean burrito . . . anyway, an hour ago I got these killer cramps. Gordo wanted me to hold out so he wouldn't lose the rest of the day, but I got to take a crap so bad. He told me to shit in the suit, but that's too gross."

AJ had an out-of-body experience. When he returned to earth, however, Manelo was grunting in pain and farting like an AK-47. Getting a few additional shots today wouldn't make the difference. "Bobby, take care of yourself. I'll handle it."

After calling Slaughter and ordering him to wrap, AJ grabbed his overcoat and headed to the garage. It was forty-three degrees and gray in Los Angeles; the weather fueled his doom as he drove to Stan Kamen's house. Until a year ago AJ hadn't heard of AIDS, and his friend still refused to admit he was dying of it, which gave the visit another surreal edge.

"Damn lymphoma's killing me," Stan whispered. He was emaciated, his complexion so waxy AJ wondered if the undertaker had gotten a head start. Stan stuffed a gold Rolex watch into AJ's hand. "It was McQueen's . . . he gave it to me for making him a star. God knows, you did half the work."

AJ leaned close. "Stan, I'm going to take advantage of the fact that you don't have the strength to tell me to shut up. Thank you for believing in me from the start. Thank you for being the best boss I ever had. And thank you for showing me that an honorable guy can make it in Hollywood."

Kamen reached out to hug him. AJ managed a tentative embrace. The man was flaky skin and brittle bones. AJ was grateful when the phone rang. "I'll get it." He couldn't believe the caller. "It's Mike Ovitz."

Fury stoked Kamen's embers. He grabbed the receiver. "Come on, Mike, I know damn well what you're doing!"

AJ caught snatches of the CAA chief denying that he'd poached Stan's clients. Whatever argument Mike offered caused Stan's blood pressure to spike. His cheeks and lips flushed against his white pallor. "Isn't there enough business out there for all of us?" Kamen slammed down the phone. After several minutes of wheezing, he regained control. "Tell Mike Simpson . . . watch out. Ovitz having . . . dinner tonight with Al Pacino." Ashes to ashes, dust to dust—William Morris to CAA.

=

"Ride 'em, cowgirl!"

Sean Devine's words were all the incentive Jessie needed. He held on to her waist while she gunned a snowmobile thirty miles per hour through the forests of Sun Valley, finally emerging onto a blinding field of fresh powder. A glance over their shoulders confirmed that they enjoyed a twenty-second lead over an army of other machines. The race was the pièce de résistance of a weekend competition organized by Sean and his cadre of baby CAA agents. The attendees were a score of young agency clients, executives, and producers destined to own the future, which in Hollywood's half-life was five years or less. The beknighted ate and drank, skated and skied for forty-eight sleepless hours.

Jess wasn't sure if she'd been invited as Sean's girlfriend or one of the "hot execs." Suddenly nothing seemed more crucial than reaching the finish line first, so she opened the throttle on her Arctic Cat. They would have made it if the snowdrift dead ahead weren't a mogul. Back at the lodge Joel Silver, who produced action films, offered to hire them as stuntmen in his next production. The miracle was that Jess and Sean crawled from the wreck unharmed. Matt Margolin, the boy-wonder head of production at Paramount, bestowed a nickname, "Crash" Jastrow—sure proof that she'd arrived.

At two A.M. they climbed the stairs to a moment of truth. Jess considered Sean sex on a stick but had resisted making love with him until she knew he really cared. The only four guys she'd slept with previously were steady boyfriends. "I'm really sorry for almost maiming us," she said upon reaching her door. "I was an idiot and you were a great sport." She kissed him lightly on the bruise above his lip.

"Everyone tells me I'm lucky to have found you. But I'm way ahead of them. I've never felt like this about any woman."

That was good enough. She grabbed his cable-knit sweater and tugged him inside, where they tumbled onto the bed. Sean was a delicious kisser. While making out with abandon, she rushed to get naked.

The ski boots delayed things, so he knelt patiently to unhook them. "Would you like me to see if I have something in your size?"

"I'll take whatever size you have."

His tongue excited her wherever it touched. She'd never been so turned on. It might be ten below, pitch-black, and snowing outside, but Jessie romped in the sun. Later, as he lay in her arms, she discovered that Sean snored. That small imperfection was her final delight.

=

At eight A.M. the fax machine beeped in the J² office. AJ and Andy leaped to grab the incoming transmission. NRG's tracking study for Monday, January 27, would predict how *The Scholarship* was going to fare at the box office when it opened on Friday. AJ was so anxious he wrenched his back reading the page as it inched out. Two numbers were as salient to movie marketers as systolic and diastolic blood pressure readings were to doctors. "Awareness"—the percentage of moviegoers who'd heard of *The Scholarship*—was seventy-three. "Definite Interest"—a surrogate measure of how many people would actually *attend*—was twenty-six. The first number was decent, the second disturbing. Both trailed *Down and Out in Beverly Hills,* the Bette Midler–Nick Nolte comedy that was to premiere the same day.

"We're in deep shit."

"It's too early to tell," Faddiman countered. Since they'd started their television campaign only five days ago, the bulk of the commercials would appear this week. And the awareness number suggested that people had noticed the film.

"They noticed, but they're not buying. You were right all along—we should switch to the comedy spot."

Andy had argued to sell *The Scholarship* as a comedy, even though it played as a drama. A funny hooker was appealing, but a real one was a turnoff. AJ wanted to stay true to the film, fearing that moviegoers anticipating laughs would be disappointed. And Megan hated the comedy spot because it trivialized her story. But pragmatism dictated making sure the movie got open *before* worrying about word of mouth—or getting laid. Andy was on his feet. "I'll call the networks to make the change. We'll catch most of tonight's schedule and the rest of the week."

AJ tried reading a script, but it was so vapid he couldn't concentrate, and watching yesterday's dailies on *The Coney Island Maniac* depressed him more. Retreating to his desk, he compulsively scribbled numbers with dollar signs on a legal pad.

J² Costs: *The Scholarship*

Negative	$11,000,000
Domestic Marketing	10,000,000
International Marketing (est.)	5,000,000
Prints for Theaters	2,000,000
Interest, Residual Payments, etc.	2,000,000
Total Costs	$30,000,000

If *The Scholarship* grossed forty million dollars at the box office, twenty million went to the theater owners and twenty to J². With video sales and foreign revenues of ten million, they would just recoup their investment. Their current tracking scores, however, suggested a fifteen-million-dollar gross. How ironic that the volatility, messiness, and magic of making movies yielded in the end to something as immutable, precise, and earthbound as a profit-and-loss statement.

=

Dinner with Sally Shumatz was a disaster. AJ tried to sell the *Premiere* editor on doing an article on J² but was interrupted every ten minutes by executives wishing him luck on Friday. The bastards all had access to NRG's tracking and their pats on the back were bullshit condolences. He felt like a dead man walking. Sally was too smart not to pick up their funereal tone. When she inquired about the prospects for *The Scholarship,* he said he expected a modest opening but a big second week. She didn't buy a word.

Disappointment multiplied by shame equaled humiliation. By the time he arrived home from Mr. Chow's, he was desperate to bury his head and hopes in a pillow. No woman had ever thrown anything at him, so he was lucky to duck the vase that winged by his ear and smashed into the wall beside the door.

"You lying son of a bitch."

"Megan."

"Don't 'Megan' me. It's everything I was afraid of."

"What is?"

"Did you see *Cagney and Lacy*?"

"How could I see it? I was out to dinner."

"There was a commercial for the movie that made it look like *Porky's*. You promised me you weren't going to run the comedy spot. You've lost faith in the film. Every promise you made to me was bullshit."

For the next half hour he conducted a course in movie marketing. She understood his reasons and didn't give a damn. AJ hated going to sleep angry, but when he tried to cuddle with Megan, he found a knife rather than a spoon beside him.

At eight-thirty the following morning, he heard her sobbing downstairs. The television was blaring when he stumbled into the family room. On the ground at Cape Kennedy in Florida a network correspondent was trying to regain her composure. AJ knew that something awful—worse than the movie's tracking numbers—was afoot but was unprepared when NBC cut to videotape of the *Challenger* exploding in an orange ball.

"That teacher, that Christa McAuliffe was on board," Megan stuttered. "The kids in her class watched."

AJ rocked her in his arms. The tragedy should have put things in perspective. Life, death, sacrifice, heroism, fate, connection—those things mattered. So he hated himself when he calculated the personal consequences, even as the rocket's fiery descent played from different angles. The inevitable blitz of television coverage would continue, preempting several of J²'s spots and creating a ghastly mood for selling a movie. Given *The Scholarship*'s already precarious chances, NASA's hopes weren't the only ones up in smoke.

≡

On Friday evening a minibus bearing ten J² executives pulled into the parking lot of a multiplex in Sherman Oaks. Filmmakers frequented theaters on opening night to monitor real-life reactions to their film, but it was unique for a company to attend en masse. AJ had organized it to acknowledge the effort made by his colleagues. Most of them were kids like his daughter, and he knew that if *The Scholarship* bombed, it would be better for them to mourn together. As the bus passed a line of people stretched around the block, he looked heavenward and prayed they were ticket holders for his movie. At the hiss of the brakes, they hurdled out like a high-school football team taking the field against its archrival. Unfortunately, the people in line waited to see *Down and Out*. Megan ran back to announce that the audience for their movie was already in the theater.

AJ sneaked into Theater 2. In the brief seconds it took to adjust to the dark he sensed less than a hundred people scattered among the four hundred seats. They looked as lonely as he felt. Cheryl Davis's character traded sex for money, but unlike in the earlier preview, the scene generated no thrill.

Andy whispered, "*Now* we're in deep shit."

Jessica stared daggers and disbelief. "You're not giving up already, are you?"

The pros averted their eyes. Tonight should have been sold-out. Movies targeted to a young market performed best on Friday nights. The weather was ideal and there was no major competition for their demographic. If *The Scholarship* performed poorly in the San Fernando Valley under playbook conditions, it surely struggled everywhere.

"Maybe it will build," Jess offered plaintively.

"Maybe." AJ spoke without conviction. In prior years, when studios released movies initially in a few theaters, a film with positive word-of-mouth could overcome a weak opening. But *The Scholarship* was already playing in twelve hundred theaters. Exhibitors would kick it out on its sprocket holes before word of mouth could spread. The opening weekend was now the tyranny of the movie business. In an attempt to anchor their films, marketers increased and front-loaded advertising dollars. And to offset the greater risk, production executives selected movies *because* they were easy to sell. A movie with a concept that could be grasped in a thirty-second spot stood a better chance of getting made than a film that was complex and character-driven.

AJ crunched numbers: J^2 faced a ten-million-dollar defeat. He gathered his team in front of a Penguin's Frozen Yogurt outside the theater. "Welcome to the movie business. It's the best in the world . . . and it can be cruel as hell. We made a fine movie. We sold it well. But the audience chose not to buy. Injustices even out. Believe me, if we do our jobs in the future as well as we did them on *The Scholarship,* J-Squared will be fine." He wasn't sure if he believed his own proselytizing.

Megan sat in the back of the bus, her eyes closed, her head against the window. AJ decided not to console her. Pete plopped down next to him. "If you combine our loss on *The Scholarship* with the write-off on *General Assembly* and add in our overhead, I figure our bottom line to date—"

"Is more than fifteen million dollars in the red. That means that the Keikus can legally override my decisions." AJ sighed. "I recall who said

I shouldn't accept the 'samurai clause.' Tomorrow I'll listen. But tonight I'm just going to feel sorry for myself."

CHAPTER 43

The canopy of Cuban cigar smoke wafting over the ballroom of the Beverly Hilton could have choked a customs agent. But the two thousand businessmen at the "Predators' Ball" didn't give a damn about import bans—or any governmental regulation that meddled with their God-given right to amass and enjoy wealth. They came to swap deals, sip '61 Pétrus, and listen to Michael Milken's gospel of greed. The lights dimmed, the theme song from *Dallas* blared, and Larry Hagman, dressed as J. R. Ewing, appeared on the screen above the dais flashing his Drexel Express Titanium Card. "It has a ten-billion-dollar line of credit, so don't go hunting without it." Rupert Murdoch, Ted Turner, Steve Ross, Barry Diller—the entertainment industry's high and mighty—cheered his spoof of the American Express commercial like kids at an *Indiana Jones* matinee.

Ricky whooped it up with them, despite ranking as the poorest person in the crowd. After existing in the company of struggling artists, he found power intoxicating. Nobody told these moguls they were too short or too tall, too ethnic or too bland. Nobody rejected them after five callbacks, and nobody blamed them for a rotten performance that was the fault of the asshole who wrote the lines. These men wrote their own lines. He grinned at the man on his left. "Thanks for inviting me."

"My pleasure, pardner." Dillard Cass was a kick-ass young Texan, complete with twang and cowboy boots. In six months of managing Grandma's money, he'd increased her net worth by thirty million dollars. Those were hard numbers to ignore, so Ricky checked out his action. The guy was like a keen-eyed agent, but instead of actors, he targeted deals—everything from golf-course developments in Scottsdale to wind farms in Modesto to hot penny stocks. Intrigued, Ricky joined a couple of meetings at the office, a few lunches and dinners, then a field trip to a gold mine in Brazil. As an actor, he always researched his parts. Playing a businessman was a kick. Dill's bankers were wilder than Ricky's acting buddies—and they could afford better coke.

After the ball, a limo drove them to Bomba, a club in downtown L.A., where they met a model Ricky knew from acting class. She sat her billiard-ball butt on his lap and made a call on her cell phone. Ten minutes later three Xerox copies of her arrived. The evening looked promising. As the girls giggled off to the john to throw up and snort, Ricky pounded the black granite table to make a point. "You see, they're indispensable."

Dill seemed skeptical. "I'll tell you after I dip my wick. I finger-fucked the redhead and she's kind of—"

"Not the babes—the cell phones." They were the next big thing, Ricky was sure of it. "My neighbor's an engineer and he took a job at McCaw Communications—"

"He was there tonight, Craig McCaw."

"I know, I introduced myself while you were chatting up Milken. Anyway, my guy says the FCC's going to expand the bandwidth these cellular companies can use. When congestion decreases, sales will go nuts. It's already like that in Europe. Shit, I made this movie in Hungary last year, and people on the streets had them. Hungary, for Christ's sake, where they can't afford a sausage."

Cass sat back with a smile. "What the hell, we can invest a few mil, see what happens."

That's what Ricky loved—if you wanted to try something, you tried it. No fucking screen tests.

=

AJ prayed the next reel would be better. But there was no better—only worse—in Gordo Slaughter's cut of *The Coney Island Maniac*. Instead of a taut horror movie, the director had assembled a turgid two-hour drama about a tortured soul. Slaughter's pretensions outstripped his talent, and in the twilight of his career the schlockmeister had chosen to make a statement about the human condition rather than scare the pants off teenagers.

When the lights came up, Gordo misinterpreted the reason his employer had turned ashen. "Pretty terrifying, isn't it?"

"To say the least."

"I know it's a tad long, mate, but I think I can remove three minutes without hurting the quality."

AJ silently talked himself off the ledge. There *was* a movie in the mess. Slaughter wasn't the first director to stray off course. He would agree to make the necessary changes when he understood the problems. But the facts outshouted AJ's soothing inner voice. *Water, Water*

Everywhere had just opened to modest box office and would ultimately generate a million-dollar profit. That put all the pressure on *The Coney Island Maniac*. If it failed, J² would lose twenty million dollars in its first year, killing any chances for a second. A calm, measured response was for some other time and place. "Gordo, the movie is atrocious."

The brutality of his comment shocked Slaughter. "I . . . I don't know . . . uh . . . what to say. Perhaps you didn't see what I went for."

"What I saw was a fucking embarrassment!" AJ's spit splashed the man's face. "Do you hear me?"

"The dead can hear you. I obviously don't agree, but perhaps we should test the film with an audience."

In a town that feasted on failure, AJ knew that lousy preview results would leak, crippling Andy Faddiman's efforts to book the film. "You have the right to a screening under the DGA rules. If you insist, I'll arrange it this week. But after the movie bombs, I'll fire your ass and ruin your reputation at every studio in town."

Slaughter's eyes popped. "You'd do that?"

"No one will hire you to direct a game show on television. But it doesn't have to be that way. If you waive your right and allow me to fix this mess, I'll swear you did a great job." A confident director would have shoved the deal up AJ's ass, but Slaughter secretly feared he was a hack.

"Maybe you should take a crack at it."

"Thanks, Gordo, I appreciate your openness."

=

AJ spent the next nine days and nights parked in an editing bay with Jimmy Millman, who'd begun the 1970s cutting Roger Corman movies and ended the decade with an Academy Award. The two men ate enough pizza, Kentucky Fried Chicken, and Chinese food to gain five pounds apiece. After watching Bob Evans refashion *The Godfather*, AJ knew what miracles could be wrought. With their hack director out of the picture, they found the real *Maniac* within the mass of existing footage. Slaughter's attempt to tell a Frankenstein story created ambivalence. To clarify the emotional line they adjusted scenes so that the audience would hate the Maniac rather than pity him. And they gave people someone to root for by restoring scenes that enhanced the character of the teenage girl who fought the Maniac in the end. Their recut version was thirty-three minutes shorter and ten screams scarier.

But a critical problem remained: the special effects. All they lacked were "Zap!" and "Pow!" in bubbles above the actors. When AJ screened the movie for his senior staff, the cheesy shots ripped them out of the movie.

With film cans in tow, AJ and Millman boarded a plane for the Bay Area to seek the cure at the movie industry's Lourdes. If anyone could enhance the images in *The Coney Island Maniac,* it was Industrial Light + Magic. The chief doctor and priest was Tony Adamo, a boy-man with a peach-fuzz goatee and thick glasses. "You should sue the guy responsible for this crap. It's malpractice."

"Tell me something I don't know," AJ replied.

"I can save it . . . I think."

"You think?"

"It's going to take at least a hundred new effects shots. If someone else can give you a guarantee, take it."

"How much."

"Two million dollars."

AJ maintained a poker face. The number was double his estimate—and a quarter of the movie's original budget. Because it was the last week in April, ILM couldn't complete the job for a summer release, though they could make Halloween—if AJ proceeded *now.*

"There are a lot of filmmakers out there who need our help," Adamo noted noncommittally.

If he were buying a car, AJ might have bargained. Instead, he impulsively shook Tony's hand. "Let's get going."

A musty odor assaulted him when he entered his house just past midnight. During his immersion in the editing room, Megan had traveled to location to do an on-set production rewrite on *8 Million Ways to Die,* the new movie by legendary director Hal Ashby. AJ threw open every window. Today's decision was tough, and *everyone* would scrutinize it in light of his recent run of mistakes, from Kinison to Slaughter. But he was a dead man, AJ told himself, if he succumbed to self-doubt. This reassurance didn't work, and he remained too wired to fall asleep, so he rummaged through his closet until he found a Baggie filled with a stash of marijuana. Slipping into bed, he inhaled a joint. The stuff was potent. Hey, fuck *everyone.* He was the hire-wire act.

=

The last time Jessie had visited the Paramount lot she'd been a ten-year-old with braces and her daddy had been vice president of production. For her return at twenty-five she splurged on a Calvin Klein suit and a haircut at Christophe, since today's appointment was with Matt Margolin. Jess hadn't spoken to him since Sun Valley, but last week he'd invited her for lunch. They ate in his newly redecorated office— at least Margolin did, because Jess was too busy voting thumbs up or down on a list of thirty movies whose titles he read off in rapid-fire succession. Reclining in his custom-made Le Corbusier desk chair, he harrumphed and applauded her answers. Meanwhile, Jess gulped down her Cobb salad, trying to ignore how his ears made him look like a Volkswagen with its doors open.

"I was a twelve-year-old picking dates on a kibbutz when the Six-Day War broke out." His non sequitur startled her. "I grew up outside Tel Aviv. You know what that experience taught me, Crash?" Was this another quiz? "It taught me that life is war. The movie business is life, ergo the movie business is war. Rival studios will swarm Paramount like a pack of Arabs unless I've got soldiers willing to die to defend the Melrose gate. In Sun Valley I saw a warrior who fought like that. You remind me of Israeli women. They're great in the trenches and in bed."

"I wasn't aware of that."

"Your preferences on the Margolin Movie Test indicate pent-up aggression. I intend to unpent you." It sounded vaguely dirty, but Jess didn't mind, because Matt offered her a job as a vice president.

Marching back to her car, she wondered if he'd assessed her correctly. Admittedly, her competitive instincts had become sharper. Playing doubles last week, Jessie had slammed an overhead that almost broke the nose of her friend Stacy Snider. As the Paramount patrol officer waved her out, she saluted smartly, then dissolved into unmilitaristic merriment.

Over dinner at a steak joint called Dominick's, Jess shared the news with Sean. "Margolin said everyone touted me as brilliant—even Ovitz. You were behind this, weren't you?"

Her boyfriend was uncharacteristically self-effacing. "Hollywood has no secrets when it comes to talent. Matt asked my opinion, I told him he couldn't do better—and he can't. When do you start?"

"You think I should take it?"

"Of course you should."

"Do you trust him?"

"Why do you ask?"

"His background seemed fascinating, so I did some checking. The only time he spent on a kibbutz was one summer after the seventh grade."

"What difference does that make? He's a star—so are you, so am I, so are our friends. We're going to run the business five years from now. Being a charter member of the club means everything."

She felt like an idiot missing the obvious. He took her hand. It was stupid how so small a gesture turned her on.

"You're afraid of leaving your dad, aren't you?"

" 'Afraid' isn't the right word."

"If he knew you had this opportunity, he'd urge you to grab it."

Jess wasn't so sure.

=

Pete stood on the threshold of his boss's office, a document in each hand and a frown on his face. AJ smiled. "All you're missing is the scythe. Okay, what's the problem?"

"It's not funny," Leventhal replied. "In the last hour ILM faxed a bill for payment of two hundred and fifty thousand dollars. They've commenced work."

"Good."

"Not good." He waved the other piece of paper. "This is a registered letter from Hiroshi Hama. Keiku Enterprises has refused to authorize the additional two million dollars. We don't have the money to pay ILM."

AJ rubbed his eyes, but the dilemma only loomed larger. "What if I get on the phone? Can I convince Seiji?"

"You won't even find him. He's on an inspection tour of his whaling fleet in Guam."

"I'll burn the negative before releasing *Maniac* in its present form." AJ pounded his desktop. "Why can't they see you have to spend money to make money?"

"They see the spending part."

"Koji poisoned the waters by bad-mouthing the project before we even started."

"And now he's bored with the movie business. His new deal is racing cars." Pete's voice shook. "It's over. It was a crazy idea to begin with—start a studio, go up against the majors. Both of us must have been out of our minds."

AJ slid open his drawer, removed his leather-bound checkbook, and wrote a personal check for the ILM deposit. "Wire this now."

"What?"

"I'll get a second mortgage on the house for another quarter million and borrow the rest."

"You can't do this," Pete pleaded. "Nobody in our business uses their own money."

"Nobody in their right mind, but as you so eloquently pointed out, I don't have a right mind."

=

A Brancusi and a Giacometti had joined the collection of Rodins and Henry Moores in Ray's sculpture garden. It made AJ feel less guilty about asking for a handout. Still, he fought back tears when Stark handed him a check for half a million dollars. "Thank you."

"Forget it. Have you got enough?"

"I FedExed Seiji Keiku a letter explaining that J-Squared will put up half the cost of the bailout. My sacrifice will look like an honorable sacrifice—and a sign of the importance of the work. He'll come through with the second million."

Ray's housekeeper arrived with iced Red Zingers, and the two men sipped them in silence, enjoying the afternoon sun on a warm spring day. The grandeur of the bronze and marble made Stark contemplative. He often came out to the garden to remember his son Peter. "You're going to miss her a lot, aren't you?"

AJ looked puzzled. "Miss who?" The Rabbit's ears drooped. "Miss who?"

"Oh, God, I thought you knew. It's Jess—she took a job . . ."

Stark had to be wrong. He was old and had misunderstood. But he babbled on till AJ screamed "Shut up!" Shut up? To a friend who'd just loaned him five hundred grand? He ran from the garden. There was another explanation for this treachery. He was sure of it.

CHAPTER 44

AJ tailgated the rush-hour traffic into West Hollywood. Stark had heard the news from Jack Rapke at CAA, who'd heard it from Frank Mancuso, the chairman of Paramount. But AJ didn't care that he was the last to know—he cared only about losing Jess. His fury at her dissipated by Beverly Hills, replaced by anger at himself for blowing it. He was too autocratic. J² was a sinking ship. A stint at a major studio could advance her career more than an apprenticeship to a failed father. It was all of the above—and none of his business. Climbing the steps to his daughter's apartment, AJ debated how to initiate the dreaded conversation. Casual, don't make a big deal out of it—even though he couldn't imagine a bigger one.

"What's wrong?" She stood in the hall, hands on her hips, concerned, suspicious.

"Why does something have to be wrong?"

"Surprises aren't your thing. And you sounded like a game-show host on the intercom."

He handed her a pizza and a bottle of Barolo. "I happened to be in the neighborhood and wondered if I might tempt you with sausage and anchovies."

"Consider me tempted." While setting the table, Jess rattled on about the lousy quality of scripts. "If I read as many books or magazines, I'd be the most informed woman in the world. But reading screenplays lowers my I.Q."

"Don't worry about it."

"Why?"

AJ popped the cork on the wine. "Paramount will provide someone to read them for you."

Jess burst into tears. "Oh God! You heard about the offer."

"Honey, I was being a wise guy, it's okay, really—"

"I should have said something, but I felt so guilty!"

"It's okay," he reassured her, gently prying her hands from her face. "I'm proud that the town's learned what I've known for a long time." She wanted so much to believe his words. "Jessica, you didn't say anything because you're afraid of being disloyal. But you're not. Of course I wanted us to work together forever, but the most important thing is doing what makes *you* happy."

"Dad . . . I'm so confused."

"If you want, I'll help you screw Paramount on the deal."

She laughed at his black humor. "You think I can make it out there?"

"I think you'll be one of the great producers in the history of Hollywood." It was true, he knew it was. To have to watch her triumph from afar . . . to see her sail till she was out of sight . . .

"If I leave, you're absolutely sure you'll be okay?"

"I'll be fine." Hold it together, AJ. "It's not like you're moving to Europe or joining the Army."

"I'll learn to play golf so we can spend Sundays together."

They hugged. He wanted to hold her—for the moment and all time. Instead, he broke apart from her. "Can we eat before the pizza gets cold?"

=

Maggie decoded her son's cadence. Short and sharp sentences meant massive anxiety. Like that time . . . it was over forty years ago . . . Harry was away in the war and they were listening to *Amos 'n' Andy* on the radio. Out of the blue AJ asked how much a vase cost. That same faux-casual voice, a few octaves higher, as if the price of crystal was a normal curiosity for an eight-year-old. His eyes widened at her estimate, and she saw him calculate how many weeks of allowance it would take to replace the Lalique he'd broken throwing his Spaulding high bouncer against the wall. He admitted his mischief and all was forgiven. Another time, another place.

Not a word had passed between them since Leon's funeral. The pouches under his eyes, the creases by his mouth—as vain as he was, Maggie guessed plastic surgery was in her son's immediate future. He was aging faster than she was—like his heart, his skin had less resilience. AJ made no move to hug or kiss her, and she felt no urge to embrace him. No love lost here—amend that, *all* love lost.

"Mother, I find myself in a situation I tried desperately to avoid."

"A situation in which you need my help."

"Exactly." He hesitated. "The last time we spoke was terrible. I've thought of it often . . . I still do . . . the craziness. . . . Our clashes always got out of hand."

"That's why I don't intend to participate in another."

"Mom, in the past whenever we disagreed, I felt frustrated if I did what you wanted, but if I did what I wanted, you cut me off. I always wished that you'd support me . . . that you would love me . . . regardless."

"What else did you wish for?" The question escaped from the dungeon where she had locked it after Harry's death. In those dark days she'd known what her son wished. He didn't need to say it—she read it in his eyes each time he ran to his room or passed her in the hallway. AJ wished that she had been the one to die.

"What do you mean?"

His concern was so smooth, so empathetic—so utterly false. "Nothing. 'If wishes were horses, beggars would ride.' "

"Let me explain—"

"Your Japanese partner refused your request. You need a million dollars or you'll lose your company."

"How did—"

"It's a small town and I'm one of the biggest people in it. I'm not sure what I would have done if you'd apologized for your sinful behavior to Ricky. But you did not."

"You don't know what went on with him. You don't know—"

"About Thailand? He told me. Your son was a horny teenager. He wasn't responsible for your stroke. It happened—like your father's death happened—like all the good things in your life happened. But you have to blame someone, so when they repossess the furniture from your office, blame me."

=

His mother's hatred left AJ numb. In another age, he had no doubt, she would have exiled him to a distant isle or placed him in a tower or, on an especially bad day, ordered him beheaded. But the reality of his dilemma made self-pity unaffordable. He flew to San Francisco to tell ILM to cut short its work because J² couldn't make its second payment, but after seeing their progress, he kept his mouth shut. *The Coney Island Maniac* played like a real movie. Why not one last college try at raising money?

His mood was upbeat when he returned home, anticipating his reunion with Megan, who had just arrived after spending three weeks on the set of *8 Million Ways to Die*. At first she'd found the experience heady and cool. Not only was she rewriting Oliver Stone but she was also collaborating with Hal Ashby, who'd directed *Shampoo* and *Coming Home*. Every morning a production assistant waited in the hall outside her hotel room to rush the pages she wrote to the set. Megan felt like a brain surgeon performing a lifesaving operation. But at dailies it was clear that the patient was dying.

"Honey, I'm home!" Before taking off his coat, AJ turned on the oven to reheat the crab rolls he'd brought back from Fisherman's Wharf. She entered looking as sexy as ever in her jeans, a wineglass in her hand. "Oh, did I miss you."

All she offered was a cool kiss and a stiff hug. "We have to talk."

That was never the best first line of a conversation. "Now?"

"I slept with Hal Ashby."

It was a swift kick in the balls. "You did what?"

"I made love to Hal . . . for a couple of weeks."

This was no overwrought apology but a bold declaration. "Can I ask why?"

"Because he's a great artist."

"He's a druggie and a burnout."

"Okay. Because I wanted to!" Megan paced. "Because it made me feel sexy . . . and special. I don't always know why I sleep with a guy."

"In our case I thought it was because we loved each other."

"AJ, don't tell me you loved everyone you slept with. I'll bet you see women every day you want to take to bed."

"But I don't." A cold fog crept over him—perhaps Ashby wasn't her only fling. "How many . . . who . . . ?"

Megan hurled her wineglass at the refrigerator. "Stick your third degree up your ass!" The dripping Merlot on the kitchen tiles suggested a murder scene.

"Why are you yelling at me? And why are you admitting all of this?"

"I couldn't get into bed with you under false pretenses."

"You can screw around behind my back, but you won't lie to my face?"

Tears welled up. Maybe she had remorse. But as he moved toward her, Megan violently shoved him away and ran from the room. AJ was incredulous. The slam of the front door brought him to his senses, but by the time he gave chase Megan's taillights were a red glow down the street. Her purse remained on the counter, so he figured that she would soon return—but then what? He found the answer in their bedroom. Propped on a pillow was her engagement ring.

=

On May first, AJ sat in the corner of Alice's Restaurant in Malibu, sipping Perrier. He needed his wits about him. A Maserati squealed to a halt in the parking lot and his lunch date hopped out like a Formula One driver.

Koji ordered a double Dewar's. "Why the hell did we have to come out here? I got better things to do with my time than drive halfway back to Japan. And what's so important that—"

"I can't let you guys off the hook. I need your million dollars."

He snorted. "Hey, man, read clause 5-12. You lost the money, and that means we don't *have to do* shit. When J-Squared got started, you promised to teach me the business, but the minute you got my father's money, you didn't give me the time of day. I told you *Maniac* sucked, but I was an idiot. So you went around me. Now there's only one place for you to go—go fuck yourself!"

AJ pushed a plain manila envelope across the table. The young man apprehensively slit it open. Inside were a set of glossies of him passed out in the bathtub in Sam Kinison's apartment. The heroin and needle were clearly visible. Included was a Xerox of the police report with a statement by a fourteen-year-old girl that Koji had forced her to perform fellatio. "This entire file will go to Tokyo *Shimbun*—along with an interview from me—if I don't get your check for ILM. Call your dad, tell him I showed you footage and you now believe the film will be a hit."

Koji closed his eyes and imagined his name smeared across the headlines for millions of *Shimbun* readers in his hometown. "This is blackmail."

"I don't see it that way. You and your father acted within the strict letter of our agreement, but you forgot its spirit. Consider this a reminder. And if you're thinking of going to the cops, remember that in Hollywood I have cinematic immunity. It comes with twenty years of hefty contributions to the Patrolmen's Benevolent Association."

Despite the cool breeze off the ocean, Koji broke into a sweat. "You like to think of yourself as a good guy, AJ, but you're a total scumbag." Clutching the contents of the envelope to his chest, he exited the restaurant.

AJ listened impassively to the stripping of gears, then paid the check. He had no memory of the drive back to the office, but upon his return, his assistant announced, "I have Seiji Keiku calling from Guam."

"Give me a second." AJ was preternaturally calm. The distance in

Seiji's voice surpassed the ten thousand miles separating the two men. "Jastrow-san, I have just wired you one million dollars to finish the movie." AJ nodded in quiet relief. "My attorneys have also sent formal notification of our intention to terminate our partnership. We no longer wish to be in business with you."

It was a fair trade—the last word for the chance to save his dream. "I will accommodate your desire." He buzzed his daughter to announce the good news but was told she had left the office. No one knew where.

=

Jessica had known Mike Ovitz for half her life. She had even baby-sat his kids. Familiarity helped her stay calm in a storm that would have swamped a normal young woman in the movie business. The CAA chief faced her on the sofa, while her boyfriend slumped in a chair by his boss's side. The surroundings were comfy, but Mike wasn't as he criticized her delay in accepting Paramount's offer. His pitch was about power. All the creative talent in the world was useless if it lacked muscle behind it. In Hollywood, muscle was money. The studios had the resources to make things happen, while independents like J² did not. "I admire your dad for what he tried to do, but it's too difficult."

"We have a lot of great projects in development." She sounded like the company cheerleader.

Mike smiled tightly. "But if *The Coney Island Monster*—"

"*Maniac.*"

"If J-Squared folds, you wasted the past two years. Paramount will never fold."

Jessie shot an accusatory look at Sean, who was the only person with whom she'd discussed the movie's shortcomings. He'd broken her confidence, and since CAA was the town crier, the world would soon know the news. Jess tried mightily to convince Mike that the movie would be wonderful.

"We certainly hope it will be, because it's good for us to have more buyers in the market—especially ones as important to us as AJ. And I understand your concern that Matt Margolin has an abrasive personality. But we're going to make him a star. Opportunities like this one only come once. It's hard for me to say, Jessica, but those of us who love you feel that you will be much better off where the action is."

Jessie watched his eyes trail over to the phone on the end table, as if willing her to dial Margolin. But something about Mike's hard sell didn't. "Those of us who love you"—that was the tip-off. Nobody in this room loved her. With mounting anxiety she discerned someone else's fine hand at work behind the scenes.

"Mike, I understand, but I worry about the effect that my leaving might have on Dad—you know, with his history of the stroke."

"I understand. But rest assured that your grandmother believes this is the right move for you."

Jess had to get out, so she promised Mike a positive answer to forestall more badgering. She hyperventilated in the elevator, frightening the other passengers, until Sean Connery offered to call a doctor. As she unlocked her Honda, *her* Sean appeared. "Get away from me!"

"What's wrong?" He knew.

"Do you take me for a fool? What am I saying—I am a fool. This was Maggie's idea, wasn't it?" Sean remained silent. "Tell me the truth or so help me God I'll never talk to you again."

"She called Mike—"

"Of course. Grandma hates Dad for what happened with Ricky. What better way to punish him than getting me to leave the fold? Ovitz gave you the job of getting me to quit, didn't he?"

"I'm sorry."

"Sorry about what? Having to sleep with me? That must have really made you sorry."

"Okay, I had ulterior motives when I started seeing you. I didn't want to do it but—"

"But you do whatever the Great God Ovitz says. It's funny, actually. You're like that guy in *The Godfather,* the one who tries to kill Michael, then tells him it wasn't personal, only business. Except you . . . you made love to me."

"I was a jerk. But my feelings are real. Otherwise, do you think I would have fucked you for the last six months? And Margolin really wants to hire you. He thinks you'll be great for Paramount."

Jess dodged his embrace, then struck him with an uppercut that left a welt below his eye and fulfilled the prophecy of her warrior soul. Or maybe not—since she cried all the way home. What she'd unearthed was too embarrassing and too revolting to repeat. And if Dad ever learned about it . . . she couldn't allow that to happen. Jess would stay at J². He would never suspect a thing.

CHAPTER 45

J² spent the summer of 1986 on life support. Under the divorce arrangements the Keikus agreed to meet payroll until the end of the year but refused to fund new script development or production, leaving most of the company's seventy employees with idle time and sinking spirits. Both trade papers reported that J² teetered on the edge of bankruptcy. Agents ceased calling, while creditors fought to get their bills paid promptly.

Under the circumstances, her father's unflagging "Have a great day" attitude alarmed Jess. He was too young for dementia and too . . . AJ to believe.

"What do I do?" Shelly asked her, following a staff meeting in which AJ had told Shelly to start preproduction on *The Sky's the Limit,* an epic air-race movie set in the 1920s. "We don't even have the money to do a budget, much less make it."

"Go through the paces," Jess replied. "AJ's so busy finishing *Maniac* he'll forget he asked."

"Has he found us another investor?"

"Not that I know of. But he's got me brainstorming ideas for new movies." Jess pressed Shelly's hand. "They say that just before people die of asphyxiation they get giddy."

"That's sick."

It was. She checked her bulging Filofax and penciled in a visit with her father over the weekend to make sure he was okay. But despite the deathwatch at J², Jess suffered no pangs over Paramount. That was a bullet dodged. "Bullet Dodged." Kind of an intriguing title for a film, she thought. Maybe a thriller about a woman who knows she's about to be murdered . . .

=

Playing the delightful Dr. Jekyll at the office took its toll on AJ, but he refused to let the troops down until the bank closed the doors and threw them onto the street. So it was with perverse relief at night that he reverted to Mr. Hyde. He spent his hours at home boozing and blaming the people who'd betrayed him: the Japanese, his hack directors, Megan, his mother, Ricky, Ovitz, and those faux Hollywood friends who covertly rejoiced in his imminent failure. He wished for them to live long enough to see *their* dreams disappear. Regret and anger exploded into a rash that first appeared on his elbows, then spread over his arms. He entertained no illusion of martyrdom, however, feeling instead like the guy who had won the lottery, only to misplace his ticket.

Today was his last chance. The frame-by-frame reconstruction of *The Coney Island Maniac* had required a month longer than Tony Adamo had predicted, so this was the first screening of the finished film. If it worked, maybe he could convince someone to back his play for one more year, a few more movies. AJ slipped on jeans, his old Weejuns, and an oxford shirt and drove to the screening room at Todd-AO. Hopefully, his old boss's spirit still lived there. The only other attendee was Gordo Slaughter. AJ wished him luck, then sat back for the next ninety-three minutes—no longer in command of his own creation.

In the yarn he'd recounted over the years, the Maniac's mayhem was spooky but fanciful. Unfortunately, the original effects in the movie had completely defanged the character. When viewed in a darkened theater on a giant screen, however, the new visual effects had the opposite impact. When the Maniac murdered a girl and ripped out the eyes of her boyfriend, both director and producer winced. With ILM's enhancements—smashed eyeballs, empty sockets, and severed optic nerves—the act seemed savage. And it was only the first atrocity.

When the lights came up both men remained silent; Slaughter was too terrified to voice an opinion and AJ couldn't make up his mind. As a responsible adult he felt guilty at delivering a movie too disgusting for the young people who were its target audience. If Ricky and Jess were still kids, he would have banned them from seeing it. As for reviews, *The Coney Island Maniac* would provoke anti-Hollywood sentiment among critics, parents, and educators wherever it played. So why did his groin twitch with excitement, not dread? It was because *Maniac* had the same shock value and gore that had made *A Nightmare on Elm Street* forbidden fruit for teenagers.

There was no time to test the picture to see if it was over the top. By this afternoon Deluxe Laboratories had to strike seventeen hundred release prints—prints that would literally be wet when the shippers packed them into film cans and sent them to theaters. The rush was necessary because the movie's release was only eight days away. Andy had begged him to delay until January to take the time to market the film properly, even offering to work without salary when money ran out. But AJ had refused, believing the ghoulish spirit in the week before Halloween created the ideal climate for *Maniac*.

In spite of the time crunch, America knew the movie was coming. Standees in theaters, billboards, bus shelters, and newspaper ads teased, "The Maniac Is Loose." In a potent radio spot a young girl screamed, "No, don't . . . please, don't . . . no . . ." followed by five agonized seconds of silence; then the announcer intoned, "On October twenty-fourth, the Maniac is loose in your neighborhood." Deprived of actual film footage, Andy had filmed the character talking directly to a TV audience and superimposed his image over three teens walking home from the mall. In a demented hiss—ending with a kiss—the Maniac apologized for the things he intended to do. A scythe swept down toward the heads of the unsuspecting youths. After a bloodcurdling cry, the screen faded to red.

When he arrived at the office after the screening, AJ grabbed NRG's tracking report. The campaign, especially the TV spot, had revved up the testosterone of young male moviegoers to a fever pitch. Their awareness of *The Coney Island Maniac* stood at 91 percent, definite interest at 70, with the bulk of the advertising to run in the five days prior to release. The movie was scary as hell, the audience primed. Given the modest negative cost—even with the additional ILM work—all he needed was forty million dollars at the box office. He fiddled with the numbers. But if they could do fifty million . . .

"Boss, we're screwed."

AJ saw anguish on Andy's face. "What now?"

"NBC pulled the spot off the air. Their head of Standards and Practices got complaints from the local affiliates saying our commercial was too violent. They want a substitute."

"We don't have one."

"I know," Faddiman replied. "NBC's forty percent of our buy till opening."

The *Challenger* was one thing, but this. . . . "I want to see the joker."

"I thought you'd say that. We've got an appointment in Burbank."

An hour later Carl Lundegren ushered the two J² executives into his office. A Marine brush cut and steel-rimmed glasses didn't augur well for clemency, but AJ respectfully explained how important it was to his company to keep the commercial playing on NBC. He could see the man's impatience, so he ended his appeal by arguing that the spot wasn't offensive to the overwhelming majority of viewers.

"Mr. Jastrow, I could blow smoke up your ass, but that's a waste of our time."

"Mr. Lundegren, maybe I wasn't clear how critical—"

"Forget it. Your spot's got our affiliates on the rag."

"This means everything—"

"My bosses care a shitload more about their happiness than about your fucking company."

AJ searched for the guy from *Candid Camera*.

"What kind of changes do you want so we can run the commercial?" Andy asked.

"Tame the actor's performance. He's a cut-rate Dracula. Then lose the scythe, the scream, and the red background."

AJ grunted. "Excuse me, Carl, that's the whole spot."

"No shit, Sherlock."

AJ rose to leave. "And no offense, asshole, but you've fucked us royally."

Lundegren laughed. "Hey, I don't make the rules."

"Yes, you do," Andy countered. "I'll change the direction of the scythe so that it's not aimed directly at the kids."

"Uh-huh."

"I'll replace the red background with orange."

"Make it blue."

"Black," Andy compromised.

Lundegren clapped. "Now we're talking turkey. But you've got to change the cocksucker's scream."

"Aaaahhhhh!"

Andy's demonstration brought Carl's secretary in on the run. "It's okay, Flo," he assured her. "We're negotiating."

AJ could see this was what Lundegren lived for. Faddiman tried again. "Aaahhhh!"

Thumbs down. "Nah, still too scary."

"Fuck it, I'll try," AJ piped up. "Uhhhhhggggg!"

"Too guttural." Lundegren stood up as if he were backstage at the Met, but what escaped his pipes was more squeak than scream, unlikely to arouse a G-rated audience.

AJ and Lundegren screamed at each other like the tenor and baritone in a bad opera. Finally, AJ couldn't go on. That his future had come to rest in the potty mouth of Carl Lundegren was a joke worthy of Hollywood. Years of tension shook him to the core, inciting a laughing jag so primitive he melted onto the floor, more protoplasm than producer. His body heaved until his toes were shaking and tears soaked his face.

"Fuck me!" Lundegren turned white, certain that AJ was suffering an epileptic seizure. "Open your mouth!" He shoved in a pencil to keep AJ from swallowing his tongue.

"I'm ffffine!" AJ spit it out, spraying Carl. He tried apologizing, but couldn't force anything intelligible through his hiccups.

Lundegren realized that the joke was at his expense. "Get the fuck out!"

Driving back to J², AJ broke down again and pulled into an Arby's parking lot to recover. A song from his youth popped into AJ's mind—"Que Sera, Sera." The hell with the spot—they had tried their best. Whatever will be, will be.

=

Steph concentrated as if the words coming from the cassette deck of her Volvo conveyed the wisdom of the ages. *"Cocinar en el horno a cuatro cientos . . ."* Bake in a four-hundred-degree oven. She mimicked the Spanish perfectly.

The kudos for the Siamese Cat had whetted her appetite for professional success. Her new idea was to reinvent south-of-the-border cuisine for L.A. diners, so she was embarking tomorrow on a two-month trip to Mexico, Guatemala, Honduras, and Panama to learn the techniques and recipes of provincial chefs. But after lunching with her daughter and hearing about the importance of the opening of *The Coney Island Maniac,* Steph decided to stop by AJ's house to wish him luck before she left.

He loved her surprise present. "These are just about the only good things left from the old days," he observed, relishing the last bite of his Pink's hot dog. "Then there's you."

"Me?"

"Yes, you. You're better."

His flirtation caught her unawares. Steph emptied her second beer. "I was a size four. Now I'm an eight. But what the hell?" She polished off the last hot dog.

"Remember how you used to inhale those ribs at the Formosa?"

"Jesus! You're a stroll down memory lane."

"How about this?" AJ got up, blew the dust off an LP, and switched on the turntable.

Steph was a sucker for Judy Collins—and she was as tipsy as AJ was nostalgic. But there was one name that would cool him down. "Ricky told me records and tapes will be obsolete in five years," Steph said. "It's all going to be these compact discs. Talking to him these days . . . it's like listening to a guest on *Wall Street Week*."

He ignored her diversion. "Come dance with me."

"No . . ." Reluctantly, she got to her feet. "I think someone's missing his young girlfriend."

"Not in the least. And you should have told me I was making a fool of myself."

"You weren't. Everyone thought you and Megan made a cute couple."

"It was against the laws of nature." He pulled her close.

"What's gotten into you, besides the brew? I thought you'd be crazed with the movie opening."

"Maybe it's you." He stroked her hair, then gently kissed her lips. "Definitely you."

Steph wondered why she wasn't nervous, why she wasn't running for the hills. "Who Knows Where the Time Goes?" Even Judy urged her on.

=

At seven A.M. AJ teed off—still tasting last night. He had wanted Steph not because he had once lost her or was horny or on the rebound, but because it felt right. Now, walking down the fairway, he surged with optimism, which was a terrible sign because he never felt good on opening day. His attempt to get anxious by conjuring empty theaters and booing audiences failed. He played better than expected for a man whose professional life was on the line. But on the sixth hole things got real. He hit a perfect six-iron to the par three. It was in line to the pin, and AJ was milliseconds from his first hole in one. But the ball struck the flagstick, ricocheted to the right, and plopped into the sand trap in the middle of the green. That kind of luck was more like it.

He quit after nine and had just returned home when the phone rang. It was Mel Brodsky, J²'s head of publicity in New York. "You know where I'm standing?"

AJ heard blaring horns and jackhammers. "Not in your office."

"The corner of Fifty-fourth and Seventh."

"Outside the Ziegfeld?" It was the midtown Manhattan theater playing *The Coney Island Maniac*.

"Exactly, but I'll bet you don't know what I'm looking at, because I'm looking at it and can't believe my eyes."

AJ did a quick calculation, but it didn't make sense. It was just past noon in the East and the first show wasn't until one P.M. "Do you intend to tell me?"

"A thousand disgustingly dressed, pimply-faced adolescents. They should all be in school, but they're not—they're standing in a line around the block! The first show's already sold out. It's bedlam. I wish you were here. The manager said we're going to do forty grand today alone!"

=

Andy had convinced AJ to let him book *Maniac* into the National Theater in Westwood, even though the place was a barn. Now every one of its twelve hundred seats was filled for the seven P.M. show with the same kind of moviegoers Mel Brodsky had described. Business in the East, Midwest, and South approached capacity, but for AJ the acid test was seeing for himself how the film played. To save J^2, *Maniac* needed more than a strong opening—it required a long run fueled by repeat business. That meant word of mouth was crucial.

So he paid particular attention when the Maniac stuck his hand down the throat of the captain of the football team and pulled out his heart—bloody and beating. The crowd roared. When Bobby Manelo ate it and belched, they cheered, "Man-i-ac! Man-i-ac!" AJ found himself cheering along. And when the Maniac vomited up the heart and ate the pieces—slurping the veins like strands of spaghetti—it was like watching a tornado barrel into town.

"Whoa!" Their ferocity impressed Jess. "NRG can save their cards tonight." She squeezed her dad's hand. "It's going all the way, isn't it?"

AJ nodded. "Keep watching. Let me know what happens."

Slipping into the lobby, he started figuring . . . they might do six million dollars tonight alone, which meant seventeen or eighteen for the weekend. He heard cheering from inside. Jesus! If the film played this well everywhere, the bottom line was . . . the bottom line was: stop calculating.

Through the glass that fronted the street AJ saw the line for the nine forty-five show. The kids looked jazzed. They expected to have a blast—and they would. And it was because of him. His imagination had given birth to *Maniac* and his perseverance and guts had kept it alive. "Yes! Yes! Yes!"

The youthful theater manager interrupted AJ's solo victory dance. "That's awesome, man—an instant classic. It'll play forever. When's the sequel?"

The question lifted AJ to a new level of reality, as if there was any reality to the movie business. "The summer of eighty-eight."

"That's so cool! What's it called?"

"The Maniac Is Back."

Stoked, the young man walked away to spread the news.

Jess ran out to announce that the destruction of the roller coaster had generated the biggest reaction yet. While everyone high-fived, AJ dreamed. In his vision the J² logo stood proudly next to Paramount's mountain, Universal's globe, Fox's klieg lights, and MGM's lion.

The Maniac was back.

THE
UNCIVIL
WAR

When it came to klieg lights, AJ was moth to flame. At first sight of the beams crisscrossing in the night sky he powered down the window of his stretch limousine, only to get smacked by a zero-degree windchill. Not to worry—a thousand people lined Chicago's Michigan Avenue to salute the opening of the most outrageous movie theater built in America in the last half century—a theater he'd inspired and paid for. Exiting the car to a barrage of flashbulbs, AJ reached out his hand for his wife. Steph stepped forward bundled in a black mink, her hair gracefully gray. He barely allowed her time to absorb the scene before whispering, "What do you think?"

Before her rose an imposing sandstone pyramid around which architect Tikvi Andasaang had wrapped more than a mile of polished titanium shaped to look like a tangle of thirty-five-millimeter film strips. Bombarded by strobe lights, the strips created the illusion that the film spooled continuously. A black silk curtain was draped strategically over the marquee. AJ kicked at the ice on the pavement until she spoke. "It's stunning."

His sigh of relief escaped in a puff. "You're not just saying that?"

"I love it."

He romped ahead like a kid taking his best friend to a secret hideaway. "Come on, let me show you the really neat stuff."

The metallic walls in the lobby sloped majestically to a shimmering crystal chandelier suspended a football field above. Below the glass-brick floor was a lower lobby serving seven theaters, to which moviegoers descended on a pair of sweeping escalators. In the main theater the screen was as big as one in an old drive-in, with a sound system and acoustics that matched those of an opera house. Above the eight hundred stadium-styled seats hung a row of glass-fronted luxury suites.

The occupants could adjust the sound and climate, phone for delivery of food and drinks, and, if the movie was a bummer, play the latest video games.

AJ stood center stage. "Now I understand why men build monuments. This is a rush."

The audience delighted in his joy—and his creation.

"When I was growing up, the most thrilling night was the night we went to the movies. Theaters were palaces. At J-Squared we believe that people still wish for that experience, so it's our plan to construct flagship theaters in major American cities. We proudly chose Chicago as our inaugural site because I spent a happy decade of my life here as a refugee from Hollywood."

AJ gestured to the box in which Steph sat next to Mayor Richard Daley. "But there's a second reason for me to celebrate. Those of you who have visited Los Angeles may have tasted my wife's cooking. In my unbiased opinion, her restaurants are the best in the city. Stephanie and I have been married since 1958—with time off for my crazy behavior. If you subtract those fourteen years and two months, then tonight is our twenty-fifth wedding anniversary."

A live television feed from the front of the theater appeared on the screen behind AJ. "In honor of that occasion, I'd like to dedicate this building to a sexy woman, a dear friend—and a great wife." The curtain over the marquee rose majestically, revealing the theater's name in electrohieroglyphics: THE STEPHANIE. AJ shouted above the applause, "I can't see you, Steph, but I hope you're as happy as I am."

The house lights dimmed for the premiere of J²'s *Lady Icarus,* a drama about the first women astronauts. As AJ hurried to join his wife, he heard the opening chords of "Hey Jude" beep from inside his tuxedo pocket. It startled him until he remembered that one of his aides had lent him a Powerline cell phone, which sang rather than rang to signal a call. It was Pete Leventhal in L.A. "Terry Mangiarcina is issuing a 'sell' recommendation on our stock this Friday."

"Can I talk her out of it?"

"Let's hope so. I arranged a breakfast for tomorrow at the Regency. The jet will fly you to La Guardia at six A.M. Call me after you finish."

=

"The Assassin" demanded coffee from the waiter before bothering to say hello to AJ. Terry Mangiarcina had earned her nickname through her brutal critiques of studio mismanagement. With a night-school degree from Temple, coarsely sexy features, and a body that preferred pasta to Pilates, she was pure South Philly. But that hadn't derailed her from becoming a vice president at the investment firm of Wahlberg & Sparrow and the most influential equity analyst covering the entertainment industry. "I've always respected you, Jastrow, because you weren't like those other self-promoting Wizards of Oz who run Hollywood."

He offered a wary smile. "Did I catch the past tense?"

"You've pissed me off," she growled. "When J-Squared started, you aimed your movies at the youth market and kept budgets down. It was a smart business plan—and now you've abandoned it."

"We've expanded it."

"By going after adults—an audience your staff can't hit with a bat. You used to break new directors, but now you throw millions at the A-list. Your budgets have skyrocketed, and so have your risks—case in point, *The Older Woman.*"

AJ had originated the idea of a love story about a fifty-year-old doctor who marries a girl of twenty-five, only to then fall in love with a woman his age. It had died at the box office. "We've already written off that loss, Terry."

"Hah! Thirty million dollars—poof."

"We couldn't find a marketing hook, but it was a fine film and I'd give it the green light again."

"Those are your emotions talking, Jastrow. And there's no place for feelings in the film business, not when the investments are of the magnitude they are today."

He sat on his impulse to tell her to go to hell. Breakfast was about damage control.

Terry attacked her kippers with gusto. She was the only person AJ had seen order that breakfast entrée in fifty years. "More coffee," she ordered a passing waiter. "And then that crazy decision to buy theaters. You took all that cash from the *Maniac* sequels and blew it."

He guessed that this was her principal peeve. In 1992 AJ had begun to vertically integrate J² by building and buying theaters. It was the studio model his father had argued to maintain before the Supreme Court. The Bush and Clinton Justice Departments had approved his plan, and his company now owned twenty-three hundred screens. "We're getting terrific synergy between production and exhibition."

"Synergy's as real as a unicorn."

"I disagree. Take a look." He removed a set of charts from his attaché case. "We're experimenting with varying ticket prices on some of our movies. When it's a presold title, like *Maniac V*, or has a star like Tom Cruise in *Animal Instincts*, we charge up to fifteen bucks a ticket. But when it's a low-budget film with unknowns like *Cattle Call*, we drop the price from seven dollars to three. In the test markets people seem to prefer paying less when the risk is greater and don't mind paying more when they know what they're getting. Our revenue is way up, and we're going to roll it out across the country in the near future."

Terry shoved the papers back across the table. "Your only future is on the sidelines. The mortgage payments on your theaters are crippling you. Your interest expenses have tripled. Last quarter they sent you into the red. Now with that new white elephant in Chicago—"

"You've never even seen it."

"It cost twice what it should. You've built great theaters, but so have Pacific, AMC, and every other chain in the country. The overcapacity's a killer."

The woman was either savagely smart or psychic. Last year J^2 had reported ten million dollars of net income, down from sixty-one million in 1995. Pete's estimates for 1997 anticipated a loss of fifty-one million, reflecting the drain from the theaters. Terry was also correct about the competition. The breadth of their building programs worried AJ. "The underlying real estate is worth our investment."

"Bullshit. But why are we arguing?"

"Because what you say sways 'the Street.' You know that."

"My only concern is protecting shareholder value." Mangiarcina's transparent innocence infuriated him. "But if you announced publicly that you were going to divest your theaters and reorient your production philosophy toward teens, I might withhold my 'sell' recommendation."

This time AJ grabbed the waiter—for a check. How could this woman, who produced nothing more creative than criticism, have the chutzpah to dictate his strategic decisions? "Theresa, do what you have to do—I've got to run my business. We'll see how it all comes out in the wash."

After his guest departed in a huff, AJ stalked Park Avenue to cool off. At the opening bell, the price of a share of J^2 stock on the NYSE was sixty-three dollars. Post Mangiarcina's announcement it would fall at least ten points. Given his one million shares, it was the most expensive breakfast AJ had ever eaten.

≡

Maggie Ginsberg ran out of patience halfway through Dr. Neil Abromovitz's hemming and hawing. "What you're saying—or not saying—is the cancer's back and there's not a damn thing you can do about it?"

"Yes." As the leading oncologist at Cedars, Abromovitz hated to fail any patient, especially one who had donated a wing to the hospital. And having treated Maggie for colon cancer seven years ago, he'd grown to admire her spirit. "I can't answer your next question." She stared him down. "Truly, I don't know how long you've got to live."

"Will I see my ninetieth birthday? That's my target."

"You're—"

"Eighty-three." When he missed a beat, she poked him. "Screw you. Now you'll have to dance with me at the party . . . and I'll want a tango. You won't mind, Neil, will you? I don't have many people left to dance with."

Abromovitz hugged her. "I look forward to it, Mrs. Ginsberg. And I'm signing up for lessons, because I never bet against you when your mind is made up."

Maggie held her chin high. Two hip replacements, the cancer surgery, and chemotherapy had left her frail but unbowed. As she navigated around gurneys, walkers, and wheelchairs, a searing pain radiated from her liver, where they had detected the newest tumor. Maggie gritted her teeth, smiling at the patients and hospital workers who recognized her from the TV days. She had to bear up because the pain medication Neil had prescribed left her so spacey she barely knew day from night.

Death was no big deal. The afterlife was an invention. There was nothing out there, so why worry about nothing? But what bedeviled her was how little time was left to ensure the happiness of the person she loved most. Ricky—no, he preferred Richard—was CEO of Powerline, the family business. The position placed him among the executives leading the technology revolution, and when Maggie died, he would inherit her stock, which would make him fabulously wealthy. He had a model family—a beautiful wife and two equally adorable girls. But despite possessing all the trappings of success, he remained as troubled at thirty-nine as the six-year-old who'd tried to burn down his elementary school.

As Maggie walked out of the hospital into the warm May afternoon, she realized that she might never see another spring. Her chauffeur opened the Bentley, but Maggie reversed directions. She needed to make absolutely certain that Dr. Abromovitz kept his death sentence to himself. No one could know until she was ready to tell.

CHAPTER 47

On the cover of May's *Vanity Fair,* to the right of a beefcake shot of Johnny Depp, the promotional copy advertised "Why Every Woman Should Want to Be Jessica Jastrow." In her flattering profile, screenwriter and journalist Delia Ephron provided ten delicious reasons:

1. As president of production at J^2, you're the third most power-ful woman in Hollywood, behind Julia Roberts and Sherry Lansing.
2. Your calendar shows lunch with Tom Cruise *and* Antonio Banderas.
3. There's no limit on your American Express card.
4. Giorgio Armani invites you to Milan for a private showing of his fall collection.
5. Your personal trainer meets you at work, where you shower and apply makeup in your personal office bathroom.
6. At thirty-six you remain a to-die-for size two.
7. Your only boss is your adorable and adoring dad.
8. TV hospital heartthrob Billy Gonzalez cooks you his paella on Sunday nights.
9. Your enemies are jealous but admit you're great at your job.
10. Your friends are jealous but admit you're wonderful—and great at your job.

As Jessica relaxed poolside at the legendary Hôtel du Cap on the French Riviera, after a lunch of crudités and kirs with Pierce Brosnan, she added an eleventh reason: "You're the princess of the Cannes Film Festival—as long as you can grant the go-ahead to their movies."

Two tables over, Dino De Laurentiis twirled pasta and promoted a movie about a plot to kill Stalin to French director Jean-Jacques Annaud, Spanish actress Penélope Cruz, a Japanese distributor, and an executive from the BBC. "Globalization" had assaulted the film business—make that "Babelization," since none of these players understood what movie the others were talking about. No one cared, however, because the real meal was finding the money to make it. Jess noticed a photographer crouched at table level taking candid shots of the delegation with a Leica set on motor drive. She almost whistled. The guy was her age, with shaggy hair, a lean body, and a two-day shadow that made him dangerous enough for an afternoon fantasy.

That's exactly what she needed, because for all the myriad reasons to be Jessie, an active sex life was not one. Billy Gonzalez was a great chef, a sweet guy, and a closet homosexual. At times Jess wished she were a lesbian, because as a mating pool, Hollywood men were workaholics, connivers, phonies, narcissists—and so scared of her power they never asked her out. As for asking them for . . . it made her feel like a predator, and if they said no . . . God, she'd die of embarrassment. Her closest friends shared her emotional problem and had suggested a technological solution. Jess retrieved her beach bag and scampered to her private cabana, situated among the tall pines dotting the grounds. Nestling in a chaise longue, she switched on the Pocket Rocket. It resembled a Magic Marker and was just long enough to contain a double-A battery, but in its case, size didn't count. When Jessie wanted to experience a bone-crushing orgasm, all she required was the Rocket and a fertile imagination.

She chose the crouching photographer for inspiration. His first name would be . . . André . . . no, Gilles, and he'd been wounded covering the Gulf War for *Le Monde*. Gilles was at Cannes on assignment to photograph Jessica for an exhibition on the sexiest women behind the camera. They were alone in her suite when he unstrapped his camera and knelt down on the Oriental carpet, where she posed in a black silk T-shirt and tight jeans. He freed the top button, now another . . .

Jess pushed aside her bathing suit and felt the hard, cool plastic of the vibrator. Its insistent pulses made her shiver as she luxuriated in how perfectly Gilles comprehended her body. Jess pressed her bottom against the cushion. The orgasm jolted her. Her shallow breathing had just returned to normal when someone knocked on the door. Through the window of the cabana she saw that her visitor was none other than the photographer himself. Not even Lucy in her most inspired moment had matched her double take.

"Hi. I'm Patrick Shanti." So much for fantasies—his accent was red, white, and blue. "I recognized you by the pool and wanted to say hello, because . . . uh . . . it happens we have an unusual connection."

He didn't know the half of it. "How so?"

"My mother's a photographer. Her professional name is Naomi Riordan."

"She's wonderful . . . and courageous." New York's Whitney Museum had presented a retrospective of Riordan's portraits of the "Combatants of the '60s," revolutionaries like George Jackson and Abbie Hoffman and reactionaries like Bull Connor and Spiro Agnew, who fought them at the barricades.

"My mom photographed your dad at his bar mitzvah reception," Patrick explained. "She eventually published a book, called *Boys to Men,* which compared her photos of young men and her sketches of how they would look at midlife with the real thing."

"I remember my dad posing for her . . . it must have been ten years ago. He got kind of strange."

"I was helping her out and the vibes in the studio that day . . . I thought Mother was going to jump him. She's been known to do that—I have eight stepbrothers and -sisters from three marriages after my father."

Jessica's cell phone rang with breaking news from her office. Not wishing to intrude, he waved good-bye. She hit the cancel button and called out, "Your dad was Avril Shanti, the Indian musician?"

Patrick stopped short. "You listen to sitar music?"

"We used two of his songs for one of our films. They were so haunting I played the soundtrack every day on the way to work."

Patrick grinned. "Better you than me. The sitar grates on my nerves."

"Would you like to . . . I don't know . . . maybe have a drink?"

"Thanks, but I've got to get back to work."

After he left, a copy line from a commercial popped to mind—"Is it real or is it Memorex?" The afternoon was filled with meetings and a dozen more distress calls from L.A. Everyone making movies for J^2 huffed and puffed about *something.* But Jessie remained unflappable and arrived at the Palais des Festivals for the evening's premiere of Ang Lee's *The Ice Storm* dressed flawlessly in silk pants and a red-and-white beaded jacket by Mr. Armani.

The photographer had faded from her thoughts when she saw him again. Actually, she heard his motor drive, because Patrick was preoccupied shooting the crowd. Or so it appeared, because as she approached he turned the lens in her face and snapped. "Don't develop that," she pleaded.

"Why? You look beautiful."

"No." Jess blushed. The picture would betray more interest in him than she cared to reveal.

"I'd like to put you in my book."

She hadn't heard that line before. "And what book is that?"

Before he could answer, Jamie Klooz, a twenty-something agent from United Talent, sidled up, displaying a smile so white he must have swished his teeth with Clorox. "Hey, Jessie, you're a ten on the babe scale tonight. Bought any films?"

"Not yet."

"Smart cookie. These foreign flicks are pretentious crap, but the food's totally awesome. A group of us are helicoptering to Saint-Tropez tonight. Why don't you join us?"

"No thanks. Jamie, this is Patrick Shanti . . . Patrick, Jamie Klooz." Klooz sensed Patrick was a civilian and ignored him. "Crash, I need you to put the pressuroonie on your business-affairs guy to close the Daryl Hannah deal on *Strangers.*"

"I'll do what I can."

Klooz proffered his cell phone. "Any chance you could do it now?"

"Absolutely none."

When he moved on, Patrick observed, "You have a really hard job."

"I appreciate your compassion. But you still haven't told me about 'the book.' "

"If you cool it with the 'pressuroonie' and have dinner with me after the screening, I'll explain." Jess apologized that it would have to be her second dinner, since she had a nine P.M. meal scheduled with the men who distributed J²'s product in South Africa. He smiled. "Just have the first course."

They ate at Le Machou, a restaurant on an alley up from the harbor. Over the best steak in Cannes Patrick described *Markets,* a coffee-table book that captured the staggering range of worldwide markets. He had already shot the rare-bird market in Djakarta, the commodities pit in Chicago, the thoroughbred yearling sales in Saratoga, and a dozen other locations. Cannes made sense because it was the world's number one film market.

"This must be culture shock for you," Jess offered.

"Not really. Regardless of the *kind* of market, people tend to behave the same way. They're on the make, they're excited, they're hopeful . . . they just don't dress as well as you folks. My favorite thing is catching people bargaining with each other. Are you good at it?"

"Yes, if it's for the company, but if it's for me personally, like at a flea market, I'm a hopeless softie." He posed questions until Jessie realized she had told her life story. That was unusual because she was normally a good listener—and men usually couldn't stop talking about themselves. By the time they'd wandered down to the square to where her car waited, there was no time to turn the tables. Patrick was leaving the next morning for Kazakhstan to photograph arms dealers selling weapons to Third World countries.

"I had a great time, and you're very special." He kissed her on both cheeks.

"We've got great farmers' markets in southern California."

Patrick mounted his motorbike. "I love fruits and vegetables." He smiled and drove off into the night.

On the ride back to the du Cap, Jess checked her voice mail and found twenty messages. That meant another hour of aggravation before she could climb into bed and lie awake wondering if she'd ever see Patrick Shanti again.

=

"Roll sound," the assistant director shouted.

"Sound speed."

"Scene 75 Alpha, Take one. Mark." The common clapboard cracked for seven cameras.

"Action!" Director Curtis Hanson's voice boomed over a loudspeaker and five hundred soldiers in gray Confederate uniforms began their attack on four hundred men in blue Union uniforms. Next to the director, perched atop a tower overlooking the rolling hills of West Virginia, stood AJ. He riveted his attention on the reenactment of Pickett's Charge during the bloody Battle of Gettysburg.

He liked to say that J²'s epic production of *Lincoln* was fifty years in the making, all the way back to his visit to the Memorial with his dad. AJ had become a student of the sixteenth president and hatched the idea of a film about his White House years after the election of Lincoln's antithesis, "Slick Willie." Although Clinton left the public cynical about government, AJ was sure the audience craved a portrayal of greatness in Washington. When the first draft of the screenplay raised goose bumps, AJ journeyed to Spain, where he convinced his old friend Michael Douglas to play the lead. The movie had been shooting for the past four months in Virginia, where Hanson and his production designer had re-created the buildings and the culture of nineteenth-century Washington.

Today's extras were Civil War buffs whose hobby was acting out battles, and they fought with a savagery worthy of members of a family who hated one another. With computer-generated crowd multiplication in postproduction, a thousand soldiers would swell to twenty-five thousand. A bank of TV monitors displayed the shots from the ground, crane, and helicopter. Hanson lacked only the epaulets as he yelled instructions through the speakers at his mock soldiers.

AJ glanced skyward. Clouds raced to cast a shadow over the sun in the middle of the scene. That would mean coming back tomorrow at a cost of a quarter of a million dollars. With a budget in excess of one hundred million, *Lincoln* had to be a blockbuster to succeed. Money was on AJ's mind these days. Following Terry Mangiarcina's downgrade, J²'s stock price had declined by a third. Wells Fargo, the company's principal lender, had imposed new restrictions on building additional flagship theaters. And the fact that their last four movies had performed poorly at the box office had aggravated the crunch. Time stopped, and AJ imagined he was Lincoln in the Oval Office, hunched anxiously over a telegraph machine, awaiting reports from the front on a battle that would turn the tide in the Civil War.

"Cut!"

With exquisite timing, it started to drizzle. The extras quit fighting, brushed one another off, and listened for further instructions. Like hyperactive eight-year-olds, most hoped to do it again. After studying the replay on each camera, the director announced, "We got it. It's a wrap." AJ breathed an audible sigh of relief. But as he started for the ladder to return to earth, he heard Hanson say, "Just one more shot."

The soldiers faced the tower, removed their caps, and sang a spirited "Happy Birthday." AJ broke into a broad grin. It was his sixty-second, but the only one who knew . . . this was his daughter's doing. A group of soldiers with real weapons fired a twenty-one-gun salute. It was a perfect antidote to AJ's bunker mentality. He thanked everyone and waved farewell to his "troops."

=

". . . And as the third regular feature each week I plan a segment called 'To Grandma's House We Go' in which I visit with a grandmother who immigrated to America. We'll make one of her secret recipes from the old country, together with her granddaughter." Steph paused to peruse her stack of three-by-five cards. "I think that about does it."

"I would say." Joe Lanaman popped his tongue into the side of his cheek. "The Food Network's only on the air fourteen hours a day."

She blushed. "I've never pitched a television program before, but my husband said I should make sure it didn't seemed like a whim. Too many courses, huh?"

"Not at all. Mrs. Jastrow—"

"Stephanie, please."

"Do you have a name for the show?"

"Taste Buds."

"Have you thought about how much time this would require? The hours and effort can be punishing."

Steph had mulled that question in her mind since flaming out from fatigue in the kitchen. Sixty-three was as good an age as any to call it quits, so she'd sold the Siamese Cat and Ole to Restaurant Associates. But she rarely talked to Ricky or her grandchildren, Jess was a workaholic, and the idea of taking up golf or going back to school had proved more theoretical than practical. Soon Steph was sleeping past nine, gossiping on the phone, surfing the Internet, and feeling irrelevant.

One morning she'd put a video camera on its tripod and taped herself making matzoh balls from scratch. AJ had claimed that the fifteen minutes proved Steph had a TV personality. "I'm prepared for the commitment," she assured Lanaman.

"Then I'll put you together with one of our producers and go to pilot. If it works, we'll have you on the air in the fall."

CHAPTER 48

AJ co-existed with marketing research, but the numbers he'd just heard were too appalling to swallow. "Twenty-seven percent of all moviegoers under the age of twenty-five have never heard of Abraham Lincoln," Andy Faddiman reported. "Another twelve percent claim to have heard of him but didn't know he was president of the United States."

"No fucking way."

Andy brandished the glossy green cover of a report by the National Research Group. "Read it and weep. Even adults over thirty have trouble identifying who fought in the Civil War or when Lincoln became president."

"The man's on the penny. How can people not know?"

"No one uses pennies anymore." Faddiman ceremonially dropped the document on the conference room table. After a quarter century of kissing the asses of ego-inflated filmmakers, convincing overpaid stars to appear on Leno, and appealing to the lowest common denominator, he had little hair or patience left. "When they showed stills of Michael Douglas in a stovepipe hat, people thought our film was a goof, like *Bill & Ted's Excellent Adventure*. We face a humongous marketing problem."

How the hell had the nation succumbed to this stupidity? AJ blamed the cowards who ran the public schools—they had given in to kids' demands for "relevance." That was why audiences accepted the mediocrity of today's movies—they had no basis for comparison because they were ignorant of the classics. But now wasn't the time or place to indulge his outrage. Instead, AJ mustered a measure of indifference, tossing the book aside. "I memorized the Gettysburg Address at the age of twelve. I guess that today's twelve-year-old would look it up in a phone book."

His line drew a stony stare from Andy and a collective "I told you so" from the other members of the longest-running executive cast in Hollywood. His daughter had counseled against the film, Shelly had sought to cut the budget by ten million dollars, and Pete had proposed sharing half the risk with a cofinancier. In each case AJ had overridden the advice.

Jess stepped to his defense. "We've had tough movies before."

" 'Tough' is *all* we've got these days."

Andy's were fighting words to the woman responsible for mounting the production slate. "If you've got a problem with what we make, then say it," Jessica shot back. "But spare us your wiseass asides."

"Well, my dear, I do have a problem. Where the hell are our action films? Where's our sci-fi? We need franchises with presold titles, not another Meryl Streep movie that costs ten million dollars more than it should."

That zinger engaged Shelly. "We made *The Widow* on a budget a lot tighter than your ass, Faddiman."

"Excuse me, I wasn't talking to you." He lectured Jess. "Our comedies are either too dumb or not dumb enough."

"*Insult to Injury* was as funny as any movie in the past year. But you scheduled it against *Liar, Liar.* Get your department in order before you attack mine."

"Can't we all get along?"

Andy laughed derisively at Pete Leventhal. "Thank you, Rodney King."

This is what happens, AJ decided, when people take hits in their 401(k)s. Over the years J² executives had received a hefty portion of their compensation in stock options rather than salary or bonus. At the market's peak they'd become paper millionaires, but with the recent dive in the price, they'd suffered in comparison to their counterparts at other studios, whose portfolios had soared with the bull market. It wasn't only pocketbooks that hurt. Faddiman's lover of seven years had just left him for a hunk on *Baywatch.* Jessica was mooning about the void in her romantic life. Leventhal's son had barely survived a brain tumor.

"Pete's right," AJ interrupted. "We are not going to turn on each other in a crisis. *Lincoln*'s in the can. And regardless of the research, I predict it will be the entertainment event for next Christmas." His colleagues listened to his pep talk, then raced back to their offices to check J²'s closing price.

=

AJ drove down Michael Eisner's private driveway like a burglar making his getaway. Dinner with the chairman of Walt Disney and his key executives hadn't agreed with Steph or him. "I'm sorry for putting you through that."

His wife massaged her temples. "Does Michael talk about anything other than business?"

"Never."

"And the one-upmanship . . . my God."

"Substitute Rupert Murdoch, you get the same meal. That's the fanatical focus you need to build an empire." AJ shook his head. "I remember when Eisner had a passion for movies. Now they're a profit center. Intellectually, I understand, but emotionally. . . . I must be suffering from a case of arrested development."

"Don't get over it." She touched his hand. "We're so lucky we spent our careers in 'happy' businesses."

"Huh?"

"Theaters and restaurants—they're both places people go to have a good time. Can you imagine being an undertaker, or even a doctor or a lawyer?"

"Everyone you encounter is dead, dying, or fucked." AJ felt his eyes mist. Tonight he'd caught his reflection in an antique mirror. Even in the flattering light, the years were turning *him* into the antique. He peered over the edge of Mulholland Drive to hide his frailty from Steph. When he looked back, her eyes were closed. She loved to sleep when he drove. However many days, months, or years were left, they'd better enjoy them now.

CHAPTER 49

From the eighteenth floor of J²'s Century City offices Jessica enjoyed an eighteen-hole view of Los Angeles Country Club. Actually, Dad enjoyed it—he could look at the manicured fairways for hours. To her, they were just acres of lawn. Two foursomes had putted out on the sixth green while Holly Ballsky pitched a story about a man and woman who meet at a dog park when their identical poodles get mixed up. Scrunched in a plush easy chair, Jess chewed intently on the pencil she used to take notes. "I like the idea, but it's predictable. The audience is so saturated with romantic comedies they get ahead of the characters, which means they'll only come if there's a fantastic marquee."

"My agent says Julia Roberts loves animals," Holly offered. "And so does Harrison Ford."

Writers could be amazingly naive. "They're both booked for the next two years. And we don't want to be in the business of begging two stars to take twenty million dollars apiece. Our goal is to develop scripts that are so original we can make them even if we don't get perfect casting."

"Oh."

Jess was a sucker for a forlorn writer. "But you're truly funny, so how about a crazy variation of your idea? Instead of another boy-meets-girl movie, let's do *Upstairs, Downstairs*—from the dogs' point of view."

Holly stopped packing up her belongings. "You mean the dogs talk to each other?"

"Absolutely. They know all the romantic aches and pains of their masters, and in the process of trying to solve them—"

"The poodles fall for each other."

They continued finishing each other's sentences and were plotting the big beats of the three acts when the Amtel on Jessica's coffee table leaped to life and the message from her assistant typed across the screen like a hot stock quote. "Pat Shanti on 08 . . . wants to know if you're ready to go shopping." Her train of thought derailed in a crush of anticipation, and she hustled Holly out like the last customer at closing time. "Come back at the end of the week and if we're both still excited, I'll run it by my dad and move ahead." Jess closed her door, checked her makeup, then punched the blinking button.

A week after their encounter in Cannes, Patrick had e-mailed a greeting, which was all the encouragement Jess needed. She flew to the tulip market in Rotterdam, where they spent a randy weekend. Postcards and letters followed, stamped from the likes of Samarkand, Shanghai, and Ouagadougou. A framed photo on the edge of her desk was her favorite keepsake. Against the black lava landscape of an island off the coast of Iceland, white stones spelled out a twenty-foot "jess." Patrick knelt to the side of the second *s* with one hand on his heart, the other outstretched. She liked the corny affection—and loved the talent. He had shot the picture on time delay, but its composition and lighting were stunning. Witness the puffs of steam from the still-active volcano that seemed to erupt from the *j,* creating the dot on the lowercase letter.

The brilliance of his work was in the details: Jess knew this because she obsessed over almost every picture Patrick had published. It was immaterial if her man had a fat wallet or powerful position, but he couldn't be mediocre. Just last year Jessica had dated a UCLA film-school professor who was cute, lovable, and treated her like a princess. But just as she was imagining marriage, he gave her the galleys of the book he had written on the movies of Howard Hawkes—two-hundred-page proof that he was a hack without an original idea. They broke up a week later.

"Where are you? How are you?" Jess blurted into the phone.

"Japan. I'm fine, if you like someone who smells like a tuna." Patrick was photographing the Royin, where the top sushi chefs in Tokyo journeyed each morning to compete for the fattiest *toro.* "If you're interested, I can stop over in Los Angeles tomorrow on my way back to New York."

"I'll pick you up at the airport." You'll never leave, she told herself.

After making the arrangements, Jess was too antsy to work, so she headed down to her dad's office to kill time and tell him she was taking a long weekend. He was in conference with Leventhal and Henry Borkin, their investment banker. Jess flopped into an easy chair, sensing that she was the only one in a good mood.

"Someone's quietly acquiring a significant block of J-Squared stock," Pete explained.

"How do we know?"

Borkin played with his handlebar mustache. "My team noticed some suspicious trading patterns. There's unusually high volume, always occurring when the quote slips a few eighths. Then the buyer backs off so as not to drive the price up too much."

"And this means . . . ?"

Her father finished a perfect practice swing with a seven-iron. "It means that someone is trying to take over J-Squared."

"I don't think we should assume there's a bad guy," Pete countered.

"Of course there is. Do you honestly think some pension fund woke up and decided we're a good investment?"

"We are." Jess and Pete spoke in unison.

"I wish Wall Street agreed with you," her father noted sadly. "Hell, I wish *I* agreed with you. For the next two quarters we're in the red. If *Lincoln* succeeds, we'll have an okay year, but if it fails . . . disaster. No one's buying our stock to clip coupons. My guess is Disney's after us."

Borkin shook his head. "I think it's Polygram. They've gone as far as they can in the record business. Acquiring J-Squared instantly makes them a player in the movies. The only thing discouraging them till now was your high stock price."

"If you're right, I wind up working for a paranoid French CEO of a penny-pinching Dutch conglomerate with a thuggish South African chairman. No thank you. Henry, you and your firm need to turn over every rock until we find out who's got his hand in our pockets. Then we're going to cut it off at the wrist."

Jess sighed. When Dad went to war, no one got any business done.

=

Two hundred fans of Megan O'Connor's packed Book Soup on Sunset to hear her read passages from *The Main Line,* a tale of heroin addiction among wealthy Philadelphians. She looked like a stunning off-

Broadway actress in black leggings and a gray cashmere sweater, her hair savagely pulled back from its roots. At the edge of the crowd AJ leaned precariously against the towering self-help section. His invitation had included a scrawled note about how much his attendance would mean to her. It was irresistible because the former lovers hadn't set eyes on each other since Megan had slammed out of his house—and the movie business—a dozen years ago.

Like her three previous books, this newest novel exposed the sordid fantasies and agendas of its pampered characters. It had already garnered critical acclaim and a low toehold on the *New York Times* bestseller list. When she hit her last period, people barraged her with books to autograph. AJ was slipping off when Megan's publicist came over to escort him to the front of the line.

"Hello, AJ."

"Hello, Megan. It was good . . . to hear your voice. I'd forgotten how stirring it can be."

"Eleven years?"

It seemed as impossible as this meeting. "Time's been kind to you."

"Would you have dinner with me tonight? Eight-thirty, my suite at the Peninsula?"

She probably wanted advice on how to get bigger bucks for the sale of her books to the movies. He felt the impatient crowd pressing behind him. Refusing would require a longer explanation than it was worth. "Sure. It'll be good to catch up."

To kill time before dinner he walked to the AMC multiplex to check how the trailer on *Lincoln* was playing. The weeknight audience watched politely but the trailer generated none of the whispering and frenzy that greeted *Titanic*'s coming attractions. With a budget as splashy as the ocean liner itself, Jim Cameron's epic appeared to be the Christmas blockbuster that AJ hoped for—and desperately needed. Expectations were everything. Take dinner—after the way Megan had dumped him, he thrilled at the prospect of rejecting whatever she might want.

When the door to the suite opened, her hair had fallen free to her shoulders. She was barefoot. A person had replaced a performer. Room service delivered a selection of his favorite appetizers, but how had she guessed his new preference for cosmopolitans? AJ slathered beluga on brown bread with a dollop of sour cream. The poor publisher who reimbursed her expenses was in for sticker shock. "You were a triumph tonight. I would have bought the book without the dinner."

"I enjoy these tours. They're my only interaction with the world. After this it's back to the Poconos and the blank page."

"Eschewing the world for your art—Thoreau would have approved."

"I hardly think so. I have a hot tub, a microwave, and a killer stereo system." She settled on the sofa, sipping Courvoisier while he finished his snack. "Does *The Main Line* have potential as a film?"

"Any drama is an endangered species in Hollywood if its audience is postpubescent."

"So I shouldn't expect an offer from J-Squared?"

"We're not classy enough. Didn't you once call us commercial hacks?"

She laughed ruefully, like a woman seeing a snapshot of herself in seventies clothing. "I was a handful in those days—but I did hate that comedy spot. Maybe time has changed both of us. I saw the coming attractions for *Lincoln* and thought it looked very classy . . . and quite moving."

"Thank you. Why am I here?" He scored first, cutting off her trivia at the pass.

"I don't like my writing these days."

"No one else agrees."

Megan dismissed his compliment. "I seduce the critics. They mistake my meanness for . . . *The New Yorker* calls it 'furious energy.' But it's getting old." She hugged a throw pillow. "It's been a long time since I loved anyone . . . and it's showing in my work."

Too late he remembered that she was a writer, poised with plot twists and armed with wistful words. "You're not intimating that I was the last?"

"No, the best."

"I don't have a clue what to say, Megan."

"I'm the one who has something to say. I'm sorry, so sorry, for hurting you and spiting myself. You terrified me . . . your intensity, your acceptance of my craziness. I was too young and scared."

"Now I'm too old and married—happily married."

"I know. Don't think I haven't had spies check out your availability. We can never be together, I know that, but . . . God, this is . . . I feel ridiculous . . ."

He could have resisted tears, but not the empty space. He moved to her side. "It's okay."

"No, losing special people is not okay."

He comforted her in his arms. She fit like old times. But this wasn't comfortable . . . it was strange—and arousing. She looked up, inclining her face until he kissed her lips. It was the same sensation he'd experienced the first time, back in his office. They couldn't stop touching.

"Fuck me." Only a few women had ever said those words to AJ without sounding silly or vulgar or playacting. None spoke them more passionately than Megan.

He tore at his clothes and hers, fearful that his excitement would overwhelm him.

Driving home, he tried to make sense of what had happened to him—no, what he'd done. He had betrayed Steph, but not out of frustration, as in the past. Maybe he'd revenged a hurt suffered at Megan's hands and reaffirmed his potency in the face of old age. His explanations were as dry as they were irrelevant. It had been a one-time-only sale on passion, and he was too avid a shopper to resist.

$$=$$

"Can you try not to laugh?"

Posing was tougher than Jessica had imagined. And her boyfriend wasn't as fast with a brush as he was with a camera. But the idea that he wanted to paint her nude was her fantasy come to life. She spent an hour dressing, then fifteen minutes getting off on getting undressed. The best thing was that modeling for Patrick gave them extra time alone. Two weeks together wasn't nearly enough, especially since she had returned to work and had only been able to spend nights with him.

But what fantastic nights! The man had mastered the foot massage, to say nothing of its aftermath. And he cooked. Every night of the week he made an exotic three-course dinner from scratch. After sampling one of his meals, her mother, who was incredibly picky, said Patrick had the makings of a chef. He didn't smoke, he always called when he said he would, and he enjoyed listening to her complain about work. . . . How in her mad world had she found a brilliant artist who was also a good guy?

Maybe that was the doubt that rattled in her mind like a loose pebble. Suppose Patrick was an extraterrestrial? Suppose he received a message to phone home? She quivered, this time with anxiety rather than excitement.

He adjusted her face. "Now you're frowning. It's not easy painting a schizophrenic."

Great—he knew exactly who she was.

===

AJ was hefting his Biggest Bertha on the front lawn before heading to Riviera for his Saturday tee time when he spotted a guy in a uniform wandering the grounds of his Bel Air estate. "Can I help you?"

"Whoa, dude, this is some spread."

"Thanks."

"What's it go for—three point two mil an acre?"

Only in L.A. could the FedEx messenger nail property values. "Something like that. Have you got a package for me?"

"A letter—if you're Albert Julius Jastrow."

"I am." It was odd because the only people who used his given name were shills from Publishers Clearing House—and they used bulk mail.

As he signed, the messenger tested his club. "How much is this—four hundred?"

AJ's dirty look sent him fleeing. As he slit open the cover, the sound of a horn startled him. "I'll be back by five," Steph shouted. She was on her way to meet a crew that would tape her preparing pancakes and lingonberry syrup with some Swedish grandmother in Sierra Madre. *Taste Buds* was more consuming than a fledgling restaurant, but she thrived on the buzz.

Disbelief hit as soon as he saw the Powerline logo:

Dear Albert,

    This letter serves as official notification of the intent of Powerline to acquire all the assets and to assume all existing obligations of J². We are offering to purchase your stock at forty-five dollars per share. We would appreciate it if you would consider our proposal and reply by close of business October 17, 1997. A follow-up document from our investment counselors, Wahlberg & Sparrow, will provide details.

Sincerely,
Richard Jastrow

Was this a practical joke—or a cosmic one? Ricky, who called himself an executive even though he'd inherited his power and every cent from his grandmother, had just announced—in seven fucking lines—that he intended to steal his father's life's work. Did the arrogant prick actually think he could succeed? Did he imagine that AJ would take him seriously? Or was this Maggie's handiwork—a belated parental punishment for not being the dutiful son all these years? He tightened his grip on his driver as he realized he had to respond seriously. Christ, Powerline probably already owned 5 percent of J². He hurled the Bertha. It flew forty yards before hitting the garage door.

CHAPTER 50

AJ took two days to corral J²'s board of directors for an emergency meeting, but only two minutes to inform them of his response. "Unless there are objections, I intend to send Richard Jastrow a letter rejecting his offer. Then the only way Powerline can win will be to wage a proxy fight, and that's a long row to hoe."

Stan Hurley toyed with his Phi Beta Kappa key—the last man under eighty to wear one. "I can understand your anger."

"But . . . ?" AJ half-expected a defection from the chief operating officer of Wells Fargo, the bank that had lent him six hundred million dollars. Powerline's promise to pay off J²'s shaky debts at one hundred cents on the dollar could save Hurley's butt.

"But I think we need to study this offer more closely. Martin . . . ?"

"You make an excellent point, Stan."

Bye-bye, Martin Tessinger. The singular passion of the chairman of Union Life Insurance was making money, not movies. After AJ, his company owned the largest stake in J², and he regarded Powerline's fifteen-dollar-a-share premium as irresistible.

"Perhaps we ought to negotiate, see if we can transform it into a merger rather than a takeover." The speaker was General Mack McCall, deputy secretary of defense under Jimmy Carter and J²'s Washington lobbyist.

"Your strategy didn't work for the Iran hostages, did it, General?" Ray Stark asked facetiously.

"What the hell does that mean?"

"It means you don't negotiate with the devil," AJ interjected.

"Come on, guys, get real." Leo Dorman had the foresight to imagine the home entertainment center before anyone else, and now his company, First Run, ranked as the nation's top distributor of videos. "Powerline doesn't know a damn thing about film. Haven't we seen too many train wrecks occur when companies barged into our world without the instincts or experience to manage the movie business? We owe our stockholders more than a quick buck."

"I agree. Movies are magic time. AJ and his team understand that."

"Thank you, Jack." AJ had met Jack Lemmon making *Save the Tiger* and they competed together annually at the Pebble Beach Pro-Am. Although he was the least business-savvy board member, Lemmon's face sold the annual report. By AJ's count he now had seven votes: Dorman, Lemmon, Ray, Steph, Henry Borkin, Jessica, and himself. Powerline couldn't touch J², so he could afford to be magnanimous to his opponents. "I'm going to have Pete Leventhal, Henry, and our attorneys review the follow-up letter and we'll talk again on Wednesday before I respond formally."

After the outside directors departed, Pete clapped AJ on the back. "It's a good thing Dorman and Lemmon value management."

"You're right." He smiled for the first time since opening the letter. "Otherwise this battle would be uncomfortably close." AJ longed to go home, open a bottle of Bordeaux, and watch *Dr. No* for the fiftieth time, but it wasn't to be. There was only a half hour to dress for a dinner at Spago for Goldie Hawn and Meg Ryan, whom Jess had coaxed into playing sisters in a mystery comedy called *Dead Certain*. They might be wonderful in the movie, but as dinner companions . . . maybe he *should* sell Ricky the company—the bullshit of running it would be his best revenge. As he grabbed his coat to leave, he noticed his daughter curled into the sofa, staring into space. AJ balanced on the arm. "Difficult to believe, isn't it?"

"I'd planned on sending Ricky a Christmas card as an olive branch," she admitted.

"Save the stamp. Anyway, I'm betting your grandmother's behind this."

She slumped against him. "Why can't we just stay distant enemies?"

"We're a family, we're Jewish, we're in the movie business. No matter how you add those up, they can never equal 'distant.'"

≡

Jess stifled a burp. The damn smoked-salmon-and-goat-cheese pizza hadn't agreed with her, but it was her boyfriend's behavior that was giving her heartburn. While Patrick prattled on about how smart Meg was and how much he'd enjoyed Goldie's stories, she worried about his nascent crush on Hollywood. Did he intend to find a job as an on-set photographer? Good-bye, art. She dropped her keys on the kitchen counter and rooted through her cabinets. The new housekeeper insisted on hiding things, and Jess had to make coffee to stay up long enough to prepare script notes for tomorrow's meeting. The backlog at the office was impossible.

"Need help?"

"No, I'm fine." Their idyll had screwed up her schedule. If she'd worked the town instead of posing for a portrait, maybe she could have found the company another movie.

"I like your family."

"Part of my family. The other part are terrorists."

"I stand corrected. I like your father and mother. Talking about mothers, mine's visiting San Francisco Tuesday for an exhibition of her photos. How about flying up with me to meet her?"

"To see if she approves?" Jess knew she sounded churlish. But his timing was atrocious. No, worse than that: it was unconscious. Couldn't he sense how pressured she was by the recent crisis? A partner who lived in his own world was no partner at all.

The proof was how calm he remained. "I thought you might have a good time. She's nuts but interesting."

"I know enough crazy people." Jess poured beans into the grinder—and all over the counter.

"Oh, come on. She got really excited when I mentioned the idea."

"You shouldn't have. Now I'll look like the villain."

"I only said you might come."

"With what's going on, you know I don't have the time now to go gallivanting."

"Twenty-four hours in San Francisco is hardly gallivanting."

"Oh, really? Have you looked at my schedule for that day? Work is my priority." She left the "and you're not" hanging.

"You can tell me to back off without picking a fight."

Just as she'd predicted, she *was* the villain. "We're too different. You enjoy the luxury of 'observing' the world. But I have to get involved and mix it up."

That hurt. "You're right about one thing. I'm not going to 'mix it up' with you." Patrick shouted over the whir of the Krups. When it shut down, the silence was sad.

"You know the old saying, 'If you can't stand the heat . . .' " Her eyes trailed through the French doors to the guest house beyond the pool.

He walked out.

The drip of the coffeemaker hypnotized Jess, and it took all her energy to retrieve the script from the towering pile in the bedroom. A deranged teacher kidnapped a group of prep-school kids and held them for ransom in an old missile silo. By page 10 Jess knew who would live and die, who was the traitor and who was the hero.

Her fight with Patrick had gone from zero to sixty in one second flat. A person who accelerates that fast pulls a lot of g force. And she knew the effects of that. When they'd shot *City at Sea,* Jess had taken off in a jet from an aircraft carrier. Her eyes and mouth sucked back, her body slammed forward against the harness, her mind blanked. Defying gravity had distorted her beyond recognition.

She should apologize, but for what—for being honest? It was good that he saw who she really was. If they were meant to be together, he would get through it. If not, maybe she wasn't meant to be with anybody. At least that would spare future generations another mad family. His car roared to life and drove off the property—not quite doing sixty, but damn fast. That was the answer she'd expected. Jess gulped her coffee but immediately spit it out. She'd forgotten her two Equals, and the Viennese roast was too bitter to swallow straight.

=

Maggie couldn't fathom why her grandson had bought a house in San Marino. Only her boring Republican friends lived this far to the east. And though the property enjoyed a magnificent view of the San Gabriel Mountains, the low-lying haze made them invisible half the year. In an earlier time she would have found a way to dissuade Richard, but now he was too sure of himself for her to interfere. Or maybe she could no longer muster her old certainty about where—or how—someone should live his life. All that mattered was that he and his wife loved the place.

As she sat by the pool, Maggie watched Amber knitting ski caps for her children in preparation for a Christmas trip to Austria. Even in a bikini, which she wore beautifully despite two cesareans, the woman maintained the protective shell of those who'd grown up in military families, where discipline damped emotion and the dislocation of base moves discouraged intimate relationships. Still, Amber was a loyal partner and a dedicated mother. Nina and Molly swam in the shallow end. They were solemn girls, and Maggie considered it a victory to win one smile per visit. A laugh was a bonus.

"Are you sure you don't want me to put up the umbrella?" Amber asked.

"No, dear, I think I look sexier with a suntan." The two women broke into girlish laughter. Maggie stopped abruptly when an ice pick stabbed her stomach. She forced a reassuring smile. "Don't worry, I'm fine. It's the price of growing old, but the alternative is worse. You look a bit drawn yourself."

Amber nodded. "I'm not sleeping well. This business move Richard is planning . . . do you approve?"

"It's not my place to approve or disapprove. He controls our affairs these days."

"But he's become so grim, even with the girls." Her frustration was palpable. "Who cares about the movie business? I don't like those people or the films they make."

"This isn't about business, no matter what he says. You can't imagine how deeply your husband suffered at the hands of his father. I want him to be free of that pain. This fight had to come."

Amber shivered. "I don't like fighting. I don't even like raising my voice."

"Sometimes you have to yell like hell. There are wars worth fighting."

"Worth it or not—I don't want my family to be the casualty."

Maggie closed her eyes at the new wave of pain. But this time she retreated to the bathroom. It felt like she was losing her insides. When the stabbing nausea abated, Maggie looked into the toilet bowl and started to cry. Blood was everywhere. She knew that she was dying.

=

AJ was mid-bite into a pastrami sandwich when he noticed that Ray hadn't touched his corned beef. "I brought that from Nate 'n Al's."

"I'm contemplating the fat," Stark deadpanned.

"We sound like characters from a Doc Simon play."

"I think *The Goodbye Girl* was the best movie Neil ever wrote."

It was a privilege of age to wander wherever the hell you wanted, so AJ gamely followed. "Whatever happened to the kid who played Marsha Mason's daughter?"

"Quinn Cummings? She's washed up—like me."

"You're not washed up. At least you'd better not be—I need you. You've always been the best consigliere in the movie business."

"Can you believe Begelman?"

Another left turn. It was two years since the studio chief had checked into the Century Plaza Hotel and blown his brains out with a shotgun, but the event still disturbed Stark. "He couldn't face his gambling debts," AJ said sadly.

"I would have lent him the money," Ray replied.

"He was beyond asking."

"Your mother's dying."

"Aren't we all?"

"I'm serious," Stark insisted. "We have the same urologist, and he said Maggie won't make it to Christmas."

AJ chewed deliberately on a pickle, then took a sip of soda. All he could taste was . . . annoyance. Through the corporate grapevine AJ had learned that, counter to his presumption, Ricky had instigated the takeover in the face of his grandmother's reservations. His son would soon possess even more power and money to pursue his plan.

"Are you okay?" Ray asked tentatively.

"It's like hearing that Nixon died."

"Jesus, that's cold."

AJ shrugged. "She died for me a long time ago."

≡

"We have to talk!"

Andy Faddiman vibrated like a tuning fork, while AJ tried conceiving a new marketing disaster. "The agency forgot to place our ads? They found Charlie Sheen in bed with—"

"You won't guess."

"But you're going to tell me?"

"This friend of mine, whose name I cannot divulge, asked me to have lunch with an investment counselor named Sparrow."

"Roy Sparrow?"

"You know him?"

"Of him." AJ glowered. "Go on."

"I thought he was going to talk about rebalancing my portfolio—or what's left of it, thank you very much—but this birdie had a different agenda. Sparrow explained that he's working with the future owner of J-Squared—none other than your firstborn—and that Richard feels I've done an unbelievable job of getting some real dogs open. They think I should head production rather than the 'bimbo' who's got the job because of nepotism."

In that moment AJ knew his fight was far from over. To end it, he would have to drive a stake through his vicious prick of a son.

"Then Sparrow claimed Richard had empowered him to negotiate a three-year contract for me, as well as cash out my stock options at a premium. The one condition—wait till you hear this—was that I quit today." Faddiman reached into his pocket . . .

A letter of resignation?

He removed a pack of Merits, lit one, and took a deep drag. "Whoever outlawed smoking doesn't know the meaning of *fartootst*. I told him I was in the midst of a critical marketing campaign, and if Ricky ultimately bought the company, he would want *Lincoln* to be a hit. But Sparrow said, '*Lincoln* hasn't got a chance in hell. It's not worth your effort.' That doesn't make sense."

It did to AJ. If the movie failed, Ricky would find it easier to convince Leo Dorman and Jack Lemmon that AJ's management team wasn't worth supporting. And because Andy was sharply at odds with Jessica, he was the most vulnerable mark in the company. "How did you leave it with him?"

"I promised to give him an answer in a few days."

AJ couldn't afford to lose his marketing guru, but he couldn't grant the authority over Jess that Faddiman desired. So he stalled. "I appreciate you giving me a heads-up."

"Before I tell him to wipe his tush with the offer, I want to make sure you don't need me as a double agent . . ."

AJ's sigh of relief revealed his doubts.

"Oh my God! You thought I was going to . . . ? Shame on you. I've known you for over twenty years."

"I apologize, Andy. I don't know what I was thinking. These days I trust no one. . . . I should have—"

Faddiman silenced him with a hug.

But as AJ headed back to his office, another doubt crossed his mind. He beelined to his Rolodex and flipped through until he located the name of Logan Clark, a private investigator whom J² used regularly as a consultant on movies. "This time I need you for a real job."

"I handle shit like this all the time," Logan assured him after learning of the mission. "I'm assuming you're just seeking confirmation, not elimination?"

"What? Are you—"

"Kidding, I'm kidding."

With a guy who had served as much time in Special Forces as Clark, you could never take the chance.

THE UNCIVIL WAR ||| 355

"*I acta alea est!*" Caesar's declaration as he crossed the Rubicon on his march toward Rome was etched in Richard's memory. Twelve years ago he'd shouted the English version—"The die is cast!"—during an audition for an ABC miniseries. But not until he'd personally sealed the bid to take over J² did he comprehend the thrill of charging into a coliseum from which there could be no retreat, no negotiations, no outcome other than victory or ignominy. Until then it had all been acting, a game, mental masturbation. Lying on his bed with the shutters drawn against the early-morning sunlight, Richard imagined again and again the impact of his terse takeover note: his father's bravado, fury, and, inevitably, fear. Now he was an hour away from outflanking his foe, driving him from his corporate lair into the open, where he could be hunted and destroyed.

"Nina is wetting her bed again."

He opened his eyes to the sight of his wife gripping damp sheets. Marriage on the rebound was a god-awful idea. "Don't make a big deal out of it."

"She's nine. We have to get her help."

"That's the worst thing we can do. It will make her feel like a freak." He rose and headed to the bathroom to shave.

She followed him. "End of conversation?"

"I'm sorry if I can't be more comforting, but I'm about to start a meeting that could determine the fate of my entire venture."

She exited without another word. That was one of Amber's problems—she composed speeches but rarely delivered them. He cared about her concerns and his daughter's lapses, but there was a time and place to deal with both. The buzz of the security gate captured his attention. First, he had to seal a grand alliance.

Mike Ovitz's power had peaked in the early 1990s, when CAA dominated the agency world and he spent his days brokering the sale of studios. But after the departure of his partners, Bill Haber and Ron Meyer, Ovitz had wearied of the ceaseless hand-holding of the talent. He'd accepted a post as Michael Eisner's second in command at Disney, but Eisner had never given the relationship a chance, axing his "friend" after sixteen months. Richard, however, had seen an opportunity in his former agent's setback. If he could persuade Ovitz to be president of J², that announcement would win over the undecided voters on his father's board of directors. Mike had ultimately declined his offer, claiming it was too soon for him to jump back into corporate life, but he'd immediately conceived an inspired alternative.

After *Don't Tread on Me,* Russ Matovich had directed twenty movies whose cumulative box office exceeded four billion dollars. The secret of his success was recognizing that young audiences didn't care about being moved or improved—they wanted action. So Matovich dealt them a visual rush with visceral state-of-the-art spectacles. Only Spielberg ranked higher in the Hollywood pantheon, a reality that drove Russ so mad with envy he hired a publicist whose job was to contact anyone doing a feature on Steven and sell him instead. But when Spielberg cofounded DreamWorks, Russ sulked. How could he compete with a man who owned a studio?

Mike proposed an elegant solution. If Matovich became president of J², Russ would get his studio, Richard would sign up a pro, and Mike would siphon power from both. They had agreed to every major point in prior negotiating sessions, but when Richard proposed formalizing the deal, the mood shifted.

Matovich smiled. "I've thought about this a lot, Ricky—"

"Richard. I prefer it."

"I remain intrigued, *Richard.* But I won't be your deputy. Maybe it's too many years calling the shots—I've got to be totally in charge." He leaned across the coffee table. "That means the power to make every decision that affects what movies we make, how we market them, and how the theaters operate."

This was massive betrayal. Forty-eight hours ago Matovich had signed off on a power-sharing arrangement in which Richard exercised fiduciary controls, as well as maintaining approval over key decisions. With Powerline spending a billion dollars to acquire J²—and billions more in the future—Richard damn well intended to keep himself intimately involved. Matovich's demand was out of line, and in any event, Powerline's board of directors would never abdicate autonomy. He glared at Ovitz, as if to say "Do something—and do it now."

But when Mike began to stroke, he targeted Richard, not Matovich. "Although it may not seem so on the surface, what Russ is seeking is precisely what you want. Ceding him control will prove how much control you have, because really powerful men exercise their power by not using it. If people ask, you say that you want your studio run brilliantly, and the only way that can be accomplished is for a single guy to manage the show, like in the days of Zanuck and Warner. Point to Lew Wasserman as a role model."

The former agent spoke with such utter conviction that it took Richard a moment to grasp that every word was a lie. He wanted to banish both men, but that would gain him nothing. He didn't have an alternative to Russ in the wings, and without a splashy CEO, all Richard had was too much J² stock and the scorn of his father. "Russ, I'll guarantee ten million dollars more in your pay package if you'll quit being a control freak. And I give you my solemn promise to stay out of your hair. I've got better things to do than run a studio."

"You're sure?"

"As God is my witness. And there's no other way this can work."

Matovich extended his hand. "Then we've got a deal."

=

AJ credited Leo Dorman and Jack Lemmon for their guts. Rather than phone to say they'd switched their support to Powerline's takeover, they came to his office to abandon him in person. His son's recruitment of Matovich had convinced both that the prospective owner was committed to building a vibrant new J². "They're a mighty impressive team," Lemmon piped up. "The kind of guys you'd like to have join your foursome."

"If you like sandbaggers," AJ replied.

"When we met with him yesterday your son described how Hollywood can program the Internet," Dorman gushed. "It's a potential gold mine, and Russ said he'll personally devise the content for a new entertainment site that will only be available through Powerline.com. We're talking original movies with A-list directors and big names. Jack's agreed to star in one."

"Please!" AJ brushed aside the idea with a wave of his hand. "We're years away from using the Net to distribute movies—or anything other than information."

Lemmon smiled sadly. "We're survivors, my friend, but we can't allow ourselves to get stuck in the past."

"I'm not stuck in it, but I am a student of it. My son's off base. It took thirty years after the invention of television for people to figure out how to make it work commercially. Give me another two quarters to raise our stock price," he pleaded. "The reason it's fallen so far is because Terry Mangiarcina slaughtered us in the financial press, and she only did it so that her firm could cash a twenty-million-dollar investment-banking fee from Powerline. We ought to haul their asses up in front of the SEC."

"That's part of the game," Dorman countered. "And as of tomorrow Powerline's increasing its offer by four dollars a share."

Flop sweat seeped from AJ's brow. "That's nineteen dollars over the market. I don't believe it."

"They're making the announcement at their annual meeting. On behalf of our stockholders we have a duty to accept a fantastic deal."

"This is my company, Leo! Mine!"

"I understand," Dorman replied. "And I discussed that point with your son. I know there's sour history, but he's willing to forgive and forget. He promised me he was open to keeping Jess as a consultant, and if you wanted to remain on the board . . . well, you'd have to be willing to see things his way, but this could be a wonderful reunion."

"That's the dumbest fucking thing I've ever heard a smart man say."

Dorman's eyes bugged. "In my entire career, Jastrow, no one's ever spoken to me like that."

"I don't give a shit! The vote will be five to five, Leo. According to our bylaws, in case of a tie I make the final decision. So tell Ricky he can offer a hundred dollars a share—his offer will still meet the same fate."

"You're inviting lawsuits from stockholders."

"Fuck them."

Lemmon looked aghast. "It's going to be a terrible mess."

"That I didn't cause." AJ threw open the door to his office. "Get the hell out of here."

≡

Jessica had been among the last to arrive for Sean Devine's memorial service. Two weeks ago a neighbor had found him—and his German shepherd—sprawled on the Spanish mosaic tile in the bathroom of his Beachwood Canyon home, both victims of heroin overdose. She'd rejected a request by his former CAA colleagues to eulogize their good times together and had debated the wisdom of even attending. Except for kidnapping his beloved dog into the next world with him, her ex-lover's burnout was no more unusual in Hollywood than a mud slide after the winter rains.

"Mind some company?" she asked, settling on the sofa in her father's office later that morning.

"Not if it's yours." He sat catty-corner, his feet propped on the coffee table. "I never liked Sean—not when you two were dating and especially when I learned about the job scam."

Jess stared. "You knew?"

"I learned a year after the fact."

"He was a charmer, that's for sure," she observed sadly.

"It doesn't take an evil person to do despicable things."

"Six months ago Sean said lying to me was the worst mistake he ever made. He begged me to forgive him. But I couldn't."

"And you shouldn't have."

She smiled thinly. "I thought forgiveness is a virtue."

"An apology doesn't erase a betrayal."

"Dad, I'm lost."

He selected an apple from the fruit bowl on the coffee table, casually tossed it in the air, then took a loud bite. "I don't buy that. Maybe you haven't found what makes you happy, but that doesn't mean you're lost."

"You're playing with words. I'm thirty-six and you're my only confidant? That's 'lost.' "

"No, it's lonely. Jessica, all men aren't Sean. You have to be willing to take a chance." He paused. "Why don't you call Patrick?"

"It's too late."

"Think about Mom and me. It's never too late."

Jess returned to her office annoyed by her father's simpleminded advice. But then she saw Holly Ballsky waiting patiently with her *fourth* pitch of the dog story. The writer looked so determined, Jess took heart. If she could track Patrick down, if he wasn't clicking snapshots in the Andes or the Arctic . . . maybe it was worth the try.

=

"Please give a warm welcome to the heart and soul of our company, the indomitable Maggie Ginsberg."

Her grandson's introduction to stockholders attending Powerline's annual meeting produced the kind of whooping, cheering, and foot stamping heard at a rock concert. Out of the corner of her eye Maggie saw CNN swivel their cameras to catch her. It took all her strength to switch on the microphone. That's what death ate first, consuming her power in chunks while saving the skin and bones for dessert. Thank God for OxyContin. The potent pain pill kept her from being tethered to the hospital during these waning days. The second she began to speak, however, *Miss Mayhem* was back on the air. Her voice was vibrant and her eyes leveled every member of the audience.

"This meeting marks my tenth anniversary as chairwoman of the Powerline board. It has been a wonderful capper to my career. So it is with considerable regret I declare that it must also be my last."

Groans attended her announcement.

"I feel totally confident that Richard Jastrow will continue to lead us forward. Our company is poised to become one of the most effective media giants in the world." She turned and smiled at her grandson. "It better be, because I'm counting on our stock to help support me in my old age—when it arrives."

Dozens of hands shot into the air. Richard pointed to a reporter from *The Wall Street Journal.*

"Madam Ambassador, does your departure at this juncture suggest that you disagree with the attempted takeover of J-Squared?"

"To the contrary. A few years ago members of the financial press castigated us for diversifying from our core cellular-phone business and building Powerline.com. But our Internet portal has doubled the company's market value. It's been our goal to acquire a producer of content, especially movies. Since we're well down that path, now is an ideal time for me to leave." Being an actress saved the day.

An elderly gentleman shouted, "Isn't fifty dollars a share for J-Squared highway robbery?"

"For those of us who survived the Great Depression, sir, the price of milk is highway robbery and the cost of a Toyota is the Brinks job. I wish the acquisition could be done for less, but I've urged Richard to proceed."

CNBC's Ron Insana pressed forward. "We've heard rumors from various sources that AJ Jastrow used blackmail and extortion to build his company and that he's ruthless and abusive to his filmmakers and employees. Do you think he's fit to run a public company?"

Maggie caught Richard exchanging a glance with Roy Sparrow. They willed her to blast away. "My son is self-serving, self-absorbed, obstinate, and over the hill. I have no doubt he's bullied and screamed at people. But if you're asking if I think he's a criminal . . . no, I do not." Leaving no opportunity for further questions, Maggie rose from the table and walked from the room. Her exits had always been art.

CHAPTER 52

Steph rolled over in bed to find tangled covers, pounded pillows, and a sweaty void. For a beat she couldn't distinguish if the footsteps on the stairs were headed up or down, but the bedroom door failed to open, a sure sign her husband's vigil had just begun. It was three A.M., right on time.

AJ always read reviews. No matter how obscure the publication or distant the channel, he knew what critics thought of his movies. But in the current crisis his habit proved masochistic because every business publication vilified his behavior. Under the headline A THRILLER IN HOLLYWOOD: FAMILY FEUD FUELS REVOLT, *The Wall Street Journal* had anointed him the black hat for ignoring the interests of his stockholders. *Forbes* and *Fortune* had outsavaged each other to agree. Their thumbs-down had driven J²'s stock into the ground and incited a blizzard of lawsuits aimed at him and the board of directors.

Steph tracked him to the den, where he was rewinding a tape of Terry Mangiarcina's interview on *Moneyline*. "She accused me of being the spoiled kid in the school yard who won't let anyone else play with his ball."

"Forget it—the woman's a bitch. How did it go with G.E.?" At Borkin's suggestion AJ had contacted Jack Welch in hopes that he might become a "white knight." When AJ hadn't returned from his meeting by eleven, Steph thought they might have struck a deal.

He pursed his lips. "Welch was interested, but won't come close to matching Powerline's bid—it's ridiculously rich."

"You still have the votes."

"How about us going far away . . . maybe Tahiti? By the time we return this will have blown over."

"It's not your style."

"You're right, there's no golf."

"I meant running away."

He waved brusquely. "You just can't take time from your television career. You're like my mother."

"Bite your tongue." Everyone was his enemy—or on their way. Over forty years she had steeled herself to provocation. "Are you worried about the lawsuits? Pete said we might be personally liable."

AJ tossed her an envelope. "I'm not sure he's the best judge."

The cover letter was from that lunatic Logan Clark, who'd helped install the security system in the house. He'd insisted they buy geese because the birds were more reliable than dogs, lasers, or alarms, but had forgotten to mention that they would cover the front lawn in goose shit. AJ had slipped and fallen in it, which had made her laugh . . . but what she read in Clark's summary wasn't amusing. "This can't be."

"*Et tu, Brute?*"

"AJ, I'm sorry."

"Feel like reconsidering my offer?"

Far away didn't sound far enough.

=

The first image on screen was pure John Ford: a bald eagle soared above an endless Indiana cornfield bisected by train tracks. But it was an incongruous element that made the frame memorable—people, not crows and hawks, perched upon the trackside telegraph poles. A steam-belching locomotive with red, white, and blue bunting slowed long enough for a tall man in a stovepipe hat standing on the platform of the caboose to wave to his fellow citizens. They could tell their children they'd seen Abraham Lincoln traveling to Washington to swear the oath as the president of the United States. Hollywood's makeup and effects geniuses had added years and inches to Michael Douglas, but it was his actor's craft that enabled him to become the man. As he locked eyes with the eagle, the main titles rolled. The scene sent chills through AJ and the audience attending the premiere of *Lincoln* at the Motion Picture Academy.

Faddiman sidled over. "We're home free, boss."

Despite the staggering cost of the film and its release in the midst of the takeover, reviews were rapturous and the tracking positive. AJ kissed Andy on his bald pate. "I'll always remember how you didn't quit on me or the film."

An hour later AJ took an unprecedented step—he sat down next to Steph rather than pacing. "Are you sick?" she asked.

"They say the legs go first. This is my favorite part. I wanted to share it."

Secretary of the Treasury Salmon Chase came to the president to urge him not to run for reelection in 1864. Brian Dennehy played Chase as a self-important schemer, warning Lincoln that his unpopularity would doom the new Republican Party. "Who might take my place?" Lincoln inquired. Chase threw back his head as if posing for Matthew Brady. "If the bugle calls, I will answer." "Well, Mr. Chase, I wouldn't spend too much time listening. When I commenced this job, I tried to please everybody, but it soon became clear that no matter what I did, I couldn't please anybody. So I've decided to please myself. Come next fall, I'll be running."

The audience erupted into applause. Lincoln had nailed it, AJ decided. Forget the fatuous advice or distraught pleas of pollsters and pundits, analysts and editorialists, stockholders and speculators. A true leader does what his gut tells him.

When the movie ended AJ felt like Lincoln's agent. A hundred people rushed over to tell him how much they admired not just the movie but the man. *Admiration.* In Hollywood it was a word long ago displaced by its perverted half brother and sister, *envy* and *jealousy.* That was what made it so ironic when Pete Leventhal indicated he needed to talk.

"I spoke to Gary Hirsch," Pete said hesitantly. They stood in the now deserted Academy theater. "He said your mother is failing and before she gets any worse, she'd like to see you."

"Tell her to give me a call—if she remembers the number."

"Do you think it's appropriate to be so—"

"Abrupt? Cavalier? Tasteless?"

"Gary and I have been trying to strike a compromise. As your mom's lawyer he has a lot of sway. To tell you the truth, I think her overture could be the opening we need."

"Did you say the *truth*? *You* want to tell me the *truth*? Go ahead."

"What's eating you?"

"Don't insult my intelligence."

"I don't know what you're talking about."

"Okay, we'll do it the hard way. Explain your fifteen calls to the offices of Wahlberg and Sparrow."

Pete chuckled. "Is that it? I tried to get Terry Mangiarcina to support our stock."

"Really? Did you also try to get Roy Sparrow's support when you called him four times at home in Scarsdale? How about when you called a beach house in Kona rented by my son?" Pete's eyes narrowed. "That's right—Logan Clark got your phone records. The hits keep coming. Would you like to see the FedEx log of packages you sent to Ricky's home? You slipped him every one of our forecasts—that's how Mangiarcina knew to downgrade us. And while we're at it, how about autographing a photo of you having dinner with Russ Matovich? Was that to negotiate your next job? When Powerline magically knew to approach Faddiman, I was sure we had a mole. When I realized it was you . . ."

Leventhal lowered his head—and his cover. "You're going to lose."

"Thanks for the inside scoop." AJ turned to leave.

"Don't you want to know why I did it?"

"Your wife counts everybody's money. You're worried about retirement. I don't know—maybe you've got a mistress to support."

"It wasn't the money."

"Bullshit."

"It was the respect—the respect you've never shown me in fifteen years."

"Concoct whatever rationale you want, you're a goddamn weasel."

"You don't get it, do you?" Pete jumped in AJ's face. "I respected you from the start, and I didn't mind being your number two. But I wasn't even that. I was . . . nothing. Every piece of good advice I offered for twelve fucking years—the Japanese, Kinison, Ricky, the theaters—all went in one ear and out the other. You were the genius. It took me all my life to realize I'm as smart as you are. You never gave me the chance because you're an arrogant prick."

Leventhal had been pissed at somebody or something since AJ first met him. "And you believe Ricky and Russ see what I didn't?"

"Yes. They respect me."

"You poor bastard—they don't even respect each other. Get your stuff out of the office tonight. I never want to see your sorry ass again."

=

An early winter storm hit Los Angeles the Tuesday before Thanksgiving. Pelting rain and fifty degrees—that was what it had been like back in Brooklyn on the first Turkey Day in AJ's memory. He must have been only four and a half, but proud that he knew how to peel chestnuts and could help make the stuffing. He loved the smell in the kitchen—and seeing his mother in charge. After their move to California, oysters had replaced chestnuts, depriving AJ of his role. Maybe that was an omen, he mused as he arrived at the house that Leon Ginsberg had built for his queen. The paramedics had parked their truck in the circular driveway and were playing hearts on a gurney, waiting for their call to arms. AJ considered asking for a hit of oxygen. In agreeing to the meeting, he'd insisted that no one else be present, so as he approached the bedroom, the nurse took a seat on a chair in the hallway.

He hadn't seen his mother in person for . . . he couldn't remember. But the near skeleton propped up on a hospital bed shocked him into the present. He could count the strands of her once luxuriant hair. Her cheeks were hollow and her breath came in uneven gasps that made him fear each was her last. Despite a fan that blew lazily, the air smelled sour.

"That's me—I'm the thing that stinks."

She had seen his grimace. "Hi, Mom," he murmured, dropping his resolve to maintain distance. "You've never had much patience for dumb questions, so I'll skip asking how you're doing." He was by her side without the memory of a single step. "I'm not sure what scares me more—how much we have to say to one another . . . or that we have nothing to say." She laughed—at least he thought she did, although her lungs barely produced a sound.

"I brought such a handsome boy into the world."

Was that a compliment or self-congratulations? He fought the paranoia that would surely doom the reunion. "We were a great pair," he said softly. "Remember sitting on the plaid sofa watching those Joan Crawford weepies?"

She drifted back to the afternoons of *The Million Dollar Movie*. "I liked you as a child."

"But I grew up."

She willed herself to the point. "You and Richard . . . it's gone too far. You'll have to settle this on your own. I root for him, but . . . the fight's almost reason to stay alive."

"The next time we meet, I'll let you know how it turned out."

"I have something I need to say."

The doctors had warned him that she had sores the size of silver dollars in her throat. "You don't have to speak."

She spit up specks of blood, which AJ caught in a Kleenex. "I loved your father."

Of all the admonishments, advice, and adieus AJ had anticipated, this deathbed revelation—was it a confession?—hadn't made the list. "Mom—"

"Listen to me!" She spoke rapidly, her vocal cords distended. "Before he died . . . we had words . . . ugly words. Maybe he thought I didn't care. You looked at me that way . . . as if you were the only one who cherished his memory. That hurt me . . ." She reached out to draw him closer. "I loved him . . . I swear I did."

Fifty years of guilt—unburied, as they were poised to bury her. Was it release or regret that made her cry? AJ took her hand. "Dad knew. He loved you more than anything in the world." His mom fell asleep before she heard. He couldn't bear to wake her, so he slipped from the room.

=

Maggie Jastrow Ginsberg passed away on December 3, 1997. According to the press announcement, her grandson was by her side. In reality, the idiot doctor hadn't given sufficient warning and she died alone. Having presented a brave face to the world, Richard retired to the solitude of his den, where he remained for the next twelve hours. His grandmother was the best friend he'd ever had. When he was a child, she was the only adult who'd believed he was more than dirt. And through all the years she'd never disappointed him.

In her waning days, as cancer sapped her will, Grandma had developed a wisp of sympathy for AJ, instigated by his manipulative visit. With her gone, Richard could now pursue the J² takeover unfettered. Time was against him. Only yesterday Roy Sparrow had warned ominously that Powerline's bid was losing momentum in the face of AJ's intransigence. Richard needed to deliver a message.

When his parents and sister arrived for the funeral, they found their names excluded from the guest list. In astonishment people watched as one of Hollywood's most respected leaders complained in vain to an off-duty cop. Once he'd had the pleasure of seeing AJ thoroughly humiliated, Richard signaled Maggie's lawyer, who conveniently appeared, pleading ignorance at the oversight. He seated AJ in a row behind the minor dignitaries. As the congregation rose to recite the mourners' Kaddish, Richard glanced back. The old man was too consumed with rage to chant.

CHAPTER 53

"Y ou've got mail!"
AJ clicked, dreading his daily barrage of "Drop dead!" "Sell!" and "Don't be an asshole!" from irate stockholders. But only fifteen messages appeared. Were his opponents losing hope? Just in case, he graciously replied to each with an explanation about why they would fare richer in the long run backing management than siding with Powerline. Next came a "wish you were here" from Roger Donaldson, who was freezing his ass off directing a J² adventure movie in Alaska, then one from his Atlanta theater manager reporting steady repeat business for *Lincoln* among African-Americans. But when AJ scrolled down he noticed that his final correspondent's address was RJ1@Powerline.com. His son's glee rocketed through cyberspace:

Dear Albert,

Sorry we didn't have a chance to speak at Grandma's funeral. I know you think the Internet is overrated, but what a fantastic way for old buddies to communicate.

As you are aware I intend to enter the movie business, and it's never too early to procure commercial material. Attached you'll find an article I commissioned. It's got a great hook. The writer received five million dollars.

I'm planning on selling it to a magazine before making it into a film. Given the notoriety of the principals and the current popularity of soul-bearing confessionals, I expect at least three publications to bid. My first move, however, will be e-mailing it to your wife and daughter for their comments. Of course, if a smart producer saw its potential and wished to preempt by purchasing the rights, I'd consider a deal.

As always,
Richard

P.S. I'll agree to call you AJ if you'll drop the Ricky.

Macabre curiosity enabled AJ to unfreeze his fingers long enough to download the file. The title read "Designing Dad," the byline Megan O'Connor:

> I am a woman whose chance of getting married, according to statisticians, is fractionally greater than dying in a plane crash. That doesn't faze me—I enjoy my single life. But I wanted to give birth to a child, and after thirty-six the chances of a natural pregnancy fall off the shelf, so time crowded me. I also wanted to choose my child's father, but I exhausted the files of every sperm bank I visited. Then I realized who the dad had to be. I've succeeded in my quest, but whether I have sinned or not you shall judge. . . .

What followed was a fantastic reinvention of his illicit night with Megan. In her version she asked him to be the father—with no strings attached—because she loved him and wanted her child to bear his spirit and genes. He agreed, willingly, enthusiastically. They required only one night together, she speculated, because of the depth of their connection.

AJ sat in awe. It was so monstrous a lie and Megan so compelling a liar that the article was sure to fascinate the prurient public. No doubt, it would sell. He longed to shout "Rape!" but why go hoarse? Despite his former fiancée's crime, his consent was her defense. And Ricky had phrased his e-mail carefully. It would be difficult to prove extortion, and in any event, Steph would immediately learn the truth—and revile his horny self-delusion. It wasn't the prospective disruption of his life or the community property or the public scandal that made that option loathsome. He simply loved his wife too much to contemplate losing her. The computer presented the new version of a rock and a hard place: "Reply" or "Delete"?

=

It was here somewhere, it had to be—buried in a walk-in closet under his bronzed golf clubs, his All-Around Camper trophy, a canoe paddle signed by his bunkmates, leather-bound copies of scripts from his fifty-plus movies, Todd's suit of armor, menus from Steph's restaurants, and her awards. Why the hell had he kept his ninth-grade book report on *The Naked and the Dead*? He knocked over a Bekins carton containing his Lionel model trains and one of Jessica's Ken dolls whose head had been ripped off. God only knew what affront had earned it that fate.

After fighting through the fallout from his son's coup de grâce, AJ had concluded that his first scenario—Ricky tracking Megan down and bribing her—was preposterous. A woman as independent as his ex wouldn't agree to get pregnant, even for five million dollars, unless she wanted to. The only explanation was that Ricky must have known *before* he approached Megan that she was preparing to become a single parent. Theoretically that was possible if the two had an ongoing relationship, but they'd barely known each other in the old days . . .

A good producer assumes nothing.

At the company kitchen a week ago he'd overheard two of Jessica's creative executives gossiping about the consolation prize if Powerline took control of J²: the prospective owner was a lot hotter than his father. Maybe they weren't the only ones who saw it that way. He was either terminally paranoid or totally screwed. Then he found it, covered in dust, the jacket mislabeled "Palm Beach Vacation." AJ retreated to his den, locked the door—though no one was home—and inserted the tape in the VCR.

He looked as if he'd aged twenty years—not twelve—since his fiftieth birthday. Shots of him shaking hands with Stan, kissing Julia, posing with his mom seemed like images from the silent movies. He fast-forwarded through the nostalgia, pausing every time the ubiquitous camera panned to his family. The scene was the same: Megan in kinetic conversation with Ricky. His son's date was stoned and he was off socializing with guests at each table. By AJ's thank-you speech, Megan was seated so close to Ricky that an observer would have identified them as a couple.

How far and fast had that relationship progressed? Where had she gone when she'd run from his house? Without her clothes or her purse, she couldn't have rented a hotel room. He remembered his frantic calls to friends, but no one knew her whereabouts. Now he flashed on an insane, grotesque possibility that . . . made complete sense.

=

The Powerline corporate jet banked sharply over a cornfield dusted with fresh snow. Alone in the passenger cabin Richard felt the plane level out for its final approach past the familiar brick control tower of the East Stroudsburg airport. His damp palms stuck to the cold metal of the seat belt. He had a case of the jitters worthy of a schoolboy. Own your fear, he told himself, embrace it.

The love of his life waited at the bottom of the ramp. Megan's cheeks were apple red, and the swell in her belly promised a limitless future. They kissed, oblivious to the wash of the propeller of a Piper Cub taxiing to take off. Megan obliterated the speed limit, covering the fifty mountain miles to her home in under half an hour. Then it was into bed, off with their clothes, under the duvet, and out of their minds.

They had blazed hot from that night eleven years ago when she'd appeared on his porch after finally ripping free from the old man. For the first week they'd never left the house, the lovemaking beyond any pleasure he'd known or imagined. Then, even as they held each other, Megan vanished. He guessed she sought escape in her psyche from the damage she'd suffered in her relationship with AJ.

Years passed with only letters. How could he say "only"? They were literature—acute descriptions of her inner life, vivid tales of the magnificent experience of writing her novels and the mundane joys of planting tulips. Meanwhile, Ricky married to escape the tedium of women throwing themselves at his exotic combination of brooding ex–movie star and go-go tycoon. His relationship with Amber existed on a separate plane from his longing for Megan, and it had survived intact until last year. Then, in a note he still carried hidden in his wallet, Megan had invited him back into her life.

"Do you see his hands?"

Richard studied the sonogram. "He looks so . . . peaceful."

"You wouldn't say that if you felt him kick. What do you think of the name Blake?"

" 'Tyger! Tyger! burning bright in the forests of the night, what immortal hand or eye could frame thy fearful symmetry?' " He stroked her hair. "He'll have a poet's soul."

"Suppose you hate him?"

"Excuse me?"

"Suppose he's a wicked child?"

"That can't be. We made him."

"Suppose he's like your father? Think how much you'll hate him."

He wanted her to shut up, to quit tempting fate. These provocations, these jabs—what proof of love did Megan require, what sacrifice?

"Do you think AJ understands what happened?" she asked.

"No." Compromising his father had been her idea, and though he recognized its genius, the knowledge that she'd screwed his despised enemy made that night the darkest of his life. "My father's ego couldn't accept that I succeeded where he failed."

"Too true." She rolled on top, pinning his arms to his side. "Fuck me."

The way she said it . . . he was the only one who could please her. After they climaxed, he whispered, "I've asked Amber for a divorce."

"What?"

He saw slate gray cloud the blue in her eyes. Megan was capable of savage storms, but he sailed on. "I want to marry you."

She withdrew from his arms. "How many times have we discussed this? I won't marry you or any man. After AJ and I got engaged, I suffocated. I refuse to belong to anyone."

She wasn't going to intimidate him. "I'm not anyone, and you'd never be my possession."

"Tell your wife you've changed your mind."

"Listen to me—"

"If you stop this, Richard, we can still be lovers. But another piteous plea will destroy everything we've built."

She was gone again—this time in body and spirit. Megan slammed out of the room. From the balcony he watched her wander down to the lake, wrapped in his overcoat. She stared at patches of floating ice seeking to link up with one another and freeze the surface. By the time he composed himself and came downstairs, Megan was the homemaker, scooping potato salad onto plates with ham sandwiches.

=

A migraine menaced AJ all morning, clamping down while he counted down to the appointed time. In a too breezy voice he announced that he was off to Riviera, but when an unexpected hand tapped his back at the elevator, he whipped around and nearly clubbed his secretary. Keeping her distance, she reminded him of his five o'clock meeting with Bob Rehme. The producer of *Clear and Present Danger* was wasting his time, because even if he wanted to deliver the next Tom Clancy movie to J^2, AJ had no intentions of leaving the future proprietors any asset beyond the keys to his office.

He couldn't make it to the Beverly Hills Hotel without a pit stop. In the putrid, airless men's room of a gas station, AJ dry-heaved until his diaphragm ached. After washing up with rusty tap water, he banged the towel dispenser so violently it broke apart, scattering the few remaining towels over the filthy floor. Hold it together, man. Minutes later, he handed his keys to the valet. A jet-black Ferrari with the initials RJ sat under the protection of a palm tree. At least his son was prompt. The bungalow reserved for the meeting stood in the far corner of the property. Halfway to it AJ's legs foundered. How had Robert E. Lee managed to mount the steps of Appomattox Court House the day he'd surrendered? Throwing back his shoulders, leveling his head, AJ carried on.

The door was ajar. AJ pushed it open, then took a beat to adjust to the dim light. Ricky was shadowboxing in the parlor of the suite, listening to his Walkman. He removed the headphones, allowing the nastiness of Nine Inch Nails' "Piggy" to bleed through. Cigarette smoke hung in the air. All that was lacking from the scene was cocaine and cash. AJ had asked to capitulate through intermediaries, but his son had insisted on exchanging papers in person. It was appropriate humiliation for the wanton stupidity that had cost AJ his life's work. He removed a file from his briefcase and addressed a silhouette: "Here's what you asked for."

"Sit down."

"I have other plans."

"Eighteen holes? Forget it." Ricky seized the documents as he had the moment.

"I've scheduled a meeting of my board of directors for ten A.M. tomorrow." AJ's voice was hollow. "I'll tell them that since I can't raise J-Squared's stock price in the foreseeable future, it's only fair to accept your offer."

His son checked for signatures. "I didn't think it would be this easy."

"Your mother deserves better than public humiliation. Frankly, she deserves better than you or me."

"I refuse to pity someone who's chosen to be a victim all her life."

He wanted to slap his son—no, beat him. And though he fantasized he still could, he recognized the ugliness of his decline. "The agreements are the ones drawn by your lawyers. I relinquish J-Squared, and as the quid pro quo you assign me ownership of the article and agree that neither you nor Megan will ever discuss or write about the incident described therein. I assume you have the side letter signed by her."

Ricky indicated a sealed envelope. "She told me how hot you were that night in the hotel—like some horny teenager—how you almost came before you even got inside her."

AJ suffered a paper cut opening Megan's document. "Don't expect to shock me. I had a private investigator talk to people in her hometown. They reported you two were an item."

His son stiffened. "We're hardly an 'item.' We love each other in a way you've never known. It's a shame you couldn't satisfy her."

"I managed pretty well in the end." AJ kicked himself for taking the bait.

"Yeah, stud." Ricky's laugh was a rusty saw. "Do you actually believe you impregnated Megan? Poor bastard—she's carrying *my* baby."

How could this be news—but it was. "You're lying."

"And you're pathetic. They should put you down like an old dog." Ricky circled him, a big cat savoring his kill. "I wasted decades feeling like garbage because that's how you saw me. But now I know—now the world knows—*you're* the garbage. How does it feel? Get used to it. You'll never get the taste out of your mouth. Look at you: the great mogul, AJ Jastrow. I hope that every second you've got left is filled with agony. I'll laugh over your grave."

AJ caught snatches of his son's screed. Black noise. He longed to apologize, but not to Ricky. How could he have failed so miserably in the one role he should have mastered? Could he have had a finer model? His father had understood the difference between right and wrong and had lived his life always placing equity and integrity above self-interest. The grandson he'd never met didn't even *think* in those terms. Ricky relished amorality. The responsibility for this familial descent lay squarely at AJ's feet—and he would suffer for his crime for the rest of his life. It mattered not what he produced for the screen, given what he had brought into the world.

Ricky churned forth hate. Get out, AJ told himself, or you'll drown like Dad. "We're finished, Ricky."

"We're not finished until I say we are."

"I'm leaving."

"Fuck you!"

AJ never saw Ricky lunge, but he felt a fist crunch his jaw, knocking him backward. His skull clipped a sharp object. He rolled over, spitting blood. He saw his son's leg poised to stomp, but it wavered, then fell from sight. AJ struggled to raise his head. A shocked expression was frozen on his attacker's face. Was it a last-second recognition of his madness? No, AJ realized, the expression was mortal fear. Ricky grasped at his chest, warding off an unseen attacker. But no one else had entered the room. His son's foe was his own heart.

He collapsed on the sofa, his pupils dilated. Still groggy, AJ forced himself to his feet. It was simple. All he had to do was retire from the room, return to his car, and drive off. Ricky would die by the time AJ reached his office. And it would remain his office. With him gone, no one at Powerline would pursue J². And since Megan already had her boyfriend's money, AJ had only to stuff her contractual promise of silence into his pocket for his secret also to remain his.

Murder or self-defense?

When he bent down to check if his son was still breathing, Ricky lashed out a final, furious "Fuck you!"

At least the two Jastrows had no quit in common. AJ searched for his soul with the anguish and desperation of a man who has misplaced his most valued possession. A gasp or two before it was too late he grabbed the phone and screamed for the operator to summon an ambulance. Then, laying his son upon the floor, AJ commenced the CPR he'd required all J² employees to learn. He pressed Ricky's heart, willing it to pump blood. Then he breathed air into his mouth, filling his boy's lungs with oxygen.

=

When Steph and Jess arrived in the waiting room at Cedars-Sinai, AJ lied that he had been meeting with Ricky in a last-ditch attempt to find a compromise. They were too overwrought to question him. For three hours AJ listened to conflicting rumors on his son's condition before a woman emerged from the ICU and introduced herself as Amber Jastrow. "The doctors think Richard's going to make it," she reported in the hushed tone of a person who feared even talking to them.

Steph wiped away a tear. "Thank God."

"His arteries were a mess. He was a heart attack waiting to happen."

"Is he alert?" AJ pressed. "Have you spoken to him?"

"Yes, but you can't see him—no visitors except immediate family."

"I understand."

Amber offered an ironic half smile. "I wish I did. Mr. Jastrow, the paramedics explained how you helped save my husband's life. I'll always be grateful. And maybe Richard will be too . . . in time. But right now the only thing he said to tell you was 'a deal's a deal,' whatever that means."

"Let him know I'll honor his wishes. He needs to use his energy to get well."

When they emerged, it was raining and the wind was gusting through the tunnel created by the hospital towers. AJ closed his eyes and let it wash over him.

"Leave your car here," Steph shouted. "I'll drive us home."

"Home"—the word sounded joyous. He was surprised when Jess climbed into the backseat. "Didn't you drive?"

She nodded. "But Mom and I . . . well, we've got something we need to talk to you about."

"Now?"

"We don't want you to find out in the papers." His daughter took a breath. "You were supposed to meet Bob Rehme this afternoon."

"That's right, we had an appointment. I don't know what he wanted."

"I do." She and Steph looked sheepish. "It was supposed to be a surprise."

"Hey, go for it. I've been to the mountain. Nothing you or anyone can say will shock me."

Wrong again.

CHAPTER 54

Jess had only seconds to seek shelter before a tropical cloudburst dive-bombed down the slope of Gunung Buda, the three-thousand-foot "White Mountain" of Borneo. Raindrops stitched the jungle floor as she dived into the hollow of the strangler fig tree. The space reeked of death. After the strangler's airborne seeds settled on the limbs of a banyan tree, the fig's roots began a slow descent, wrapping themselves around the trunk of the host until they "strangled" it. The corpse disintegrated in the fetid humidity, leaving behind the eerie hole in which she stood. Stranglers were indigenous to rain forests, but Jessica guessed they had a future in her hometown.

Destiny must have been at work in the weird events that had propelled her halfway around the world. First, there was her brother's heart attack just before Christmas, then his stunning recovery and her father's surrender. She'd vacated her office the day before the Powerline people occupied it. At the same time *National Geographic* approached her boyfriend with the plum assignment of photographing the massive and mysterious caves of the Buda. Patrick got his editors to provide a ticket and per diem for a special camera assistant, then called to pitch her the job. Jess was unemployed and didn't have to be back until the Academy Awards—so why not?

In forty-eight hours on the island she'd lost her identity. The local men had never seen a movie, much less a movie executive, so her day job meant nothing. They couldn't understand why Patrick kept her, since she couldn't cook, sew, or haul wood. The place was ripe—just short of rotting. Every tropical fruit she bit into exploded with juice, dripping and sticking to her till she became a magnet for insects. And the flowers, trees, and birds were too vivid, like an old Technicolor movie.

To clear her head Jessica spent hours wandering in solitude through the stark cave formations, which were beyond the imagination of a production designer or the skills of a construction crew. Deep pools of fresh water dotted the cave floor. She stared into them, as if they held the answer to the question of what she should do with the rest of her life. The image that stared back was no longer a girl but a woman who had to decide for herself.

The delight of the trip was daily life with Patrick. After her mea culpa to him last fall, they'd squeezed brief visits between his final revisions on *Markets* and her daily crises. But here in Borneo, watching her lover at work—he made it play—provided insights she couldn't have scored on a dozen dates. He had an empathy with people that crossed cultures and an unquenchable fascination with nature. Patrick embraced adventure in a way she did only in her fantasies and films. And making love in a tent—once she got the hang of avoiding roots—was delicious. But now her respite was ending. Involuntarily, Jess glanced at her watch.

"It's four P.M. in L.A.," Patrick said softly.

She jumped, still unnerved by his ability to sneak up on his subjects. The rain cascaded around them like a waterfall. Jess ran her hands through a mop of frizz. "When I get off that jet tomorrow at LAX, you can't imagine what I'll be walking into."

"What *we'll* be walking into."

She had four firm offers for production deals. Patrick kidded that studio chiefs would be waiting for her in baggage claim like limo drivers, carrying signs with her name. But the more promising her prospects, the more anxious she grew. If her father didn't decide his future soon, she would have to go it on her own. But what if she couldn't make it without him?

Now a new fear was plaguing her. "Standing here, I couldn't care less which movie did business last weekend or who got cast in what. But once I'm home, I'll always need a fix. Give me the grosses. Give me *Variety*. Give me the gossip."

"I know you're a slave to what you do, but you're not the only one. We can be slaves together. And maybe break a little free."

She sensed where he was heading. "Come on, let's make a run for it."

"No." Patrick pulled her back, then caressed her face. "No more running. Will you marry me?"

=

Humiliation was the gravest side effect of Richard's heart attack. Not only had he failed to rub his father's face in failure, he'd also given the bastard the satisfaction of saving his life. According to the stories AJ had leaked to the tabloids, he deserved a medal. Then there were the "pity the invalid" glances from Richard's business associates. They marked him as roadkill. Richard had to prove that angioplasty had made him healthier than ever and mentally tougher for having faced down death. So a month after being carted out of the Beverly Hills Hotel flopping like a fish, he was back at his desk twelve hours a day.

He reestablished his turf by negotiating a deal for Motorola to acquire Powerline's cellular-phone business, which no longer fit his vision of a "new media" company. The cash from the sale paid down Powerline's debt, leaving them lean and mean. The vultures backed off. Although Powerline's Internet business hadn't earned a dime, no one cared because the portal's subscriber base was expanding exponentially and everyone agreed that grand profits would follow. To speed up that time frame he raided the chief operating officer from America Online. That left Richard free—and ravenous—to realize the potential of his latest acquisition.

Powerline's valuation skyrocketed in anticipation of his bold foray into the movie business. On the first day he ordered a crew to sandblast the J² symbol from the front of their headquarters, chiseling in its place the new Powerline Pictures logo. After several weeks exploring the nooks and crannies of his father's company, Richard understood the old man's virtue—and fatal flaw. J² spoke quality, from the luxurious theaters to the knowledgeable personnel to the classy movies in development. His father and sister never stinted—but like hopeless suckers, they overpaid. Did every employee need to stay at the Four Seasons? Did the company have to grant motor homes to supporting actors? Why on earth did theater managers receive stock options? According to Pete Leventhal, who knew where the bodies were buried, AJ had granted these bequests like a king.

At Richard's urging Pete targeted areas in which the new management could cut costs, but Russ Matovich howled that he couldn't operate under the proposed constraints. He and his associates hadn't flown commercial or paid for a meal in a decade. Instilling discipline was key. When Russ arrived to bitch, Richard gave him "time out" in the outer office. But the new president would need sterner measures, since he was still seething. Russ had mastered the tantrum as a technique of intimidation. Out of disrespect he sat on the edge of Richard's desk, then screamed, "Are you out of your mind? Do you honestly think I'm going to put up with interference? How am I supposed to turn this place around if I've got an accountant up my ass?"

"With your talent, you can do anything."

"Fuck you and the horse you rode in on. Read my contract."

"I have." Richard leaned across, poking his finger in Matovich's chest till he retreated. "I know exactly what your rights are. You're an excruciatingly high paid *employee.*"

"Huh?"

"That's right. Your bullying and bullshit are history. Let's get this straight, Russ, I'm going to be involved—deeply involved. Forget my promises, like I forgot most of the pretentious acting tips you used to give me. If you can't stomach Richard Jastrow over your shoulder, breathing in your ear . . . quit. It's that simple."

Matovich couldn't still the flicker in his eyes. Quitting meant forfeiting a huge upside. And where could he go? He had lost his enthusiasm for directing, and twenty younger guns framed more stylish shots. If he wanted to continue as a factor in the movie business, this was it. "I don't mind dealing with you, Richard. But I need help with Leventhal."

"We'll see." They pored over budget items until Matovich was too bored to fight back. Then Richard struck his killer blow. "I looked over your proposal regarding Ovitz."

Mike had planned a new company, called the Artists Management Group, which would represent actors, directors, and writers. "He's going to own this town again," Russ waxed enthusiastic. "So if we invest twenty million in AMG, we'll get a share of his profits and preferential treatment with his clients."

"Pass." Richard waited a beat before looking up from some meaningless document. "Anything else?"

"Pass? Just like that?"

"Just like that."

"Mike loves you."

"And I love him, but he'll never command the power he once did. There's the stench of failure about him, and we don't need that rubbing off." He winked.

Involuntarily, Russ winked back.

Richard spun around in his father's old desk chair. The fit was perfect. After owning J² for two months, he understood why the old man had fought so hard to keep his company. His only regret was that Grandma wasn't around to see her dream come to glory. As always, she had called it right after Uncle Leon had died. With the Internet about to link the world, the possibilities were infinite for a company that created content.

=

Kirk Kerkorian's suite at the MGM Grand in Las Vegas was more opulent than the Sun King's palace at Versailles. The gold leaf in the drawing room alone could have funded a movie studio. It would be a relief, AJ reflected, to have deep pockets to rely upon, permitting him to take risks on projects without fear that failure meant doom. That would be the situation if he accepted the financier's offer to be chairman and CEO of MGM–United Artists.

Kirk sucked on a Turkish cigarette. "I have to admit, I secretly rooted for Powerline."

"Sometimes honesty is not the best policy."

"Consider it a compliment. If you had to relinquish J-Squared, I knew I could bring you here. MGM hasn't had a real lion since Louis B. Mayer."

AJ was too sharp a salesman not to know when the other guy was pouring it on, but too vulnerable not to love the dousing. Of all the calls he'd received—with their messages of sympathy and solicitation— Kerkorian's was the most welcome. The guy was Wall Street savvy in ways that AJ couldn't imagine, but he had no interest in actually operating an entertainment company. Uncontested division of labor promised a perfect partnership. But one doubt remained. Kerkorian had bought and sold Metro twice before, and AJ wasn't interested in playing a shill for another of his "slam bam thank you ma'am" encounters with the business. "As long as you're baring your soul, Kirk, are you in it for the long haul?"

"Let my lawyers prove it to you."

Direct was a dead end. This guy was too smart to reveal any agenda other than enthusiasm. But AJ wanted no surprises about *his* plans. "If we proceed, I have a two-pronged strategy. First, we'll carve a niche with the adult audience that wants quality product with complex stories. At the same time we'll focus on family entertainment, G and PG movies that parents can take eight-year-olds to see. The other studios can kill themselves targeting teenagers with action and special effects."

Kerkorian appeared delighted. "We're on the same page."

Yeah, yeah—it all made sense strategically. But what had AJ ready to jump was the promise of action. He could envision it. Outside his office executives, agents, and all manner of talent were already lined up, bidding for answers to their questions and requests. Lights blinked on every phone line. He was in conference with Jess, in battle with Andy. Fifteen times a year he'd dispatch filmmakers to the corners of the world, imagining the genius—and havoc—they might produce. Every day meant new deals, new dailies—a new lease on life. With a million things to do, he would have no time to think.

MGM was here and now, up and running. Every other offer would require building from scratch. He didn't have the patience for the years it took to generate a production slate, much less a new studio. The morning he took over at MGM he'd be a force again, which was the only way to live in Hollywood in your sixties. As for the chance it would provide to kick his son's ass sideways . . . well, he had never run from a street fight—and had rarely lost one. Finally, the Mayer bullshit aside, seeing his name on that hallowed letterhead would be a gas.

AJ allowed a mischievous smile. "It's intriguing."

"We can get this done in time for you to announce it on your big night." Kerkorian extended a hand with manicured nails and tobacco-stained fingers. "What do you say?"

=

"Are you going to be sick?"

AJ jerked his head from between his legs and smiled wanly at Bob Rehme. "In front of a billion people? Relax, I'll be fine." But his oatmeal complexion and glassy eyes gave the president of the Motion Picture Academy of Arts and Sciences small comfort. In Oscar's history there had been indelible embarrassments, from Sally Field's ditsy "You really like me" to Sacheen Littlefeather's harangue on Indian rights while accepting for Marlon Brando. But those disasters would pale in comparison to the recipient of the Irving Thalberg Memorial Award passing out at the podium.

"Forget 'a billion people,' " Rehme counseled. "Think 'a few friends.' "

"Right." How could he explain that stage fright wasn't the source of his anxiety?

As the broadcast paused for commercials, Jessica hurried over. "We're next, Dad." Although Gil Cates, the show's producer, had argued for a celebrity presenter, AJ had insisted on Jess, and Cates had acquiesced, rationalizing that the father-daughter schtick would play for the female audience.

"He looks like Albert Brooks in *Broadcast News,*" Rehme whispered to his daughter.

"You would too if someone was blowing hot air in your pants." She pushed aside the man with the dryer. "It's dry and he looks fine." As an afterthought Jess grabbed a powder puff from the makeup table and gave his forehead a final pat.

"Thirty seconds." An assistant shepherded them into position.

AJ heard the show's host, Billy Crystal, make another lame joke about *Titanic*'s director, Jim Cameron. Time twirled. He was dropping a seven-year-old Jess off at ballet . . . but then she was walking across the stage with the polished grace of a woman.

"AJ Jastrow probably deserves tonight's honor simply for surviving forty years in the film industry." She won the audience with her opening line. "But he's used his time well, energizing our business like the pioneer executives of our golden age. Ladies and gentlemen, a great producer—and a great dad."

The room darkened for the *Reader's Digest* version of his life, replete with clips from his movies, plus tributes from actors and directors with whom he'd worked. And then Ray Stark, a past Thalberg winner—and the man who had nominated him for the award—spoke to the camera. "Congratulations, AJ. Your dad would be so proud of you tonight. I'm proud to be his stand-in." The audience rose in ovation, and AJ stepped forward into his paragraph of movie history—without an idea what he was going to say.

Jess smothered him with a hug. "Knock them dead, Daddy." She handed over the statue, then slipped into the background.

Stick to the script. A recitation of thanks, sufficient self-deprecation to caramelize his teeth, perhaps a choked-up pause, then a coy line like . . . "What a happy coincidence that the award I'm holding was named for the legendary head of production at MGM—the studio that I'll be heading next week." After an outburst of spontaneous applause, bow humbly and shake the Thalberg in the air. It would be so easy.

Except for that damned broken faucet. AJ had been freshening up in the backstage men's room when it had exploded, soaking his tux trousers. He'd dabbed at the mess with towels but still looked like a guy who'd pissed himself. His memories and imagination kicked into gear. In the mirror AJ's reflection morphed into the desperate figure of Barney Balaban as he left the witness stand . . . stained in the same place. "I'll never let that happen to me"—or words to that effect—wasn't that what AJ had vowed in that Manhattan courtroom? But tonight he wasn't an old mogul who'd stayed too long at the party. He was in his . . . late prime. Then again, was that your delusion until they bounced you out the door?

Screw letting fear call the shots.

Steph would be his inspiration. She was the reason he was here. If he hadn't been so in love, he might have quit the business after Todd's Garden Party. Third row center on the aisle. But in the glare of the spotlights, he couldn't see her face.

It wasn't just fear.

And his doubts weren't just a whim of the last thirty minutes. They had hovered since the second act of his life had ended at the Beverly Hills Hotel. What the hell was he going to do in his third act? MGM was comfortably more of the same, but he had worked on too many movies not to know: repeating action was a recipe for disaster.

How long had he been standing there? Long enough, he guessed, to give Rehme and Cates a heart attack. He already knew that experience. The tension in the Shrine wafted up to the stage. The loyal J² crew must be bowing their heads in prayer. Even those cynics who regularly rooted for train wrecks willed him to speak.

He glanced down at the statue. Cast from bronze, it was stumpy but heavier than an Oscar. Thalberg looked intense—not a guy having a very good time. Jesus, the genius kid had also died of a heart attack.

As always, his daughter stood behind him, waiting calmly and loyally—a position that no longer felt right. And because it didn't, AJ smiled. He knew exactly what he wanted to say—not just in his head but in his heart.

"You would think that someone who spent his whole life in the movie business could learn his lines. But occasionally, it's better to toss out the script and improvise."

The audience relaxed.

"I have already told all the people dearest to me—the ones responsible for this award—how much I love them. So I'll skip that part . . . and the next, which was boilerplate you've heard a thousand times. In fact, I'm going to take that long-standing Hollywood advice and cut to the chase.

"Tonight I announce my retirement from the movie business."

People gasped. Nobody retired because . . . what else was there to do?

"I do so because it's always best to exit when you're high, and for a movie producer, there is no higher than now. I go because new opportunities beckon—although I'm not sure exactly what they are. But principally I go because the future of the business I cherish lies not with me but with the talented people of the next generation—none more so than my daughter. It's their time to step to the forefront and mine to stand back and applaud their triumphs."

AJ bowed to the audience—at least he'd practiced *that*—then took Jessica's hand and started off the stage.

She looked astonished. "A thousand bucks says you get so bored you'll eat those words within the year."

It would be the easiest money he would ever make. "You're on."

=

Steph feigned sleep. She even mock-snored. It was a convincing performance because she was exhausted after celebrating at the *Vanity Fair* party till three A.M. But her husband had awakened at seven, creating the kind of rooster racket whose sole purpose was finding company. He'd climbed for an hour on the StairMaster, showered, and dressed. But when he bombed down on the bed to tie his shoes, her charade ended. "Good morning, AJ. You're up early."

"I've slept enough."

"An extra couple of hours won't make you a bum."

"Who said anything about being a bum?"

"No one." He had—in his dreams. After the rush of his retirement speech and the bravado of bets, AJ must have realized the implications of his announcement. How sad that what should have been the most satisfying of mornings was only another Tuesday full of concern. But it was inevitable—AJ had been hard-wired for worry from birth.

"What are you doing today?"

She yawned. "Taping Wolfgang Puck giving the recipes for the dishes he made at last night's party."

"Oh."

"But I've got some time now if you want to talk."

AJ waved her off. "I might go over to a couple of hotels and get comparative prices for Jess's wedding . . . what's that look?"

At least he wasn't going blind in his old age. "I've been waiting to organize her wedding since the day she was born—"

"Okay, do it yourself, no problem." He left to sulk over orange juice and a bagel.

She rose to follow, as she had done for forty years, then realized the trap awaiting her in the kitchen. AJ wasn't seeking a sympathetic ear or sage advice. No, he wanted an accomplice to flee the scene of the crime. But she liked her life the way it was. And whatever the solution to his problem, he had to find it. Benign neglect was best for both of them.

=

AJ moped off to Riviera. It was crazy to have spoken so definitively last night. Not that he regretted passing on Kirk's offer, it was just . . . he didn't know what it was. The club was as dead as his mood. During the takeover battle his game had deteriorated, and when AJ muffed his long irons on the driving range, he fretted he was too old to find his touch again. When no fun members had shown up by early afternoon, he decided to play alone. Get used to it, he told himself.

"I'm Scotty Landis." His caddie had golf team good looks.

"AJ Jastrow. You're new?"

"New to the Riv. I caddied up at a place called Pebble Beach."

"Nice track," AJ replied casually. Stiff from last night's dancing, AJ groaned putting his tee in the ground. On the way up he detected a smirk on Scotty's face.

The insult jump-started him. The club swept back, his hips turned like a teenager's, then every muscle shifted forward in perfect sync and he crunched his drive two hundred and seventy yards down the first fairway. Striding past Landis, he noted raised eyebrows.

"What do you do, Mr. Jastrow?" Scotty inquired upon reaching his ball.

"Nothing much. I'm recently retired." The words crackled and itched like a new shirt overstarched from the factory.

"That's my goal. As soon as I can."

"What's the rush?"

"I want to have fun and I don't want to wait until I'm too . . ."

"Too old like me?" Landis blushed. "Don't worry, I won't report you." AJ boomed his fairway wood onto the green of the par five in two.

His caddie's skepticism faded. "What did you used to do?"

The kid must have been out drinking last night or watching reruns of *Seinfeld*. "I was in . . . manufacturing."

"What kind of stuff?"

"Dreams."

He sank a forty-foot putt for an eagle. AJ had visited this zone before, when his body knew exactly what it had to do and his mind was present to enjoy the experience rather than confuse it. The state rarely lasted for more than a few holes, but on this late March afternoon, the bubble refused to burst. Hole after hole he flowed. As they approached the fourteenth, the sun was cutting through the rows of eucalyptuses, casting shadows like the fingers of God in an illustrated Bible. The hole was a par three, with the pin cut behind a bunker that had beckoned like Circe to fifty years of mis-hits. He swung and the ball bored through the air, disappearing over the edge of the trap onto the green.

"You're the man!" Landis cheered. "That should be close to the pin."

"I think it's too long."

When they reached the green, the Titleist was nowhere to be seen. AJ checked the rough behind, while Scotty looked in the sand trap to make sure their eyes hadn't deceived them. They looked under leaves, behind rakes, under benches, in divots, up a tree, but all they found were someone else's lost balls. Neither said a word but both began stalking the flag. At the last instant Landis hung back, leaving the moment of discovery to the man responsible. AJ peeked one eye over the rim. Nestled in the cup was a ball with his distinctive red-stripe marking.

He waited for the jubilation, the urge to pump his fist, shout, dance a jig. But there was no surge, no thrill—just deep, abiding peace. AJ looked skyward to the person with whom he shared the triumph. "Capricious game, Dad." He shook hands with Scotty, picked up his ball, and marched silently to the fifteenth tee. He had four holes to play and just enough daylight left.

ACKNOWLEDGMENTS

I originally intended *Action!* to be a nonfiction history of the film business in the second half of the twentieth century. Jon Karp courageously gambled on my ability to accomplish that idea. A year later, when I announced over lunch that I wished to turn it into a novel, he glanced up from his salad—color still in his cheeks—and said simply, "Give it a try." As my editor, his guidance and support at every step was one of the most remarkable examples of faith that I've witnessed in my twenty-eight-year involvement in the creative process.

If you don't know what you're doing when beginning a book, then it's crucial to have colleagues who do. Scarlett Lacey and Eric Hetzel, my associates in our film production company, applied their editorial skills to every page of every draft of the manuscript. In addition, Scarlett joined me in roaming through libraries compiling the research that informs the fictional events. Their assistance proved invaluable.

As a producer I got to know Binky Urban while bidding on the terrific books she represents. It was a thrill when she cheerfully agreed to become my agent. I am indebted to her for educating me about the world of publishing, as well as for her creative suggestions.

Special thanks to the Random House team: Benjamin Dreyer, Bonnie Thompson, Carol Schneider, Todd Doughty, Dan Rembert, Ivan Held, Libby McGuire, and Howard Weill.

The fact that you're reading these acknowledgments is in large measure the work of Lynn Goldberg, Grace McQuade, Paula Silver, Suzanne Wickham-Beaird, and Mimi Zora. They did an extraordinary job drum-beating the book to anyone interested in reading it and talking about it.

Film people are wonderful storytellers. I have benefited—as well as laughed my ass off—over the years listening to their tales of madness. Their experiences provided inspiration for many of the sequences in *Action!* In this regard, I owe a special debt to Peter Hyams, Jack Brodsky, Irv Ivers, Danny Melnick, Andy Fogelson, Joe Wizan, and Norman Levy.

My former partner, David Madden, my sister-in-law Carrie Cort, and my friends Paul Michael Glaser and Linda Hawkins read early drafts of the novel, and their insights helped shape the revisions.

I can't even count the contributions of my wife, Rosalie Swedlin, not least of which was learning how to fall asleep while my computer screen glowed in the dark.

ROBERT W. CORT has produced fifty-two films, including *Outrageous Fortune, Three Men and a Baby, Bill & Ted's Excellent Adventure, Mr. Holland's Opus, The Hand That Rocks the Cradle, Runaway Bride, Jumanji,* and *Save the Last Dance.* After graduating from the University of Pennsylvania and the Wharton School, he worked for the Central Intelligence Agency and McKinsey & Company. He lives in Los Angeles, California, with his wife, Rosalie Swedlin, a manager of writers and directors.

ABOUT THE TYPE

This book was set in Bembo, a typeface based on an old-style Roman face that was used for Cardinal Bembo's tract *De Aetna* in 1495. Bembo was cut by Francisco Griffo in the early sixteenth century. The Lanston Monotype Company of Philadelphia brought the well-proportioned letterforms of Bembo to the United States in the 1930s.